THE HEALER'S DAUGHTER

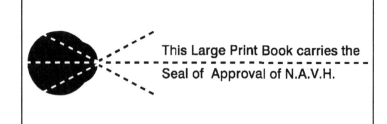

This Large Print Book carries the
Seal of Approval of N.A.V.H.

THE HEALER'S DAUGHTER

CHARLOTTE HINGER

THORNDIKE PRESS
A part of Gale, a Cengage Company

The publisher bears no responsibility for the quality of information provided through author or third-party Web sites and does not have any control over, nor assume any responsibility for, information contained in these sites. Providing these sites should not be construed as an endorsement or approval by the publisher of these organizations or of the positions they may take on various issues.
Thorndike Press® Large Print Relationship Reads.
The text of this Large Print edition is unabridged.
Other aspects of the book may vary from the original edition.
Set in 16 pt. Plantin.

LIBRARY OF CONGRESS CIP DATA ON FILE.
CATALOGUING IN PUBLICATION FOR THIS BOOK
IS AVAILABLE FROM THE LIBRARY OF CONGRESS

ISBN-13: 978-1-4328-4969-6 (softcover alk. paper)

Published in 2020 by arrangement with Harold Ober Associates Inc.

Printed in Mexico
Print Number: 01   Print Year: 2020

To the memory of all the courageous original settlers of Nicodemus, Kansas, who left the South to find freedom on the Great Plains

But let justice run down like water,
and righteousness like a mighty stream.

—Amos 5:24, NKJV

Chapter One

The feeble Kentucky moon shone on a rickety frame house two blocks away from Freedom Town, a teeming ex-slave settlement. Even though it was 1877, a full twelve years after the war, the two women living there could not afford to move a respectable distance from the blackness that lapped at the edges of their existence.

Within, soft as a haunt's breath, the air quickened and feathered across the skin of a small Negro woman sleeping on a pallet. Bethany Herbert awoke instantly, her body stiff with terror. White, all white, the filmy shroud fluttered toward her. Steel glinted in the faint moonlight. Instinctively, she rolled hard to the right. The knife plunged into the thin feather bed.

Her heart pounded, and her breath caught in her throat as she rose to her knees, pulled the knife loose, and hurled it across the room. She stood and grabbed Nancy

St. James's hands. Both women trembled with fright.

"What has come over you, Miss Nancy?"

The white woman blinked. Her skin, once the envy of all the belles in three counties, now was the off-white of sour cream. It mirrored the gradual curdling of her bright wit into torturously slow thoughts. For a moment Nancy remembered who she was — or who she once had been — and tugged on Bethany's hands, but she was no match for the fierce black woman who she surely believed had no right to nip at her like a blue heeler bent on bullying her back into line.

"Please. You don't understand," Nancy said slowly, her voice dignified, distant. "You don't understand how I've suffered."

Bethany choked back a lump in her throat, but she didn't loosen her grip. *God give me strength,* she prayed. In the beginning, taking care of this woman had seemed like the most natural thing in the world. She had been doing so all her life. But Nancy St. James had turned on her.

"I'll fix some nice chamomile tea to help you sleep, Miss Nancy. For both of us. It will help us both."

"No, please. You can do better by me. You know you can. Now let me go. Please."

Nancy turned her head, sobbing convulsively.

"Shh, now. Sleep will come. You've got to try." Bethany led Miss Nancy toward the bed, knowing they were doomed if she gave in to her own exhaustion.

She tucked Nancy under the covers, then went to the kitchen and put the teakettle on the stove. She did not want to waste the precious fuel, but if she didn't get Miss Nancy calmed down, they would be up all night. While the kettle was heating, she went back to the bedroom and sat on the bed beside the woman who had become a rank stranger.

"Please?" the white woman said.

"No. Be strong, Miss Nancy. Be strong. I've told you what happens to people who start aching for laudanum. I'm trying to keep you from slipping down."

"What you've become is an uppity nigger."

Bethany could not keep tears from rolling down her cheeks. Miss Nancy's yearning for laudanum had crept up on her. In anyone else, Bethany would have been suspicious long before. But her white mistress had always been so disciplined, so wonderfully joyful.

At first, Bethany had sympathized with

11

the headaches, the bodily aches, knowing they came from the fire, the Yankees. Then, too late, she knew she was doing more harm than good, as Miss Nancy yellowed and shriveled like a cornhusk, and Bethany couldn't tell where her skin ended and her hair started.

"Please? I can't sleep. You know I can't."

"Let the tea do its work."

"Please. You don't understand. I can't stand these headaches. I can't sleep. I am so terribly weary."

Each evening Bethany combed Nancy St. James's lifeless blond hair, now as fragile as dandelion puffs, and helped her into one of her soft, white, batiste nightgowns. Then she washed Miss Nancy's feet in lavender water, dried them, and tucked her into bed like she was an infant. Just as though they were still living on the plantation instead of in a drafty little three-room cottage. Not far enough from the colored folks to make Miss Nancy happy, but far enough so she could still hold up her head when she had to tell people where she lived. Then Bethany held her hand and sang to her, or read poetry. On nights when sleep did not come easily, she listened to Miss Nancy's memories.

"You don't understand how much I need that medicine. I have to have it. I know you

12

have more."

"No, it's you who doesn't understand," Bethany whispered gently. Other healers might dispense laudanum freely, but she had always been judicious. "I'm not being cruel. It's for your own good."

"And just who are you to presume to know what's good for me, you nigger bitch." Nancy rolled off onto the floor with a heavy thump and began moaning.

Too furious to speak, Bethany pulled Miss Nancy to her feet and pushed her back onto the bed. She ignored the woman's wild weeping, settled her back down, then went into their tiny kitchen. Steam puffed from the spout of the teakettle. She sprinkled precious chamomile leaves in the bottom of their brownstone pot. She let them steep, her arms crossed over her chest, her head dull with the burden of another sleepless night.

She filled one cup and carried it to her rocking chair. The cup was beautiful, painted with yellow roses. They only had two of them, and she feared Miss Nancy would send the other one flying, so she waited for her to quiet down. She sipped the hot liquid, keeping a mournful eye on the crazy white woman lying on the bed.

She's treating me like I'm her slave, Bethany thought ruefully. Ironically, when she was a slave she had never felt like one, and now that she was free, she did.

Before the war, for as long as Bethany could remember, her family had been held in high esteem by both the white and slave communities. She was descended from a long line of grannies — healing women — revered for their medical knowledge. The Herbert women — her grandmother Eugenie and especially her mother, simply known as Queen Bess — were gifted. Herbert women had always been at the St. James plantation.

There had never been any thought of selling them. The St. Jameses had even allowed them the luxury of using the separate surname of Herbert, although most blacks went by the family name of their owners. *Their* name came from the European doctor, Adolph Herbert, who first trained Eugenie. A talkative man, he lectured the small slave woman on every process he used as he cut and bandaged and probed and scolded. As time went on, and Eugenie's understanding of diseases and medications grew, she came to be known as "Herbert's woman." She was sent in his place to care for sick slaves. After Adolph's death, whites, too, began to seek her out.

14

Bethany warily eyed Miss Nancy, who was still sobbing. A fine mahogany dresser they had managed to salvage from the plantation dominated the tiny bedroom. Empty perfume bottles littered the top. Miss Nancy opened them often, her face brightening sometimes as she hummed and twirled.

The flickering shadows cast by the kerosene lamp comforted Bethany. If she closed her eyes sometimes, she, too, could make herself believe nothing had changed since the war.

She slowly sipped her tea, waited for Miss Nancy to calm down, and tried to count her blessings. She slept in a cot at the foot of Miss Nancy's bed, as she had always done.

Their house was small, not adequate, but the most they could afford. They had bought it through the sale of the sparse cache of Miss Nancy's jewelry, hidden from the marauding Yankees. The fire crackled, and Bethany jumped as if she had heard a distant shot. She steadied the cup and then wept. Miss Nancy had started eyeing her like she was a she-devil right after the war. Like Bethany had personally thought up the aftermath of the Late Rebellion.

Before the war, on other plantations, animosity had always been there. Gentile white mistresses' resentment of their husband's sexual attraction to slave women came out in relentless cruelty, sometimes in the form of out and out beatings, but more often through exhausting, petty demands. Then there were black women who spitefully sabotaged their white mistresses day after day. They spat in the food they were serving. They served dishes mixed with traces of urine or feces. Tiny white babies fell prey to mysterious illness, and everyone in the slave community knew why.

But this kind of carrying on had never been true on the St. James plantation. Those slaves viewed their owners as moderately decent people. Not perfect, but far superior to most whites.

Miss Nancy weakly lifted her head from the stacked feather pillows. "Bethany? Bethany, sweetie, will you come sing to me? Pretty please?"

Bethany sighed, rose, set down her cup, and slowly walked toward the bed, knowing Miss Nancy used a pleasant tone of voice to substitute for an apology. It was the best she could do.

She began crooning in a low contralto voice, finding it odd that Miss Nancy was always more comforted by the words of "Swing Low, Sweet Chariot" than by songs of her own culture. Next would come the poor woman's cascade of memories, as though the agonizing recital could restore better times.

"Remember that lawn party, Bethany? Remember how I wanted a bright coral dress, but Momma insisted the color was too strong for me? She wanted a soft blue. It was you who talked me into the blue." Then Miss Nancy fell into a fit of weeping again.

Some nights Miss Nancy could stand to speak of her fiancé, who had been killed at Gettysburg; some nights she could not. Finally, Miss Nancy fell asleep, and Bethany went back to her own bed. Sleep eluded her, as it did most nights now.

It will never be the same, she thought bleakly. *Never, never, never. I'm young. I still have my health, but I won't have, if I keep trying to take care of this woman.*

CHAPTER TWO

Every Wednesday night, Bethany attended services at the African Methodist Episcopal Church, an easy walk from their house into Freedom Town. The parishioners took great pride in the snowy exterior of the white frame building. There was not enough money among them to furnish the interior with more than rough benches. But the pulpit was an exception — it was a stunning work of interlocked woods, finely crafted by one of the members.

Bethany brushed the sleet from her cloak and carefully wiped her feet. She was late. The service had started, and she had to sit closer to the speaker than she liked. She was a quiet woman, not shy, but she did not like to attract attention to herself. Her face was a delicate oval and peaceful with the dark honey tint of an oriental Madonna. Her fine brown eyes were almond-shaped and thickly lashed. Her nose was narrow and delicately formed like others with her West Indies ancestry. Cherokee, too, in her face, and more than a hint of randy white masters who had visited the slave quarters. She was known for her great beauty as well as her medical skills when she would have preferred to serve in the shadows.

She could never pass for a white woman, but her lighter complexion set her apart from most of the persons gathered here. They ranged from blue-black to polished mahogany sheens. However, her cinnamon skin was darker and more frankly Negroid than the scattering of "high yellers" in the congregation who had a mere trace of black blood.

Kerosene lamps flickered, throwing eerie shadows across the room. There was a pungent smell of unwashed bodies. Some of the luckier ones had coats — although torn and ill-fitting — and real shoes with layers of newspapers to cover the holes in the soles. Some used blankets as shawls and had fashioned crude moccasins from old cloth. A poorly vented cast-iron stove sent a puny layer of coal smoke into the cold air.

Despite the obvious poverty of the people gathered and clutching old, worn Bibles, there was a curious anomaly. Some of the women, defiantly and with great pride, wore bright, huge hats adorned with feathers and flowers and ribbons and even grasses gathered from the countryside. No one of this group wore the bandanas or white turbans previously the only legal headdress for slaves.

Bethany squeezed in next to a mother nursing a small child. She smiled, nodded, then neatly arranged the skirt of her dark-blue homespun dress. She always felt curiously isolated wherever she sat. Trained by Queen Bess to question, ponder, and scrutinize from the time she was a small child, she lacked the simple faith that buoyed the people around her. She had reached a serene truce between those parts of her that yearned to be understood and her self-protective private nature. She came to these meetings because she needed the music, the noise, and a chance to be away from Nancy St. James.

People stood, their hands raised in supplication. The walls pulsated with yearning. "Yes, Lord, yes, Lord."

Strangers occupied the preaching platform: a small white man, and a large, scar-faced black. Bethany's stomach tightened with resistance to whatever their message was. Greedy intentions — she would bet on it. More strangers out to fleece the flock.

20

The white man sat in a chair by the lectern with a derby hat balanced on his knee. He had a trim mustache, eyes like raisins, and small, neat hands. His head bobbed to the words of the black man in the pulpit. The preacher's voice boomed as he swayed backwards and forwards to the rhythm of his speech.

"Ain't gonna study war no more," the preacher thundered. "The lamb will lie down with the lion. In the Promised Land there will be no more tears."

Caught up in the heat, the chanting, Bethany swayed to the call, weak with longing.

The preacher's voice dropped to a whisper. "Bible says to turn the other cheek. See this cheek? See, brother? See, sister?"

They gasped and murmured, for a brand was burnt there. Seared flesh.

"Got this for learning to read and write. This was punishment for wanting to know. But ain't gonna turn my cheek to white men any more. Going to turn it to the black man in love. Going to a place God picked out just for us.

"And it called Nicodemus, and I'm going home, Lord. Home to Nicodemus. Where the black man can be free."

"Going to the Promised Land," the people chanted.

"Not just men," the preacher called back, his voice a deep rumble, "but women, too. And there's land all around. There for the taking. And the people going to praise you. Welcome you. It's not like here, where there's still bloodshed. Still sorrow. Still terror.

"Come to Kansas, where there are no white-sheeted devils waiting in the shadows. Come to Kansas, where there's no night riders, no demons. No need to study war no more. And there will be land. Land a-plenty. Land for God's people. Not a piddling forty acres and some broken down mule, but one hundred sixty and clear title in five years."

Land. The promise of land jolted Bethany back to her senses. *Another huckster.* She looked around at the hungry eyes focused on the speaker. She kept her thin, elegant hands tightly clenched in her lap, resisting the allure of the treacherous calling man. The church was full, despite the cold north wind clattering against the siding of the building.

Bethany retied her bonnet strings, as though she could anchor her head more firmly on her thin shoulders and sort out what was real about the oratory. In her heart, she wanted to believe, but her head knew she was hearing another foolish promise foisted on foolish people.

"Come to Kansas," the bawling fool pleaded. Although she appeared to keep her eyes closed, her head meekly bowed, she risked a quick, hard look at the visiting preacher. He had close-curled, black hair and good, white teeth. His shoulders were large, developed, and she would have thought him a field nigger were it not for his ability with words.

"Come to the home of John Brown. The home of avenging angels. Come to wide open spaces and skies so blue the angels are jealous that it can't be matched in Heaven. But we talking about more than just land. We come to tell you about a town we're setting aside just for you."

There was a sharp collective intake of breath. Light flickered across whites of eyes yearning, yearning to believe.

"Yes." The preacher lowered his voice to a soft drumming cadence. "Not just land, but a town. And that town's name . . . and that town's name . . . and that town's name is Nicodemus."

"Tell us 'bout Nicodemus," the people chanted back. "Tell us 'bout this man."

"Now Nicodemus was a slave."

"Just like us, Lord," a woman cried. She started to chant, sing out the wonder of the

23

legendary African prince who was the first slave to buy his freedom.

"Yes. Nicodemus," called the preacher. "A black man. One of our own who warned the white man he would suffer for chaining God's children."

"He suffer all right," the woman shouted back. "Lord, he going to suffer."

"Nicodemus said —" thundered the preacher.

"And Nicodemus said . . . Yes, Lord, yes, Lord. Amen and amen."

"Telling 'bout a town."

They echoed the preacher's words. "Telling 'bout a town."

"A town for the colored man." The preacher paused after each phrase. "A town where you can make your own laws, lift up your own kind. All around, crops spring from the ground like they were blessed by God. Land . . . your land. Your own land."

Your own land, Bethany thought cynically. Once again all it had taken was hearing the word "land" to jolt her from the hypnotic call to consciousness of the vulnerability of the people around her. Bitterness welled up from her stomach like rank sorrow. Sometimes she felt like vinegar and gall was all she'd been offered after the disastrous war.

She'd hated it when it started, hated it

24

when the flaming blue-coated liberators burned the home she had always known, hated it when the lying Northerners came slinking around afterwards with their sharp Yankee teeth and shifty, greedy eyes.

She wanted to get up and leave, but she didn't want to attract attention.

"Your own home . . . your own place. Come home, come home. Come to Kansas. The land of John Brown."

Again, she shuddered and swayed, caught up in the rhythm, the call. It swept through her soul like a vibration from within.

The land, the free land.

"Your own home, your own place."

She imagined herself in a little log cabin under blue, blue skies, gathering plants to heal her people, walking along gentle creeks. She would dye her dresses indigo. They would have babies in Kansas, same as here. She would still be called to deliver babies, to heal the sick.

Against her will, the cabin came to life in her mind. There was a huge fireplace, with a pot of good stew hung from a tripod. There were quilts made by her own hands, for herself, herself, her own free self. The patterns and colors formed a backdrop for the walls.

Her status would be the same. She was

revered and feared here for the knowledge passed down from her mother and grandmother. She cultivated this fear. Fed on this fear. Her mother had led the way.

A woman's ecstatic cry, "Yes, Lord, yes, Lord," jolted Bethany. Warily, she opened her eyes and looked at the wailing black woman, work-worn and high hipped, her hands clasped above her head, strung out like an old pullet ready for the chopping block.

Bethany wanted to leave. She was not up to an evening of people being caught up in the Spirit. Still unnerved by Miss Nancy, she could not stand another night of wild emotion. She shook her head and scolded herself back into grim reality. She looked about at the yearning faces.

They believe, she thought with wonder. *My people always believe. It's a curse, this stupid happy ability to believe.* If the white man had been standing at the pulpit instead of sitting down, maybe they would not believe. But a black man was issuing these promises.

She no longer believed men of any stripe or color. Too many blacks had turned out to be simple dupes and white men evil manipulators. She believed in herself — and God sometimes — when she was having a

26

good day. She used to believe in Him a lot, before the foundation of the world shifted.

She had also once believed in the St. James family. Now she knew the white people who had owned the plantation she had always lived on were the sorriest excuse for humanity she ever come across. She had been far happier as a slave than she was now, trying to care for Nancy St. James. Sometimes she scolded herself for being so judgmental of these people who had lost everything they owned. But she felt betrayed. These were the same white people who had lectured about courage, who thought they were heroic people, bonded to lofty ideals.

They thought they were entitled to their grand lands, their fine houses, and their exquisite possessions. Entitled because they were white. Entitled because they were English. Certainly entitled because they possessed superior virtue. Well, the Yankee hordes had changed all that. The young mister St. James had fallen at Gettysburg. The elder St. James had died of grief and Miss Nancy might as well have.

At first, after they settled into their little house, Miss Nancy kept up the pretense of providing for herself by gallantly taking in sewing. In truth, Bethany provided for all their financial needs by doctoring white folks. Mostly ex-aristocrats who could no longer afford their European-trained doctors.

Bethany had never married, never taken a lover. Grannies often stayed single. Before the war, she had been too young to attract the attention of lusty young white men, and afterwards, her calling kept young blacks at a distance. Now, trying to slither around Miss Nancy's profound depression was wearing her to a frazzle. She had neither the time nor the desire for courtship.

She willed herself to shut out the preacher and let her mind drift back to happier days when both she and Miss Nancy were free. Not trapped like they were now.

Miss Nancy St. James had been a dazzling beauty. Superbly confident of her place in the world, the natural order of things as willed by God, she cared deeply for the Children of Ham. Her slaves had not wanted for food, or clothing. They were never beaten unless it was absolutely necessary.

The St. Jameses immediately culled out sadistic and stupid overseers. They encouraged family bonds and were not likely to sell or trade away men who had "jumped the broom" with a St. James female.

Grief for the woman Miss Nancy used to

be swept over Bethany like a wave. Her throat tightened, remembering how the Herbert women had kept the plantation going in ways other than medicine.

Her great-grandmother, Tillie, had been in charge of the vast domestic production needed to feed and clothe all the white and black persons living on the plantation. She organized the spinning, the weaving, and the final working of thousands of yards of cloth. Overseeing food production was her Aunt Faith's job. When Bethany's mother, Queen Bess, received her call from God to take Eugenie's place as a granny, it was swift and terrible and accompanied by an awesome ability both to diagnose and to heal.

The preacher pounded on the pulpit, and Bethany started. His voice blasted. She closed her eyes, then opened them and looked around her with sorrow. It was not just the white people who had suffered great loss from the war. Some days, she would even give up her precious freedom to have the old life back.

Miss Nancy veered about like a blind mule. Sometimes cheerful and determined, then given to fits of weeping. The vibrant white flower of Southern womanhood had faded before Bethany's eyes like clothing hung too close to a window. She had faded in spots and pieces, her mind a collage of suspicion and tatters. Bethany could live with that. What she could not abide was Miss Nancy peering at her over her handwork, her eyes filled with hate, as though Bethany could no longer be trusted.

The service ended. Bethany didn't like either of the two men at the pulpit. She hoped the persons there that night would not be duped. She re-tied her bonnet strings and prepared to plunge into the cold night air. Greeting people as she walked down the aisle, she moved quickly, hoping to avoid any discussion of going to Kansas.

She was nearly to the door when she felt someone watching her. She raised her eyes, swept the room with her gaze, and saw a small, grizzled mulatto man shamelessly staring at her. Her eyes did not waver, but she didn't smile.

He wore a tattered hat and a gray frock coat. His wrinkled homespun pants were too long, but his vest fit well. He might have needed a haircut; she couldn't tell. On the other hand, he might have preferred the bushy length. Might have thought the long, gray locks looked just right with his short, grizzled beard.

He looked ancient, or ageless. His face had heavy wrinkles and stains like an old burlap sack. His eyelids drooped over his amber eyes. His nose was distinctly African, but his skin had a yellow cast, like a drying tobacco leaf.

He removed his hat and came toward her. Surprised by his boldness, she waited.

"Ma'am."

That was all. He did not blink. He was pine tree straight, but self-conscious like he had just won the right to hold himself so pridefully and would never bend his head or bow his back again for anyone.

Flabbergasted, she could only look at him. Then, bewildered, she stiffened. "Sir, I don't believe we have met."

"No, ma'am," he said solemnly, "we have not. However, I have asked for one of your abilities and have been informed that Miss Bethany Herbert is the finest granny in these parts. I came with these men who occupied the pulpit tonight."

"You're with them?" she asked.

"Yes, ma'am, I am. My name is Theodore Sommers. And I am a townsman. I help folks get started." Sommers clutched the lapels of his coat. He did not flinch from her unswerving gaze.

"A townsman?"

"Yes, ma'am. I come to help these folks start a town. I can help get land for folks, too, if that's what they wants. But not all our people are just dying to farm," he said. "Brings back memories. Bad ones."

She laughed. "Yes, I expect it does."

"Too many of our people ended up a different kind of slave after the war, chasing after land. Working ground, picking cotton all their lives didn't do them a lick of good when it come to understanding how money works. Money is a white folks' game."

"And towns? Why would they do better at towns? We don't have any background for that, either."

"We know how to do things white folks don't know how to do. Think about it. On big plantations, our blacksmiths used to be just blacksmiths. Our teamsters just teamsters. Our sawyers just sawyers. White folks out West veer around from job to job. Try to do it all themselves. I can promise you, we sure enough needed. White folks going be begging us to help them."

"And where, pray tell, would we get the money for this venture?"

"From the town company. They going to sell us the lots on credit and loan us the money to get started."

She stared at the people flocking around the black preacher and the energetic little white man. Her throat tightened with despair. For all of them. It was time for her to face the north wind, the cold street, and be done with this stranger. Put him in his place, if he had one. If any of them did now.

"You do our people no service, sir, with these promises. However, they will all undoubtedly follow like sheep. I, for one, will not."

"Look at me, ma'am. Couldn't anybody mistake the likes of me for a flim-flam man. Not likely, now is it?"

She laughed then. "No, I reckon not. Have you been to Kansas? This place where there will be no more prejudice, no more terror?"

"Not just been there, I live there."

"You have your own home?"

"My own home. In a town called Wyandotte. It's east of where we going, but I'm going to sell it and come live with y'all in the new town. Might file for land, too. It's there for the taking. Yes, sir, a place in town and a place in the country."

She had doubted the other two men, but there was something about this one. Perhaps it was his humility, the infinite patience in his kind, weary eyes.

"I'm not a farmer, sir. I'm a healing woman, but then you already know that."

"Don't matter. The land's there for the taking. For you to use. Kansas law says you

33

can claim one hundred sixty acres. You have to live on it, but it don't say what else you have to do with it."

She noticed a neatly darned spot in Sommers's old gray coat. He had cleaned his aged, heavy brown shoes with care. A careful man speaking careful words didn't always have careful ways, but Sommers clearly knew how to take pride in what he'd managed to grab hold of.

"There's plenty of people here tonight who would die for such a chance, Mr. Sommers. But I'm not one of them." She tugged on the strings of her bonnet.

The wee upright old man proved he could read her soul. "In Kansas, ain't no one going to tell you what kind of hat you have to wear."

She started. The women here tonight gloried in owning a hat, once an emblem of status in their native Africa. After the war, Bethany had chosen to wear bonnets, strictly forbidden headgear for slaves. Even though many other healers still wore the traditional white turban, she refused to do so.

"I would love to be truly free, sir. But I depended on white people before the war, and I do now. Most of the women who actually pay me money are white people. They trust me because my family has always been in this county doctoring and delivering babies. I can make a living. It's a poor living, but we have survived."

"We? You have children, then?"

"No," she said. "I live with my white mistress, who lost everything in the war. I lost everything, too."

He nodded. "And so now you taking care of her?"

"Yes. As best I can. She believes she's still in charge."

"And you help her keep up this act?"

"It's getting harder and harder. Sometimes I think when she looks at me she sees the whole black race standing there. She thinks I started the war, burned her house, turned on her."

"That's why our people must leave. The same people that used to beat us ain't gonna just love us now that the war's over. What Northerners dreaming up don't make sense. They think the white folks and the black folks are somehow just going start working together. Won't happen. Not in this man's lifetime."

Bethany was impressed by his common sense. She missed it. Her people used to be full of it. This kind of intelligence was highly prized — motherwit — a type of intuitive thinking that had allowed her race to survive. Nowadays she could just swear every ounce of her people's brains had drifted heavenward in the smoke of the burning plantations. There wasn't enough sense left to outsmart a possum.

"Are there women in Kansas? Having babies?"

"Some, but not enough to keep a doctor busy."

"And how would you have me live? Just breathe the fine air these men have been telling me about? Drink the pure, fine water? What would I do for food?"

"Don't want you to just doctor for a living. I want you to start a school."

"A school?" Her heart lurched. She felt the sudden rush of blood to her cheeks. "A school?"

"Yes, ma'am. A school. Our people need schools."

"Don't I know that, Mr. Sommers. Dear God, don't I know that."

She and Miss Nancy had been born nine months apart. She had never lived in the slave quarters. She had never asked her mother who her father was. She and Miss Nancy had discovered each other when they were about three years old. They had played together, laughed together, and when the tutor came to teach Miss Nancy, it had been understood that it was "just fine" with the St. Jameses if Bethany listened in. It wouldn't hurt a thing.

The tutor, Mister Jeremiah Epstein, was a Jewish man with liberal ideas about scholarship for women. He saw no reason to spare females rigorous instruction. One day he noticed Bethany paying rapt attention when he read Greek mythology aloud.

When he quizzed Bethany on the meaning of the story, he was at first amused, then stunned at the depths of her insights. He was careful to give glowing reports about Miss Nancy to her parents — but her companion! He could not resist stretching the mind of the remarkable Negro child.

Bethany looked at Theodore Sommers, her eyes filled with tears. Of all the advantages she had had, it was schooling she prized the most. She knew the difference it would make for others of her race.

"I want you to file on homestead land," he said. "Even though we're starting a town, I want us circled by land of our own. Then start a school. Our children need a school."

"I could never, never leave Miss Nancy."

"You can, and you must, Miss Herbert. It won't never be the same again. The white folks that used to love some of us have thrown in with the white folks who've always hated most of us. The free blacks that always looked down on us are scared to death they will get mixed up in people's minds with Negroes who have just been freed. Some folks that thought they wanted freedom wish they could go back to what they had before. Ain't no one, nowhere, happy with the way this war turned out."

"Do you trust these white folks, Mr. Sommers? The ones who are backing this town company?"

Time seemed to stop as he carefully considered this question. He twisted his shoe on the floor like he was squishing a bug. Then he lifted his head and looked her squarely in the eye.

"No, ma'am, I don't suppose I will ever really trust a white man."

"Then how can you possibly, possibly ask us to take this chance? Leave our people, our homes?"

"Because the folks that were plumb worn out thinking of ways to be mean to us colored folks done got a second wind. Time for us to go. Don't trust them, but I trust us. The government wants people in that state. Wants them bad enough to give land away. Has to be some reason they wants us."

"And what could that possibly be besides our strong backs and untaught minds willing to believe any lie they choose to tell?"

"Has to be money," Teddy said promptly. He twisted his hat in his hands. His gaze faltered for the first time. "Can't see how. We ain't got none, and ain't going bring them none that I can see. But when white folks show up dangling prizes for black folks, money always changes hands. There's them what does the fleecing and them what gets fleeced. Don't guess I have to tell you which we usually is. But this time we going to stay one step ahead of them."

She heard Nancy St. James's weak, whimpering voice before she even opened the door. The poor woman cowered in her bed, her eyes wild with fright. "State your name, sir," she called.

Bethany gave her a short, dark look as she whisked into the room. "Shh, now. It's just me. Surely you remembered this was my church night."

"You don't have the right to go gallivanting. You know how sick I am. Get me my tea. I feel a headache coming on."

"Yes, ma'am," Bethany murmured. Resentfully, she took her time, and by the time the tea had steeped, Miss Nancy was asleep.

She undressed quickly but was too stimulated by the service at the church to fall asleep instantly. Hours later, she was still mulling over the old mulatto's words.

"It will never be the same," he had said. "You can't go back. What our people need is learning. Come to a new clean state, and make a fresh start. Kansas. The home of John Brown. They understand freedom. The land is free. The people are free. You'll know what the word means at last."

The next morning, she rose while it was still dark and dressed quietly lest she wake Miss Nancy. Worried about a patient who was still bed-ridden after a difficult birth, she wanted to see if the woman was getting her strength back. She picked up her bag of medicines, then heard a wail of protest.

"You can't be leaving. I haven't had breakfast yet."

"I'll be back soon, ma'am. Go back to sleep. I have a few people to see, then I'll make you something special."

"Uppity nigger," Miss Nancy mumbled. Then in a flurry of new-found strength she swung her legs over the bed, swayed to her feet, grabbed a nearby broom, and held it like a club over her head and rushed toward Bethany.

Bethany easily sidestepped as Miss Nancy stumbled clumsily over the coal bucket. Her momentum sent her crashing onto the floor. Stunned, Bethany stared down at the helpless bundle of flesh. She stretched out her hand and helped Miss Nancy to her feet.

She could no longer pretend it was night terrors. That Miss Nancy didn't really know what she was doing. That she couldn't help herself. Truth was, this crazy woman — once dearer to Bethany than life itself — wanted to kill her.

"Get dressed," Bethany said coldly. "You're coming with me."

"You don't understand."

Bethany didn't reply. She lifted the blue dress Miss Nancy had worn yesterday off the nail holding her daywear, then fairly yanked off the frilly white nightgown. She roughly thrust the dress over Miss Nancy's head and stilled her own trembling hands long enough to manage the rows of buttons. She plopped Nancy down into the nearest chair like a rag doll and shoved her feet into her useless, just-for-show shoes without bothering to fasten them properly.

Bethany walked over to the dresser where she kept their cache of money, counted out half, and tucked it into her medicine bag. Then she grabbed Miss Nancy's hand and pulled the stumbling belle of the St. James plantation down the streets of Lexington to a house off the main street. A small sign in one of the windows read Milliners.

The shop belonged to the Mueller sisters, distant aunts of old Mister St. James. Poor relations. They had come to the plantation once, years ago, and Miss Nancy had made it quite clear that they were just barely members of the family.

Once inside, the sharp-eyed woman in charge gasped when she saw her niece.

"Miss St. James is ill," Bethany said curtly. She unfolded a piece of paper. "Here is the deed to her house. She owns it outright. I have been taking care of her. I can no longer do so."

Her mistress stood there, slack-faced and expressionless. Drained of will.

No fool she, Nancy's Aunt Winona quickly took the deed to the house. "You're Bethany Herbert?"

"Yes, ma'am."

"You're well known. We are grateful for the care you've given our darling niece. We thought she was doing just fine. We had no idea. Of course she's welcome to live with us and there's a place for you here, too. We insist."

Knowing it was the money her doctoring skills would bring in that prompted the invitation, Bethany looked at her incredulously. "No, ma'am. But I thank you kindly."

"Nonsense." Winona's face mottled with anger. "Where will you go? What will you do? You need a white family to protect you."

"I'm going to Kansas."

"You are out of your mind."

Bethany said nothing.

"You belong to us, you know." Then, infuriated by Bethany's silence, Winona added, "We'll find a way to bring you back. You'll never get away. Not really. There's ways to deal with people like you."

Bethany slowly raised her eyes and beat back the knee-weakening terror that swept over her. It was replaced by a trembling fury she had never felt before.

"Ma'am, I'm off to Kansas."

CHAPTER THREE

Teddy Sommers wished the sun would shine. The haze was pulling everyone down. It was one thing to talk bravely in halls and churches and homes and quite another to board a boat leaving for a mythical promised land. This new unknown was as frightening as death. Some had burst into tears, a few had changed their minds and hadn't boarded at all. Most had gone trembling quiet.

The four-tiered Anchor Line packet boat was barely visible through the heavy fog. These shallow-hulled, broad-beamed steamers seemed miserably unbalanced, but they were cleverly constructed and the workhorses of river travel. Even so, the *War Eagle* looked like she could sink at any moment.

The *War Eagle,* a stern-wheeler, was built to navigate the shifting sandbars of western rivers. The main deck housed the boiler room and engine room and had cargo space. Passengers and animals were on the next tier. The lucky persons who won out in the dive for sleeping room on decks teeming with children and animals got to rest on thin cornhusk mattresses. The third tier housed the crew, who were only slightly better off than the human cargo. Above this, the square pilothouse perched recklessly like a top hat on a dandy and gave the navigating captain a clear view of the river.

Teddy finished overseeing the boarding of his group of fifty ex-slaves who would become part of the new colony in Kansas. They were packed in with over two hundred other persons — both white and black — bound for other places along the river.

It hadn't gone well. By the time his people moved around and shifted to accommodate crates of chickens, squealing pigs, bleating goats, dogs, and tools and utensils of the trades they would start in their new town, there was hardly room to move. Each family guarded their possessions like jewels. Folks looked penned up; trapped.

A bleating horn echoed across the scummy water. Black and white dock hands cursed and strained to ease bales of hemp and cotton into the hold.

B. R. Wade, the small white man who accompanied the eloquent A. P. Harrington on the preaching tour, stood on the dock. He was talking to a huge black man wearing the most peculiar set of clothes Teddy had ever seen. His mustard-colored jacket topped tattersall pants, and his black hat looked ridiculously small on his large head.

Wade spun his derby hat on one finger as he gestured with his other hand. He saw Teddy, nodded his head, then waved in a casual salute.

Teddy headed toward him. He'd been mulling over some things. He had been haunted by Bethany's question ever since they'd met that night at the church. "Do you trust these men?" she'd asked.

Truth was, he didn't. He never really trusted any white man not to sell him out if it were in their best interests. But he could always find a way to twist their deals around to where black folks got something. Not much, usually, but something.

He was troubled because he couldn't figure out the angle that would make white men lure his people to Kansas. There had to be a reason. He was sure it had to do with money — it always did — but damned if he could see where Wade could make a cent off of poor, starving, scared-half-to-death Negroes.

Yelps from two half-starved mongrels

fighting over a dead rat rent the air. The waterfront smelled of grease and decaying fish. As he walked toward the men, he decided sticking out his hand might be seen as too uppity and settled for respectfully touching the brim of his hat.

"Mr. Wade."

"Mr. Sommers. Fine day, for a fine trip." Wade turned toward the large black man standing by his side. "I want you two to get acquainted. This here is Paul Tripp of Nicodemus. This here fellow can sing the bird out of the trees. You can count on him to make the town go."

Teddy reached for the huge extended hand. "Pleased," he said tersely.

"Everyone accounted for?" Wade asked. "Captain says we'll be on our way in another hour."

"Yes, sir. We will. We will for a fact, if the sorry excuse of a boat stays afloat."

Wade laughed. "Never knew of one to sink right next to the dock. Could happen, but not likely."

Despite Wade's easy words, Teddy saw the flicker of irritation in the speculator's eyes. Dismissing him. Annoyed at having to make conversation with a wrinkled old black man who didn't amount to much.

"Just making sure I'm telling these people

the truth, Mr. Wade," Teddy said doggedly. "Still a short jog up the Ohio, then on up the Mississippi to the Missouri?"

"Rivers don't change, man." Tripp laughed heartily. "What you worrying about? Looks like we got us a fretter here, Mr. Wade."

"I know you want to be thought of as a man of your word, Mr. Sommers. Everything is in order. Tickets bought and paid for. Then after you reach Wyandotte you'll go by rail to Ellis. Those are paid for, too. Courtesy of the town company. Then I'll have wagons waiting to take you to Nicodemus. Just a short ride under God's blue sky to your own town."

"Everyone on that boat came up with five dollars," Teddy said. "Not all is courtesy of the town company. You need to know, sir, I been listening. Some of these people going to want more land than just a tiny square of a town lot."

"Both doesn't work," said Wade sharply. "You folks have got to stay right there in that spot. Can't work a homestead and get up a business at the same time."

"Mebbe not. Just telling you, these people free now. Land hungry. Not everyone going to stick with a town. Everything better be there just like you said. That's what I want you to know. We is counting on you, and, truth is, you is a rank stranger." He looked Wade in the eye, stopping short of saying, *white stranger at that.* "And mebbe we'll want to pick a different spot."

"I picked the place for that town myself, by God," snapped Wade. "That's the one thing I won't allow. Switching townsites. I tramped those fields barefoot and asked for divine guidance. The Lord Himself led me to that divine spot. I'm telling you I saw your people ascending and descending up a golden ladder in that very spot just like Jacob's angels in the Bible."

"That's the God's truth," Tripp agreed solemnly. He swept his little hat off his head and began turning it around in his huge hands. He fixed his black eyes on Teddy. "God's solemn truth. He told me so himself."

Teddy swallowed hard. His mouth was parched. Mothers scolded their children, and their urgent voices echoed across the water. Birds skimmed over the brown surface of the river. The odors of oil and sweat and dead animals trapped in the heavy water wafted from the landing.

He stared at the two men. It was no problem to control his temper; he had been doing so all his life. What he was trying to keep at bay was a warning flare of despair triggered by their easy use of religion. Assuming that was all it would take to make him shut his mouth.

"Angels is nice," he said carefully. "But horses and plows is better. Even if we don't farm, we gonna need food. Gonna need a garden. Gotta stir up some land to grow food."

The two men laughed as though delighted with Teddy's wit. "Now that's a fact, Mr. Sommers," said Wade. "Angels aren't as good as plows. Everything will be in place. Mr. Tripp and I will be coming along behind you. We're taking a separate boat. If you beat us to Nicodemus there are already people there waiting for you."

Teddy wished them a good day and watched them walk off. He soured with the sure knowing that these two men weren't about to be stuffed in with his smelly, crowded collection of humanity. They would be on a better boat.

He turned to go back on board, then stopped. A tall, slender man with mahogany skin nearly identical to the coat of his Morgan mare watched without bothering to hide his interest.

Teddy stared back, then walked over. "That is one fine horse."

"The best. Bar none."

The man's fine, intelligent eyes were a luminous light gray. Teddy had never seen eyes this color on a black man before.

"Looks like you've put quite a crew together," the stranger said. "Been watching you load up."

"Going to Kansas. Going to Nicodemus. Want you to have this here flyer." He shoved it at the man. "Be glad to help read it to you, sir, if you've a mind," he said kindly. "Name's Teddy Sommers. Some folks call me Pappy. I'm a townsman."

"Jedidiah Talbot," the man said cordially. He grinned and looked at the circular. "Seeing as how I'm a lawyer, I'm supposed to be able to read it myself."

Teddy laughed, glad to know the man wasn't a poker player, because with those eyes giving away every thought, he couldn't imagine Talbot would fare very well. Doubted if they did him much good in a courtroom either.

"Strange place for a lawyer to be hanging around."

Talbot's smile faded. "Just been collecting information. Talking to people. Trying to figure out how we can still live in the South."

"We can't. That why we leaving. Place for you out West, too, if you've a mind."

"Not that desperate yet. Might be, but not

yet. You watch yourself, hear? There's some mighty funny goings-on to keep people from bolting from this part of the country."

"Funny usually means no good."

"Mean things. Things you wouldn't believe. Men are getting killed just for thinking about going to Kansas."

"Why they want to do that? We no good to them dead."

"No good to them free, neither."

"That's a fact, sir."

Teddy eyed the canteen attached to Talbot's saddle horn. It was stamped with the insignia of the United States army.

"Guess you was a soldier," said Teddy, realizing Jedidiah Talbot with his magnificent horse might have been part of a cavalry unit. Quality animals. Both of them.

"54th Massachusetts," Talbot said tersely. His eyes clouded.

"Lord God Almighty," Teddy said. His mouth was dry as cotton. Words failed him. He could barely recall his own name. He wished to God he was entitled to salute or show some sign of respect worthy of this man instead of standing there slave dumb.

The 54th had changed history. Proved blacks could fight. Proved they were just as fatalistic as whites when it came to obeying senseless orders. Teddy knew he was looking at one of the few survivors of the doomed troops commanded to take Fort Wagner.

"Lord God Almighty," Teddy said again.

Talbot gave him a weak smile and picked up his reins.

A horn sounded through the fog. "I best be going." Teddy shook Talbot's hand, then reached to pat the horse, who jittered to one side. "You can keep the flyer, sir."

"That I will, old man. Godspeed to you all."

Teddy joined his people. They all gazed at the fog-shrouded shore. A wave of wild, mindless grief, for what might have been in their own native state, swept over them like a tidal wave.

Some of the women had all their worldly possessions tied in bundles and balanced on their bandana-wrapped heads. There were eating utensils, carefully guarded and, for a fortunate few, needles and bits of thread. Some wore the traditional white turbans, and some had on men's fedoras. With the exception of about three women, they were all clad in the same dresses they wore when they first came out of slavery. Some had worn plaid aprons, but the dresses were gray and brown and patched over and over again.

A large, calm man with the clear, brown eyes of a young horse came up to the deck and stood beside Teddy.

"Gotta be better," the man said slowly. "Gotta be somewhere on God's green earth where we're safe and white folks ain't gonna covet the poor miserable life we cobbled together. That war surely was for sumthin'. Can't believe those white boys died for something that ain't never going to happen."

They didn't take their eyes from the water and strained to see through the fog.

"Name's John More. Know who you are. Guess everybody does."

"Guess so," Teddy said.

"Funny, I never thought it would matter, but I'd like to see the damn place for the last time."

"Don't reckon it's my last," Teddy said. "I'll come back for more folks. I always do. I wouldn't like it much either if I was seeing Kentucky for the last time in a cloud of fog."

Later, when the rag-tag group talked about the trip, some thought it was better, leaving when they couldn't see their green homeland clearly one last time, their blessed shades of green in full sun. But their dreams would be haunted by memories of grass and trees and water like it was a part of their skins, like their blackness.

The fog, the gray, was the color of death, and like a lover denied viewing the body of their loved one, later they were bedeviled by the vision of a gray shroud hovering over the South when they wanted to be brave and needed the memory of green.

"Miss Bethany."

"Yes?"

"We need your help. Already, ma'am."

Bag in hand, Bethany followed, quickly skirting the clusters of black people packing the deck.

"This happen before," Teddy said. "Ain't never killed nobody."

"What's happened?"

He was silent for a moment. "No name for this. Just happens." In his own mind, he had always called it the African Terror. "I'll take you to her."

People parted to let them through. An old lady lay on the deck, trembling, her eyes rolled back as she twisted from side to side. A woman who had been trying to restrain her struggled to her feet. "You the healing woman?" she asked.

"I am," said Bethany. "What's happened here?"

"I don't rightly know. She bound for

Kansas, same as us, but when we got under-way she got fitful."

"Happen before," Teddy said. "Gonna happen again. She old. She scared. She heard stories her old granny told her mammy and her mammy before her about the big trip years ago. White men rounded them up, and their own people helped. It in their bones. Their mammy hexed them so they can't never forget. Comes back to them when they get on a boat. They 'fraid they gonna die. 'Fraid their own black people has lied to them. 'Fraid white people lied to them. 'Fraid they gonna be thrown down a black stinking hole and never come back out. They is hexed."

"They're not hexed," snapped Bethany. "We're not going to start off that way." She pulled the woman to a sitting position, then snapped her fingers in front of her eyes. The frightened victim focused on Bethany's face as though she had come back from a long journey.

"Praise the Lord," said the woman who had been caring for her. "Yes, Lord, I praise thee. She going to be just fine."

"She would have been just fine with just what you were doing," Bethany said. She eyed the nursing woman, whose skin was gray-brown as tree bark without a bit of sheen. Her homespun dress had been colored with black-walnut dye. Her hands and face could have been one with her clothes were it not for the dusky circles under her calm, brown eyes. Her plum-purple lips were the only variation in her sameness. She kept her strong, ready hands neatly clasped over a dingy, gray apron.

"You did just fine." Bethany rose to her feet. "I'm Bethany Herbert."

"I know that, ma'am. I is LuAnne Brown, and I is traveling with my husband and my two youngsters." She swiped at her hair, which was trying to frizz away from the bun at the back of her neck. "Old Mr. Sommers, he make sure we all know we got a healing woman coming along."

"Made sure there was some of us, too, instead of just ignorant field niggers."

Bethany stiffened at the words, turned, and looked into the pale, hazel eyes of a woman who was the color of weak tea. She had a lavish sprinkling of freckles over her fine, high cheeks. Her dress was a light tan with the hint of a bustle in back. Her matching bonnet had stiff little pleats along the brim. She extended her slim, elegant hand to Bethany.

"I'm Dolly Redgrave."

Bethany suppressed her anger. She knew

to the marrow of her bones what this arrogant woman had meant by "some of us."

She couldn't remember how old she'd been when she first became aware of the hierarchy of color among her people. She'd always known people stepped away from her mother not just because she was a granny, but because Queen Bess's blackness was the color of their night terror and eyes gleaming in the dark woods. From the time she was little, she'd known there was something about her own light-brown skin and dark, straight hair that set her apart.

Bethany had loved Queen Bess and her royal all-knowing soul above all things on earth. She trusted the kindness of the dark and her mother's blackness. There was a meanness to light-skinned ones, a harshness that came with the pale skin, and these people were not her own despite her own generous dollop of white blood. Because she had always known that, even if she wasn't as black as Queen Bess or the field niggers, she was plenty black enough.

Dear God, she prayed, *don't let us carry this to Kansas, too. Let us leave all this behind.*

Pretending not to understand, she shook Dolly Redgrave's hand. "I surely do admire your dress," she said. Dolly's face glowed with pride.

"I'm a dressmaker," she said. "I plan to open a little shop in our new town."

Astonished, Bethany looked away, then caught the eyes of LuAnne Brown. The gray-brown nursing woman, she noticed, was equally amused that Miss Dolly Redgrave believed ex-slaves would have the money to hire a dressmaker. Both women managed to keep straight faces as though they were partners in a conspiracy.

"You by yourself?" asked LuAnne easily, as though she had not heard Dolly's first remark.

"No, I have three youngsters," Dolly said. She looked around and shrugged. "Hard telling where they've took off to. Reckon you all will get to know them soon enough."

"Maybe they managed to find mine," said LuAnne. "I have two — a boy and a girl." She shielded her eyes and looked around the deck. "There they are. With my husband." She looked in the direction of a man leaning over the rail, pointing at something in the distance.

"Reckon I'll see what mine are up to," said Dolly. They watched her make her way along the deck.

"Reckon I'll do the same," said LuAnne. She didn't bother to hide her broad smile as she nodded to Bethany and headed toward her family.

Bethany strolled along the deck. Folks were chatting and passing around their cherished circulars describing Nicodemus, as though they were holding the Bible itself.

The town was located on the Solomon River. Not all the buildings would be completed by the time they arrived, but they would be finished by September. There would be homes for them all, and they would be set up for the business of their choice.

Wade had promised a church. Saloons were outlawed for five years. There were plenty of trees and an abundance of water. Excellent water, in fact. As pure as the river flowing through the Garden of Eden. Just laying around on top of the ground was a kind of stone used to build houses. So easy to cut, children could do it.

They would be happy and free and even rich. Rumors of wealth for the taking flew around like bluebirds.

But when nighttime came, there were darker rumors. Tales out of Africa sweeping the ship. Even brave men trembled at the ancient memory bred in their bones, and when a night bird called it was the gray ghost of one of their own ancestors. *Warn-*

ing, warning.

Bethany put her own blackness aside; the knowing, the knowing, the blessed sure knowing. That part of her that was white and rational rushed forward from group to group reassuring little clusters of people.

Then her stomach tightened. Suddenly she wasn't at all sure she had done the right thing in leaving. The part of her that loved books and learning and could think knew Teddy was right — things would never be the same. They had to leave.

But there was a cold fear working at her guts. Worse even than when Winona Mueller told her she could never really get away.

CHAPTER FOUR

Bethany sat on the seat of one of the heavily loaded wagons. Unlike the ones used for long trips, these did not have canvas tops, and she yearned for shade. Two days ago, after arriving in Ellis, she had relaxed for the first time since she turned Miss Nancy over to the Mueller sisters. It seemed like years had passed instead of a mere five months since she decided to leave for Kansas.

Gathering up her few belongings had been a simple matter. A couple in her church offered her lodging until the departure. She was ready to leave in a heartbeat, but some of the people heading for Nicodemus had to sell their land, and their belongings. A lucky few of them had done right well after the war.

The train ride had been swift, almost pleasant. Most wondrous of all, the town company had kept its promises. At each step of the way, all the necessities for completing the journey were there waiting. There were tickets from the Mississippi River transferring them to the Missouri, then a man waiting to see them safely aboard the train from Wyandotte to Ellis.

At Ellis, there were wagons pulled by heavy-footed work horses furnished by the Nicodemus Town Company. So, compass in hand, Teddy gleefully pointed west. The children were ecstatic. Their spirits rose after they got off the boat. They were on the last leg of the two-day overland trip and would see Nicodemus by nightfall.

Giddy with excitement, they had camped out on the prairie the night before. But the sun came up like a burst of fire this morning. As they moved across the prairie, away from Ellis and toward Nicodemus, the horizon wavered in the heat. Bethany felt like she had descended into a fiery furnace.

There was no breeze, no trees. The hot air seared her lungs. Toward midday, a mild wind began to blow and then turned harsh and scalding, bending the vast sea of grass. Rather than cooling them, the wind was malevolent, pushing more heat before it.

The people turned inside themselves. Turned jumpy like a herd of spooky cattle. God knew most of them had been hot before, but there was no name for this wicked wind. No song or chant to ease its hold. No devil's blacksmith to clang away the blistering gusts.

They did not speak or sing. Children did not bolt away from the wagons as they had the day before. They simply pushed on, with Teddy grimly consulting the compass from time to time.

About twilight, when they would have been hearing hoot owls and cattle lowing and mothers softly calling their children home to supper in Kentucky, they came over a little ridge. Before them were three tents centered around a small campfire with a tripod in the center.

Five black men stood there in a line as though they were waiting to receive the queen of England. One of them called to Teddy.

"Hello. Hello, sir."

Teddy stopped, looked at them, and waved. "Hello to you." He climbed down from the wagon, flexed his stiff knees, and tugged at his coat. "I'm Teddy Sommers, and who might you gentlemen be?"

One of the men gave a nod. "I'm A. C. Jones, and these are my colleagues. Welcome to you all. Welcome to Nicodemus."

Teddy's hand froze in mid-air. He couldn't

speak, couldn't breathe. He'd supposed these men were just strangers journeying to another place. He'd thought they would spend a pleasant moment or two chatting about this fine state before he and his people went on.

"The circular said there would be buildings and a church and stores in place," he said slowly.

"And there surely will be. Meantime, we're here to help you get started."

Teddy wheeled around and walked away. He rested his head against the flank of the exhausted horse who had pulled the overloaded wagon across the difficult thick grass without so much as a trail to find their way. Through air so hot it seemed like the breath of a dragon bent on incinerating them all.

He could not bear to look his people in the eye. People he had led into this merciless cauldron of flames. He could not bear to think of the home in Wyandotte he had sold, where there were trees and water and people. Civilized people who went to meetings and church and visited one another. People who sat on their porches in the evening.

People who could breathe.

He slowly lifted his head and looked around. He had been lied to. He was used to that. But what he could not figure out was how white folks thought they could make any money off of them. He could not bear to look at Bethany Herbert.

Overwhelmed with fear, Bethany drew deep breaths to quell her panic. When she heard the words "welcome to Nicodemus," she looked around over the vast empty prairie and fought a surge of nausea. What would they eat? Where would they live? Was that pathetic measly trickle in the distance a creek? Was that the Solomon River promised in the circular?

Slowly she turned in her seat and looked as far as she could see in every direction. Where were the plants she would need to keep her people well? Where were plants to stop bleeding? Draw out poison? Keep babies from coming too fast? Where were plants to doctor a burn, or stop pain or cure a stomach ache? She clutched the nearly empty medicine bag closer to her side.

Teddy straightened, gave her a look, and something passed between them. The sure knowledge that they alone could keep the whole group from collapsing.

He turned to the stunned people sitting in the wagons.

"This is it. This is Nicodemus."

"Can't be," said John More.

Then Jones stepped forward. He was a tall man, easy with words, with the face of a wise old ram. His hair stuck out in white tufts on the side of his bald head. He had staked out a homestead himself a couple years earlier. He had no use for folks — black or white — who weren't up to Western Kansas heat. No truck with weak people who couldn't stand a little breeze now and then. Folks who carried on about the wind.

"Reckon this is a moment you've all been waiting for," Jones said. "Reckon this is the time to show you we means business. Want you all to climb down off those wagons. Want you all to line up. Want you to look north a little with me."

Exhausted, all the men obeyed. When they were all grouped, Jones waved his hand toward a set of stakes sticking up over the grass.

"Now close your eyes tight, and just let the picture fill your head. See that church. See that school. See that hotel, that lumberyard. See all those fine homes."

A woman sobbed. A child wailed.

Jones paused, his gaze wavering under Bethany's angry glare. None of the women had their eyes closed. The women seldom did. Bethany looked around at their sad, weary faces. There were thirteen children among the fifty-five people gathered.

She swallowed her tears and looked away from their despair, remembering her gentle Kentucky with its soft swelling hills — where the sun was bright and kindly — not this merciless molten disk rimmed with red.

"Now I want you all to open your eyes," said Jones, "while I give you something you can hold in your hands. Something of your very own that you can keep. Want each man of the household to step up here. Gonna give you something. Something more precious than gold."

And the men obeyed that command, too.

John More was the first in line. Bethany's eyes brimmed with tears. They had talked on the boat. At the time she had been deeply moved by his expectations, his soft, brown eyes alive with hope.

"Can you write your name?" Jones asked him.

"I can," he said proudly.

The four other black founders had formed a crescent around Jones. Behind them was a board spanning two barrels. On it, a hammer kept a stack of papers from blowing away.

Bethany glanced at the few trees growing along the creek bank. The undersides of cottonwood leaves sparkled silver in the fading rays of the sun.

"Good!" Jones said. "We want the first person to be someone who can sign his own name." He cleared his throat. "Gentlemen and your loving wives who have journeyed from your Egypt to this here promised land of Kansas, we commend you for your vision, your courage. Like Moses of old and Joshua after him, the Lord is rewarding you for your obedience to the natural laws that move us all. And now, Mr. More, I present to you the very first certificate of membership in the Nicodemus Town Company of Graham County, Kansas."

John More slowly extended his hand and, with wonder, received the precious piece of parchment.

"Sir," he said, "I can't read this here writing. I can scratch out my name. Can't read much of anything."

Bethany quickly stepped forward. "Allow me, please." She quickly scanned the certificate. "Says here they were printed in Topeka." She looked up at Jones.

"That's right, ma'am. There's lots of them. We have faith in what we're doing here. No way we could have time to hand-letter all those pieces of paper."

"But it would take a great deal of money to have things like this printed." She knew her own words sounded foolish. But she was growing more confused with every passing moment. Then she slowly began to read aloud.

"It says, 'State of Kansas, Graham County. This is to certify that —' There's a blank space here for your name, Mr. More," she said. She looked up at the trembling ex-slave, ex-field hand who was now clasping his arms around his chest, his hands tucked under his armpits as he swayed back and forth.

" 'This is to certify that John More' — that's after you fill in your name, John — 'of Graham County, State of Kansas, has this day paid the sum of Five Dollars, being the full amount of Membership Fees in the Nicodemus Town Company of Graham County, Kansas, and that said John More is entitled to any vacant Town Lot on the town site of Nicodemus, Graham County, Kansas, at the time said party arrives at Nicodemus.' "

"Um, um, um," murmured More. His eyes were still closed, and he still swayed. "That be me, sure enough, and I have arrived. I have, indeed."

" 'The said Nicodemus Town Company,' " continued Bethany, " 'giving their obligation to make Title to said lot as required by

70

law. And it is further agreed that no intoxicating liquors shall be sold on said lot within five years from this date. Dated at —' — another blank here, John — 'this day of 1877. Not valid until countersigned by W. R. Wade, general manager.' "

Her voice wavered, and she spoke the last words softly. Everyone was clustered around her now. " 'Nicodemus Town Company.' "

Tears streamed down John More's face. "Glory be to God," he said. "Glory be. I'se a gentleman now. Better than a land owner. Got me a place in town. A real honest-to-God place."

They clustered around More as he proudly held the certificate aloft and waved it in the still scorching night air. He whooped and jumped as he clutched the piece of paper.

"I is truly free now. Glory be. I gots a place. Says right here I get to choose my lot first." More's hands shook as he allowed the emigrants to have a look. Then they all lined up to receive their titles to their new lots in their new town in their new state.

Bethany looked at the vast open prairie dissected by the feeble little creek and a few spindly trees, and thought she was losing her mind.

There was nothing here. Absolutely nothing here, yet these grateful souls saw homes and buildings and a chance for real freedom. The cry, the yearning since creation, was for a place of one's own.

They wanted the reality and the paper. That blessed piece of paper printed in Topeka, which took money after all. The money paid to print the certificate made it official somehow that someone, somewhere, was willing to invest in them.

Someone was willing to take a chance.

Teddy walked over to Bethany. "You want to help the others get signed up, or you want me to do it? Some of them just going to be able to make their mark."

"You do it. I don't want any part of this . . . this sham."

"Yes, you do," he said sharply. "Better be glad these folks seeing what they see. It's all we've got."

"Do you still believe, Teddy?" Her words were careful, even, but she looked straight ahead as though she couldn't bear to hear the answer.

"God help me, I do," said Teddy. "I surely do. Not all the time, but most of the time. Ain't no good for nobody these days when I don't. But I knows this for a fact. There's some things about white people that our folks gotta start thinking like. Been studying on that some. Our people usually see what's there, and white folks think about what oughta be there. Our people's smarter, right enough, but white folks are the ones who gets ahead."

Bethany nodded. "We're only capable of imagining when it comes to Heaven." She turned and looked Teddy fully in the face.

"Well, we're here," she said grimly. "And now we'll all have a piece of paper saying here's where we belong. We will just have to make the best of it."

Teddy stepped forward and helped sign names for people who could just make their mark. By full nightfall, every family had their certificate, and as the emigrants built a central campfire for the night, a sense of anticipation. They were here. They would no longer have to think about loading up again.

They were home in Nicodemus.

CHAPTER FIVE

The next morning, directed by the five black founders of the Nicodemus Town Company, the men started staking out lots in the town. The women began setting up a semi-permanent camp.

Bethany stood beside Teddy as he rested his sledgehammer on the ground.

"How big are these lots?" she asked.

"Don't rightly know." He wiped the sweat off his forehead. "I do know that most folks starting a town company get a whole square mile."

"How much does it cost them?"

"About eight hundred dollars."

"So figuring six hundred forty acres and eight lots to the acre, that would be . . . ?"

"Be 5,120 lots," Teddy said quickly. "In some places they're getting $100 a lot. That's a hell of a lot of money. About a half million."

"But not here," said Bethany. "Not here.

At five dollars a share, that's just a little over twenty-five thousand dollars for this sorry place, and then they loaned us the money to boot."

"That's still what's bothering me. Folks gots to be figuring to make money off us, but I can't see how." He stared into the distance.

Bethany fingered her skirt. "Where are we supposed to live? They can't be expecting us to build frame houses, because there aren't any trees. And all the fine stones I've been hearing about. The ones that are supposed to be so easy to carve. Where are they? They're not just lying around on top of the ground like the circulars said."

Teddy shook his head. "Don't know."

"I'll ask one of our esteemed town sponsors," she said bitterly.

"Morning, ma'am," said Jones as she approached.

"Good morning, Mr. Jones. Some of us women were wondering about our new homes."

"Reckon you are," he said easily. "Going to show you my place. Gather up the womenfolk, then come along with me."

He led them toward the Solomon River and talked constantly as they walked. "Those trees there are cottonwoods."

"They're beautiful," Bethany said. "And huge."

"Yes ma'am, they are. They spring up natural along the creeks out here. Nothing can kill them. They bend, and they break, but they still keep going. Kind of like us." He led them over the next rise and pointed to a door built into the side of the hill.

"That's a dugout," he said. "That's how y'all will be starting out. I've lived here for three years."

"You expect us to live in a hole in the side of the hill? Where it's dark as a dungeon?" shrieked Dolly Redgrave. The other women were shocked into silence.

"I'm a seamstress. Gotta be able to see. Can't sew in no hole in the side of a hill."

"It's where you going to have to live to start out," Jones said flatly.

One of the women, Sister Liza Stover, stepped forward. She had joined the group when they passed through Topeka.

"It ain't so bad. Not as good as I was used to in Kentuck, but better than what I had in Topeka. Filth there and disease. Thought I was going to die. I truly did."

Beside her was an old woman stooped from field work. "They cool," she said. "Cooler than picking cotton. Supposed to be warm in winter. Don't know. Ain't tried that yet. Just know they cooler than picking cotton. But it a fact that only the worse masters made his niggers sleep on the floor. Now you trying to tell us we is blessed."

"Don't care how cool it is." Dolly's voice was shrill above the creek. "I won't live in a hole like a spider."

Jones held open the rickety door and gestured toward the interior. "You're welcome to look. It's right homey inside. Best we can do for y'all until we can put up soddies."

Bethany was small enough to enter without stooping through the doorway. It was dark and dingy but indeed cool, just as the old woman had said.

She felt safe in this peculiar earth dwelling. There was no window, but there could be one in front. She could sleep with her back against the far wall and never ever worry again about someone slipping up behind her. No more would she ever fear that hands — black or white — could invade her bed in the middle of the night. There would just be a front door.

"Wanted to live in a cave, I'd never have left Kentucky," said Dolly. "Wanted to live in a hole, I'd have stayed where the hole was high and dry and the floor was stone."

"Won't be this way forever," Jones said.

"Just till you get going."

"I won't live in such a no-count trashy place," Dolly said flatly. She whirled around and walked off with a few like-minded women trailing behind her.

The next day Dolly found three men to help build a lean-to. Some of the women had located a scant pile of wood. Dolly grabbed an axe and cut down small striplings to weave a top for the roof.

There was no siding to cover the framework of small branches she tied to the four corner logs. But she wove together small cottonwood strips and covered them on one side with an old sheet. When she finished, everyone clustered around and admired her ingenuity except for Sister Liza Stover, who hung back in polite silence.

Two days later, a high wind came, ripped the sheet from the framework, and sent it sailing. Then all the woven branches skittered across the prairie like fall leaves.

"Tried to tell her," Sister Liza Stover muttered. "Heard folks talk about this wind."

Dolly ran off to the creek bank, threw herself on the ground, and sobbed. Bethany watched in dismay but decided it was better to say nothing.

Several days later, after she had a chance to think, Bethany took Dolly aside.

"We'll start a dugout for you and your children right away. At least part of it will be above the ground. Even though we all need a place, we sure don't want wind or rain to spoil all the supplies and cloths you brought."

"Knew someone would surely come to their senses. Stop lumping us all together. Do a little sorting."

"Make no mistake," Bethany said coldly. "Everyone is equal out here. It's just that you might be able to provide a little income for Nicodemus. The whole community. We'd be foolish not to protect your goods."

Dolly said nothing.

"Now please pull yourself together and show a little appreciation."

The next day, five men left off staking lots and came to build Dolly's home. They staked off a fourteen by fifteen-foot area at the top of the edge of a ravine formed from an ancient creek that had once flowed through the soil. Then they dug a six-foot hole. A large group watched the building progress. Some worked from the bottom and some worked from the top of the ground. They dug out steps descending to the bottom and constructed a front wall of sod bricks. Bare earth formed the back and sides.

They set a ridge pole and carefully covered the roof with woven branches from cotton-woods. They covered the branches with a little layer of sod, then another heavier layer, going in the opposite direction. The roof soon supported a heavy layer of sod.

If any of them resented the least grateful and congenial among them being the first to get a new home, no one said so.

One of the women, Carrie Williams, who would be delivering in a couple of months, watched every step of the process. Bethany walked over to ask if she was still troubled by heartburn. She clutched Bethany's arm like they were best friends.

"Miss Bethany, my baby's going to have a real home," Carrie said eagerly. She was a small, mahogany-colored woman with nar-row bones and frizzy, wooly hair neatly covered with a kerchief. "They said so. Mr. Jones and Mr. Tripp and Mr. Harrington. They'se all promised. Soon as they can get their hands on a sod cutter, they going to build an above-ground house just for us in honor of our new baby."

"That's just wonderful," said Bethany. *More promises,* she thought grimly.

They had been there five days, living in

tents just as they had done on the trip out. Several more days of relentless heat had given way to a couple of cooler ones. Rather than comforting them, the variation kept them on edge. They never knew what to expect.

"Do you think I'll have any trouble?"

Bethany quickly looked at the ground. She had a sour taste in her mouth. She was terrified at the coming birth, but she didn't want Carrie to know. Every day since they arrived, she went out on the prairie looking for plants. She couldn't find the ones she needed and didn't recognize the ones she did see. Truth was, she no longer had plants to stop pain or bleeding.

"You'll be just fine," she said. "Just fine. Now go home and rest while you have a chance. After the little one gets here, sleep will be hard to come by."

Carrie's face brightened. Bethany mashed her fist against her mouth as she watched Carrie lumber toward her tent. She closed her eyes and took deep breaths.

She was running out of medicine. People's trust was as important as the medicinal properties of the plants themselves. Without that, she was nothing.

She stared at the prairie. The shimmering waves of grass. The land promised and then withheld. One minute it seemed to teem with everything they needed, and in an instant, the same landscape appeared bleak, stingy with its favors.

Then she caught her breath. Far away, she could see a herd of wild horses. *They're real,* she thought with wonder. They were coal black with huge manes and tails that touched the ground. The herd whirled and pounded away as if hearing a distant signal.

"We can't catch them," she whispered. "Never, never." The three sorry nags they had arrived with certainly wouldn't be up to chasing down wild horses.

What in the world were they supposed to do for food? They were all skilled people. When they had lived on plantations, like most slaves who were not field hands, they all had some trade, but there wasn't a farmer among them. She was struck with the irony that there wasn't one single person among them who knew a thing about growing food.

Land was there for the taking. Land for crops and cattle spread out so far they couldn't see the end of it, yet there wasn't a person here who knew a thing about growing a variety of food crops from start to finish. A few knew a little bit about growing tobacco. A few knew a little bit about growing cotton.

Couldn't eat tobacco. Couldn't eat cotton.

They were a collection of people who had been worth their weight in gold on plantations and whose value had plummeted when poverty-stricken Southern whites ruined by the war suddenly started competing for the jobs blacks once had to themselves.

She sighed. Even if someone among them did know how to farm, they didn't have the tools to do it with.

"Miss Bethany?"

She turned. Teddy gestured for her to come look at a piece of paper. His hands shook as he wordlessly handed her a circular.

" 'To the Colored Citizens of the United States,' " she read. " 'We, the Town Company of Nicodemus, Kansas, are now in possession of our lands.' "

She skimmed through the rest but faltered when she read about members being permanently located on claims and that there were "ample provisions for them all."

"Are they out of their minds?" she cried. "We can't even take care of the people who are already here."

"That's not the worst of it," Teddy said. "Here's another one." He shoved another piece of paper at her. The wind whipped her skirt, and she turned her back to read the circular.

" 'All colored people that want to go to Kansas on September 5th, 1877, can do so for $5.00.' " Her eyes raced over the page. The Nicodemus Town Company had consolidated with another colony in Kentucky that was bound for Kansas.

"This can't be, Teddy. There can't be more people coming."

Bethany's stomach plummeted as she stared at a jack rabbit in the distance. Food. Food aplenty, but could they catch it? Where was the easy game that was supposed to be available?

In the middle of September, there was a subtle vibration in the earth. The ground trembled and throbbed with a pulsating beat. The day was Kansas blue, crystal clear air shimmering with anticipation. The townspeople heard the singing-chanting before they even saw them.

There were some three hundred people making their way across the prairie. There were goats and chickens and little children hopping around and dogs barking and old mules and cobbled-together wagons with mismatched wheels and spokes spliced together.

There were women in white turbans and bonnets and a few women balancing hats they had made themselves, and they would have made them tall enough to touch the sky if they could have found enough red. They came with drums and anvils and musical instruments and washboards and all manner of tools and the expertise to use them.

What there was not, was farmers. What there was not, was horses and plows and mules and food and fuel and seed. There was hope, and that in abundance.

When they saw the cluster of black people standing on the prairie, they shouted in relief. Then some of the group began running. Several knelt down and began to pray. Some just stopped and looked as though they were seeing a mirage. One of the women saw her cousin and gave a cry, and they stumbled toward one another.

Bethany immediately counted fourteen pregnant women. Fear swept over her like the tricking wind blowing across Kansas. Fear had been pushing at every crack and cranny of her soul, looking for a place to shove through ever since she left the South. Now fear plucked at her openings until she could no longer keep it out of her terrified heart.

Dear God, she didn't know enough. Her lips trembled until her teeth chattered, but there was too much joyful excitement for anyone to notice a small black woman shaking in the wind.

Pull yourself together, girl. Her mother's words echoed in her mind as surely as if she had been standing by her side. *Pull yourself together.* Bethany eyed the crowd. They looked healthy, well-fed. *Good thing,* she thought grimly. That wouldn't last long.

Reverend Harrington stepped out to meet the new arrivals.

A large man stepped forward. He had a sleek, small head atop a neck so long it made him look like a gleaming eel. "Where is we? Who might you be?"

"Welcome. Welcome to Nicodemus. I'm the Reverend Harrington."

"Name's Henry. Henry Partridge." He added his surname with the clumsiness of a man not used to using it. His scarred hands trembled as he reverently held out a varnished print. Bethany was close enough to see the image. It was a chromolithograph. She had seen one once when she was tending to a wealthy lawyer's wife in Lexington.

It was cruder than most chromos — the vivid colors had been inked and stamped with a stone — but the meaning was clear

86

and geared to slaves who couldn't read.

It was titled "The Freedman's Home." There was a Negro man in a charming cottage looking out floor-length French windows and relaxing in the rosy haze of the Kansas sunset. His wife played the piano. Deer, there for the taking, grazed outside the window in a grove of shade trees. Turkeys flew past the window.

"This ain't what we was promised," Partridge mumbled, looking around at the barren prairie. "This here can't be Nicodemus." Partridge had three fingers missing from his right hand. The little finger and thumb formed a crude claw, and he rubbed the scarred center as though wishing and rubbing could make fingers sprout. As though wishing and rubbing would make a town appear.

Stunned, the people looked around.

"Where is Mister Wade?" a man called from back of the group. "He's the lying bastard who promised us the freight would be paid to Ellis from Wyandotte."

A tall, gangly man stepped forward. "Name's Earl Gray," he announced to Harrington. "Don't suppose you care much who I is, but they is plenty of people here who will be happy to tell you. I sold a right smart parcel of land to get here. Was starting to get a hold on things back in Kentucky."

Gray wore overshoes without any boots underneath and a tattered blue hat without a bill. His face was hard, lean as a worn-out mule, the whites of his eyes mottled cream and yellow.

He punched his fist into the palm of his right hand. "Wade was supposed to pay our freight. That's what he promised, all right," he called back to the crowd. "Didn't he?"

"Got that right, brother. Wade said. He surely did."

Gray took another step toward Harrington. "When we get to Ellis, no one had paid for the freight. Railroaders took two of our horses and most of the corn we was going to plant. He was supposed to meet us when we got off the train. Supposed to take us on to here 'stead of just letting us stumble off on our own."

"He's coming," said Harrington. He turned, dragged an old rag from his back pocket and wiped sweat off his brow despite the fact that it was a cool day. "First things first. Reckon most of you is hungry. Gonna see to that first." He turned and quickly started giving directions to the women of Nicodemus. "All of you that's got fires started, hurry up and get some food down these poor folks." Then he walked away as though he couldn't be bothered with such minor details as a missing town.

They were all too weary to do more than start unloading their freight. Then Harrington peered at a speck on the horizon.

"Wade's coming yonder. Driving like Jeshu. He's the only one hereabouts that has white horses. He'll explain everything."

The group quieted and waited in eerie silence. Wade drove up with a flourish, then jumped down and walked forward with his hand outstretched, his derby shoved back on his head. "Greetings friends, and welcome."

"Where's the buildings? Where are the churches? Where are the homes? The fine homes you promised? Don't look like no promised land," Gray said.

"They are all forthcoming, I can assure you. I have another town to worry about, too. About thirteen miles from here. All white same as this is all black. But you don't see white folks complaining. This is a chance to show that you're as good as white folks."

"We know we is as good as white folks. Never been any question about that. We not as dumb as they is, though," said Henry Partridge.

Wade flushed. "Now look here . . ."

"No, you look. You lied to us. Pure and simple. What we got here is more of white folks' lies."

"Don't call me a liar, you black bast—" They all knew what he had been about to say. Wade started easing toward the buggy. Then he bolted and leaped into the seat. Reins in hand, he smartly slapped the leather across the horses' backs.

There was no help for Wade out here. No white sheriff to back him up. No night riders for him to assemble. No jury-rigged courts to take away a black man's land. With a cry, a few of the men began to run after the buggy. Taking the law into their own hands just as white men had been doing forever.

A man whose skin shimmered like coal ran toward Harrington's horse. The startled horse reared, but Sidney Taylor had been a groomsman for many years and was one of the few elegant riders among the new arrivals. He vaulted into the saddle and raced after the terrified Wade.

Another man unhitched one of the mules that had been used to haul their wagons and joined the chase, although at a slower pace. Several ran after Wade on foot carrying pitchforks and shovels, and a few luckier men followed on worn-out mules and horses.

■ ■ ■ ■

B. R. Wade had a fine start, but there was nowhere for him to go. Wade City, the little embryo of a town he had started, only had a couple of residents. Wouldn't do him a bit of good to go there.

He headed toward the nearest dugout. The colonists were a good mile behind. He slammed through the door. Mrs. Lawlis was a huge woman who could not move quickly. Wade came hurtling into the room.

"You gotta hide me," he blurted.

"Indians?"

"No, blacks. No time to explain."

"Well, mister, there's no place to hide you. None at all in this here house. Just look around."

"Can't let them catch me. They're going to hang me."

Mrs. Lawlis stepped to the doorway and shaded her eyes with her hand. A dusky horde was heading toward her dugout.

"Whoever they are, and whatever they plan to do, they're going to be here pretty quick." Nervously she looked at Wade, who was running around like a rat in a cage.

She waited, watching the group approach, then gasped as she felt Wade creep under her skirt. Her face burned with shame. The riders raced toward her soddy. Wade's horses and buggy were loose in front. The team was tearing the heads off her precious marigolds.

Sidney Taylor jumped off his horse and headed for her doorway. "Good afternoon, ma'am," he said.

She clutched the doorway for support. Taylor was blue-black and huge. She would put a bullet through her brain if she was about to suffer the fate worse than death. She cursed her husband, who had decided to go to Ellis, today of all days, leaving her here alone to face a mob of crazed Negroes.

"We're looking for a thief by the name of Wade."

"No Wade here. You can see that for yourself. No place to hide here."

Bewildered, the man looked around the room, then turned and looked again at the fine team Wade had abandoned.

"Don't see how he could have gone anywhere," he said.

"Don't see how he could have, either."

"Looks like he just vanished into thin air."

"Does for a fact."

Sidney tipped his hat and walked over to his horse, mounted, and eyed the team and buggy. They would about cover the amount the railroad had taken for their freight bill. He looked at them for a long time.

"Don't do it," said Elijah Woodrow. "Ain't gonna be worth it." Elijah had been a field hand. He knew when to cut his losses and just keep hoeing.

"He stole from us first," said Taylor.

"Did for a fact. But stealing's stealing. Won't no good come of it for nobody."

"Maybe not. Not gonna steal them. Just going to hold them as collateral 'til that thieving Wade does right by us."

Sidney climbed into the buggy and defiantly looked around at the group. "Someone can bring my horse on in," he called. He slapped the reins across the team's backs and headed toward Nicodemus.

"You can come out now," Mrs. Lawlis said tersely when the last black man disappeared over the horizon.

"My apologies, ma'am," said Wade. He looked out at the yard. "Did you see that? They stole my horses. People I gave every break in the world. Treated 'em just like I'd treat my own children."

"Don't know what the world is coming to when black people would think of hanging a white man," mumbled Mrs. Lawlis. "They scared me plumb to death. When my man gets here he'll hide you in back of the wagon and take you to Stockton."

" 'Preciate it," said Wade. His lips were tight in his pale face. Embarrassed that he had hidden under her skirts, neither of them could stand to look each other in the eye.

"We may have to make a few concessions to the damn niggers now, but after we get their vote for the county seat, they can all go right square to hell."

Henry Partridge stood before the wary group of immigrants and waved his claw hand in the air. "Quiet down, now. I called this here meeting 'cause we got to figure out what to do. And fast."

Night was coming on, and they were looking for places to stretch out their pallets on the long-stemmed blue grass.

"We gotta eat," Henry said. "Not just now and the day after. But from now on. This ain't Heaven, and ain't no manna gonna drop down."

He turned to Harrington and Jones. "Did any of you sorry people know how you was gonna feed us after you got us here?" He trembled, scarcely able to contain his fury. "Did you? Since any fool can see we can't chase down those rabbits, and the deer ain't hardly gonna just stroll right up to us and let us hit them over the head with a stone."

Harrington and Jones looked at each other helplessly.

"Wade promised to bring over wagonloads of supplies," Jones said. "Food and tools."

"Well, guess that ain't gonna happen now, is it?"

Henry whirled around and yelled across the crowd. "Gotta eat. No one here is gonna feed us," he said bitterly. "Might have known. Should have known. Dumb nigger that I am. But there's little children to feed. Best we not waste time."

Bethany closed her eyes and said a quick prayer of thanksgiving. A practical man. The Lord had sent them a practical man who knew how to move things along. He didn't waste time brooding on the white man who had chopped off his fingers or the white man who had given him the lying picture promising a paradise in Kansas.

"There's a creek over yonder," Henry said. "Supposed to be a river. That's what they called it in this here piece of paper." He waved the circular in the air. "Says it's the Solomon River. Yeah. That what it says. I say it's a creek, and I say it's the most pitiful dribble of water I've ever seen, but that is what we got. Got to make the most of it. Let's see if there's a fish in it."

■ ■ ■ ■

Hesitantly, Bethany approached Dolly's dugout. Over one hundred people had turned around and gone back. Worse, they were the most prosperous ones who had the means to leave.

Bethany was determined that there would be no more broken promises in this community. The latest promise that she had some control over was that the menfolks had promised the first child born in Nicodemus would be born in a real home. They did not have much time. Carrie Williams was just a month away from giving birth.

"Hello," she called softly. Dolly was sitting outside in the sunlight, stitching a patch on a piece of cloth. A sunbonnet protected her light, freckled skin. Her dress was a faded, soft, blue-calico print. It was worn and raggedy but, for all that, far better than the drab gray and brown linsey-woolsey dresses worn by nearly all the other women.

"Hello," said Dolly, not bothering to warm her voice.

Bethany sighed, knowing she had antagonized this woman on the boat by her refusal to form a light-colored alliance. She hadn't gone along with Dolly's sense of superior-ity. Her temper flared suddenly at having to cater to this selfish woman. She got straight to the point.

"I've come to ask a favor of you. Would you consider turning your home over to Carrie Williams? We're running out of time, and we had no idea there would be so many people coming in so soon." Bethany fingered her skirt. "The thing is, we've promised Carrie a proper home for this new baby."

Dolly's eyes widened, and a sly smile crept across her face. She laid her sewing quietly in her lap as though she were the queen asked to give up her throne to a peasant.

"I think you already know the answer to that."

Bethany whirled around.

Teddy Sommers had hunkered down and waited for the sky to fall after the men had come prancing back with Wade's horses. What had these crazy niggers done? What were they thinking?

A week later, two men pulled up with a wagon load of supplies. "This here's what you were promised from Wade."

Clyde McCall spoke the words in a monotone, like they pained him. He stared into the distance as though the men gathered were beneath being honored with a look.

"This here is to see you through the winter," he said slowly. He turned his head and shot a stream of tobacco. "If you all ain't too shiftless to figure out how to make do."

In the back of the wagon were sacks of flour, a few sacks of sugar, several barrels of lard, and bags of wheat and seed corn. No meat. Barely enough to feed twenty-five people for two months.

Henry Partridge stepped toward them, but Teddy reached out to stop him. "Let me," he said.

He took off his hat before he spoke. "Don't mean no disrespect, sirs, but can't make it on that. You knows that. Black, white, or yellow. Not enough food. Not enough nothing. You folks have got to show a little mercy here. If we'd of knowed what we was getting into, we would have come with more."

"White folks would have found out what they needed to know before they came." With a superior smile on his face, Clyde winked at his companion. "Didn't come here to chat. Came to give you people this generous offering from Mr. Wade and to take back what belongs to him."

McCall jumped down from the wagon and

unloaded the sparse cargo. He walked over to Wade's horses, untied them, hitched them to his buggy, and set out across the prairie with his friend driving the other team and wagon.

Winter was coming. There were no houses, no lumber, and the meager supplies they had on hand would soon be depleted.

Teddy scouted the countryside and came back one day hauling a plow in the wagon he had borrowed from Harrington.

"Traded some fixing for a week's use of this here contraption. They showed me how to use it. A week won't be long enough to get very much done, but long enough to build a nice place for Carrie's baby."

They completed a half-sod house, half-dugout. Teddy studied the wistful faces of the womenfolks as they helped Carrie Williams tote her meager belongings inside. Shyly they offered little treasures — a cup here, a coveted piece of cloth there — as though they were contributing to a place of their own. Honoring their own first child.

Teddy called Henry Partridge aside. "Need to talk. Got to get this sod cutter back on time. But wasn't nothing said about what we had to use it for."

"Gonna be used for homes. That plain.

We can't put the women and chillum in snowbanks. Don't cotton much to the idea for myself. What you got in mind?"

"No time to build places for everyone. I want to build a big place for us all. Use it for everything and everyone. Meetings, church, school, sick place. Belong to nobody and everybody."

Henry scratched his head with his claw hand. "That a fine idea. Give folks a place to go they own themselves."

They worked furiously cutting sod. The men worked all day and during the moonlight, and if the nights were cloudy, some of them carried lanterns and guided the way for the man plowing. A number of the women, hardened by field work, could match their physical strength. Their axes flew after they scoured the banks of the Solomon for dead cottonwood limbs. They framed in two windows and a door on the long side of the dugout.

"Poorest wood I've handled," grumbled Teddy. "Might as well be using plant stalks."

"You want oak, go back to Kentuck where they knowed what a tree was," Henry said.

Before the week was out, they had built a thirty by fifty-foot sod building. Seeing the happiness on the faces of the women, Teddy turned to Henry.

"We done good. We done the right thing."

"Too big to keep warm. No stove," said Henry. "Man can still freeze to death there. Still got to hollow out fire ditches so folks can eat and stay warm."

"Point is, Henry, women need something to give them hope so they stick around. That building's going to make them stick. Now let's figure out how to keep them alive."

Then as the nights grew colder and the children shivered around the tiny clusters of campfires, the men frantically carved little caves into the sides of the creek banks with hoes and, in some cases, just their hands.

Bethany dug furiously. Dug like a field hand. Cold blazing anger was new to her. She had first felt it when she was dealing with Miss Nancy, and it boiled anew over Dolly's refusal to help Carrie Williams. She worked until her hands bled, barked orders to the other women, then fought back frustrated tears.

Doctoring women couldn't afford to make enemies.

Autumn fell heavily on the menfolks, for black women were watching women. Used to escaping into the fields or their trades, there was nowhere for the men to go. The women watched them all the time.

Like the coyotes they could hear off in the night, the women were a silent accusing presence. There were no woods to slip off to when their souls needed peace. There were just the watching eyes of the women in the dugouts.

In Kentucky, there had been a trembling worry that owls stole their souls some nights. Here in Kansas, the men would be glad to fly away into the peace of the night. Just for a while.

There were no trees on the prairie, so there were no owls to trade souls with. Nowhere to slip away to.

On the barren prairie, the womenfolk could see them anywhere.

Chapter Six

The campfire flickered with a puny smoky haze and was barely brighter than pine-tar torches shedding light on the face of the speaker. They had started off burning old cottonwood branches at the public meetings. Then the colonists realized wood was too valuable to light the face of someone who was probably just going to stir things up anyway.

But having been forbidden to meet in large groups since America was founded, there was a magical attraction to these gatherings. Despite the cold and the dark.

Bethany sighed and splayed her fingers across her face. She looked down at her feet. Paul Tripp irritated her more than anyone else. She hated his voice, his clothes, his arrogance, and most of all his ideas.

Tripp's face gleamed in the light from the campfire. He had a thunderous voice and a way of making people believe.

"White men owe us," he hollered. "Owe us back wages for all our years we were enslaved. Owe us for our blood."

Bethany loathed the gatherings when they dwelt on the horrors of slavery. A man told of night riders chopping off his uncle's hands just for wanting to come to Kansas. Another sobbed through his father's hobbling — cutting the Achilles tendon so he couldn't run away.

She didn't doubt the validity. She knew of terrible things just from doctoring in the slave quarters. But all these memories did was stir up hatreds she knew they should set aside. The stories were a terrible legacy for the children, and she wanted them all to move on.

She listened with an aching heart. They spoke of cruelties that had come about in the new South that would never have been inflicted on blacks when they were someone's property. Before the war they had been too valuable. What would have been the point in chopping off a slave's hands and rendering him useless?

She watched Tripp sway the group. Now he wanted them to ask the state of Kansas for aid. "We got it coming," Tripp said. "You know that. White folks have lived off our sweat long enough."

Teddy came up beside her.

"Are you going to speak out against what he's proposing?" she asked. "Someone has to."

"No," Teddy said. His voice was solemn, his face dark in the shadows. "No, he's right, Miss Bethany. We've got to have help. Too many people on short rations now. Been studying on that waking and dreaming and every other way. Can't let the children starve. We done did ourself in when those men tried to hang Wade. He might have come through."

"And then again, he might not have," she said quickly.

"Well, one thing for sure. The food he promised ain't here and ain't never gonna be here."

"Teddy, we can't start off begging. People will think we can't take care of ourselves. That we don't know how to plan."

"Well?"

"Well, we can, and we would have if someone had told us the truth."

"Maybe we should have been smarter in checking out the truth. Truth is we got here too late to plant crops even if we'd of knowed how to plant them or what to plant or what it took to pound a hole in this miserable piece of earth."

"There's got to be another way."

Miserably, she looked around at the faces illuminated by the fire and knew there wasn't. They had to get more food for the community. For the children.

"It's just that I can't stand to hear 'dumb nigger' one more time in my life." She looked at Teddy, not bothering to hide the tears streaming down her face. "I know we've got to do this, but I just hate it."

Bethany huddled in her bed against the back wall of the dugout. Wrapped in every quilt she had managed to bring from Kentucky, she was still chilled to the bone. However, she was better off than most of the settlers. Only the people arriving with her in July had built decent dugouts. The ones coming in September had run out of time before the soul-freezing cold weather hit.

They didn't have the tools or the time to cut the tough sod, so they were reduced to hacking away at the sides of the hills until they had literally dug out wide, deep burrows for housing. Most had entryways covered with hides as there wasn't finished lumber to make real doors.

The community just barely completed the promised half-house, half-dugout structure for Carrie Williams before she gave birth to a fine son. A blessedly trouble-free birth. Bethany doubted she would be so lucky next time.

The food shortage was bad enough, but fetching water was a miserable ordeal. The town was located far enough back from the Solomon to escape flood waters, but the walk with heavy buckets was exhausting.

There were simply too many people coming all at once. Come spring, some of the families planned to get their own land instead of trying to live in town.

The Browns had begged Bethany to live with them. "You family, girl. No point in staying by yourself."

"Oh, but there is," she said. "I'm called away all hours of the night. I'm used to it, but you folks would be worn to a frazzle."

Her dugout was her very own place in the world. Hers alone. Giddy with joy, ignoring the dirt, the bugs, the bleak black walls, the dampness, she had made it as homelike as possible. She hacked off twigs from dead cottonwood branches and pounded them into the walls. Then she wove vines into cords, strung them between the sticks and draped her colorful quilts over them. Most quilts owned by former slaves were made of old tattered cloth, but Miss Nancy had let her draw from her finest silk scraps, so Bethany's were vibrant with blues and reds and purples and yellow.

On another length of vines, she had hung thatches of dried herbs and tiny cloth bundles of seeds, carefully labeled. There was a pleasant aroma from sage and orange blossoms.

She used flat rocks to make four squat wide pillars to support a bed frame. She had bound four poles together with vines to make a stout rectangle, then wove a base from the long, tall grape vines she had found growing in a thicket along the Solomon.

She was warm at night, sandwiched between layers of the feather beds she had brought with her. To her surprise, after the first snow, the dugout became warmer. The huge drifts provided extra insulation.

In the daytime, she propped the bed against the wall and laid a board across two of the rock pillars, which served both as an eating table and a work table.

Most of the people still cooked outside. But some had dug a shallow trench in the bare ground inside their dugout. It was usually just two feet long and wide enough to set a skillet on. While it worked well enough, Bethany worried about effects of the smoke during the winter when the houses were all closed up.

Although she'd hated to part with the money, Bethany had bought a stove from one of the September families who went back to Kentucky. It was one of three in the whole community. Now she gave thanks that she had done so. The flames visible through the gleaming nickel grate always soothed her.

She had started rabbit stew early in the morning and added a handful of the wild onions she had gathered and strung up on the wall to dry. They were one of the few plants she recognized and knew were safe to eat. If there were people who needed doctoring that day, she would take food with her.

She smiled. This poor hole in the world was a far cry from the cabin of her daydreams. In the corner were stacks of buffalo chips for fuel and a whole pile of hay cats — twisted hanks of grass and straw — that provided quick, hot fuel. They burned quickly, but some mornings they were just right to take the chill off the room.

The stovepipe jutting out of the ground provided fresh air. She had tied a jaunty strip of red cloth around it. It warned travelers to stay away from the roof of the only home she had ever had in her entire life. It also served to thwart birds and animals, who stayed away from the flapping cloth.

Burrowing deep in her blankets, she began to hum. This was the only time in her life she had had the luxury of total rest. When she was a slave, she worked constantly. Other people always told her what to do from one moment to the next. Here in Kansas, no one cared.

The colonists had pooled all their food. The scant amount delivered by Wade to get back his horses and buggy wasn't even enough to keep a fourth of them alive. Thankfully, Tripp and Harrington had left for aid before the blizzard hit.

Wind-driven snow was covering the ground with high, treacherous drifts. She felt like a woolly bear hibernating for the winter. She burrowed deeper and slept again. There were no windows. It was difficult to keep track of time. She didn't mind. Sleep was still a heavenly luxury. She dozed off.

A fierce clanging on the stovepipe jarred her awake. It was followed by a muffled voice. "You there, ma'am?"

"Yes," she hollered.

"I'm coming in after you. You're needed. A woman is having a baby."

110

"I can't get out." When she had tried to push the door open that morning, it was blocked by the snow.

"I can see that. I'll dig you out."

She got out of bed, quickly combed her long hair, and twisted it into a bun. She stuffed a supply of herbs into her cloth satchel. She grabbed her cloak and wrapped it tightly around her body.

No one in the community was close to having a baby. It had to be someone passing through. She waited for the man to clear the drift. Just as she was shoving from the inside, he gave an enormous tug, and she fell across the threshold at his feet.

"Beg your pardon, ma'am."

She looked up and up and up at a huge man, dark as a panther, with the most powerful shoulders she had ever seen. His broad features were set off by a close crop of kinky hair. His powerful thighs strained against his homespun pants. He took her hand and silently helped her stand up.

"My name's Jim Black. You Bethany Herbert?"

She just had time to nod a quick reply before he tugged her to the waiting horse. The wind howled, and the snow blew around them in blinding swirls.

He swung into the saddle, then reached

111

down and picked her up as though she were a feather and settled her behind him. Sheltered by his broad back, Bethany drew a painfully cold breath as they headed out across the prairie.

She peered around the man when the horse began to slow. Ahead was a covered wagon, nearly invisible through the snow. It was drawn by a team of work horses, their heads drooping. Statuesque, as though they were frozen in place.

"Oh no," she said. "Please, God, no. Let her be alive." Clearly the horses could not move. The wagon was icing over.

Jim Black reined up, dismounted, and carried Bethany to the wagon before she could point out that she could walk on her own two feet. He practically shoved her through the opening. She drew a sharp breath, then turned and looked at him, her eyes huge with accusation.

A white woman.

Even though she had assisted at many white births, the consequences of things going awry were terrifying. Tight lipped, she reached for the woman's hand. Then her heart plummeted to her stomach.

The woman was much too cold, but her eyes fluttered open. Bethany gave her hand a little squeeze. "I'll take good care of you, ma'am," she said.

The woman gave a little moan of despair and then was wracked by a strong contraction. She held Bethany's hands in a death grip.

"Leave this wagon for a bit," Bethany said curtly to Jim Black. The minute his feet hit the ground, she pulled up the woman's dress. If birth was imminent, they were doomed.

The woman was not fully dilated. There would be a little time. Several hours, maybe. Time enough to get her back to Bethany's dugout. But that was impossible. They couldn't use the wagon. It would take hours now to dig it out. The woman could not bear to ride back on Black's horse, either by sidesaddle or astraddle. Bethany could not risk bringing on bleeding or speeding up labor. Yet she had to warm this woman and calm her down.

There were no children around. If this were the woman's first child, Bethany could count on the birth taking a bit longer. Time enough to get them back to her dugout? But how?

Desperately, Bethany looked around. She saw several boards turned on their long edge, wedged against the side of the wagon.

"Mr. Black," she hollered. "I need your

help to loosen this board."

He climbed back inside. They tugged it away from the bundles of tools packed against it.

"I need you to fetch several lines of the harness from the horses. Let's strap her to this board and get her back to my dugout."

Black nodded, then threw the board out onto the snow. He grabbed a hammer and some nails from inside the wagon and pounded them into one of the short ends of the board. He removed a harness strap from the team and attached the leather to the board.

"We don't have time to do this right," Bethany said. Her teeth chattered from fright and from the cold. "We're going to lay her flat and rig up something for her to hang onto so she won't fall off. I'll hand you the harness after you get back on the horse, and I'll guide the back end."

Jim Black scooped up the woman, and they placed her on the makeshift sled. "We have to stay on top of the snow," he said. "Or it won't pull right."

Bethany turned to the woman and patted her hand. "Ma'am, just hold on. That's all we ask. We're going to get you to where it's warm and I have room to work."

"Her name is Suzanne," Jim said.

114

"Miss Suzanne," said Bethany. "Just hold on. I'm less than a mile from here."

"Best you ride," Jim said, shaking his head. "I'll keep her steady."

He helped Bethany climb into the saddle. She pivoted around and reached for the ends of the leather strips fastened to the nails. They set off, pushing slowly into the swirling clouds of snow.

The horse shied, and the board started to tip and edge down before they had even gone a hundred feet.

"Wait," she called. "It's not going to work. Her blanket keeps falling open. She can't hold it shut and keep hold of the straps at the same time. Let's trade places. I'm no rider, and this horse is used to you."

Black lifted her down. She handed him the reins and ran to the back of the board. "Can you see where to go? Can you make out the way?"

"Yes," he hollered. "I can see where we broke through when we come to the wagon. But I'll go back for more straps to put on back so you can pull up on the bottom. I can hold the front straps up with one hand."

The big man lunged through the snow and quickly returned with more harness and the hammer. Suzanne groaned as he pounded nails into the far short end and attached the leather lines. He looped extra lines of harness over the saddle horn.

The woman's face was pale and waxy. Frightened, Bethany felt for the pulse in her throat. It was weak.

"Help me lift her," she said. Jim cradled Suzanne against his chest. Bethany whipped off her own cloak and placed it on the sled. Then she used the end of one of the nails to rip a four-inch width from the bottom of her skirt. She quickly tore off the strip of worn material and used the binding to strap the cloak around Suzanne's body.

"You gonna freeze yourself now," Jim said. He took off his own thin coat and handed it to Bethany. She accepted it, knowing he would fare better in the relentless wind than she would.

Bethany lifted the back of the board. Jim twisted in the saddle and, grasping the front straps, raised the front end. When they set off, with Jim awkwardly keeping an eye on the faint trail in front and the women behind him, the makeshift slid skimmed on top of the snow instead of veering from side to side or sinking.

Bethany only went about fifteen feet before she had to reposition herself. The wind was like a deadly wall, and her breath came in short, icy bursts.

Jim reined up abruptly. "Let's shift places," he yelled.

"I can't ride," she hollered. "Never had to."

He didn't bother to reply, just scooped her up onto the saddle and gave her the reins. Bethany did not have the strength to hold up the front end of the sled and guide the horse. Jim removed the extra lengths of harness from the saddle horn. He quickly retied all the lines, shortening the length of the front ones so that the horse bore the weight. Then he took Bethany's place behind the board.

She spurred the horse, knowing they would go faster now if she could figure out what to do quickly. With each foot they gained, she gave thanks for anything and everything she could think of. She gave thanks that it was afternoon, and they had daylight to work with. She gave thanks for the stove keeping her dugout warm. She gave thanks for the bright little red flag that had shown Jim Black the way. She gave thanks for her quick mind and the willing hands of this man who could see at once what needed to be done.

The horse stopped and shuddered. "We're nearly there," Jim said, pointing in the distance.

When they reached the dugout, Jim lifted the woman from the sled and carried her inside.

"Here," said Bethany tersely, pointing to her bed in the corner. She pulled back the quilts and spread a thin sheet on top of the feather mattress. Jim laid Suzanne on top. Bethany covered her, then went to the stove and added hay cats for a quick blaze under her largest kettle. She moved the stew toward the back.

She studied the little cloth sacks hanging from the various lengths of twine on the wall. She untied the one labeled *arnica Montana* from the main length. It would help stop bleeding if Suzanne had complications. But even in Kentucky it was hard to come by. Other arnica plants that looked a lot like this were deadly poison. Would she recognize the right ones on the prairie?

She absolutely had to find plants to control bleeding. She could resort to reciting Ezekiel 16:6, but she wasn't that kind of a healer. It wasn't the way she'd been taught. She lacked the sure belief it took to lay on hands. She knew all the right words: "When I passed you by and saw you squirming in your blood, I said to you while you were in your blood, 'Live!' I said to you while you were in your blood, 'Live!' "

The words didn't work for her. She knew healing women that could stop bleeding cold by just saying that Bible verse three times, but she couldn't.

Her throat tightened. There were only a few sacks of herbs hanging on the wall. When her precious supply of laudanum ran out, she had no idea how to replace it.

She lifted the woman's head and gave her a sip of hot tea. Then she poured some hot water into a pan and began to wash Suzanne's face and rub her arms and legs. She would do the best she could for this poor, thin, little blond-headed waif. She went to the crate in the corner of the dugout and took out a long, white gown.

"I'll need to wash her down and try to warm her up," she said to Jim.

He nodded, glad to have a woman in charge. "I'll step outside."

"No need. You'll be too cold. Just turn your head."

"I don't mind, ma'am," he said with a small smile. "I don't mind at all."

"I'll call you when I'm done."

Bethany slid Suzanne's dress over her head, then covered her again with the blanket. Her lids fluttered open.

"Thank you," she said. "Thank you. Oh, thank God."

"You'll be fine, Miss Suzanne. See, I even know your name. I've delivered many a baby, and you're doing just fine." Bethany eased the white gown on over her head. "Right now, we need to get a little food in your stomach. I have some good stew."

She went to the stove and ladled some stew into a tin cup. She wanted to brew a separate tea of willow bark to help this woman with her pain but hesitated. It was a bad choice if Suzanne was a bleeder.

Bethany lifted Suzanne's head off the pillow and let her have sips of the hot liquid. "No meat, just yet," she said. "I'm just going to give you a bit of broth at first."

Suzanne nodded and sipped the hot broth. Then as her body warmed, she eagerly reached for the cup.

"Slow, now," said Bethany. "Take your time swallowing. Then try to sleep for a little while. What is your last name, Miss Suzanne?"

Suzanne looked at her blankly as though totally bewildered by the question. She started to cry. "I was Missus Mercer. Am I still Missus Mercer? Or Miss. I don't know what I'm supposed to call myself now."

" 'Was' Mercer?"

"We were going to Denver. My husband was going to start a lumber business." Suzanne's eyes filled with tears, and she turned her head as she bit her lip. "He died. He just died about a week ago. What am I supposed to call myself when my husband's dead?"

"How did it happen?"

"He cut himself, trying to fix the wheel on the wagon. It was just a little cut, but all of a sudden it got big and red, and he was taken with fever, and then he just died."

Bethany's heart sank. It would be a miracle if this woman could keep her wits together long enough to help with the birth.

"Now I don't know what to do, or where to go. I just want to die."

"Shh, now. You're going to have a little baby to live for."

"He wanted a son. I swear to God if it's a little boy, I don't know how I can stand it."

"A little boy will need lots of love. You're warm now. You're safe now. Your husband is safe now. Safe in the arms of Jesus." Bethany kept her voice low and rhythmic. "Safe in the arms of Jesus." It was both a song and a chant, meant to soothe.

Suzanne Mercer relaxed her death grip on Bethany's hands. Her eyelids fluttered. Her breaths were deep and easy. Exhausted, she dozed.

Bethany wiped her hands, then opened

the door and called to Jim Black. "You can come in now. She's sleeping. Gathering strength."

He sprang to his feet from where he had been crouched down against the side of the dugout. His mouth looked grim and tense.

"You've done well, Mr. Black," she said softly. "Don't know how anyone could have done better by this woman."

He didn't speak, but his eyes reflected his profound gratitude. He ducked and entered the dugout.

"Now, let's take care of you," Bethany said. "We need to warm you up. Stand over here by the stove. I have some stew. I imagine you're hungry."

"Yes, ma'am, I am at that. But first, you said there was something you wanted me to do?"

"Yes," she said. "I want you to fill this dishpan with snow, and I'll set it on the stove. I need a lot of hot water."

He took the large tub, went outside, filled it with snow, carried it back inside the dugout, and set it on the stove. Bethany ladled a bowl of rabbit stew, making sure he got plenty of the rich meat.

"I didn't make bread," she said. "I wish I had something to go with it. As soon as I'm done tending her, I'll fix us all a decent meal."

His hands trembled as he finished off the bowl in huge swallows, scarcely bothering to chew the meat. Silently, she refilled it four times. He glanced at the pot, then thanked her. He easily could have eaten the whole thing.

He sat on the floor, his great legs extended.

"Were you heading for Denver also, Mr. Black?"

He nodded. "I'm a blacksmith. I heard they were in short supply there. I knowed the Mercers were going west, so I decided to hook up with them. Knowed them from before the war."

He shuddered. The muscles in his jaw jumped. "They're good people. Her husband died so fast I couldn't believe it. One minute he fine, the next he dead. All over a little cut. You is a healing woman. Could you have done for him?"

"I could have tried. But sometimes, there's just no help for it." Her voice faltered.

"The cut was dirty," Jim said. His voice was heavy, as though he felt responsible for the man's death.

"Can't always save someone from a dirty cut."

"We was trying to fix that wheel," he continued, looking at her with guilty eyes. "He slipped. Just cut his hand a little. Next thing I knowed, he took terrible sick. Next thing I knowed after that, he dead. Miss Suzanne and I had to keep on. No smart place to quit."

"You did just fine. It's a miracle that you found my place. Please rest now. You look like you need to rest as badly as she does."

They edged toward opposite sides of the wall, and he sat on the packed earth and again stretched out his long legs. Bethany took the only chair. She quietly studied his wide, high cheeks, his broad nose with a scar across the bridge.

Any black man traveling with a white woman was just asking for trouble, let alone one of his enormous size. What would they do? Where could they go? For that matter, what would she do with the woman after she gave birth? Suzanne Mercer wouldn't want to stay in a colony of black people.

"We're in desperate need of a blacksmith, Mr. Black. Would you consider staying here?"

"Don't rightly think I could make a living." He glanced toward the bed. "I want to do right by her. Don't know what I'd do about her."

"I know. I've been thinking as soon as she can travel, there's a town about twelve miles from here called Wade City. I don't much like the man who founded it. But we can buy there."

"No laws against black folks being in stores out here?"

"No, not out here. Teddy Sommers has been there, and he didn't have a lick of trouble. Teddy says we can buy whatever we have the money for. He got the impression that not all the folks there think that much of Wade, either. We can take Mrs. Mercer there as soon as she and the baby can travel."

"Good," Jim said. "That woman is worrying me half to death for more than one reason."

"Taking her to Wade City will give us a chance to see how folks out here feel about us as a group. Can't really judge that from just having Teddy go. No one feels threatened by Teddy. I know you haven't met him, but as soon as you do, you'll see what I mean. He helped start this place; I don't know what we would do without him."

Jim gazed at the white woman on the bed. "It would ease my mind plenty if she takes to the idea. Up to her, though."

"Why don't you sleep on throwing in with

us? Staying right here in Nicodemus. I know we don't look like much now, but we're going to make something of this town."

He nodded. "Thank you. I'll think about it." She handed him a blanket, and he quickly fell into an exhausted sleep.

CHAPTER SEVEN

Bethany jerked awake at Suzanne Mercer's cry. She leaped to her feet. Dazed, Jim Black, who had been sleeping soundly, raised up from the floor.

"Perhaps you'd better step outside for a while," Bethany said. Her voice was calm, belying her anxiety. She hated birthings where she didn't know her patient at all. When Jim pushed open the door and edged out, he let in a blast of cold air.

Bethany bowed her head and centered her thoughts. Praying constantly, she went to Suzanne Mercer's side. She drew deep calming breaths and checked her patient. Suzanne was fully dilated. In a short time, she would begin the last stages. Bethany went over to the stove and stoked the fire. She turned at a sharp cry and went to tend to the woman.

She could see the baby's head, and as long as there was no trouble afterwards, it would be a normal birth with no complications. *Praise God,* she thought.

Minutes later, Suzanne Mercer began to push. Her guttural cries filled the room. The birth was surprisingly easy for a first. Bethany praised God when the infant let loose its healthy cry. "It's a girl," she said softly to the new mother as she laid the baby on Suzanne's stomach. Now if there were no complications with the afterbirth, she could rest easy.

With a long fork, she lifted string from the hot water and eased her hot knife onto a cloth. Then she turned back to the bed, neatly tied the cord twice about an inch apart, and sliced through the middle. The afterbirth followed only minutes later. She cleaned up Mrs. Mercer and the baby and then called for Jim Black to come back inside.

He grinned broadly. "Guess you might know how happy I am, for more reasons than one." He blew on his gigantic hands to warm them.

"If something had gone wrong, it would be terrible for all of us."

"How long will she be down?"

"Ten days. She and the baby can stay right here, and I have friends who will be glad to put you up. In fact, I'll speak to the Browns about you spending the winter with them if you decide to stay."

"Been thinking about it."

"Why take a chance on what you'll find in Denver?"

"Depends on what we can get done with Miss Suzanne. She can't stay here with a bunch of blacks. You know that. If we find a place for her, I done been thinking favorably about staying here in Nicodemus."

"I'm so glad." She couldn't find the words to tell this strong, good man how much she admired his actions during the last twenty-four hours. He was just the kind of person Nicodemus needed.

He looked at her hard. "Want you to know I is just a blacksmith. Ain't got no tricks. No fancy magic."

"Didn't figure you did. That's not why I asked you to stay." Blood surged to her cheeks. Some of the old folks who had come to the St. James plantation from Africa believed blacksmiths were favored with a special knowing. They kept the fire. Molded the people. Talked with their anvils.

"Just so you know what you is getting."

"Understood."

He nodded. "Now tell me where y'all keep your oats. I'll round up some help and go

129

fetch that poor team before they freeze to death."

Two weeks later, Bethany, Teddy, Jim Black, and Suzanne Mercer — holding Baby Abigail — set off for Wade City. That morning they had hitched up her fine team, which was the envy of all the men. The snow from the early blizzard had melted. Although the grass had died with the onset of late fall, the ground was firm and easy to navigate.

Suzanne's bright-blond hair was concealed by her sunbonnet. She was a small, talkative woman who naturally expected to fit in wherever she went. After her baby was born, she had been seized by crying fits for her dead husband. Then her natural resilience bubbled up. Now that she was on her way to an established town, she was mulling over ways she could make a living.

"I could sew, of course, I like to do that; but I'm a better cook, and good cooks get to meet a lot of people. 'Course, if Danny had lived I wouldn't need to think about any of this. He was going to start building for folks, and I was going to cook for all the help he was going to hire. But I've got a little dab of money to get started. I'll have even more income from the sale of his tools and supplies. There's sure to be town lots in

Wade City."

"You can count on that," said Bethany. "And I think an eating place is a fine idea. Have you thought about combining it with a boarding house? As more people come out here looking for land, they will be short on places to stay. You have a wonderful advantage in that you have some money."

"I know. Can't think of anything unluckier than losing my Danny, but thank the Lord, I'm not broke, too." Tears brimmed in her eyes. "I'll spend more time crying later. Right now, I have this wee one to think of."

She smiled down at the tiny baby in her arms. "There's no way to repay you and your people for all you've done, Miss Bethany. If I start my café and boarding house, all of you will be welcome anytime. Want you to know that. Is there any other way I can repay you? Anything at all?"

Bethany started to say "no," just her thanks was enough. Then one of the horses tossed his head, and a thought crossed her mind as though she had been struck by a bolt of lightning.

"Yes," she said firmly. "The people who came out here in September had their horses stolen." She quickly decided not to go into details damning Wade. "Would you please loan us your team for a week? That

131

would speed up making proper dugouts and soddies, and allow us to break a little land."

"Well, of course," said Suzanne. She beamed at Bethany. "Of course I'll do that. Longer, too, if you need them."

"Thank you," Bethany said. "I can't tell you how much I appreciate it." Her throat tightened with tears, and Suzanne squeezed her hand.

They both were silent as they looked across the prairie. There were no roads, no signs, no indentations in the grass to guide them. They depended on Teddy's unerring sense of direction. Bethany studied the countryside, hoping to identify some of the plants as they traveled. But all that was visible were dried stalks poking above some of the dried grass, and it didn't do her a bit of good.

By the time they got to Wade City, she realized the vast distances in Kansas were so different from Kentucky that she would have to learn to ride. For the sake of her patients, she certainly couldn't just walk as she had always done.

Wade City was sparsely populated. There were a few scattered sod houses and businesses, and several tents and half-dugouts sticking up where there was an incline.

There were no frame houses, but there were mounds of cut rock lying around as though the people intended to build something more substantial in spring. There was a limestone combination hotel and saloon.

"We're laying these people in shade already, Teddy," said Bethany. "Just look! I'll bet we've got four times as many people."

Tears filled Suzanne's eyes as they pulled up in front of the cobbled together half-sod, half-limestone mercantile store with a rickety board sign hanging down from the roof. "I guess I was expecting more." She drew a deep breath as Bethany reached for her hand. "It'll get better," she said.

"That's what they keep saying. Yes."

Teddy jumped down and tied the reins to the rail. His face was sober. Apprehensive. They had come from a state where white people killed their kind for just looking at them the wrong way. The men of Nicodemus had come close to hanging the man who started this town. They'd taken his team to boot. Be just their luck if Wade was there inside.

Jim Black helped Suzanne Mercer get down from the wagon, then Bethany handed her Baby Abigail.

"Jim, just put my things right here," Suzanne ordered. "I'll have someone inside this store tote them to where I'll be staying. You folks will be taking this rigging back, so I don't want to overlook anything I might need this week. Would you like to borrow Danny's tools for a while?"

Jim drew a deep breath, scarcely believing his good luck. "Yes, ma'am. That's mighty generous of you."

"Nonsense. Just consider them on loan for now like the team and wagon. Bring them back later. There's no need to sell them until you're through."

Jim glanced over at Teddy. They would never be through using good tools. "Much obliged, Miss Suzanne."

He handed down all her belongings and stood awkwardly beside the wagon, waiting for her to say goodbye.

"No sense just standing here. Let's go inside where it's warm."

Bethany gave Jim a look and cleared her throat. "Perhaps it would be better if you went in by yourself, ma'am." Her delicate eyebrows arched with pride.

"Absolutely not. You're my friends, and I plan to introduce you just like I would any other friends. You've saved my life. And my baby's life. If people give you a speck of trouble, they'll have to answer to me."

There were several men sitting around an

old stove at the back. Wade was not among them. They stopped talking as soon as the door opened.

Bethany blinked, letting her eyes adjust from the bright sunlight to the dark interior. There was an odor of coffee and dried apples. On the shelves were bolts of cloth and tinware and a king's array of goods she yearned to touch and hold and smell.

"Gentlemen. I'm Suzanne Mercer, and this is my little baby, Abigail, and these are my friends from Nicodemus, Kansas: Mr. Teddy Sommers and Mr. Jim Black and Miss Bethany Herbert. These people saved my life, and I've come to inquire if there is a place in this town where I can stay until I can start a boarding house."

Well there, now, thought Bethany, covering her mouth with her hand to hide the trace of a smile. *Couldn't be more direct than that.*

Behind the counter was a tall, thin man, clean-shaven with neat, brown hair and sideburns. He spoke. Bethany felt a little lurch of apprehension at the Southern accent. *A Georgia man.* She would bet on it.

"We're pleased to meet you all." He nodded politely in the direction of the blacks. "I'm Josiah Sinclair. And will your husband be coming along later, ma'am?"

"No. I'm a widow." Her eyes brightened with tears as she told of Danny's tragic death. "And if it hadn't been for these fine people here, I'd have died, too." She praised Jim Black for his steadfastness and then Bethany for her medical skills. "And of course you all know the esteemed Mr. Sommers," she added. "Cabinetmaker and the prominent landsman from Kentucky."

Again, Sinclair simply nodded politely and stood ramrod straight. "I'll get my wife, Mrs. Mercer. I'm sure you and the baby must be exhausted from the long trip." He looked at the cheeky trio of Negroes as though he could not figure out his next move.

Bethany smiled. She was used to confusing white folks. She had learned from Queen Bess to stand straight, look people in the eye, and state her business plainly and in decent English.

A man who had been sitting by the stove rose to his feet. "I'm Stanley Bradley. We would be glad to help you, ma'am. Proud to have you stay with us 'til you get started. No point in paying anyone. My wife and I just started a livery stable and feed store. We have two young 'uns. Our oldest girl just got married and moved out."

"That's very kind of you." Suzanne's face

brightened.

"You helped her with that baby, ma'am?" Stanley asked, turning to Bethany.

"Yes. I deliver babies and do other kinds of doctoring."

She yearned to tell them what the people back in Kentucky thought about the Herbert women. Wanted them all to know that her training was special. That she knew many things that some of the country-trained white doctors didn't know, because the St. James people had always called on physicians with the most advanced methods.

She wanted them to know that she put her supplies in boiling water, because it cut down on infections. And she hadn't learned that from any white doctor, either. Queen Bess made her do it. Told her folks were more likely to live. She didn't know why. But Queen Bess was a watching woman, and she knew it was so. She'd seen.

But it would all sound like empty bragging, so Bethany kept her mouth shut.

"We've tried to get a doctor to come here, but it's a little hard to talk anyone into it. This here's Fred Phillips and Zed Wooster," Stanley said easily, as though colored folks strolled into the store every day.

Perhaps Wade hadn't told anyone of his misadventure, Bethany thought suddenly.

Maybe they were starting with a clean slate after all.

"And the fellow over by the wall is Aaron Potroff."

Potroff stepped forward from the shadows. He tipped his hat, but Bethany was chilled by the look in his eyes. She felt it in her bones when someone hated her because she was black. Or because she was a woman doctor. Or just because she was alive.

"Charmed, I'm sure," Potroff said.

Bethany felt the room spin. Her stomach lurched. She reached for the counter to steady herself. Where had she heard the voice before? She had never been out of the South, and this man did not have a Southern accent. He was a Northerner.

I could not possibly have heard this voice before, she thought.

She kept her eyes lowered as Suzanne chattered brightly and told them all her plans. Potroff kept his gaze fixed on Bethany. He was tall, with a balding head fringed by silver hair. His face was the off-white of rancid bread dough. Puffy lids hooded his cold, gray eyes. He kept his head tipped to the right, as though he were listening intently to whatever anyone said. He held his hands high on his chest, his fingers neatly interlaced.

Bethany felt his eyes on her and kept studying the floor. *Do what the white man says, honey. Say what the white man wants you to say. Figure it out. If they say the grass is blue, say they smart, they is genius smart.*

"Old Potroff here is the real brains behind most things out here," teased Stanley. "Wade thinks he is, but he ain't."

Just then, Josiah Sinclair returned from the back room followed by a tall, painfully thin woman. She had white, liver-spotted skin and stringy, brown hair skinned back into a skimpy bun. Her light-blue eyes were oddly pale, as translucent as a fish's fin. Bethany closed her eyes for a second, recoiling from the sickly aura emanating from her.

"We don't serve niggras here," she said at once. "Your kind isn't welcome."

"Beg your pardon, ma'am," said Bethany, knowing it would not be smart to antagonize her. "We have been tending Mrs. Mercer here. We're with her."

Then something steeled inside her. Times had changed. They were free now. She didn't have to lower her eyes to anyone. Not this rude woman and not Potroff, either. She wouldn't do it any longer.

"I'm Bethany Herbert. And you are?"

Dumbfounded, the woman responded before she could stop herself. "I'm Estelle

Sinclair."

"Pleased to make your acquaintance, ma'am. I'm from Nicodemus, and you'll be pleased to know that your kind is welcome in our town. Long as your money is good, we will be more than happy to buy and sell to you."

Two dark splotches stained the woman's cheeks. Her mouth tightened, but before she could compose a reply, Bethany noticed a poster tacked on the wall.

"I see y'all are trying to start a church," she said pleasantly. "Certainly a worthy endeavor, and we do wish you well. In the meantime, you're more than welcome to come worship with us, also. We have two denominations for you to choose from. Baptist and Methodist Episcopal."

Heartened by the amused flicker in the eyes of two of the men around the stove, she hid a smile and turned to Suzanne Mercer. "Please send for me if you get sick. And the best of luck to you and your little Abigail. We'd best be getting along."

"Don't want you to be strangers, now, hear?" Suzanne said. "You plan to stay a while when you bring back my team."

Bethany wrapped her cloak tightly around her and walked out the door with Teddy and Jim Black. She could feel Estelle Sinclair's eyes on her as they climbed into the wagon and drove off.

Later, she would realize how strange it was that on the way home, although they all discussed everyone in the store and gleefully compared Nicodemus to Wade City, they didn't say a word about Aaron Potroff.

And, for the life of her, she couldn't account for such a violent reaction to someone she had never seen before.

CHAPTER EIGHT

Josiah Sinclair headed for the half-limestone, half-sod building where Aaron Potroff spent his time. There was a sign calling it a hotel, and there were indeed grand plans in the making, but in the meantime, a couple of extra pallets that would be welcomed by only the most desperate of travelers were all the accommodations available.

As usual, Potroff sat at a poker table in the corner, no doubt conjuring visions of a bustling community as soon as he figured out how to lure more people to Wade City.

Sinclair had the devil's business to do, but his wife had practically pushed him out the door, insisting it was his duty to let Potroff know of all the misery he was bringing to this county. Sinclair didn't much care for Potroff, but he was quickly learning that prosperity on the plains called for strange alliances.

Potroff looked up from his hand of solitaire. Josiah paused, miserable at the thought of getting into yet another argument with this man. He reckoned Potroff was forty-something, and if he had ever been married, he hadn't said so. The man was duded up like a gentleman, but he was not one.

Josiah figured he should know. He came from Southern gentry himself. No amount of slick tailoring could hide Potroff's flabbiness. His arms were unusually long and lacked muscle. He looked like a pale, intelligent hog. Josiah knew better than to underestimate his capacity for malice.

Before the war, he had overseers like Potroff.

Before the war, he could devote his time to books and finer considerations.

Before the war, he would not have dreamed of marrying Estelle with her stingy Yankee mind.

But his destruction had been so complete that he latched on to the first woman of means and allowed himself to be led West like an old ox. It may have been Estelle's idea that they speculate in lots in a town on the prairie, but he had taken one look at the vast empty space and decided at once that it suited him.

He had not seen opportunity, but rather

the burying place for dreams. A landscape of infinite sameness that did not nurture hope. He did not believe he could stand to have hope rise again, or any other giddy emotions he had once taken for granted. He followed Estelle's orders like he was another man from another world.

He sighed at the thought of having anything at all to do with the shrivel-hearted man sitting before him. However, Wade City needed Potroff to survive. He was their money man.

"Hope you noticed you got yourself a reading nigger, Potroff."

"Ain't my niggers."

"You're the one who brought them here."

"Them?"

"The Nicodemus niggers."

"Wasn't me; it was Wade."

"We all know better. You're the money behind this."

Potroff grinned. "One that can read, you say?"

"Didn't you notice that wench reading that church poster? Hard telling what kind of notions they will get. What they can do. It causes trouble, I tell you."

"You don't say."

Potroff stopped working his cigar. When the cigar stopped wiggling, it meant he was planning something.

"Well, what do you think they're going to do, Josiah? Start a revolution?"

"No, but if they can read it might not be as easy as you think to get them to vote this town in as the county seat. Wouldn't that be a deal now?"

"Don't you worry about them darkies. I brought them here for their vote. Wade says they're like sheep. Little lambs. We'll just lead them to slaughter when the time comes."

"Don't be too sure. I grew up around niggras. You'd be surprised how smart some of them are. And as for the sheep idea you've got in your head, that tells me you haven't had much dealing with them. They've got more ways of going against a white man than a dog's got fleas."

Potroff bristled at the suggestion he wasn't smart enough to keep on top of slaves or rich enough to have owned them. Though he was from Illinois, he knew, in the South, a man's wealth was measured by the number of slaves he had owned.

Was measured. He smiled. Was measured.

But it was hard to keep these Southerners whipped. Despite their defeat in the Late Rebellion, as they quaintly referred to it, Southerners were quick to work into the conversation just how many slaves they had owned before the war. How many acres of cotton they had grown. The size of the old plantation.

"Well now, Josiah, I think you're underestimating how grateful these people are. And I'm sure you're mistaken about how well any of them actually read. A little poster ain't that big a deal. All they would have to do would be to recognize a word or two to get the gist of a poster. And, even if they can read, you're overlooking a small detail. There's no other town around that's a contender for the county seat. Wade City is it."

Josiah shook his head in wonder. "There is another town, Aaron."

The man looked at him blankly and removed his cigar from his mouth.

"Nicodemus," said Sinclair. He wheeled around and walked off.

Aaron Potroff stared at the cards. There were no plays left. All the kings were at the top. The aces were set, but the little cards wouldn't fall into place. He swiped them all off onto the floor. He picked up his dead cigar from the edge of the table and tried to relight it. His hands were plenty steady, but the flame wavered. Annoyed, he looked around at the bleak room, but he couldn't see the source of the air current.

He rose and brushed the ashes off his vest, then knelt and picked up the cards. When he straightened, he caught sight of himself in the cracked mirror hanging over the basin. He looked seedy. There were stains on his jacket that couldn't be sponged off. The cuffs of his shirt were dingy. What the town really needed was a good washer-woman. It was hard to make a good impression on newcomers if a man looked seedy.

He walked outside and looked at the bleak collection of buildings scattered along the muddy street. Having the county seat was everything. Railroads came through county seat towns. People bought lots in county seat towns. Those towns became business hubs. Kansas was ablaze with county seat fights. Fortunes were made or lost on the county seat gamble. He intended to make his fortune right here, and he wasn't going to let anyone steal it from him.

He wasn't worried about anyone taking Nicodemus seriously as a county seat contender. But what if another white town sprung up to compete for the black vote? He didn't dare let that happen. People jacked up houses and business on the prairie and moved them to new locations without batting an eye. Whole towns could be dismantled and re-made in a heartbeat, with the old town sites deserted. Until Josiah Sinclair came calling, it had not occurred to him that someone might start a new town under his very nose. A new town would need the Nicodemus vote also. Maybe he'd better start buttering up the darkies.

He pulled on a top coat and stalked off to the livery stable. Since the night the niggers had turned on Wade, there hadn't been a soul in Wade City who had a good word to say about Nicodemus. Then Suzanne Mercer came along playing like her rescuers were black angels.

Well, he wanted Nicodemians to know how much he cared about their welfare. He surely did. He would put up a little money to tide them over, see how they were doing. And, most of all, see how many palms he would have to grease to make the vote go his way.

Potroff slowed his horse and buggy and stared at a large sod building, with a stovepipe clearly projecting from the roof. Several men, then women, came out of dugouts and silently watched him approach.

"How do, Mr. Potroff," said Teddy Sommers.

"Good day," Potroff said. "I see you folks haven't let any grass grow under your feet. See you've found yourself a carpenter."

"It's our new meeting place," said Teddy proudly. "This here's sort of a church and a town hall and gonna be a school, too. Nobody's building. Everybody's building. Belongs to all of us."

Potroff climbed down from the buggy and walked around the new construction. Not only was it large, but the sod blocks had been laid with precision, and it had a difficult "car" roof unique to Kansas. A car roof involved incorporating three beams, then springing boards into a bow, secured with sod blocks. It involved a considerable amount of knowledge and a great deal of skill with construction techniques.

The windows were covered with greased buffalo hides that could be rolled up in summer. The house faced true north, and the door frame was hung plumb. It was top-notch carpentry. Someone here was a whiz at building. Taking care to hide his surprise, he scratched his chin before he spoke.

"Yes, sir, it looks like you folks have been busy," he said finally. "Looks like you're doing all right for yourselves."

"No thanks to Wade," Teddy said. "No thanks to that lying Wade. He your man?

149

Folks say he is."

"Just an associate," Potroff said quickly. "Not close enough to call friend, even."

"He done us wrong. Can't expect us to think kindly of him. He sold horses out from under us to pay for our freight. Promised us food and tools. Didn't deliver. Left us to pert' near starve."

"Well now, I can see where you folks might think he's been a little neglectful. That's why I've come today. Heard about that. I know you folks got off on the wrong foot with a man from our town, and I want to make it up to you. Help you out a little."

"We is doing just fine now," Teddy said. "On our own. Soon as we figured you folks gonna leave us high and dry, we knew we was on our own. Two of our people gone back east to Wyandotte to ask for help. We doing just fine. Things are a little short right now, but our men are due back any time."

"You can do better, a lot better, and I want to help you out. That's how we do things out here on the prairie. Folks help each other out."

Their faces were black and sullen.

"Take those windows there in that house. Fine as that carpentry is, think how much nicer that place would be with real glass. I would be pleased to donate a glass window."

"Don't need your glass," Jim Black said. "Where were you before Tripp and Harrington went for help? When you first knowed we needed food and our horses needed hay?"

"No need to get riled," Potroff said quickly. "I had no idea you folks were in that bad a shape. No idea atall, or I would have helped. Wade should have told me."

He didn't like the men's steady advance. Didn't like the look in their eyes.

Bethany Herbert stepped forward. Like she was somebody, he thought. Stepped right out into men's business just like she had at the general store when she plopped Suzanne Mercer in their midst.

"We don't need your help," she said. "We're just fine. You brought us here, you dumped us here and had your man tell us to make do, and we did. Now get out. We're here, and we're staying. You're too late to help us, and nobody likes you."

His eyes smoldered. The group took another step toward him, and he took another step back. It wouldn't do to turn and run, but he wanted to get the hell out of Nicodemus. When he reached his buggy, he swallowed hard and then turned back to the group.

"Sorry there's still hard feelings." He

nearly strangled on the words. "Real sorry, but you know Western Kansas is hard for all of us, not just blacks. Lots of white folks walked into something they weren't expecting."

Bethany's eyes brightened with agreement for an instant. So he addressed his words to her. "Don't think everything that happens to you is because of the war and your race. The prairie kind of makes us all equal. Not in a good kind of way, either. If some of you want to start a business, let me know. I can help. I loan money. I loan to white folks, and I can loan to you folks. You're going to need me. You'd better start thinking ahead."

Knowing he had made his point, he climbed into the buggy, flicked his reins across the horse's back, and drove off.

There was quiet jubilation among the men, knowing they had stared down this powerful white man. Teddy walked up to Bethany, his hands clutching the lapels of his old suit.

"Guess we know he means trouble." The lines in his mottled old face deepened.

"He's up to no good," she said bitterly. "I know his kind. I've known them all my life. I just don't know what he's after right now. But he's right about one thing; we've got to think past just making it through the winter.

We can only trade so much back and forth. We have got to figure out how to get some real money into this town."

"Can't start no businesses now," said Teddy. "Could have if this place hadn't drained us to start with. Some of our folks had a little money. Ain't got none now."

"We've got to figure out what white folks need enough to pay good money for. And then we've got to figure out how to make them trust us enough to give us some work."

"How we going do that? You know good and well white folks think we they equal in just one way. Think we can lie with the best of them. That's a fact. Think nobody as good at lying as a lying nigger."

The wind came up and batted a tumbleweed against their sod building. Teddy never allowed trash to light there. He walked over and sent the bush on its way across the prairie.

Bethany trailed after him, still talking. "We're not going to lie. I won't have it. And I have an idea for getting the white folks in this county to give us a chance. I want to print flyers. They worked to get us folks here. But what we say is going to be the truth. When folks come to Nicodemus to check us out, they are going to find things in place."

"You just going to conjure up paper? A printer?"

"No. A couple of weeks ago, when Jim Black was out gathering wood, a man stopped to talk. A New Englander. Right friendly, too. He said he was going to start a newspaper. A new town, too, maybe. An editor would welcome a print job. I'm sure of that. If he doesn't, I'll buy some paper and hand-letter them." She twisted her apron and watched Teddy's face.

"I'll call a meeting for tonight," he said.

Bethany sat huddled under a blanket in front of the campfire. There were too many coming to fit inside the new sod building.

It was twilight, and usually Kansas sunsets were a wonder to her. She loved watching the flaming hues ebb and drift across the sky like floating gauze. In Kentucky, the setting sun had been obscured by the trees. Tonight, she was too troubled to enjoy the colors. She looked up when Teddy came toward the fire.

"Looks like we got the best seats," he said. He threw a couple more cottonwood branches on the fire.

"They'll all be here plenty soon enough," Bethany said. "It's going to be a reach to come up with the words to get these folks to have anything to do with whites."

Teddy looked at her sharply. "Can't say as I blame us."

"I know we came here to get away from them. I get along with them better than most of our people. You do, too. But most folks here would rather die than have anything to do with them at all."

"White folks is a fact of life."

"I know that, Teddy, but I don't know how to make our people understand. If we don't move forward, if we don't have money to buy seed and tools and get new horses, the white folks in this county will never see us as real people. As human beings."

"No guarantee of that anyway. That they gonna see us as human beings."

"No. No guarantees. We're probably going to be dealing with people out to lie to us or trick us. It's going to take all our wits just to keep from getting fleeced. Just like back home." Bethany smiled, stood up, and brushed her hands against her skirts. The people of Nicodemus were drifting toward the fire. When they all gathered, she took a deep breath, then walked to the front.

"Teddy and I asked you all to meet here tonight to see what we're going to have to do to bring in some money. Before now, all we've talked about is how to stay alive. Now we've got to figure out how to make it up to the next level or we're going to get crushed by white men here, same as we were in the South."

"You wants better," said Patricia Towaday. "Just you." She had worked in the fields all her life. She no longer had to worry about beatings or the threat of being sold off. Nicodemus was heaven.

"You wants the glass windows and the fancy books. You wants to start a school and take up fancy white ways." Patricia looked around, then quieted at the lack of approval.

"Yes, I want all that. Others here want that for their children also. But it's not a matter of wanting books and glass." Bethany's voice was steady, but her stomach was aflutter. As she talked, several of the men nodded their heads.

Teddy said firmly, "She right. Right as rain. Can't just stand still. Won't work to tread water. We've got to sink or swim."

"What you have in mind?" Jim Black asked.

"I want us to start getting some of the white folks' money," said Bethany, "so we can start making this into a real town."

"Didn't come here to be no servant. Or a slave," said Patricia.

"I didn't either," said Bethany quickly.

156

"None of us did." She told them about her idea for flyers. "Let's put our heads together and figure out what we can do for hire that white folks are going to want."

"There's a crying need for good blacksmiths around here," said Jim Black.

"And I'll bet people need seamstresses." Bethany nodded toward Dolly. "I know they are going to need doctoring and babies delivered. But remember, we can't trade goods or services. We need cash money. We've proved we can stay alive. Now let's build a town."

"There's not a real hotel in this county," said Silas Brown. "No place for folks to eat. Potroff House ain't nothing. Just a flea bag big enough for the king flea himself. Let's start a hotel with real food."

"Wouldn't that be something now," Teddy said, "if the only decent café and hotel in the whole county was put up by ex-slaves?"

"You're getting the idea," Bethany said. "And when you bring in some real cash money, I'm asking you to put twenty percent in a fund for the promotion of Nicodemus."

"Twenty percent of nothing ain't hard to come up with," LuAnne Brown said.

"Won't be twenty percent of nothing for long," Bethany said.

"We don't have a sod cutter," said Jim

157

Black. "Can't start no hotel anyway this time of year. Ground is too froze for plowing. The hotel's out until spring."

"No it's not," said Henry Partridge. He pointed toward their community building and waved his claw hand. "I hereby declare this place Hotel Nicodemus. Guess I've learned how to do some things from those lying sons-a-bitches who brought us here. This here is everything else. Might as well call it a hotel, too."

John More was the first to laugh. Then it spread.

"Well, why not?" Bethany said. "Why not? It's sure better than Hotel Potroff."

"I'll make a sign," said Jim. *"Hotel Nicodemus."*

"I'll cook if someone comes," said Lu-Anne Brown.

"That's thinking. That's the kind of thinking I want us to do," Bethany said gleefully.

Millbrook was little more than a gleam in a speculator's eye. Millbrook was composed of a few hastily built dugouts and a tiny sod building that sold a few essentials. There was the start of a livery stable and a surprisingly good corral used by all the residents. Millbrook consisted of twenty-five people. But they had a paper and a second-hand printing press.

Norvin Meissner, editor of the *Millbrook Wildhorse,* was a sometime lawyer and full-time abolitionist. He had one suit of dress clothes. His daily dress alternated between two shirts and two pairs of pants that he washed himself.

He was of medium height with mild, blue eyes. He had muttonchop sideburns after the manner of Van Buren, although the style had long passed. A cheerfully wrong-headed man, he naturally and honestly veered toward the most controversial side of any argument.

He had tried a wife, but found the practical side of married life too confining. He wanted to spend his days in the world of ideas, and his wife wanted him to make a living. So they had parted — she with great bitterness. He had barely noticed her leaving and was greatly surprised when one day he noticed the small stash of food she had prepared in advance was gone, and so was she. He cared enough to check, but was greatly relieved when he found she had returned to her parents, and he was free to return unhampered to his books.

When Teddy Sommers came across the prairie riding his old mule, Norvin thought he was seeing a wee, brown ghost. Like many transplanted Yankees, he had had very little personal contact with "people of color," as he delicately referred to them.

Teddy climbed off his mule, and Meissner immediately rushed forward to take the reins and tie them to the post himself.

"Let me do that," he gushed. "Are you from Nicodemus? I've heard about your town. You do our little community honor. Come in, come in."

Teddy immediately recognized Meissner's eagerness to please a member of the Negro race. The man was a cousin to the editors who referred to Indians as the Noble Savage without knowing nary a one.

Teddy smiled broadly. "Name's Teddy Sommers, and I is come to see if you is agreeable to printing something. 'Course, we expect to pay cash. Just inquiring right now." He handed Meissner the sample copy of Bethany's hand-lettered flyer.

"Of course. Do come in, come in. I have coffee. Real coffee. May I offer you a cup of coffee, sir?"

"Well, now, I sure enough would like a cup of coffee. That sure do sound agreeable."

Teddy stood straight as a sentry and puffed out his scrawny chest. He tugged on his vest, newly mended for the trip. Dolly had shortened his straggly old pants and brushed and patched his jacket. Puttin' on de massa was second nature to him anyway, and Meissner was like putty.

The editor steered Teddy to the best, and in fact the only, chair, then carefully poured coffee into a tin cup. He perched on top of a barrel and watched anxiously as Teddy took a small sip.

"This is fine brew, Mr. Meissner. Right fine. Good as I ever had." It was the second time in his life he had tasted coffee.

Meissner read the list of services Teddy offered. "You have a midwife?" he asked in astonishment. "Does she do other kinds of doctoring?"

"She's a wonder," said Teddy. "Just a gem."

"And a blacksmith? You have a black-smith?"

"The best." Teddy grinned. "A lot of my people is the best at what they do. White folks make us learn it right."

"I knew about your town, of course, but I had no idea there was such a splendid ac-cumulation of talent. Of course I intend to write an article about your settlement."

Somewhere in the conversation, Teddy forgot Meissner was white. Forgot all thoughts of using him. He was no longer "putting on de massa." He could not recall another time in his life when he had forgotten he was a black man and the other person was white.

Meissner came to Nicodemus the very next day. Teddy introduced him to Bethany, to Jim Black and Henry Partridge.

The editor could hardly contain his excitement. Everything Sommers had said about the town was real. Most of what Meissner wrote about Millbrook wasn't exactly the truth. But everything Sommers had told him about Nicodemus was.

The *Millbrook Wildhorse* was desperate for news of any kind. No one paid for subscriptions, and there was rarely money available to pay for advertisements. Meissner's paper was sponsored by a town company, as were all the other papers on the prairie. He had just barely set up shop and was preparing to give Wade City a run for the money. While it was unthinkable that a black town would be a contender for the county seat, Meissner quickly realized he needed to get on the good side of this group of people. If for no other reason than to get their vote for Millbrook.

Teddy rode back over to Millbrook a week later to pick up the edition of the paper that contained information about Nicodemus. He whooped when he saw the headline.

New Town of Negro Immigrants Galvanizes the County

The illustrious citizens of Nicodemus bring a level of skill and industry unrivaled in this county and, indeed, in Kansas. Never has this editor had the privilege of reporting such a contribution to the quality of industry and civilization on the prairie. They have a blacksmith whose skills are second to none, and, by the grace of God, this county now has available Miss Bethany Herbert, who possesses formidable skills as a midwife.

The intrepid Miss Herbert was tutored by her mother and grandmother before the war and assisted white doctors at some of the finest plantations. People in this area would be well advised to keep her abilities in mind.

Meissner went on to praise Teddy's abilities as a carpenter, then raved about the quality and convenience of the hotel and the outstanding food he had eaten. He went on in that vein so extravagantly that Bethany and Teddy just shook their heads with wonder. Meissner had advertised their talents far better than the planned flyer. Now they could channel their money into a circular to attract more blacks.

The next week, a homesteader came to their town and asked Jim Black to repair a wagon wheel. While he waited, he bought a meal at the new café and hotel. He paid Lu-Anne Brown cash for the meal and then paid Jim Black for the wagon wheel. Between them, they made five dollars.

That evening both of them went to Bethany and handed her twenty percent. She solemnly recorded their names in a book. "You'll get this back in a year," she promised, "at six percent interest. Just like a bank would pay."

The next morning, she made the long walk over to Millbrook, clutching the precious accumulated dollar.

"I want to order some handbills," she announced to Norvin Meissner. "How much would they cost, please?"

"How many?"

"About one hundred fifty."

He swallowed. That was a bunch. Back East it would be a decent-sized print job. Here it was enormous. And expensive. "I'd have to order in paper. I don't keep that much on hand." It seemed indelicate to bring up the subject of money, but he would need some to get the project started.

"We can pay," Bethany said softly. "Would a dollar down get you started?"

"Just barely." When he agreed to come here, he hadn't realized there weren't any people around to read his paper. No one to read it, and no one to buy it. His job was to start a town, but he didn't understand how hard it would be. They were giving away land, for Christ's sake. You would think folks would just come pouring in. Instead they sent scouts who went back with bleak reports of little water and no trees. The only chance any settlement had to survive was by getting the county seat and attracting a railroad.

"What do you want it to say?" he asked.

"We want other colored folks to come to Nicodemus. We want them to know we'll help them get started out here."

Meissner's face brightened. Thunderstruck, he knew how he could help the blacks. The town company sponsoring him would put up money for this handbill in a heartbeat if it brought in enough colored people to swing the vote.

"I can do this. And I'll be glad to write everything up for you."

"I'm going to write it up."

"Oh, Miss, there's an art to this. An art, I tell you."

"There's not going to be any 'art' or exaggerations or lies. Nothing made up at all." Bethany's gaze was stern. "The handbills we send down South are going to be the truth. God's own truth, that's all. No lies."

"I wasn't suggesting lies."

"Good."

"I'm saying that I want to help you get it just right."

"I understand that. We want black folks to know what they will find, and what they will need to get by. Didn't it set better with you, Mr. Meissner, when you could see what we said about our services was true?"

Chagrined, he nodded. It *had* set better. In fact, he had been surprised when he saw there actually was a hotel and café and blacksmith shop. He was pleased when Marvin Schump stopped by after Jim Black repaired his wagon wheel and told him what a good job the man had done. It gave the impression that Meissner was a man of integrity and people could trust his word. What the woman was proposing just might work. He was weary of the fury of people coming to Kansas, cussing him out for his lying ways, then turning right around to go back.

"We don't have to lie about Kansas," Bethany said. "There's lots of good things you can say about this state."

"Yes, a few good things. I'm from Ohio. Doesn't necessarily mean better, but different. Just different."

She smiled. "Yes, you mean better. I think we both know that. How do you think we feel, Mr. Meissner? We're all from Kentucky. Trees, water. Reasonable people and reasonable weather. We were used to better, too. But we're still not going to lie."

"All right," he said. "All right. We'll do it your way, Miss Herbert."

"Naturally I'll be interested in any ideas you might have," she said sweetly. "I'm sure you're a better writer than I am."

"We'll work together."

They spent an hour drawing up the handbill and getting the copy just right. He noticed her hungry eyes quickly reading the titles of the books he had stacked in the corner. He came close to offering to loan one but backed out. What if she didn't return it or something happened to it? Reading material was incredibly precious. Besides, all he had was classics, and he was sure they were too hard for her.

"We are going to start a school right away. Just as soon as we can," she said.

Incredulous, he was slow in responding. "What will you use for books?"

"I won't need books at the beginning," she said, with a quick bright smile. "Or paper, either. Until we get some money coming in, we'll have to make do in other ways. As soon as it's spring, I can teach the children their letters on the ground and their numbers, too, for that matter. They would have to be a little farther along anyway to need books right now."

Again, she glanced at the stack in the corner.

"Would you like to borrow one of my books?" he asked impulsively. "For your own, ah, examination?"

He was embarrassed by her naked gratitude, her quick tears. She rushed over to the pile. To his amazement, she reached for Plutarch.

"He's still my favorite," she said. "Plutarch taught me what liberty of one's soul could and should be."

"Yes." He was tongue-tied. There was no standard for talking with this woman. No example, no protocol. A Negress and an ex-slave to boot. It was unusual enough that they had spent the better part of an afternoon alone together and that he had lost all consciousness of her race and sex as they composed the flyer.

Then his eager intellectual bent took over. His love of ideas. "Well, Plutarch wasn't the first. Hardly the first to advance such thoughts."

"But he was the best," Bethany responded. "The first to set it down clearly so that ordinary citizens could know such principles."

"Madam, he was not," Meissner replied with delight. In his time on the prairie, he had not found one single person with whom he could discuss books. To think that his first opportunity was coming from a black woman who was an ex-slave. They happily fell to quarrelling, and when Bethany started off he called her back.

Her beautiful face was lighted by the setting sun, the slim volume of Plutarch clutched to her breast as she stood in the bluestem grass.

"Yes?" she said softly, suddenly shy.

"I was wondering. I have some extra ruined paper. Discards and misprints. It doesn't actually cost me anything. It's provided to me by the backers of the Millbrook Town Company. Would you like some for your school? For days when the weather is bad and you can't take your students outside."

Rather than accepting his offer immediately as he had expected her to do, she stood looking at him for the longest time. When she did speak, her words were simple, grave, and unadorned. Cautious, almost.

"Thank you, Mr. Meissner. I would surely appreciate that. Thank you for your kindness. But I do not want to be beholden to you. Please put a value on the paper, and we will pay you for it."

He started to assure her that would not be necessary, but something in her voice stopped him.

"Ten cents for one hundred sheets," he said. "The paper is spoiled, you know. Worthless to me."

"Thank you, that's quite reasonable, sir."

Two weeks later Bethany Herbert stood beside her desk, which was a broad plank spread across two barrels. It was late December, and the morning was bitterly cold. The settlers were anxiously waiting for Tripp and Harrington to return with food. They were watching provisions carefully, but had decided the school would be a welcome distraction for the whole community.

Bethany had spent last week setting up her classroom in the back part of the hotel.

Knowing it was important that the children have the best possible impression of the opening day of school, she gathered a good supply of buffalo chips for the stove. She wanted them to associate the school with kindness and warmth and love and opportunity.

Most of all, she wanted to instill a love of learning. She wondered if that would be possible in these crude surroundings. Her own education had been in an exquisitely beautiful room, with brocades and velvets and the scent of wax on mahogany furniture. She had enjoyed the same meals as Miss Nancy and, of course, had clean, neat attire.

She knew how the day in formal classrooms should begin. She had once accompanied Miss Nancy to a spelling bee in a small private school in a town close to their plantation. Even as Miss Nancy's girl, huddled in the corner at the back of the room, she had witnessed the careful opening exercises, with the recitation of the Lord's Prayer and the opening hymn.

When Mr. Meissner offered her the paper, she had been overwhelmed with confusion. Paper. White folks' paper for the children. She would have refused if he didn't set a price. It was their school. Not a school started as a white man's project. It belonged to the people of Nicodemus.

Nevertheless, she knew the gift had no strings attached. It was a good-willed gesture from an honest, simple man. But she could not accept the gift. The white people in the area had to see the people of Nicodemus as self-supporting and capable of carrying their own weight. At all costs, they must establish that they needed to be paid in cash, not barter, and they needed to pay for services in coin in return, or they would never be able to choose to purchase what they needed or desired. They would always have to settle for whatever people felt like offering.

She trembled with wonder at the importance of what was about to begin here this very day.

"Please stand," she said, "and recite the Lord's Prayer."

When they finished, she told them all to sit down. Her gaze faltered when she saw how instantly they all complied. It was a bitter legacy from another time, this willingness to accede to authority of any kind. And she was the school marm.

These were children of the wicked Reconstruction. They did not even have the giddiness of children born on plantations where most had food and warmth and a relatively untroubled if extremely short childhood. A time where they were cared for by grannies while their mothers worked in the field. All these children had ever known was fear and hunger and a loss of place.

Dear God, she realized. All this time she had been worrying about initiating them into the white folks' world of knowledge. Now she knew she was even going to have to teach these children how to be black.

There were only a couple of makeshift benches. Most of the children sat in a semicircle on the floor. Suddenly, Silas and LuAnne Brown pushed through the door. They were followed by the parents of the other children and Jim Black, Teddy, and Mr. Jones. The adults stood at the back of the room, watching respectfully.

"Don't mind us," Jones said quickly. "We going to leave right away. We just want to watch you get started. That's all." Tears streamed down LuAnne's face.

Suddenly Bethany was seized with joy. Joy of the morning, joy at the eager look of the bright, cheerful faces of the adults.

This was their land, their town, their people, their school in this wild, bawdy state. She wanted the children to know about their own people. About Africa and about America. About the white and black people who had died to bring them to this town and this place. This opportunity.

Most of all, she wanted them to know their own music. She turned aside from the solemn white folks' dirges and opening exercises and clapped her hands and begin an irresistible rhythm until the children looked at one another and began clapping in response.

"Children," she sang out brightly. "Children, we're going to make a joyful noise unto the Lord. Let us begin."

Chapter Nine

Bethany rose, got one of the dried buffalo chips from the corner of the dugout, poked it into the stove, and hurried back to bed. They were all hungry now. Not yet desperate, but becoming anxious as they waited for Reverend Harrington to return with food. School was conducted intermittently, when the weather permitted.

The wind raged; snow fell in great drifts. She was miserably cold, despite her quilts, and sick with worry over the other families. Several children were especially frail. She would check on them the moment the storm let up.

The snow stopped by mid-afternoon. She went to the stove, picked up a pan, shoved the door open, scooped up a pan full of snow, and set it on the stove to warm.

When it melted, she gratefully drank it. Dizzy with hunger, she sat weakly on the side of the bed. When her stomach settled, she rose and spooned some broth from her wild onion stew into a cup and sipped slowly, making it last. They needed meat.

When they were lucky enough to snare a rabbit, the children and pregnant women and nursing mothers were fed first, and it had been three days since there was meat for the rest of them. Finally, she rose and listlessly dressed to go out and see how the other colonists had fared in the storm.

She heard voices shouting. She grabbed her cloak and went outside. She blinked against the icy white diamonds sparkling across the prairie.

All of the men in the colony and a scattering of women had gathered outside. They were pointing to a wavering, long, dark line moving slowly in the distance.

"Indians," someone shouted. "Wild Indians."

The distant figures pushed through the snow. The riders were traveling single file, but as they drew closer, their profiles and paraphernalia were unmistakable.

"Get a gun."

"No, wait. Don't. Not yet."

"They can hardly move through this snow. Bet they weren't expecting it either, any more than we were. They for damn sure won't attack."

Bethany watched, her hunger forgotten. She sheltered her keen, far-seeing eyes with her hand. Several of the horses pulled riggings like the one she and Jim Black had put together to transport Mrs. Mercer.

"Those people aren't going to give us any trouble," she said. "There's women with them. And little children. They're coming toward us." She turned and looked at the pale line of smoke drifting from the pipes sticking out on top of the dugouts. "They see our smoke."

"I'm going to talk to them," said Jim Black.

"I'll go with you," said Teddy.

Five other men volunteered to join them. They put a white flag on top of a long pole and started pushing through the heavy banks of snow.

A huge Indian at the head of the line held up his hand and turned to holler a command to the group following. The caravan stopped. The Indians stared at the black men coming across the prairie.

"Believe he's as big as you are, Jim," Teddy said. "Pretty close, anyway."

As the colonists trudged toward the Indians, both groups eyed one another warily. The blacks stopped when they were about twenty-five feet away. Although all the

Indian men had bows and quivers of sharp-pointed arrows, only a few had rifles, and they were very old.

Arrow-Going-Home, the principal chief for the Hunkah, the Isolated Earth People, shared the leadership for the hunt with Sun-On-His-Wings, the principal chief of Tzi-Sho, the Sky People. He stood silently before the edgy band of black people and sniffed the air. Of all the traits of the Heavy Eyebrows, the white people's ways that were the most despicable to the Osage, the Little People, were the way they kept their revolting body odors trapped in their collars and pants. It made his stomach heave. He sniffed again. Despite the difference in color, these men were no different from white people.

He stared at Jim's blackness, then turned and called to Sun-On-His-Wings, who immediately stepped forward. Both men were well over six feet with shaven heads except for a tall roach into which eagle feathers were braided. Arrow-Going-Home's feather hung on the right side of his scalp lock with the sharp side of the feather turned outward to show that he was Hunkah. Sun-On-His-Wings wore his feather to the left with the downy gentle side facing out, showing he was Tzi-Sho.

Jim didn't understand a word the chief said, but from the wondering looks that passed between the men, he wasn't what they expected. He smiled, then touched his face. His gesture set off a flurry of hand movements from the stern warrior facing him. When the Indian finished, he looked at Jim, clearly expecting a response.

"It's sign language," said Teddy. "And I don't know it."

"Well, I sure as hell don't."

"They've been hunting," said John More. "Look what they is dragging along behind them."

"Don't make sense," said Jim quietly. "There's too many of them for a hunting party. What kind of hunters would take women and children along? And they don't have enough guns to do any good. Their horses are plumb pitiful. Worse than ours."

The Osage had been given permission to leave the reservation for their winter hunt. Each year they were forced to travel farther and farther west to find buffalo. They were the last remnant of a heroic tribe whose ownership of the vast prairies once ranged from the Missouri River to the Rocky Mountains.

Last year's hunt had been so disastrous

179

that only centuries-old tradition had compelled them to go on one this year. The Heavy Eyebrows had wiped out their buffalo to the extent that it had become nearly impossible to provide the animal skins necessary to perform the seven rites for manhood.

Now some of the tribesmen were old men before they were fully initiated. Their bows and arrows were no match for the long Sharps rifles used by the wasteful Heavy Eyebrows to slaughter buffalo. On the other hand, their arrows were swift. Deadly compared to the few pitiful firearms they carried. This year's hunt had been better.

The blacks stared at a travois heaped with slaughtered buffalo, covered with hides and lashed firmly onto the crude sleds.

"Meat, by God. Meat and robes." They began to mutter. "Food. Food for the families. Meat." Maybe enough to see them through the winter.

The two chiefs followed their gaze and spoke sharply to the other blacks. The Indians tensed.

Instinctively, Jim held up his hands to show they were empty. None of his people meant any harm. They weren't foolish enough to try to take the meat away from the Indians. *Not yet, anyway,* he thought grimly.

"Maybe it won't matter if we don't know sign language," Teddy said. "There's some things people just seem to know everywhere."

Jim motioned to the chief and walked over to the first travois. He tugged on the covering hide and exposed the mound of meat. He pointed toward it and made a circling gesture over his stomach.

The chief turned back to the men. An agile younger man jumped down off his horse and walked over the snow to join them. He and the chief started talking rapidly. Jim stood to one side. The younger man looked at the heaps of meat and nodded. The chief turned and solemnly faced Jim, then gestured toward the collection of smokestacks in the distance. He pointed toward the sky. A new storm was coming. He made a movement that Jim was sure meant the Indians needed to rest and sleep. They wanted to feed their horses. It would only make sense that men of any race needed a place out of the weather.

Jim faltered for an instant. What if they were letting a group of wild savages into their homes who would slaughter them all? But the Indians had meat, and the settlers had no guarantee that Harrington and Tripp would make it back before they were totally out of food. He looked at the chief and nodded.

The chief shouted to his people, and the Indians headed toward the large, communal, open-faced shed the settlers had dug in a ravine to shelter their animals. Stacks of hay cats in the corner were needed for fuel, and the whole colony drew on the supply to ignite their slower-burning buffalo chips. The Indians' horses began to make short work of the hay bundles, and Jim and Teddy watched uneasily.

"Guess hay for meat ain't too bad," Jim said.

"Long as they come through with the meat."

Then the chief went to the back-most travois, tugged an animal skin off, and laid it on top of the snow. He pulled hunks of meat from under the rest of the hides and laid the meat on the skin. He twisted the four corners into a bundle, slung it over his shoulder, turned, and looked expectantly at Jim.

"Praise the Lord," whispered Teddy.

Jim gestured for the chief to follow and led him to the first dugout that had a pipe protruding from the earth. Smoke drifted into the crisp winter air. Jim pointed toward others. The chief understood at once, looked around, located more smoke. Then he called sharply to two men standing to one side, and they began unloading the meat from two of the travois. They divided it into smaller units and parceled them out to each dugout.

An old woman waited by the last travois. She had spotted the thick stream of smoke billowing from Bethany's dugout when the caravan first stopped. She called sharply to two muscular young men. They unhitched the travois from the horse, hoisted it onto their shoulders like it was a stretcher, and started dog trotting toward the dugout. On the travois lay Walking Buffalo, son of Arrow-Going-Home.

Once inside, they lowered the travois to the floor, then stood attentively with arms folded across their chests as the old woman came through the door. Bethany stared into the sharp, black eyes of one of the oldest women she had ever seen. Her mahogany skin was like a dried and cracked mud puddle checkered into hundreds of squares. Her gray hair was thin and drawn into two skimpy braids. There was a red line down the middle of her scalp. Her mouth was a thin, tight line, her hands old yellow claws, as dried as cottonwood twigs, with odd black marks on the backs.

Bethany fetched a pallet of fresh straw and laid it on top of her feather beds. She would burn it afterwards to dispose of blood or seepage. Her mother had taught her well about the risks of contagious diseases. She gestured for the two young men to transfer the injured warrior to her bed.

The old woman barked a command, and they ran outside and came back carrying hide bundles, which they placed in the center of the room. They went back outside again, leaving the two women alone with the injured man. The Indian woman glanced at Bethany and quickly took in the bundles of dried herbs and sacks of seeds hanging on the wall. She pulled aside the heavy buffalo hide covering the man and knelt over him.

Bethany's throat went dry. Human bodies were alike, no matter what the color of their skin, and this man's wound sliced across his stomach. It was very deep with telltale red lines spreading out from a crust of blood and pus. The two women stared at one another. Wordlessly, Bethany set to work. She sacrificed her hoard of buffalo chips to set kettles boiling. The man lying on the bed stirred, moaned.

Bethany turned and watched as the old woman unrolled one of the skin bundles. She spread out the contents, then picked up a handful of dried, tangled roots, fine and withered like old moss. Bethany gasped as she put the roots directly over the wound.

The man tightened his lips. Pain was universal. Bethany eyed her precious bottle of laudanum on the shelf above her tied cache of herbs. There were only five doses left. She had no way of replacing it. Suddenly the old woman rose and went over to the little sacks Bethany had strung down the wall. She quickly removed and untied the first one.

"Please don't," said Bethany. But the woman ignored her as she examined the contents. She worked her way down, carefully retying each one before going on to the next. When she came to the one containing willow bark, her eyes gleamed triumphantly, and she went to the stove. She poured some of the boiling water there into a tin cup and let it steep. After it cooled, she knelt beside the man and gestured to Bethany to help raise his head. She forced some of the tea into his mouth and held it shut, forcing him to swallow.

About five minutes later, the man began thrashing from side to side. The old woman's mouth tensed. With a glance at Bethany, she pressed her hands against her temples and rocked from side to side to indicate unbearable pain. She looked at the hanks of herbs and shrugged helplessly. Bethany understood. They both knew the man's pain was sending him into shock. She could help, but that tiny bit of laudanum was all she had left. The man moaned again. His fever was breaking even as his torment increased. His forehead was drenched with sweat.

Deciding quickly, she went to the shelf, got the bottle, and offered it to the old woman, who opened it and smelled it. Her eyes gleamed with recognition.

"Is good," she said in broken English. She went to her bundle, removed a buffalo bone spoon, and carefully eased some of the liquid into Walking Buffalo's mouth.

The old woman began to chant and never took her eyes off the man. About thirty minutes later he fell into a deep sleep. Then she picked up the other leather pouch and pulled out a piece of meat. Eying Bethany, the old woman poured some hot water into a separate pot, then divided up the meat into quick-cooking chunks and threw them into the water. Bethany's stomach ached with hunger.

When it had cooked, the old woman first coaxed the wounded man awake long enough to get some broth down his throat, then she handed Bethany a bowl.

When she'd finished eating, Bethany rose and poured water over a few of the Earl Grey tea leaves she had brought from Kentucky. She offered it to the old woman, who eyed her with suspicion for the first time. Bethany looked at her in bewilderment, then realized the medicine woman had never seen these herbs before and was not about to ingest an unknown substance. A woman after her own heart, but she didn't know how to tell her this. Bethany nodded and smiled, and tactfully removed the cup.

She went to the old woman's leather medicine bundle lying on the floor, pointed toward the fine, gray moss, then gestured toward the collection of plants hanging on the wall. She wanted to know what the woman had used for the infection just now. Where could she find it? Where did it grow? What was it called?

Immediately the old woman's hands flew with elaborate movements. Shaking with frustration, Bethany could not think of a way to tell her she didn't understand.

The old woman stood and walked over to the hanging bags. She smelled them, then untied one of them, mimicked a person doubled over with stomach pain, and then held up the bag. Bethany nodded. Of course, of course, she understood. They both knew lamb's-quarter was just right for this ailment.

Bethany trembled with frustration. She needed this woman. Needed to learn from her. Supplies were becoming desperately short, and she was terrified of picking up a plant that would harm her people.

She went to the wall and pointed toward a bag. One by one, she worked her way down the row and mimicked each ailment that she used it for. She pointed to the man's stomach, then toward the wall, and shrugged to show that there was nothing there, nothing she could have used to help the man.

Once again she was helpless before the flurry of the old woman's hand movements. Bethany's eyes filled with tears. Infections were frequent and lethal, and she absolutely had to understand.

The old woman stared at her stonily, not approving of her loss of control. Bethany pulled herself together and stood rigidly by the bags of plants. Then, as best she could, she began to mimic all the ailments that she didn't have plants for. After each, Bethany made a sweeping gesture toward the wall, then shrugged, then pointed toward the old woman and held her hands out in prayerful supplication.

The old woman nodded curtly. She understood.

Bethany pressed her head between her palms and moved it from side to side, emulating an excruciating headache. Then she went to the wall and removed the bag containing ground charcoal and carried it to the old woman, who sniffed it and then rubbed it between her fingers.

She frowned and shook her head. That must mean she had never seen it, or didn't use it. Then the old woman bent over her bundle and pulled out a little pouch containing valerian leaves. Bethany could not think of a way to tell her that she, too, used valerian, but it was not enough for the one-eyed blinding headaches. Nevertheless, the old woman reaffirmed many of Bethany's herbs, letting her know that she used these, too, and the plants could be found on the prairie.

But there were so many gaps. So many plants the old woman examined in bewilderment. Clearly, they only grew in Kentucky. How could Bethany learn to substitute? What would she do? Who could teach her?

She would probably never see this Indian woman again, and even if she learned to recognize herbs in dried form, it wouldn't help her to find the growing plants.

Bethany had heard that Indians were as reserved with their displays of emotion as her own people were expressive. Not wanting to risk the old woman's disapproval again, she kept her trembling hands hidden beneath her apron. Then suddenly she sank to her knees and wept.

"Please. I must know. I'll try to find a way to come to you during the summer when I can harvest seeds and herbs. Surely there's a time when something grows on this God-forsaken wretched prairie. It can't just go from scalding heat to the dead of winter year after year." Childishly, she blurted this out to a woman who could not understand and by her scornful expression certainly did not care.

The old woman went over to the sleeping man and held the back of her hand to his forehead to check his fever. She nodded at Bethany, then went over to a corner, sat with her legs straight in front of her, and dozed off.

After Bethany's sobs subsided, she stared at the old woman's exhausted, seamed face and wondered who had taught her. Who would replace her when she died?

CHAPTER TEN

Hawk Woman's eyes flew open when Walking Buffalo moaned, then turned on the straw bed. She rose stiffly and went to his side. The light gleaming through the glass panel on the stove was enough for her to see that his forehead was dry.

Soft as a feather, she touched his cheek, hoping the dryness did not mean his high fever had returned. Satisfied that he was mending — his breath was strong and regular, and there was little fever now — she passed her palm over his face in thanksgiving, then crept back into the corner. She would not check his wound until morning when he was fully awake.

She settled back down on the floor where she had spread a buffalo robe to cushion her old bones. Then she covered herself with the quilts offered by the *Nika-Sabe* woman.

Gloomily, she studied the sleeping woman's beautiful face. For a while as she and this emotional woman had tended to Walking Buffalo, she had forgotten how much she hated the Heavy Eyebrows and even more their strange, colorful variation, the *Nika-Sabes,* who had caused her people so much new trouble.

It had taken thousands of years when they first descended to the earth for the Sky People to instill order over the chaos of the land. Thousands of ceremonies, thousands of lives lost to create the majestic Osage, the most profoundly religious of all the tribes. Even here, even now, in the presence of these peculiar people burrowed into the sides of hills, tomorrow would begin with her own people's ceremonies, their chanting to Grandfather Sun.

The fire flickered, and the shiny metal on the stove was like the Peeps in the Water disks used in trade by the Heavy Eyebrows. The woman in this dwelling was the first *Nika-Sabe* she had seen up close. Much killing had taken place over these black-skinned persons. It made no sense to her that Kansas soil was stained with Osage blood over these people when they were as scarce as buffalo on the prairie. The Civil War had split her own people in two, the Great Osage band fighting with the Confederate Army and the Little Osage fighting with the Union.

She understood wars and colors and tribes and blood, for it had always been so. Her people fought their enemies with mad abandon to protect their land. For centuries war had kept them powerful and lordly. What she did not understand was how her people had been seduced into fighting this white man's war. Her people had been shoved and shoved and shoved farther west from the time the Heavy Eyebrows first invaded, but through this worthless, silly war, they had lost even more of their tribal land.

Over the *Nika-Sabes.* Slaves.

She knew the word. She understood far too many of the white man's words. Her people often took Pawnee as slaves or traded them to the Heavy Eyebrows for guns. Slavery she understood.

But *ga-ni-tha,* chaos, again! Over and over, a legacy of the Heavy Eyebrows. She loathed the bastardization of the Little People — the contamination of their customs, the confusion. Now her people even dressed their brides in long coats with brassy buttons and silky golden braid jutting out from the shoulders. The coats were prized souvenirs from the white man's war, and Osage maidens wore them over their traditional dresses. They also now wore top hats with feathers to their weddings. Osage warriors were buried in generals' dress tunics with United States flags draped upside down over their cairns.

The Little Old Men, their priests, would say chaos was always present on the earth. It had always been so. Peace came from above. The movements of the heavens were regular, restful, predictable. But Hawk Woman knew no force on the earth had been as swiftly destructive as the disorder brought by the white man.

Her eyes glistened in the dark. She was a holy woman descended from a long holy line. One of her own lineage had been the very first shy, trembling woman who had woven the covering for the sacred hawk bundle. For four days, this woman, this weaving woman, had stayed at her loom and chanted and followed the instructions for the design given by the Little Old Men. Just so, she herself had worked and wailed and gone without food.

Hawk Woman glanced at the sacred hawk bundle beside her. She should not be carrying it. A holy man should carry the magic of the Sacred Hawk. But *ga-ni-tha,* the Heavy Eyebrows' chaos, had seeped into

195

Osage religion, too. Many of her own people no longer knew who was holy or who was Hunkah and supposed to wear symbols on the right, or who was of the peaceful Tzi-Sho clan. Even though they still fasted and chanted, they were no longer sure. Some of the tribes had even started including the white man's Christ in their morning chants.

Hawk Woman stared at the sleeping *Nika-Sabe.* She, herself, could sit for days huddled in a buffalo robe in perfect silence, still as a mountain. Unmoving as the North Star. But this woman, this *Nika-Sabe,* would never sit. She would be up soon, doing, doing, charging about with Heavy Eyebrow energy, despite her dark face.

Hawk Woman knew how to put her own dreaming aside and care for her people. To be completely in the world when it was necessary. But this woman didn't have a bit of the Sky People in her. She would not know how to sit.

Hawk Woman could teach this small *Nika-Sabe* woman many things. Teach her the healing chants, teach her how to seek the gifts of the animals, but last night when the woman first asked her help in learning the plants, Hawk Woman knew at once she would reject all that was in the sacred hawk bundle. Reject it, and reject all the ways that mattered most. This woman would recoil from the animal wisdom, would loathe the white man's scalp contained within.

She had seen the look on the *Nika-Sabe*'s face when she noticed the red line on Hawk Woman's scalp. Hawk Woman freshened it each morning. It marked the path for Grandfather Sun to follow.

She extended her hands toward the fire and studied the spider tattoos — a mark of great prestige. Her father had sacrificed many horses and robes that she might have these sacred spiders. She in turn had honored her family by only uttering the permitted ceremonial cry when she was overcome by pain.

By her side, wrapped on a spool, was her ever-present burden strap. Her husband had made it and presented it to her in a sacred ceremony years ago. A burden strap made and sanctified in this manner was as important to her people as the Sacred Hawk shrine was to the men. When her people saw it, they knew she was a traditional woman who prized virtue.

What did this *Nika-Sabe* woman know of virtue and ceremonies? But, for that matter, what did the Osage know of ceremonies by now? While they were carrying Walking Buffalo into the dugout, Hawk Woman had noticed the clamor, the shouting, the disagreements, the posturing of these *Nika-Sabe* people. There were too many egos and no leader and no way of agreeing. Chaos again.

One woman had been standing in front of a place that was fancier than the others. Three children were at her side. A white-faced woman. A woman of two worlds. She had turned away when she saw Hawk Woman watching her, tracking the naked envy on her face as she stared at the *Nika-Sabe* medicine woman.

Watchers watching watchers.

Once when Hawk Woman was in a mission store, she had seen a white cup on a shelf with the profile of a black person. It seemed to her a curiously frozen, fearful pose. Now, she remembered the cup.

For all her yearning to understand the medicine in the plants, this sleeping *Nika-Sabe* woman was full of fear. Fear surrounded her. Hawk Woman could see it stalking her like a great gray wolf. This *Nika-Sabe* ran out charging like a small dog full of false courage, then fear sent her scurrying back to safety.

Hawk Woman did not have the words for something she knew in her bones; this *Nika-*

Sabe woman was on the wrong path. Her fear came from taking the wrong road. Given a few more days among these burrowed people, she might be able to pinpoint the source of the danger.

Hawk Woman's face softened before she drifted off to sleep again. Despite her fear, this *Nika-Sabe* woman had helped Walking Buffalo. During the night, she had given him the very last drop of the precious medicine from her bottle. Hawk Woman knew its power from the time she had spent in the mission infirmary. It was highly prized. It could not be replaced. She felt indebted.

The next morning, the band of Osage prepared to return to the reservation. They gave the settlers more meat in exchange for the lodging and hay for the horses.

To Bethany's great relief, the Indian man's wound was less angry. He ate everything she gave him.

She helped transfer the warrior onto the travois again and watched as the old woman gathered her medicine bundle and the other bundle she had never unwrapped.

The snow sparkled under the dazzling sun. Everyone clustered outside to say goodbye. Bethany clutched the blanket draped over her head and shoulders and blinked back tears. The one person who could help her was leaving, and she would probably never see her again. She turned away and pressed her fist against her nose, trying to regain control.

As she did, she saw Dolly Redgrave cross over to one of the travois and reach toward a bundle as though she were helping adjust it. Dolly quickly removed a spool and hid it in the folds of her skirt.

Too stunned to react, Bethany let the moment pass and turned back to the caravan. Clearly, the old woman had seen, too. Although her face was still, her black eyes glittered with rage, and they did not blink as she stared at Dolly. Bethany's hands trembled as Dolly's eyes widened, and she returned the old woman's look with a sly, defiant smile.

Daring her, daring her.

Bethany swallowed. Despite last night's camaraderie, these people were warriors. Used to killing.

Hawk Woman seethed, and her heart pounded in her frail frame. The woman of two worlds had just taken another woman's sacred burden strap. A word, all it would take was a word from her. Just a word shouted to Arrow-Going-Home, and these accursed *Nika-Sabe* would be no more.

But then the Heavy Eyebrows would retaliate, and then there would be even more killing. Her people had begged to make this hunt. Begged to be allowed to leave the reservation. She would not risk the fragile bargain to hunt even over a sacred burden strap. They had promised the Heavy Eyebrows this would be a peaceful excursion.

There were other ways. She knew them all. The woman of two worlds would soon understand her mistake.

Sun-On-His-Wings shouted for them to leave. Hawk Woman checked the lines lashing Walking Buffalo to the travois, then looked stiffly ahead. At first, she did not look at the small *Nika-Sabe* medicine woman when she ran over to the travois and stood there, helplessly clutching at her blanket. Trembling with worry.

Bethany's voice quivered through her chattering teeth. Her steamy breath hovered in the morning air. "Ma'am. I'm sorry. I'm so sorry we can't talk. Thank you for trying to teach me. I'm so sorry for what happened just now. I know you saw. I did, too." Her tongue thickened with misery. "I wish you could understand me."

Hawk Woman did understand. She had

been educated in a cruel mission school where the Heavy Eyebrows tried to exorcise the ways of the Osage from their very bones. She understood only too well the words and the intentions of these invaders no matter what their color.

But for many reasons, it was important that she as a keeper of the sacred not be perceived as offering more than token help to this group. A little meat, a few robes exchanged for hay, that was fine. But teaching this woman to heal would expose ancient rituals outsiders did not have the right to know.

"Thank you," the *Nika-Sabe* said again.

Then Hawk Woman softened, remembering the medicine sacrificed to the last drop simply to help Walking Buffalo bear the pain. This wee woman had trouble enough living in the same village with the woman of two worlds.

She turned then, pointed toward the wounded warrior, and chose a word that would be meaningless to her own people. No one would remember her saying it. "Bartholomew."

"What? What did you say?" Bethany called after her as the long line of Indians started off through the snow.

"Bartholomew," Hawk Woman shouted back.

CHAPTER ELEVEN

A gaunt Negro woman in Saint Louis, Missouri, read a flyer from Nicodemus, Kansas.

She walked.

She walked out of the white folks' house where she had been washing clothes. She left work pants a-soaking and delicates still submerged in the rinse water. She walked back to the hovel she shared with the pitiful colored family she had seen through a short, miserable round of influenza. She wrapped her collection of medicines and cures and her precious needle into a white, raggedy old apron and tied it to a pole. She did not add any food because she had none.

She didn't have a change of clothes. When she washed her raggedy dress, she did it in her old shift at night when the dark would hide her disgrace. Then she put the old dress on wet and removed the shift and washed it. She was not a natural born thief, or she could have done better.

She walked through the town and across the levee leading to a packet boat bound for Wyandotte. She walked right up the gangplank just as though she had every right to do so. She stationed herself about three paces behind two white women. The crew assumed she was part of their entourage.

Even if this had not been so, only the most courageous would have dreamed of crossing her. Her face was fierce and dangerous. She had queenly posture and angry, black eyes.

She understood subterfuge and stayed slightly behind the white women. They, in turn, could barely see black people under ordinary circumstances, so in the chaos of the departure, they certainly did not notice her trailing after them. The crew fed her just like all the other people of color accompanying white people.

She disembarked at Wyandotte — the chaotic, booming settlement on the Kansas side of the Missouri River — and made her way to the colored section of the town. Her speech was markedly Southern, but accurate, and she did not have any trouble getting answers to her main question — which was how to get west.

She walked.

She washed for a family in Lecompton long enough to trade her work for a length of linsey-woolsey and two yards of cotton. She made the linsey-woolsey into a warm dress, and, from the cotton, she immediately fashioned a new turban and underwear and a new shift. Then she started again on her long walk.

Everywhere she went, she collected herbs and added them to the bundle she had attached to her pole. At Abilene, after she doctored a sick horse and earned the gratitude of a group of drovers, she got to ride in a wagon to Hays when they headed back to Texas.

They gave her credit for saving the horse's life, but she knew it would have lived anyway. Weary to the bone, for she was not a young woman, she slept while she rode. When she was not sleeping, she listened. When she spoke, it was just to ask careful questions.

None of the drovers could read, so it did her no good to show them the handbill describing Nicodemus. They dumped her off in Hays, and she walked boldly into the general store. There were no Jim Crow signs prohibiting her from entering or shopping there because there was no need. There were no scary groups of black people on the plains.

Startled by the novelty of seeing a Negro

woman in their community, a man stepped forward, read her handbill, then assured her the place she sought was farther west. Everywhere was always farther west.

"Not much to mark your way around here. It's easy to go in circles. Best to follow the faint trail north to Stockton, then head west down the Solomon. Or I suppose you could start out along the Saline River and go anti-goggling toward the Solomon." He squinted at the small type on the flyer. "But that way ain't as clear."

She listened, her head cocked to one side.

"Not many folks been that way," he said. "The quickest would be to follow the Saline a ways and then go at an angle toward the Solomon, but it's awful easy to get lost."

"I thank you kindly. Reckon I'll tarry a day or two if any of you gentlemen needs clothes washed."

She was dead tired and hungry. She would need to take food with her. Back home, her sense of the land had been so acute she hadn't given provisions a thought. She could fish, hunt game, gather plants and grains. Out here, there was just prairie. You could chase a rabbit to hell and back before you caught it. She couldn't imagine how people managed to live.

She did enough laundry to buy food for

her little bundle, and after she had rested for several days, she started off again. She had a superb sense of direction but carefully heeded the man's words about getting lost.

She headed due west, then when the stars came out, she switched to north and walked for about two hours in the moonlight. The next day she had oriented herself well enough to walk northwest and was rewarded by the sight of the new river.

She was always more comfortable when there were trees around and a chance to catch some fish. She knew how to manage when she was around water. Scornfully, she looked at the muddy, bleak ribbon of water in front of her. What they called a river in Kansas was a pitiful thing by Southern standards. She began following it due west.

She walked.

Bethany was the first to see a person coming across the prairie. It was toward evening, a time for looking west, as the sunsets were incredibly lovely. They stained the evening sky like spilled paints. The snows had stopped. It was still winter, but the air had quickened, and it would soon be their first spring on the prairie.

Last month, Tripp and Harrington had

returned with two wagonloads of food, clothes, and seed. Hope soared as the earth warmed. Music floated around the campfire at night.

Blessings always came from the east. Each evening before she went inside for the night, Bethany instinctively turned her face east toward a certain spot in a little line of cottonwood trees standing across the Solomon. She saw the sunrise there every morning after the Lord saw her safely through the night. Her high energy rekindled with the dawn and ebbed toward late evening.

The light was beginning to fade, but her eyes picked out a shape moving toward her. When the speck grew to the size of a person, she could see the traditional white turban and knew it was a woman.

Then as the woman came closer, her heart nearly stopped in her body, and she caught her breath. Blinded by joy, she blinked hard to see if she was conjuring up a vision.

"Momma," she called wildly as she ran to meet the woman. "Momma."

The woman started to run toward her. "Bethany? Bethany? My own angel girl? You here? In this town?"

Bethany rushed to meet her. Tears streamed down her face. They hugged, clung, swayed back and forth in the fading twilight. The tall bluestem grass dipped as a sudden breeze moved across the plains. A frog hurrumphed from the banks of the Solomon. A jack rabbit bounded across the prairie.

Racked by sobs, Bethany let go of her mother, splayed her fingers across her face, and bent over like she had been kicked in the stomach. Her voice came in child-like uncontrollable explosions of misery.

"Child, child. I can't hear you. Can't understand you."

"Oh Momma, Momma. I thought you were dead. I thought I was seeing a ghost. How did you find me? How in God's own name did you find me here? How did you know to come here?"

Her mother's eyes were like two sinkholes in her lined face. The whites were bloodshot, and her dress hung limply off her painfully thin body. She lifted her blue-black hands and patted her daughter's face. Felt it all over. Then soft tears started down her cheeks.

"Didn't know you was here, child. Didn't know that. Didn't know nothing about you being here. Just wanted to come to this town. Read about it in this here writing and wanted to come here where black folks could have a chance. I may be an old woman, but I wanted that chance. You're never too old for chances."

Bethany took the paper from her and stared at the handbill she had composed herself, stunned that it had brought Queen Bess to her.

"This has to be the Lord's doing," she cried. "I wrote this one myself. Wanted folks to read something, just once, that wasn't a passel of lies."

"Just knew this was something special." Queen Bess stared at her beautiful daughter, then stroked Bethany's soft, black hair. "Oh child, it's sure enough the Lord's doing. Just magic. But something was calling me. It was like I just had to come here."

"Come inside now, Momma. I have a home. You need a home. We'll have a place. You need food right away." Her mother was on the verge of collapse, and she seemed to let her strength slither into the deepening twilight as Bethany braced her and led her toward the door of the dugout. "You're going to be home, Momma. Just a few more feet. You're going to be home in Nicodemus."

Then Bethany blinked as the sun blazed as if in protest at being banished over the horizon. Her joy faltered as the setting sun became a fiery red-orange, a terrifying ball of evil in the West.

She remembered, she remembered.

Flames, flames across the land. Flames and heat and destruction. Destruction and stark terror.

It was Momma standing in front of the plantation shielding the St. James women when the soldiers rode up. And Momma, screaming at the Yankees to leave them alone, leave all the people alone. The whites, the blacks.

"This is a good family," her momma yelled. "We all has it good. Didn't no one ask y'all to come." None of the black folks wanted to be freed from that plantation.

And then there was the blue-coated man saying no black bitch was going to tell him what to do and say and how he should act, and some of the other slaves were trying to shut Momma up.

Bethany knew all about men and women even though she had never been with a man. She knew all the things that went on with black women and white men, and it was better not to provoke white folks anyway. Momma had told her it was better for her that all the young white men were off to the wars when she reached her womanhood.

Bethany knew Momma was taking a terrible chance screaming at these evil men, and it wouldn't do anyone any good, and it wouldn't stop a thing, and she would just be putting herself in terrible, terrible danger, and then the man dragged Queen Bess behind the house, and Bethany listened for a scream, but she didn't hear another word from her mother. She hadn't heard her momma speak again until now.

They had run, all of them, from the burning house, the burning barns, the screaming animals, and she did not understand why the invaders wanted to burn everything. She hated them, hated them, but most of all she grieved for her mother.

She had never seen her again since that terrible day.

Until this very moment she had always supposed Queen Bess had been left for dead. With the return of her mother, this Lazarus raised from the grave, terror limped through her doorway into her little dugout. The malevolent molten blast in the west flared triumphantly.

The fire, the fire. Feelings she kept beaten down like wayward flames threatened to blaze up and get out of hand.

She steadied herself. The sun, the sun. It was only the sun showing off at the end of the day. She eased her mother through the door and into the corner where she had hung a curtain to hide her bed from the rest of the dugout. When there were sick people who needed special care, she laid them there, and she slept on one of her straw pallets. She eased her mother onto the bed.

"Going to get you something to eat first," she said softly. "A little soup, and then sleep." Her mother's nostrils were pinched with fatigue.

Bethany went to the stove. Thanks to the aid from Eastern Kansas, she now had potatoes to add to her rabbit stews. She ladled a helping into a tin cup and sat it on the floor beside the bed. She gently lifted her mother's shoulders until Bess was propped against the sod wall, then began to spoon little sips into her mouth. Queen Bess savored the hot liquid with her tongue, then noisily began to gulp the broth.

Bethany brought her a cup of water and then lowered her down onto the bed again and covered her with her old quilt. She eased her mother's dress over her head and slipped a loose nightgown on in its place. She froze when she felt welts on Queen Bess's back.

The Yankees! The St. Jameses had never touched her mother. None of the Herbert women had ever been whipped. Mindful of the shame on her mother's face, Bethany finished dressing her. Queen Bess immediately fell asleep.

Then Bethany's heart swelled until it choked her throat. She began to cry in great silent heaves again. She rose and went outside, afraid she would not be able to control her sounds, and she did not want to wake her mother.

When she was spent, a rhythm began in her heart, a drumbeat as old as Africa. They had come home.

They were all coming home to Nicodemus. Weren't going to study war no more. Weren't ever going to know hunger or terror or sorrow or the white man's lash or blood lust or separation.

Just freedom, precious freedom.

CHAPTER TWELVE

The next morning, several of the women had already heard the news. They walked over to the school before Bethany started her lessons. They gathered around her desk. Bethany's voice trembled as she told them that sure enough, her own mother had stumbled into Nicodemus like a miracle sent from God.

"She's plumb worn out and a bit sickly. She's nearly walked herself to death. She needs to rest, but you all will meet her in a couple of days. Just want you to know . . ." Then she couldn't stop her tears. "This is a miracle. Sure enough. She found us on account of something we did. She read our flyer and knew she was reading the truth. It wasn't puffery, wasn't a pack of lies. See what we can do? Our people need the truth. See what the truth can do?"

"Lord, have mercy," said LuAnne Brown. "She a healing woman, too?"

"Is she a healing woman? She is quite simply the best healing woman I know. I had to stop myself from running through this town shouting last night." Bethany raised her hands toward heaven. "We are so very blessed. Yes, praise God. She's the best healing woman I know."

"She lay on hands?" Dolly asked.

Bethany stiffened. Either way she answered it wouldn't set right with some of the folks. Although Queen Bess was part motherwit and a sometimes faith woman, she also put a lot of stock in healing plants.

Queen Bess's grandmother had come from Haiti, and she knew some black witching she had only hinted at to Bethany. Something darker. Truth was, besides that, she had a special knowing all her own. Once she had tried to get Bethany to see the light shining around people, but Bethany was blind to this kind of vision.

Queen Bess knew the white doctors' ways, too, from when they were called to plantations. But she also knew they were mostly wrong. White folks were bled senseless to bring the four humors into balance. The more highly trained the doctor, the more likely he was to kill.

But they knew how to cut.

Queen Bess had watched them cut when

she attended their rounds. She put a heap of stock in their cutting.

Folks said she was part witch, and she didn't mind that a bit. She had told Bethany long ago that the biggest weapon they had against white folks was fear. Fear of what their slaves were doing behind their backs. They did plenty, and the white folks knew it.

"Sometimes she lays on hands," Bethany said carefully. "Sometimes."

Three nights later, the whole town gathered outside around the campfire to meet Queen Bess.

Bethany pulled Teddy forward from the back of the group. "Momma, I want you to meet the man who's made this all possible. This is Teddy Sommers. And Teddy, this is my mother, Queen Bess."

Teddy arched his eyebrows and gave a little tug of his hat as he looked frankly into the face of the blue-black woman, her skin as shiny as a gun barrel. She wore the classic white turban, a vestige of slave status. She was the only lone woman who had come to Nicodemus who had not abandoned it at once. That alone spoke volumes about her.

Everyone knew by now that Bethany's

mother had found Nicodemus from reading a simple handbill that Bethany had created. Hope and wonder rippled throughout the colony. Nearly every black family had people who had been lost or sold away. This woman had walked across the plains to find her daughter. Perhaps their own loved ones would find them, too.

Queen Bess looked at him hard, and he winced under her scrutiny. There was a nearly palpable aura emanating from this woman. Uneasily, he looked around, wondering if others could see the light, the field of pure energy. They did not shake hands or touch. She merely nodded in his direction, but her eyes did not swerve.

Bethany beamed at them both. Unable to turn away from Queen Bess's hard gaze, Teddy felt a quiet bubble of protest rising within him. It was the first time since he had come to Nicodemus that he felt uneasy in someone's presence. He closed his eyes for an instant. Trouble had just walked into their town. "You're simply the two most important people in my life," Bethany said softly. "The most important."

Teddy smiled. Implied was her hope they would just love each other. Be the best of friends. Well, he hated to disappoint her, but he could tell her right now, it wasn't going to happen. He intended to give the old woman a wide berth.

Before the meeting started, Bethany had gone from place to place asking them all to rejoice with her and bring their plates or bowls. Although food was not scarce like it had been during the winter, it was still a rare treat to eat food prepared by someone else's hands. They lined up to receive a portion of venison, spiced with wild onions she had cooked that morning. All the men sat in a group apart, and all the women wanted a chance to talk to Queen Bess.

Teddy watched and listened.

"Momma is a granny," Bethany said. "So was her mother ahead of her and her mother's mother. But Momma, she's special."

Teddy studied the faces of the other women gathered. Respectful faces, hands close and neat, waiting to serve. All eyes on this black leopard who had sprung into their midst.

"Granny" could mean many things. This woman was high quality, a healer. But on some huge plantations, the granny was the slave woman in charge of overseeing all it took to make the place run right. Feeding a couple hundred slaves, spinning wool, cutting and sewing their clothes, keeping them well, called for a right smart-thinking woman. Teddy had known a couple of these black matriarchs. Stark fact was some white women just couldn't figure out how to run a plantation. So they took to their fainting couches. Then an able black woman was the heart and brains that kept the whole place from falling apart.

Sometimes, the term granny meant the old woman who looked after the children until they were old enough to join their parents in the fields. But from what Bethany had said, her mother was one powerful doctoring woman. She probably kept things on an even keel, too. Did it all.

Teddy sighed and stuffed his hands in his pockets, one foot braced against the wall. Gloomily he looked at Queen Bess. No doubt in his mind what that turban meant — an ex-slave who wore her badge of shame like it was a crown of thorns. Flaunting it. *It mean she 'bout as changeable as an anvil.*

Dolly Redgrave had noticed him listening. Seemed like every time he turned around, that woman was peering at someone. He turned back to the menfolks.

"Come spring I'se going to plant a little corn and a little oats." John More spoke cautiously, as if hoping someone would approve.

"You say it going to be spring, boy? You

221

sure of that?" Henry Partridge guffawed. "And if it do come, how can we tell?"

"I hear say the wind switches to the south, that how we can tell."

"Corn's good. I'se going to stick to stuff my youngsters can eat." Silas Brown's limp, mottled face sagged with worry. He looked like an old tan coon dog that had taken the wrong turn. "Not taking no chances of going hungry ever again. Going to figure out how to grow food. Then I going to pick up buffalo bones and sell them to the railroad folks. They ship them back east to grind up for fertilizer. Meissner, he say they's plenty of money in that. But I going to keep the hides."

"I'm not," said Henry Partridge. "Gonna sell it all. Meissner say there's plenty of money in hides, too."

"Need them hides for covers for my youngsters and shades for my windows," said Silas. "Reckon I learned a few things this winter even if it was from a bunch of wild Indians."

"Not putting your trust in the Lord, Preacher?" taunted Henry Partridge.

"Not a question of trusting in the Lord. Proverbs got plenty to say about ants and grasshoppers," Silas snapped. "Besides, Meissner done been steering us right. He say there's money in picking up bones, I say there is, too. His little town is doing all right, and he's doing right by us. His little town is sprouting houses. He sends people here to give us work."

Silas started swaying to an imaginary rhythm. "He say they a railroad coming to these parts; I say they is, too. He say no job like a railroad job; I say it is, too. He say Nicodemus a gem on the prairie; I say it is, too."

Teddy grinned. The preacher man was about to get wound up if someone didn't stop him. But talk moved to argu-fying, as it always seemed to nowadays.

" 'Spose Tripp and Harrington going to round up anything for us this time?" Henry Partridge rubbed the cleft of his hand as he always did when he was wishing for something.

"Don't know, and can't say as I like it," said John More. "Bad thing, I say, going round to white folks with their hands out. It was different when they was going to Wyandotte. They understand hard times there. And it was taking from the kindness of our own people, but this going out around here ain't right. You know it ain't. Gonna give white folks the wrong idea. That we can't take care of ourselves."

"Well, we can't, John. That's the truth, and you know it."

"Hell we can't. Could of, if we hadn't been lied to."

"Don't care. White folks heard lies, too." Henry wasn't a man who backed down easily. "You think some of them ain't out begging just like us?"

They fell silent and stared at the fire. Then Sidney Taylor stepped out of the shadows. "I've made something. Something I wanted to do for a long, long time now. Guess it comes natural. Making barrels and then making this." Shyly the man held out an exquisite drum, beautifully shaped and covered with deerskin.

Teddy swallowed a lump in his throat. Several of the men had tears in their eyes. Teddy's hand trembled as he reached to touch the taut hide. Before the war, drums were forbidden. Even blacksmiths were whipped without mercy if their clanging sounded too catchy or too even or too uneven or too anything at all.

Masters were scared to death they were talking through those drums. Going to start an uprising. Going to kill all the white folks in their beds.

Whites were right for once. They could surely talk through those drums. They could talk with them now, if they wanted to. As they were able to do in Africa. Always Africa. Always Africa, in their blood, their background, their music. Nothing that had happened so far in Nicodemus gave Teddy a greater sense of freedom than seeing this drum. They could do anything they wanted to. Play anything they wanted to. Make their own music.

The men clustered around, admiring the highly polished wood, the taut skin.

"Reckon all we need now is someone to play it."

"Reckon so," said Teddy softly. He went closer to the open doorway of the sod house, where he could hear the women talk as well as the men. They crowded around Queen Bess, pestering her with questions.

"I like to bleed to death with my monthlies. Can you stop it?"

"My boy, he get to shaking sometimes, like he demon possessed, and I don't know what to do."

"My time will come soon. Will you help?"

Queen Bess abruptly turned to Bethany. "When did you come here?"

"Just last summer, Momma."

"No chance then to see what grows. What you can use?"

"No. And no one to ask. There was an

225

Indian woman who was part of the group of hunters that gave us enough food to see us through the winter, but I couldn't understand her. Through signing and pointing we managed to agree on the uses of the plants I already had, but I couldn't talk to her well enough to find out what she used that I didn't know about. She used a word I didn't understand, like I was supposed to know it. It sounded like 'Bartholomew.' "

"It Bible," said Sister Liza Stover. "He Bible folks."

"It still don't make no sense," Queen Bess said.

"Then there was a white woman I helped deliver who was just passing through." Bethany shrugged. "I doubt if she knew anything, because she came from back East where there's different sorts of plants."

"It soon be spring," said Queen Bess. "I'll start looking right away. I just brought a few things with me."

"The next time Teddy goes out, there's a priest he came across. He knows where the government put those Indians. Maybe the Father will let us go with him and talk to the old woman. Help us ask all the right questions."

Queen Bess spat words in a language Teddy didn't understand.

"But Momma," Bethany said. "We have to. We're all alone out here. Don't talk like that. Speak English. I can't even understand those words any more."

"I said I don't ever want to see a white man in this town. Not now, not ever. That plain enough for you? We don't need them, and we don't want them. Not even a priest."

Teddy sighed and closed his eyes. No trouble understanding this time. Not her words and not her meaning. The only thing he dreaded more than his people who just loved all white folks, were the ones who just hated all of them. No question which camp this woman fell into.

Trouble had just walked in. Big trouble. Black and blue and seething with anger.

CHAPTER THIRTEEN

Bethany passed pieces of Meissner's tattered news pages among the children and told them to duplicate the letters she'd printed across the top. Jim Black planned to make a large board they could all see as soon as he had time to plane the wood.

"Chalk stone's easy to come by," he'd said. "Plenty of that 'long the creek. Take a little longer to figure out a coating that'll hold marks and you can erase."

Bethany's thoughts strayed from the child in front of her. Seemed like Jim was right there now every time she turned around. Holding his hat, looking at her with awe. And more. She would have to be a fool not to see the more.

She walked among the children, softly encouraging those who lagged behind, stopping to guide the fingers of the little More girl who was on the verge of tears.

She had just dismissed the class when

Queen Bess suddenly appeared in the doorway. It was her first visit to the school. Bethany beckoned her to come on inside. The children filed past the crate where they stored their supplies and carefully put their papers inside. They greeted Queen Bess politely on their way out.

"Why you want to trouble these youngsters with white man's words and white man's ways?" Queen Bess said furiously after the last child left.

Astonished, Bethany whirled around. "We must learn, Momma. We must learn."

"Listen to me, girl. It's our chance to leave that world and those evil people behind."

"We have to get along with white folks even out here."

"Don't have to get along with no one, girl. Just ourselves, and that keep us plenty busy enough. Trouble with you, you didn't know you was black soon enough. Now you slow to see you're a bit too white to know how our people think."

Bethany gasped. Trained from infancy not to talk back to her elders, for a moment she was speechless. But she couldn't let this go. "Momma," she said slowly, "it's not my fault. Not my fault that I'm not completely black. It's not your fault, either. Why do you want to blame me for something I can't help?"

Queen Bess lowered her eyes. "You right as rain. None of this our fault, but child, here we have a chance. A chance. You turning up your nose at plenty of chances thrown at you, day after day. I've been here three weeks now, and I see how that fine young man, that Jim Black, looks at you. It's your chance to marry a blacksmith. A good man. And you just turning up your nose. You would have fine, fine children. You too good for him?"

Bethany's face flamed with embarrassment. "No, Momma, I'm not too good for him. And he is a fine man. I know that. But he's not . . ."

"Not white enough?" Queen Bess said softly. "He too black? Too crude?"

"No," said Bethany. "No, it's not that. It's not."

"Yeah it is, child." Queen Bess turned and left as quickly as she had come.

Bethany pressed her hands against her face. Dear God, it wasn't true. Of course she knew Jim Black would like to keep company. He was a good man, just as her mother said. Tears stung her eyes. "You'd have fine children," her mother had said, sounding like some old plantation owner matching up slaves for breeding.

She grabbed a broom and started sweeping the floor with long hard strokes. Momma was right about one thing; reading had filled her mind with all kinds of fancy notions. One of them was that she wanted to marry for love or not at all.

She leaned on her broom and looked out the window. She had rolled up the buffalo hide shades to let in light and air. No danger now of anyone being chilled. Soon they would all be complaining about the heat. She saw her mother's white turban bobbing in the distance. Every evening, Queen Bess searched for plants and herbs.

Bitterly, Bethany watched her mother disappear over the horizon. She had hoped Queen Bess would help her cultivate the baby business in the white community. There wasn't another doctor or midwife around close. But it wasn't likely she could attract customers, with Momma wishing a black and terrible death on anyone who came their way if they weren't the right color.

She saw a wagon coming across the prairie. The driver headed straight toward the schoolhouse, and she went outside to meet him.

"You Bethany Herbert?"

"Yes, sir, that would be me."

"Donald Hays," he said with a curt nod. "It's my wife. It's her time, and Suzanne Mercer said you were a doctoring woman."

"Yes," Bethany said. "Yes, I am."

"Will you come? Mrs. Mercer says you do a fine job."

"Of course. Let me get my satchel."

The man was lean and upright. Plainly dressed, with gentlemanly ways. He had a short, blond beard and keen, blue eyes. Trusting her instincts, she had no qualms at the thought of heading across the prairie with a white stranger. Nevertheless, she was glad her mother had worked her way to the creek bank where she was out of sight and wouldn't be throwing a fit.

She went back to her dugout to collect her supplies. Some of the children gathered to eye the man. She turned to Zach Brown. "When my mother gets back, please tell her I've gone to help a white woman with a birthing, and I'll be back as soon as I can."

She was uneasy before every birthing. What if something went wrong? Her mother was far more qualified than she to deliver babies. But right now, she was furious with Queen Bess and didn't trust her around white folks.

Back outside, she climbed into the wagon.

She guessed they had gone about five miles when he pulled up to a sod house. About five hundred yards to the south, the man had dug out the side of a short rise and made a three-sided earth shelter for his animals. The entrance was fenced across. He had a windmill and a watering trough. A few chickens scratched around the yard. There was a small plot of neatly plowed rows, shining and black right next to the house. A start of a garden.

Inside as well as outside, there was loving evidence of hard work. The woman had a number of patchwork quilts. Pictures hung from nails pegged into a shelf that spanned a whitewashed wall. Muslin strung across the ceiling to catch bugs lightened the dark room.

Hays led her to a bed braced in a corner. It was strung with cords to support a straw-stuffed mattress.

"This here is my Libby," he said. He took his wife's hand and gave a little squeeze. She was a young, pretty woman with long, dark hair, damp with sweat. She sat up slightly to see Bethany more clearly.

"Libby, this is Miss Bethany Herbert. The woman Suzanne Mercer told you about."

"Thank God. Thank Jesus." Libby's eyes were dark and huge in her fair face.

Don Hays took a worn bandana from his pocket, wiped tears from his eyes, and loudly blew his nose. "Don't mind telling you, ma'am, I was worried sick. Now, I'll just step outside and leave you to your birthing work."

Bethany went to the stove and stoked the fire, then went outside and filled two pans with water from the rain barrel next to the house. Setting the water to boil, she washed her hands, went over to the bed, and examined Libby Hays's swollen belly to see if she could expect a normal birth. She gently eased up Libby's gown. The woman was a ways from being fully dilated. "Everything is fine. It will be a while yet. Shouldn't be too hard."

"Lord, I'm glad to see you. I've been so scared."

"You'll be fine. I'll be right here beside you. Sleep when you can. Talk when you want to, hush when you don't."

There were two straight-backed chairs and one rocking chair. They had used planks and barrels to make a table. "Please, make yourself comfortable," Libby said.

Bethany moved the rocking chair closer to the bed, opened her satchel, and took out the quilt block she was working on.

"Oh, let me see. Let me see what you're

making."

"A log cabin, it's called."

"That's one of my quilts, too. Over there on top of that chest."

Bethany stood up, walked over to the quilt, and admired the colors and stitching. "Where did you get your cloth?"

"I had some of it with me when I came. The rest I traded for."

Don Hays stuck his head in the door from time to time. "I'll be right outside," he said. "Setting right out in front. Got a little harness to mend. Reckon I'll be better off if I keep my hands busy."

Bethany and Libby chatted easily for another couple of hours. Then the contractions became even and urgent. Even though it was a first birth, it was easy with no complications. Bethany gave thanks at the first cry of the splendid, healthy, perfect little baby boy. After she cleaned him up, she opened the door and beckoned to Don Hays. "You can come in now. And this little fellow needs a name."

"Irving," he said, his face splitting with a grin. "It's already decided. Irving after my father and his father before him."

He went to the bed, stroked his wife's forehead, and beamed with pride. He turned to Bethany. "I can't tell you how grateful we are. How long can you stay?"

"I can't," she said, although she believed in the value of a decent lying-in period. "I teach school, and I must get back to the children. Aren't there other women around who could help?"

"No, ma'am. Not a one. The lady to the east has her own family to tend to. No one lives close enough to go back and forth." Don looked at her anxiously. "We'd be much obliged if you would stay on here a couple more days. I would be glad to go back over to your place and let folks know. And we can pay you. Cash money."

"Can't you stay? I feel like I've known you all my life." Libby blinked back tears.

Bethany thought of LuAnne Brown. She would be perfect.

"I can't stay, but I know someone who might be willing. LuAnne Brown. She would be excellent. Far better than I to help with the lying-in. Her husband can tend to her children." She turned to Don Hays. "I'll stay until you can fetch her."

Hays turned to his wife. "Sounds like a good idea to me."

Libby nuzzled the little boy wrapped snugly in a new flannel blanket. "I'm sure that woman will be just fine if you say so. We'll be glad to have her."

"When you fetch LuAnne, please tell her to bring extra scrubbing cloths, and tell her to get ready to spend ten days. Her family can manage on their own."

After he left, she changed Libby's gown and replaced the damp bedding. Then she started tidying the soddy. Don Hays clearly cared about pleasing his young wife. Even the one plastered and whitewashed wall brightened the dark interior and made a lovely display for Libby's walnut-framed picture of her parents. Throughout the room, there were cheery touches.

"Books!" An assortment rested on a crate. Bethany laughed and blushed. "Excuse me. It's just that they're scarcer than hen's teeth out here."

"Go right ahead and look at them if you're a reading woman," Libby said. "Please, help yourself. And there's a *Godey's Lady's Book* and some newspapers, too. My parents live in Eastern Kansas. They send papers to me, and Don gathers up any spare newspapers for me whenever he goes for supplies. I hear some folks over in Wade City have a Montgomery Ward catalog, but I haven't been able to get my hands on one."

"I have work to do first," Bethany said. "Then if you really don't mind . . . Oh, ma'am, if you don't mind. I would just love to."

Libby gratefully ate fried potatoes and pork, and after Bethany changed her pads, she fell asleep. Irving snuggled next to his mother, breathing easily.

Bethany pulled the rocking chair next to the warm stove. There was a pile of buffalo chips behind it, and they gave off a pleasant grassy smell as they burned. Bethany set the books aside and started through the newspapers. Although she loved subtle reasoning and the nuances of classical literature, she enjoyed the inflammatory rhetoric of Kansas editors. They could skin a mule with their tongues, their words. They came straight to the point. There were no double meanings or smoke screens or even common decency. They strutted and insulted and maligned and slandered and raised lying to an art form.

She laughed aloud when she read a description of Ulysses S. Grant in the *Frontier Index*. The editor called Grant a "whiskey-bloated, squaw-ravishing adulterer, a monkey-ridden, nigger-worshipping mogul . . . hell-born satrap, a stinking aristocrat and double-dealing hypocrite and other things as well." *Well said,* she thought. *Well said.* Any hopes her people had for the paradise offered by the Yankees had vanished when Reconstruction ended.

She read with amazement that there was a newspaper in Topeka run by colored folks. Her skin tingled with excitement. There was a colored newspaper in Kansas. She had to get a copy. She would give anything to see it. Her people were coming into their own. Eagerly, she snatched up the paper again. It was the *Topeka Daily Capital*, and inside there was a quote from *The Colored Citizen*:

. . . *the truth of the matter is that the papers in Kansas are not nearly as troubled at the sufferings of the newcomers as they are about the political power that will be in the colored man's possession in the state.*

Bethany began to rock faster, eyes skimming across the page before she could settle down to read every word. She picked other papers up off the pile.

Of course! How could she not have understood this before? Negroes were becoming a political power. Thoughts swirled like puzzle pieces settling into place. If it wasn't about money and land, it was usually about politics. The people of Nicodemus had no money, and most of them hadn't had time to file on land, but according to law they could vote.

Potroff wanted them for their votes. She and Teddy had been going crazy trying to figure out why these white folks were being good to them. It made sense now. She couldn't wait to tell Teddy.

The baby boy cried out, and Bethany sprang to her feet. She smiled at the eager look on Libby Hays's face. "Reckon you two are missing each other right off," she said. "That's a good sign."

Libby laughed and reached for her son. She shrugged the gown off her shoulder and guided the little lips to her breast. She stroked the soft down on his head. "How long will it be before Don gets back?"

"Tomorrow evening, at the latest. He was lucky to have a full moon tonight. Makes traveling a lot faster. I'm sure he'll put up at our hotel, which is our school, too, when I'm around. It won't take long for LuAnne to get her things together."

"How will you get home?"

"Shank's mare." Then she laughed at Libby's puzzlement. "Means I'll walk, ma'am. I'm a strong walker. I got it from my mother."

"I won't hear of it! You will not. Don will take you back in the wagon."

"That's very kind of you, but really, it will be a full moon, and I don't mind walking at all."

"Nonsense. Don will take you, and that's final. He'll be back by nightfall and then see you safely home. It wouldn't be good for me to worry about you getting there."

"That's very kind of you. Thank you." For the rest of the evening they talked as easily as she and LuAnne did.

Bethany whisked through all the work the next morning, then settled back down in the rocking chair to read some more.

"Could I trouble you to fetch something from my trunk?" Libby asked. "I want to write a letter to my mother. There's some special paper inside. It's in a tray right on top."

Bethany went to the small, polished walnut trunk and opened the lid. It was lined with cedar. There was a box of stationery within. The sheets were a heavy, creamy vellum fit for a queen. Pure and unstained. Exquisite. She could not imagine anyone having the courage to put a pen to such fine paper.

"How many sheets would you like?"

"Just one. I'll send the letter back with you if you have a way to mail it. I want my mother to know she has her first grand-child." Libby smiled radiantly as she reached for the paper. "This little fellow changes everything. When we first came here, I didn't think I could stand the loneliness."

"I wouldn't mind a bit of lonely," said Bethany. "I was used to living with just one white woman. At Nicodemus, we were all crowded together until this spring when we could spread out some. I wouldn't mind the people and the squabbling so much, but I can't make sense of the weather. In Kentucky, a body always knew what was going to happen."

She stood quietly remembering the most recent spring storm. There was a nightmar-ish quality to being curled up in a dark hole when the wind swept across the prairie. The wind-driven rain had come with a slam of water. If it rained hard enough, fast enough, her dugout leaked, and there was no more miserable feeling in the world than to be inside a wet hole in the ground. "Here it's like the weather's plotting against us."

"You aren't married, then?" asked Libby.

Bethany looked away. "No, ma'am, I'm not." She briskly walked over to the cup-board and inspected the contents. "Reckon we'd better start thinking about dinner. Let's see what you have on hand."

LuAnne and Don came right in time to eat the fried ham and biscuits while it was still piping hot.

"Libby, I want you to meet one of the most trustworthy women I know. This is LuAnne Brown, and you won't find a finer nurse anywhere."

LuAnne shyly ducked her head and mumbled, "Just know how to do what I'm supposed to do, ma'am. But I do know one thing, that is one fine baby boy." She reached for little Irving, and her eyes shone as she crooned and swayed from side to side.

When Bethany was finally ready to leave, Don reached into his pocket and carefully selected ten dollars' worth of coins.

"That's a Lord's plenty," said Bethany. "Really. Half as much would be a fair price."

"Twice as much would be even fairer." Don glanced at his son. "Worth twice as much to get my wife and the little one off to such a fine start."

"It was my privilege." Bethany picked up her satchel. "My pleasure." She was walking out the door when Libby called her back.

"I want you to take those newspapers. I've read them over and over. And books. I want you to borrow any books you want."

"Really, you folks have been generous enough already."

"Nonsense. Can't think of anyone I'd rather loan them to. I know you'll guard them with your life. One last thing. Don, go fetch my box of stationery."

Hays went to the chest and carried the stash of paper to Libby's bed.

Libby counted out ten sheets and ten envelopes. "Here, this is for you. A gift. I insist."

"I couldn't possibly, possibly take it," said Bethany.

"I want you to have this," Libby said. "My folks gave me one hundred sheets of Parkway vellum and one hundred matching envelopes when I left for Kansas. Not to remind me of what I left behind; they're not mean people. But just so I'll remember that I'm entitled to fine things if I've a mind. We all are. And that includes you."

Bethany stood stock still, then finally raised her eyes. She barely registered the astonished look on LuAnn's face. The look of someone trying to take in a new idea. A wonderful idea.

They didn't have to just survive out here. They all still had slave ways of looking at things. Slave ways of hoping. Slave ways of keeping yearning small and manageable. Slave ways of just wanting no more than to stay alive and not get maimed or killed.

She reached for the paper.

CHAPTER FOURTEEN

Too excited to concentrate on the children, Bethany's mind whirled. The newspapers Libby had given her said the American Negro had become a powerful political force. Politics and their right to vote would be the blacks' ticket to power. And acquiring land. Land had been the key to clout since America was founded.

Potroff may have been the one who brought them here to round out his town, but he could not stop them from voting and acquiring land. There was no way to stop blacks from getting their one hundred sixty acres.

Eager to talk to Teddy, she hurried through the lessons. She found him at Jim Black's shop, watching the blacksmith as he wrestled a wagon wheel into position.

"Morning, Miss Bethany."

She mumbled a quick hello, then ran her fingers through her cascade of hair, loosened during her rush from the schoolhouse. "Teddy, what do we have to do to file for homesteads?"

Incredulous, he looked at her hard. He could not marshal his thoughts fast enough to come up with all the words he needed to tell her this was a terrible idea.

Later he would wish he hadn't tried for prettiness and just gone with his age-old gut reaction — not to rile white folks for any reason. Wished he had blurted out the first words that came to his mind. What she wanted would attract too much attention. What she wanted was dangerous. Not worth the risk.

"Why would you want to do that?" he asked softly. "Lord, Lord, Miss Bethany, why would you want to do something like that? The day we boarded the boat, Mr. Wade done made it clear we was supposed to stay put. In this here town and not go wandering off on our own."

"Because it's our right." Her dark eyes glittered. She glanced at Jim, then moved toward the entrance where there would be more light. Teddy followed.

"I honestly don't know nothing about getting land." His face tightened with misery. His body tensed like a played-out, hounded fox. "And I sure as hell don't know nothing

247

about keeping it."

Part of his soul protested at what she wanted to do, and part of him was envying her guts.

He remembered his profound sense of shame the day when he had understood what it meant to be black. He was a slave. A member of a race that was in bondage to another. He had clung to his mother, asking, trying to make sense of it all. Then he was swept with another memory — the day he learned he was part white. He had become obsessed with the color of skin of everyone he played with.

He knew he wasn't nearly as white as little Robert from the big house, but he wasn't nearly as black as little Jack whose daddy worked in the fields, either. When he asked his mother why he wasn't as black as his brothers and sisters, she sternly told him "not to make no never mind." Warning him off, always warning him off, of whatever he wanted to know. Another in the long list of things he was never to bring up again. It took him awhile to figure out that he had a lot of white blood, but it didn't make any difference in the scheme of things.

A black man was a black man.

However, he knew there were black folks, too, that had held slaves before they were all freed by Mr. Lincoln. He knew some black folks were plumb jealous of his lighter skin. Some of them who had been free before the war were madder than hell at the ones who were newly freed. Wouldn't even let them into their churches. They had hired white ministers and let folks know that "no black nigger" was welcome.

As he grew older, he decided he liked the black race better, but he knew how to get along with the white folks. He had an uncanny instinct for doing that. He knew how important it was, also. They had a chance here to live in peace. White folks would leave them in peace if they didn't go round riling things up. And what this woman was fixing to do, would rile things up good.

One thing never changed. It didn't set right with white folks to see colored folks own land.

"Do you know how mad folks will be when we start filing claims, Miss Bethany?"

Her beautiful face radiated ambition. "I don't care; it's our right."

"No one will help you. No one in their right mind will help you."

She smiled broadly and waved airily as she started back to her dugout. "I just thought of someone who will, Teddy."

■ ■ ■ ■

Norvin Meissner watched Bethany Herbert coming across the prairie. Honey-colored, her hair streaming behind her in the late spring breeze, she moved gracefully through the tall grass. Stunned by his delight in watching her move, he drew a deep breath. Abruptly, he went back inside his soddy for his pipe. He had never seen her approach before. Always she simply materialized, like a tawny ghost. Then after the very briefest exchange of greetings, she would come to the point of her visit. She always had one. She always came for a reason. Because her own time was so valuable, she was respectful of his, as though what he did was also of enormous importance.

Until this evening, he had thought his pleasure in her visits was due to the fact she was the only one with whom he could talk about books. She alone had the breadth of knowledge and learning to provide a foil for his ideas. He had come to depend on her swift, uncluttered insight, her wit, and her wild bursts of laughter when he was showing off. Testing phrases. Deflating other editors.

Now she fairly flew across the last hundred

yards toward him.

"And to what do I owe this unexpected pleasure?" he teased.

She flashed a grin at him. "Unexpected? Not likely. Who comes here more than I do?"

He turned away from her for an instant, suddenly unable to return the lightness in her tone. *So that's the way it is,* he thought. *So that's the way it is.*

However, these were his feelings, not hers. She had never given one whit of indication that there was anything else between them at all.

"As a matter of fact, you really are my most frequent visitor." He waited for her to say why she had come.

"I want you to help us get land," she blurted. "I know Potroff is set on us taking up all the plots in his town, but some of us want homestead land. I've read the newspapers, and we are entitled to it. Men and women alike can file if they're the head of a household."

"That's true." He moved to the table and gestured for Bethany to sit down. "You're going to make a lot of people mad."

"Oh Lord, you sound just like Teddy. That's the first thing he said, too."

She rose, went over to the open doorway,

and stared at the setting sun. Then she turned back to him, clearly disappointed that he didn't share her vision. Her dress fell in elegant folds on her slender body. "That's what everyone keeps telling me. It's what I've been hearing all my life. Not to make people mad. And I learned a long time ago these 'people' we were talking about were always white folks. Black folks aren't people at all, and no one cares about making us mad."

He blinked. Withered under her heat.

"Well, I don't care who I make mad. I'm not going to think that way or act that way out here. I'm just going to claim what's rightfully mine. And the law says we've got the right to land, the same as white folks that move out here."

"You have the right, Bethany; I didn't say that." He cleared his throat and looked away. "All I said was, it's going to make a lot of folks mad."

"So be it," she said. "So be it. I came here to ask if you would help us. Will you?"

His heart sank. It was one thing to rile folks with words in a paper. It was easy to stick up for black folks in an editorial. It would be quite another thing to help them file for homesteads.

Fact was, he was a Caucasian. A white

man. Damned if he wanted only black folks to like him. It was one thing to see to it they got a fair shake, and quite another to have blacks and only blacks for his friends. Whatever he decided now, there would be no turning back.

"What do you want me to do?" he asked finally.

She gave a little squeal. Although he smiled at her exuberance, his mouth went dry, like he had swallowed a boll of cotton.

"I need to know how to file for land. What do we need to know so we won't be called a bunch of dumb niggers?"

"Potroff helps people file claims," he said. "I don't understand why you aren't going to him for help."

She traced her finger in the dust on the table, then raised her eyes. "I don't want help from Mr. Potroff," she said slowly. "Let's just drop it at the fact that he's not a good person."

"Can't argue with that." Puzzled by the flicker of fear on her face, he leaned back on two legs of his chair, his arms clasped behind his head. Then he abruptly rose and went to the crate in the corner of the room where he kept various papers and supplies. He took out the paper for a land claim. It was blank. He went through it with her, line by line.

"The nearest office is Oberlin," he said.

"I'll go there tomorrow."

"Bethany, you can't. You simply can't walk into a land office, like you had the right — which you do — and demand filing papers. They'll figure out some way to stop you. It will take a man like Potroff standing at your side to make them do the right thing. But to just do it on your own, they won't let it happen. There's a thousand ways to stop colored folks; you know that."

Her eyes filled with tears. "It's not fair. I thought things would be different out here. We should be able to make a living and even prosper. God knows most of us would just love to prosper."

He thought hard about the people who were backing his paper. He thought about what she had said earlier, about voting; about the black people becoming a power in cities. States were courting their votes. Earlier, his backers had understood when he told them Nicodemus could sway the county seat vote. Wouldn't take much to make them see that if he helped these colonists get land, it would lock in their vote for Millbrook. It would be sure-fire insurance. They could help each other.

"Miss Bethany, I think I know some people who can help you. They are the ones backing my paper and this town we are trying to start. Let me talk to them, and we'll see what we can work out."

Her smile was dazzling.

"Thank you," she said. "Thank you, Mr. Meissner. I know you want to have the county seat, and I don't think there's a chance that Nicodemus will ever be taken seriously as a contender. So we'll support any town that will help us live here quietly and with dignity."

Meissner nodded. "Reason," he mumbled thoughtfully. "I'll appeal to folks' reason. And ideals. Ideals work well." He picked up a pen and started making notes.

"Most of all, I want my students to have real diplomas. Most of our people just want to make a living and live in peace, but I want our school to be official."

"You have to listen to me, then. You can't rile folks up just now. We must go about this right. But if you can get your folks to vote for Millbrook as the county seat, I think the people backing me will help you get land."

She looked at him hard. "I hope you are telling the truth, Mr. Meissner. But if you help us, we'll help make Millbrook the county seat."

CHAPTER FIFTEEN

Norvin Meissner dropped a piece of type, swore, then tediously eased it back into line. His hands could not keep pace with his thoughts. It was late spring now, and the prairie was alive with insects. Bright-yellow clumps of wild mustard brightened the landscape. White patches of cow parsnips rose above scattered short stands of bluestem where it had taken over the buffalo grass. He could see so far it was as though the earth had no boundaries.

He wasn't a handsome man when he came here, and he knew that had not changed, yet when he last shaved, he stopped mid-whistle and looked at the man who stared back at him. His normally too pale skin had darkened from long hours outside, and his body was harder. There was a new line to his jaw. To his amazement, he looked like a person to be reckoned with. Not exactly a mean son-of-a-gun, but no pushover either.

He was preparing a kindly article about Nicodemus, mixed with glowing words about the character of the people there. Surprisingly, there was an ironclad rule in the town against drinking. He spoke glowingly of the industry and temperance of the residents. He chose his words carefully, knowing exactly how far to go. He knew what would rile folks up and what would not.

When he had worked for two solid hours, doing his best with some irregular type, he looked up and saw a woman coming across the prairie. She wore a white turban on her head, and she was black as a gun barrel. She walked right up to the door, stopped, and looked at him hard, her slim-fingered hands stilled across the front of her apron.

Dumbstruck, he waited for her to speak.

"You be the man Meissner?"

"Yes." The black woman carried herself with an aristocratic bearing that would do pride to any Southern belle. Tall, straight as a pine tree. But it was her force, like an electrical charge, that stunned him. A combination of anger and intention as though she could kill through focus of will.

"I is known as Queen Bess. Bethany Herbert's mother. I come to tell you to leave my daughter alone."

He stammered. "I can assure you, ma'am, that my intentions are strictly honorable in every way."

"Ain't no white man's intentions honorable when it comes to our people. Yours ain't either," she said flatly. "If you think that, you is a fool. But I'm telling you this for your own good. Leave my daughter alone. She set apart. A healer. She has a calling. Birthing is part of it, but there's a lot more. Lots of women of her kind never marry. I never married."

His eyes flickered. Never married, yet she had a daughter.

"Oh yes, Mr. Meissner, I know all about white men. Stuff you don't want to know. The only good thing that come from me and my doings with white men is my daughter. That's all."

"Ma'am, I swear to God, such thoughts have never entered my mind." Even as he said the words, he was swept with shame, remembering his pleasure in seeing Bethany coming across the field.

"Ain't your mind I'm worried about. I'm telling you, quit sniffing around her. You is putting notions in her head."

"She's the one who's putting notions in my head, ma'am. She's asked me to help her get land for you folks. She has a right to do that." His face was hot with dismay. "I'm telling you, ma'am, she's the one that comes to me. Not the other way around. And if you think there's anything immoral going on between us, you are mistaken. Your daughter has a splendid mind. It's a great pity she's not white."

He was so shocked by his own words that he could not speak. Fixed by her gaze, his tongue thickened. Those fierce, judgmental eyes. It was the eyes' fault. They had caused him to blurt what he did not even know he had believed until that very moment.

"You wish she was white," she mocked. "You wish she was white. That's the only thing that's keeping you from my daughter. Well, it had just better keep on coming between you, if you know what's good for you."

His chin quivered. This crazy woman had come out of nowhere and made him say things he didn't mean.

"But I don't think I has a thing to worry about. You see, I know you, Mr. Meissner. I met you a thousand times before. You're white through and through and won't taint your precious blood in any way that can be found out. Ain't like panting and sneaking around in the dark on a plantation. And you ain't got the guts to go after what you want in daylight. Can't hide that kind of thing out here."

She continued to watch his face. Sullenly, he stared at the ground. Later, he wished he had talked back. Offered a word or two in his own defense. He was a man of words. He valued words; knew the power of words. But he had been stunned to silence like a bug paralyzed by a tarantula.

It came from her recognition of thoughts he hadn't even known he had. Desires that were buried deep inside his soul. She had forced him to look at a side of himself he didn't even know existed.

"Who are you?" he whispered. "What are you?"

Her smile was grim as death. "I just am, Mr. Meissner. I just am."

She turned and walked back the way she had come.

The next day, after pacing the floor, staring gloomily at the type, and starting a new column three times, he finally went outside and began yanking weeds in his new corn patch. By noon, he knew what he was going to ask of the people sponsoring his town company.

He spent the next morning composing a letter to Mr. Frank Slater, who was providing the bulk of Millbrook's money. When he had finished, he saddled his horse, rode off to Oberlin, the nearest town with an official post office, and mailed his letter.

He got a reply a week later and whooped when he read it. It was cautious, but positive. He had permission to move his paper to Nicodemus. Immediately, he started thinking about a new name for the publication. If he could persuade all the colored people trekking into Topeka and Leavenworth to come on out to Nicodemus, there was no doubt whatsoever, their town could be voted in as the new county seat.

There would be an ample supply of labor and work for all through the effort to raise up the town. Everyone would get rich, and he would have the satisfaction of helping a race he had always defended with his words.

He saddled his horse and rode toward Nicodemus. He eyed the schoolhouse, heard Bethany's voice as he passed, but did not want to interrupt her lessons. He went down to the blacksmith shop.

Jim Black looked up, nodded, then turned back to the horseshoe he was fitting.

"Looks like you're starting to get a lot of work from outside the community," Meissner said.

"It's building. Slow. Real slow, but people

are starting to come."

Meissner strolled outside, walked down the street, and took inventory. There was a sparsely stocked general store, the livery stable, the school-hotel-storage building, and Jim Black's blacksmith shop. Other business and services — such as Dolly Redgrave's dressmaking — were conducted from the settlers' homes. The town needed more people.

He watched an old woman tend to her new garden and, in his head, began to compose columns bragging on the industry and vitality of the town. His town, by God. He planned the celebration that would take place to welcome Nicodemus's first newspaper. He planned the publicity release for the Eastern presses.

By evening, everyone knew there was something afoot. Meissner waited for everyone to assemble in the schoolhouse. He envisioned a fine new school, set apart, constructed from limestone quarried from the bluffs near Nicodemus. Self-consciously he strode to the front of the room.

"Tonight, I bring you good news," he began. "Very good news indeed. My paper, the *Millbrook Wildhorse,* is backed by affluent people who have an interest in the railroads. They wish to share their prosperity with the people living on the Great Plains. A railroad is essential to a county seat, and a county seat is essential for attracting a railroad."

He straightened. Trembled with the importance of what he was about to say. "They have selected you — your town, Nicodemus — as being worthy of the all-out, no-holds-barred effort to get the county seat."

Confused, the blacks buzzed like hornets. Henry Partridge, looking even more like an eel due to the flesh-stripping winter, waved his claw hand. "Thought Wade City was going to be the county seat."

"Despite the very best efforts of Mr. Potroff and the lying bunch of thieves in back of him, he does not have enough people to petition for county organization. I see no reason — In fact, I'm quite positive, that with the right backing — and I have it — Nicodemus would make an ideal site."

He paused, bewildered that there was not the immediate joyful shout he had expected.

"I hope you understand what this will mean for the economic security of this community. Not just the economy, but the recognition you will get nationwide. It will be a Mecca and the first Negro community in the nation to have this status." He flushed. Perhaps they didn't understand.

"Nicodemus will be the county seat."

His neck reddened, and his freckles were stark against the sudden whitening as the blood drained from his face. Perhaps he should explain more thoroughly that he was offering them the opportunity of a lifetime.

"Mister, I've got news for you." All turned to look at Patricia Towaday. She was a slight woman with snuff-colored skin sprinkled with dark freckles. Her voice trembled in the manner of a person not used to speaking up. But, driven by fury, she couldn't restrain herself.

She and her husband and two children had come to Nicodemus better outfitted than anyone there. They had bought a team, a wagon, and a fair amount of seed when they went through Wyandotte. The railroaders at Ellis had confiscated it all in exchange for Wade's unpaid freight bill.

"If there's one thing our people know, it's when white folks offer us something, it time to run like hell. The last time we listened to a white man was Wade, and he told us we were going to be rich and happy. We pert' near starved to death."

"Amen," piped up Sister Liza Stover.

"Most of us don't even have the animals we came here with. We like to died during the winter. The only difference between the winter coming up and the winter we just went through is that we're a lot smarter. And we is plenty smart enough to know better than to listen again to another white man."

"Yeah," said her husband. "It took us a while, but we learned."

"You don't want my newspaper here in this town?" Meissner asked. "You don't want a chance to be the county seat?"

"We don't want *you* in this town."

Everyone turned toward the woman who had stepped forward from the back of the packed room.

"We don't want you, and we won't have you." Queen Bess did not bother to look at anyone else. Her eyes burned with contempt. "We don't want your wrongful, hurtful ideas killing what we have here. Sapping its life with little half-truths and lies."

Bethany walked forward and stood to one side of Meissner. "Momma, you're wrong," she pleaded. "You're wrong. This man wants to help us. We need to let him help us."

"We don't need to be taking nothing from white folks. Not their money, or their words or their ways," snapped Queen Bess.

Meissner stood helplessly to the side. Then Bethany turned to him. "Mr. Meissner, I apologize that your presence and your expertise should be so poorly received. More than anyone here, I know and appreciate your kindness, but you have to know I, too, am stunned that you would come riding in here and just assume we would all be tickled to death without feeling out one single soul first."

Dumbfounded that Bethany first praised him and then criticized him in front of the group, he opened his mouth to defend himself and then thought better of it.

Bethany's cheeks darkened. Her voice was staccato. Clipped. Furious. "How would you like it, Mr. Meissner, if a Negro came riding into Millbrook and announced he was going to plant himself in the middle of your town, expecting a royal welcome, and intended to speak for you, decide for you, and tell you what to do and what to think?"

Bethany looked around. Queen Bess beamed, and Teddy's eyes were alight with pride.

"That's right, child," someone murmured. "You tell him, sister. You've got it right."

"We thought you were different. I told these people you were different."

"Ain't no white person different," taunted Queen Bess. "Not at heart. They just think they are because they ain't been tested."

"The point we need to make ain't being

said so Mr. Meissner here can understand." Earl Gray's yellow, bloodshot eyes hardened with anger. He had lost his wife and child during the winter. Word was, he was planning to marry a widow with two grown children who'd come trekking into town two months ago. Word was, he was still so bitter over his loss that the widow was marrying a ghost and might as well be living a single life. But apparently there was life in the ghost after all.

"What's not being said is, we don't ever, ever want white folks living in our town. Not now, not ever. Get out."

The room was quiet. Norvin Meissner's skin prickled. Everyone in the county had heard the story about these blacks forming a lynch mob to hang Wade.

He swallowed hard. There would be no help for him. No place to hide. Stunned, he struggled to find some words to offer in his own defense, but before he could speak, Jim Black edged up beside him.

"I'se a plain man," he said. "Ain't got Bethany's ways with words, and God knows I don't have Meissner's. I make my living with my hands. Can't put my words together fast enough to always say what I'm thinking. But there's something starting up here that's wrong. I know it, and you know it.

This here man is a good man. Make no difference if he black or white. He still a good man. Ain't no call to say he ain't. He loaned us books for our school. Gave us old paper to get the children started. He told folks about this town. Stuck up for us. Ain't no call to act like he's like most white folks, 'cause he's not."

"Oh, yeah?" Gray said bitterly. "You just sidling up to him because you is starting to make a little money off blacksmithing for him and his kind."

"I'm taking money from white folks, too," LuAnne Brown said. "I'm helping these people. You all know I helped out at the Hayses when they had their new baby. I was proud to do it, and they needed me. I don't understand what's come over you people. I truly don't."

Meissner's gaze swept the room, seeing the division on their faces. They needed to slug this out without him here. He reached for his cap and pulled on his jacket. "I apologize for coming here without thinking some things through." He knew this was not the time to speak in his own behalf. He left quickly and rode home under a black velvet sky sparking with stars that winked and mocked his foolish heart.

Once inside, he poured himself a rare jolt

of whiskey and stared at nothing in particular. A poem came to mind. He hadn't thought of it in years. He could only recall a few words: "These harsh, well-meaning hands, I thrust between the heart-strings of a friend."

He went to the pile of books he had heaped in the corner and thumbed through the well-worn pages, found the poem, and read Sill's old, familiar lines over and over.

"Lord be merciful to me, a fool."

Chapter Sixteen

Teddy absently ran his fingers across his saw blade. He stood in the broad entrance to Jim Black's shop and stared across the prairie. Normally, no matter how broody he felt, it didn't keep him from working.

He had started up his coffin-making business again. It had earned him a decent living during Reconstruction before he became a landsman. Now there were three orders waiting as word was getting around that he built the finest coffins in Western Kansas.

Today, however, he was too heartsick over Norvin Meissner to rustle up any energy. The grass waved in the early summer breeze. Flies were starting up.

Jim Black swore as the shoe he was shaping refused to yield to his relentless hammer. The metal would need reheating. Horseshoeing was one of the first pieces of outside work to come in, but Jim lacked the assortment of tools and ready-made shapes he had on the plantation. He didn't have a single shoe even remotely adequate for the huge Percheron blissfully eating oats in the corner of his shop. He had tried three times to shape the new shoe from scratch.

"S'pose I should count myself lucky to have nails," he muttered.

Teddy turned to watch him ease the shoe off the anvil and back into the fire. Jim had been out of sorts, too, ever since the meeting with Meissner. His timing was off.

Hell, they were all out of sorts. There was something wrong about running off the only white friend they had made out here. Teddy recalled the day when he first met Meissner and the editor offered him coffee, real coffee, like he was quality folks. Worst of all, now they didn't have a sponsor to untangle the maze for filing a claim. He wished he could get the notion out of Bethany's head. His face tightened with worry.

He started toward his tools, then stopped and went outside. He shielded his eyes against the sun's glare. A lone rider was coming toward the town.

"Someone heading this way," he said to Jim. "Work for you, maybe."

"Maybe not." Jim manipulated his tongs back onto the horseshoe and lifted it from the coals back onto the anvil. "Could be trouble."

Jim resumed hammering, and Teddy watched the rider. Not wanting to break the blacksmith's concentration, he did not speak again until he heard the hiss from the red-hot shoes as Jim lowered them into a tub of cold water to cool.

"Well, I'll be damned," Teddy said softly. He stepped outside the doorway.

"Someone you know?" Jim called.

"I'd know that horse anywhere. That sure am one fine horse."

Jim stepped outside the shop and stood beside Teddy. The rider was close enough now for him to appreciate the elegant Morgan mare. "Cavalry man, I 'spect. They's the only ones that gots horses that caliber."

"Yeah," Teddy said. "But that man started out walking, not riding. He walked right into a death trap. Most of his bunch never made it out."

"Hope to hell he was on our side."

" 'Bout as on our side as a man can get," Teddy said. "That man yonder was in the 54th Massachusetts. Our side and our kind of people."

"Don't know nothing about no 54th Massachusetts. Just know mostly our people ain't easy riders." Hardly any Negroes had had access to horses on a plantation. The

273

danger of them running away was too great.

Teddy watched the mare, knowing she'd had to travel many miles to get to Nicodemus, but her steps were still prideful, as though her rider could barely keep her from prancing.

"Bet she's five-gaited. Never thought we'd see a horse like that out here. Or a man like him, either."

Teddy stepped fully into the sunlight.

"Surprised?" Jed Talbot grinned as he dismounted in front of the blacksmith shop. "You do remember me, I hope." He pulled a piece of paper out of his saddlebag. "Remember this?"

Teddy stared at the circular he had given Talbot at the landing the day they left Kentucky. "Surprised ain't the word for it." He looked at Jed in amazement. "Who'd of thought?" Teddy shook Jed's hand. "This here is Jim Black. Finest blacksmith you is ever going to find."

Jim mumbled, "Pleased," but he couldn't take his eyes off the horse.

"Her name's Gloriana," Jed said, smiling at the man's admiration.

"Passing through?" Teddy asked.

Talbot shook his head, and his lips thinned. "Come to stay."

"The hell you say."

"According to this piece of paper you gave me, this here place is supposed to be paradise. Why wouldn't I want to stay?"

"Well, I can't rightly claim this is paradise." Teddy laughed, bending like an old amber grasshopper as he slapped his knees. "There's a few things missing we done set our heart on."

"So I see."

Teddy straightened and proudly held up his head. "Ain't paradise, but it ain't hell, either. Sure ain't hell. Was for a while, but ain't hell now."

"That's all I ask," Jed said. "The absence of hell."

Teddy looked at him curiously, then glanced away from Jed's penetrating, gray eyes. "We most generally puts staying kinds of folks up at Reverend Brown's 'til we can put something together a little more private. Our schoolhouse is kind of our hotel, and we put passing throughs there."

"You have a school?" Jed asked. "Here?"

"And a real bona fide teacher. She quality folks." Suddenly, Teddy recalled Jed Talbot had told him when they first met that he was a lawyer.

A lawyering man. Able to sort out twisty words. Rode right into Nicodemus like he was the Archangel Michael. This man was the answer to Bethany's prayers.

"Mister I 'spect someone going to be plumb thrilled to death to meet you. Can't wait 'til you two get together."

"Guess I'se been standing here admiring that horse of yours long enough," said Jim. "I'd better get back to my shoeing. Water inside. Oats, too."

Jed followed the two men inside, then tended to Gloriana. Jim took the cool shoes from the tub and carried them and his tray of nails over to the huge Percheron. Speaking softly, he calmly lifted the huge right front hoof between his legs onto his heavy leather apron and began filing it with a large, heavy rasp and a curved knife. He trimmed the hoof so that all the ragged and dead parts of the sheath were removed, leaving a solid base upon which to nail the shoe.

He drove nails through the holes of the molded shoes into the hoof at an angle. As the nails cut out the side of the hoof, he cut off unneeded ends, then bent and pounded the nails tightly into the side of the hoof.

"You've got my business sewn up," Jed said admiringly while he watched the process of anchoring the first shoe.

"Much appreciated. Be an honor to work on that mare of yours. Now if I'm not mistaken, folks is starting to trickle out to meet you."

Jed turned. There was indeed a cluster of men outside the door, none of them bothering to hide their curiosity.

"Best you start getting acquainted."

Queen Bess watched from the edge of the crowd. Saw the tall way the newcomer had of holding himself. Didn't have a bit of trouble imagining him slicked up in a good suit and a brocade vest. Could just see him, with his lean, fine hands holding cards, or fiddling like the devil or changing into a whirlwind or a dust devil.

She knew at once from the careful look in his too-light eyes, from his fine white man's lips, and most of all from the easy arrogant way he stood — that this man was not good news. Same as Dolly Redgrave was a burden to them all. Same as her own daughter was, most of the time.

Before the slaves were freed, there were blacks who were born free. They had formed a society in America all to themselves, like they were a separate country. They looked down on the newly freed slaves. Queen Bess would just bet Jed Talbot was that kind of man. If more of his kind of people moved in, they were all doomed.

"And he's a lawyer," Teddy announced

proudly. "Nicodemus has her first genuine professional man."

Queen Bess trembled, dread-struck, as she watched everyone make over Jed Talbot.

Her daughter was still inside the schoolhouse, flogging the little children through stuff they would be better off not knowing. But it wouldn't be long before she would be fawning all over this book-learned miracle that had waltzed right in.

Bethany Herbert stepped inside the Browns' dugout that evening, expecting to meet the usual raggedy, starving derelict. They straggled into Nicodemus at the rate of two or three a week now, and she was worn to the bone trying to find enough food and clothes.

She stilled when she saw Jed Talbot, who instantly rose to his feet and removed his hat as she walked through the door. She stilled her hands, her face, but she could not still her heart, or the fluttery self-consciousness that swept over her as she looked into his luminous, gray eyes.

"Miss Herbert. I'm Jed Talbot. I'm honored to make your acquaintance. Your good friends here," he waved toward the Browns and Teddy, "have told me of your abilities."

Some days, more days than not now since she came to Nicodemus, she had started

278

wearing her hair down, held back from her eyes with a kerchief tied in back. She bit the inside of her cheek and would have given anything if she had changed into her indigo dyed dress and dressed her hair.

Suddenly she was stricken with awareness of what her life really was. She lived on a god-forsaken windblown prairie in a hole in the ground. She didn't know what she was doing most of the time, because she couldn't find any of the plants she needed. She was trying to get along with another race, most of whom would always just hate her kind.

Then that part of her which was already Kansan took over. A side she wouldn't have known existed if she had never moved to the state. A side given to illusions and prideful lies. A side that would knock the hell out of anyone who implied her life wasn't just fine and dandy.

"Welcome to Nicodemus, Mr. Talbot, and I'm sure you can see for yourself the wonderful progress we've made here. It won't be long until we are the Gateway to the West."

"I can certainly see that, Miss Herbert. This is a fine town indeed," he said, managing to suppress a smile. His color was that of a soft fawn, and his voice was rich, melodious, but not Southern. He spoke as though the right words always came easily to him. His cheekbones were high and his nose, thin and straight.

Long ago, she had learned to put her feelings toward men in their proper place. Because she could control her emotions during doctoring, it was understood by all they would be safe with her. This ability let her go into everyone's houses under special passage. But now, her mouth felt cottony, and for the first time in her life, she didn't know what to do with her hands. Embarrassed, she looked away from those remarkable gray eyes, then pulled herself together and headed toward Silas and LuAnne, who sat at the table.

"Jed here's a lawyering man. He going to help us get land," Teddy said. "He been to fine schools back East."

Her resolve to conduct herself in a seemly manner vanished at the word "lawyer." She couldn't stop smiling and stepped toward Jed.

"I'm sure Teddy's already told you, I'm the school teacher and do what doctoring folks need. I hate to pester you for legal advice right off, but if you'll excuse me, I have some papers I want you to see. I'll be right back."

She flew out the door and returned in five

minutes with the homesteading papers Meissner had given her.

Jed started reading them immediately. "This is a fairly simple process," he said. "Owning land would be wonderful. A fine move for everyone."

"Don't mind telling you, I not as hepped up 'bout all this as Bethany here," Teddy said gloomily. "Not just because whites going to hate our guts, but because we don't know a damn thing about farming this country. Never seen ground so contrary."

"You can't all be merchants or craftsmen," said Jed. "You've all got to eat. You folks came here ahead of the flood of people coming up out of the South. You don't know how bad it's gotten or the things I've seen."

Bethany shot him a warning glance and nodded her head toward the Browns' children. Silas and LuAnne were listening, spellbound. LuAnne got up from the table and shooed Zach and Mercy off to bed.

"Where are you from originally, Mr. Talbot? Where did you go to school?"

"I'm from Baltimore, and I went to school at Oberlin in Ohio. It's the first college in the United States to accept men of color. The first one to let in women, for that matter."

"You were born free, then?" Teddy asked.

"Yes, but that hasn't meant much since the war. My father has passed on. Before the war, he manufactured saddles and harness. Lot of government business."

His eyes brightened with unshed tears, and Bethany couldn't take her eyes off his face.

"And then all your father's white friends turned on him?" she suggested. "It no longer mattered if you were born slave or free? If you were born black, you were suddenly shunned by the same whites who had treated you with respect before?"

Talbot stared at his clenched hands. "That's about the size of it," he said. "We didn't face the same kind of hatred as those living in the South. But things changed. Every white man who looked at my father now only saw his black face. They all had a son or a nephew or an uncle or a brother who died for his kind."

"And when they looked at him, they saw blood and death and misery?" Bethany asked softly.

"You seem to know a lot about this, Miss Herbert."

"Oh, I have my own stories to tell about how the war changed everything."

"I'm sure."

"Let's don't get into the miseries tonight,"

LuAnne said. "My children are all ears. Won't sleep if they hear any more 'bout the boogeyman."

Jed held up the forms, abruptly changing the subject. "Nicodemus needs to decide who will file for a homestead first. Teddy says we need to go to Oberlin to file the claim and get set up. Then a surveyor will come out."

"Another thing," Teddy said, "since you is a man of words. Wish you could help us get a fellow back that didn't mean us no harm." He proceeded to tell Talbot about the blow-up with Meissner. "Never meant us no harm atall. He didn't. He just ignorant."

"Would you concur, Miss Herbert? That Meissner was simply caught unaware?"

"Oh, absolutely. He's as good a friend as we have out here. He gave us books for our school. And paper. He's tried to help. He's just . . ." Her voice trailed off helplessly, and she shrugged. "He's just Meissner, that's all."

"Then I'll call on him. See what I can do." Jed smiled. "It's always a good idea to apologize when you know you're in the wrong. Especially when that person owns a newspaper."

Bethany looked at him in wonder. She felt a burden lift.

"How do you call folks together?" Jed asked.

"Since so many have moved in, we always have to meet outside around the campfire. We ring a bell for the ones living close. And we've started using drums to round up scattered folks when it's important. One person hears, then beats on his own drum. Chains on across."

"Please call a meeting for tomorrow night, and we'll see who volunteers to be our first homesteader."

On the way back to her dugout, Bethany stopped and stared at the crystal-studded Milky Way. The full moon gleamed softly in the black, velvet sky. She blinked back tears. An answered prayer. God had sent someone. Someone had come to them who could reason and speak well and help with their legal entanglements. Someone who would be an intelligent civilized link with the white community.

Someone who had asked her if she "concurred" with Teddy's evaluation of Meissner. Someone who had known what the word meant. Someone who valued her judgment.

Then, unbidden, her mother's face mocked her. Put words in her mind.

You mean someone that's just a little bit colored. Sort of like a smoked salmon. Someone like you that white folks ain't gonna want to kill right off.

CHAPTER SEVENTEEN

Jed Talbot stood on the north bank of the Solomon. Gloriana drank deeply of the pure creek water. Dragonflies skimmed across the surface. A sudden gust of wind rippled the leaves of the cottonwoods.

He squatted and cupped his hands to get a drink. He filled his canteen, then sat propped against the largest tree, staring toward Nicodemus. Clumps of wild daisies grew in the dappled sunlight. He reached for a handful of the flowers, slit the stems, and began weaving a chain.

Many years ago, he had woven daisy chains for his little sister. But that was before the war. He shut his eyes against the pain as though not seeing the flowers would hold the memory at bay.

Gloriana whinnied and swung her head over to a nearby patch of grass. "Go ahead, girl," he said softly. "You've earned it." He had ridden many miles since morning, looking over the land surrounding Nicodemus. He had gone from town to town for the last three years collecting information for a committee of fellow blacks; trying to find a place in the South where they could live in peace. Reluctantly they had decided it was time for their people to go.

Jed knew exactly how to blend into each community. He usually took a job at the livery stable — feeding horses, mucking the stalls, running errands, or driving strangers around if they were hesitant about setting out across the prairie with strange rigs. He received lodging, usually a little money, and a lot of information.

It wasn't true that all towns were the same. Long ago, he had decided that each place called forth an angel. Its soul. Once there, it was nearly impossible to dislodge. People could come and go, and brave individuals might attempt to rid a town of an evil or an attitude, but as long as the angel hovered, nothing worked. Nicodemus had a powerful angel protecting it. He had felt its brooding presence from the moment he rode into the settlement.

Already, Nicodemus was becoming the stuff of myths — glorified, enshrined. "There is a town," the colored folks insisted. "There is a black town out on the prairie where Negroes are left alone. They are free and proud and fighters, and folks leave them alone."

You should have been a preacher, boy. You sure can talk. He had heard those words all his life, yet he knew that was not his calling. A preacher ministered to the meek, saved souls, fed the hungry, gave solace to mourners, clothed the needy, and soothed the forsaken. While he surely admired those who could and did, he had the soul of a hawk. For him, it was not enough to feed a hungry man. He wanted to attack the evil that denied them the right to grow enough grain in the first place.

It was not enough to give solace to the mourning. He wanted to send those who had caused their agony straight to hell. He didn't want to soothe the forsaken; he wanted to stop the tormenters who had made cowards of his own race.

His fellow black soldiers, friends all, had marched into a massacre when they tried to take Fort Wagner. They had died trying to claim the natural rights belonging to all humanity. He would never be free of the memory.

There had to be some place on God's green earth where blacks could live like men.

He would make his stand, put all his energy into defending that right in Nicodemus, Kansas. He would make the deaths of those black soldiers count for something. He imagined his dead comrades looking on with approval.

After Jed had made his case for people to file for homestead claims, the group fell silent. The huge campfire crackled and popped.

Then Henry Partridge stood up, cradling his maimed hand. "We all been slaves. We used to being around other folks 'til after the war. Just slave quarters, maybe, but together. Kind of figured we'd all stay together here without some of us marching off on their own. Trouble start, there no hope for some poor black man off in the middle of the prairie by hisself. No hope atall."

"I know that," said Jed. His face was solemn in the wavering flames of the fire. "That's why I didn't try to make this sound like a lark. It will take a very brave person or a family to volunteer to live alone on a homestead. It's not just a matter of race. These are strange times, and a lot of white folks get caught up in dangerous situations, too."

Patricia Towaday leapt to her feet. "So why you come a-stumbling onto Nicodemus treating us all like we was your little colony. Telling us what would be best for us and what we have to do."

He felt a vein pulse in his temple, but years of training took over. "In the first place, madam, let me enlighten you. I did not just stumble onto Nicodemus. Your own Teddy Sommers gave me a flyer the day you left Kentucky. I sought this town out. I heard about this town."

"Praise the Lord," sang out LuAnne. "He hear 'bout Nicodemus."

"Soon everyone will hear about this town." Jed glanced at Bethany. "Because it's the first black town anywhere to make it past a year, and it's doing it in a part of the country where most white towns can't make it. This won't be easy. All I care about tonight is selecting our first volunteer."

"That gonna be me."

The people parted as Queen Bess, who had been standing at the edge of the crowd, walked toward Jed.

Bethany gasped. "Momma, why? No, Momma, you know a black woman trying to live by herself is just asking for trouble."

"I have the right," Queen Bess said. She looked hard at Jed Talbot, and his eyes wavered for an instant. "I is Bethany's mother. Filing claims is my own daughter's bright idea, mister. I see she finally found someone dumb enough to help her."

"Ma'am, I can't let you do that. It's dangerous for a woman to live alone anywhere."

"You can refuse to help me with the papers, but you can't stop me." Queen Bess's dark eyes glowed with contempt.

Jed wished he had been prepared. A woman would complicate matters. There were parts to the Homestead Act that were deeply troubling. Not everyone was interpreting it the same. It read that only persons filing who had "never borne arms against the United States government or given aid or comfort to its enemies" were entitled to the precious one hundred sixty acres. Some folks figured that included Confederate soldiers; some did not. There were plenty of ex-Confederate soldiers in the area. Bearing a grudge.

"It's going to take money. Fourteen dollars up front."

"We has money set aside. Bethany said so."

"You'll have to walk a lot of miles when you come back here to visit or if you need supplies. You won't have any work animals.

You can't expect some man to just hand over his team of horses."

"I'm used to walking, mister fancy lawyer."

"You'll have to live there. Make improvements." Jed's mind raced. Perhaps she would not be a target like a man would just naturally be. Perhaps.

He looked at her hard. There was something about this old woman. Finally, he nodded. "We'll head for Oberlin tomorrow morning."

Queen Bess walked back to their dugout with Bethany following close behind.

"Momma, I don't understand. You know you're welcome to stay here in town with me, where you'll be safe. Have I said something? Done something to drive you away? Momma, please. You won't be safe there."

"You the one that's courting death. I want shut of this town before folks get stuck in things they don't understand and shouldn't be meddling with."

She stopped. Spoke carefully. "You the worst of all. You is getting way too mixed up."

"Momma, I'm not. I'm just doing what has to be done. To get along and to get ahead."

"Just remember. Remember what I is telling you, Bethany."

■ ■ ■ ■

Jed never used Gloriana as a harness horse. He had borrowed Henry Partridge's worn-out piece of horseflesh and his sorry old buckboard. He and Queen Bess plodded across the prairie. A muscle jumped in his jaw. He would rather have made his first trip to Oberlin on his own high stepping mare.

He had made several attempts to start a conversation with the woman who sat beside him with queenly posture like there was an iron rod holding her spine upright. Queen Bess answered every question with a curt yes or no, then fell silent again.

Well, there were a few things this woman had to discuss whether she wanted to or not. "When we walk into the land office," Jed said, setting his jaw, "when we walk in, they are going to show you a map of all the land that's available. You need to give some thought to where you want to settle. Usually folks choose a spot as close as to the creek as possible if there's no danger of flooding."

"Don't want to live close to water. Too many folks come to water. Won't do to have them see me right off."

Jed sighed. She was right, but she would bear an extra burden.

He took out a long list from his shirt pocket and read through it. They would have to hustle. Although there were no laws keeping them out of stores like there were in the South, he knew it would not be smart to hang around after sundown.

Besides filing for a claim, he would bring back supplies ranging from woodworking fittings for Teddy, and some shoeing nails for Jim, to a hodge-podge of sewing items and groceries for the women. "Henry Partridge wants oats," he said. "The sacks have nice prints. I want you to help pick them out."

"Just want to file my claim. Don't need to do no traipsing 'round."

"Miz Herbert," he snapped, "you are part of a community. You're not back on a plantation. You must help these people whether you want to or not. I'll be right there beside you, but you will, by God, pick out the prints on the seed sacks."

"Don't you tell me what I have to do. I do as I damn well please. Ain't no high-toned, freeborn Negro man that had it good all his life coming in telling me what I have to do."

His hands trembled, and he didn't try to control the fury in his voice. There was no one to hear him out here. No one except the two of them under the clear, blue sky. Not like being in Nicodemus, where people mulled over every blasted word he uttered, like he was Moses come down from Mount Sinai. He was going to set this old woman straight.

"Madam, there's a few things about me I would like you to know. Yes, I had it good for part of my life. And I've gathered you did, too. Then everything went to hell on me. Plumb to hell. Just like it did for everyone else in Nicodemus."

"Freeborn miseries ain't the same. Not the same as what happened to us." She crossed her arms over her chest and stared scornfully into the distance.

Abruptly he stopped the wagon, and she wavered an instant as though fearful he might be planning to throw her out.

"Madam, there's something I want to get straight. Right now." He looked hard into her cold, black eyes. "I'm sick and tired of ex-slaves feeling they are superior to other blacks and even other human beings in the eyes of God because they have suffered the most."

She blinked.

"Many people have been wronged, many times, in many countries, in countless ways.

Sometimes I think human beings were created by Satan to torment one another, and God had nothing to do with us."

She turned away, jaw rigid. He flicked the reins, and they rode on.

Suddenly, as though he could not contain the words any longer, he blurted out between clenched teeth, "It might interest you to know my father hung himself. He just, by God, couldn't take it any longer after the war. We had a nice house, and yes, I suppose, high-toned ways. We even had servants."

"Slaves, you mean." Queen Bess's voice dripped with scorn.

"Not slaves, servants. Servants. They were paid a decent wage. And after my father died, my sister, my little sister, fell into bad ways."

"You got schooling," she said, her voice terse with accusation.

"Yes, and I'm proud of it. It's carried me a long way. I was even offered a position in the state department. The state department. Because I speak French."

"Why didn't you take it?"

He tried to calm down. He could feel that he had piqued her interest. "Because, someone has to be writing down what happened to our people. I've been all over the

South, collecting affidavits and keeping a diary. In the beginning, a group of us black men were trying to figure out where we could live in peace. We can't in the South. But we will, by God, in Nicodemus."

Chagrined by his loss of composure, Jed drove on in silence. Then he spoke again. "And it also might interest you to know I became a lawyer because I thought I could do some good for my people."

She shuddered like a horse shaking off flies and looked at her hands.

A couple of miles further on.

"And just for the record, slaves did have it worse. Far worse," he said sheepishly. "And as far as my being a lawyer doing someone any good — any whatsoever — it hasn't happened so far, I have to admit. It's going to, though. I can feel it. Going to happen right there in Nicodemus."

Jed intended to witness Queen Bess's mark at the land office. He watched, trying to feign casualness as she reached for the pen. Then, to his surprise, she carefully dipped the nib into the inkwell and signed *Regina Marie Herbert.*

"Don't tell nobody," she said as they walked out the door.

"What are you worried about? Do you

think I'm going to tell someone who'll hex you if they know your real name?"

"Been years since someone learned my name."

"Where'd you learn to write?"

"That girl of mine. She bringed home lessons every night. I sneaked peeks."

"Then why are you so set against your daughter's school?"

"Not set against reading and writing. I'se against all the high-toned ideas."

He wiped his hand across his mouth to hide his smile. This mysterious Regina Marie had more secrets than a voodoo princess, and he probably had learned more about her today than her own daughter would unearth in her whole lifetime.

The clerk at the land office said a Tobias Gentry would likely be willing to survey their land, and he generally hung around the livery stable.

"Let's take care of everything else first," said Jed. He read through the list. "The mercantile store will have most of what we need."

When they entered, the clerk, Seth Leister, made a self-conscious point of ignoring their color. "Can I help you find anything?"

"I have a list," said Jed. "We'd appreciate it if you'd help us collect these items."

Queen Bess moved over to the feed sacks and chose three matching blue calico prints.

The door opened.

"Hello, Mr. Bartholomew."

"Morning, Seth."

Queen Bess turned. A tall old man with a luxurious white mustache, wearing gold-rimmed spectacles on his lordly roman nose, stood stock-still and peered at her and Jed with alert, kindly interest. His eyes glistened with curiosity. He reminded her of the old gentlemen doctors she had assisted on the plantation. She stiffened, feeling as if she and Jed were being examined under a microscope.

Then the old man did something so unexpected, Jed and Queen Bess could not think how to respond. He blushed and removed his hat, revealing a bald pate fringed in white hair.

"I do beg your pardon," he said. "Forgive me if I was rude. You are the first people of color I've seen on the prairie. I can assure you, I usually have better manners."

"Quite all right," Jed said.

Elam Bartholomew nodded, then briskly turned his attention to the shelf where the owner kept a scant supply of patent medicines. "I'm out of luck, I guess, Seth."

"You're not the only one out of luck. Not

all of us are just thrilled to be living in a town that's bone dry."

"Well, I'll come back to check your next shipment. I need that alcohol to preserve my tinctures. There's just no way to keep some ingredients from spoiling otherwise."

He looked at Jed and Queen Bess solemnly, tipped his hat again, and left.

Queen Bess went over to the clerk. "That man, that Bartholomew, he a doctoring man?"

"They say he's a botanist. He doctored soldiers during the war. He actually lives in Stockton."

"A botanist? Out here?" Jed asked.

"Yup. Out here. You find all kinds of strange people out here."

Jed smiled, his eyes widened, and he put the last of their order on the counter.

"What he mean, no alcohol?" Queen Bess asked as Jed placed the sacks of flour in the wagon.

"Just what he said. Sure none in Nicodemus, and none in this town, either. In fact, none allowed in most towns in this state. You can order straight alcohol through patent medicine people, but it costs an arm and a leg."

"Can't be," she muttered. "Never heard of a place that ain't got no alcohol atall."

"Never figured you for a drinking woman."

"Shut your mouth, fool. Not for drinking. For doctoring."

"That's a dead sure way of killing pain, all right."

"Not pain. Got stuff for that. But after I brings my medicines to life, I need alcohol to keep them from spoiling just like that old gentleman said."

He looked at her, dumbfounded.

"Got to have alcohol, boy," she mumbled. "Got to have it."

"Don't call me boy . . ." The words died as her head whipped around.

"I said shut your smart mouth. I gots to think. Sugar cane? They any sugar cane out here?"

"Might as well ask for mangoes," he said as he lifted a box of harness fittings onto the wagon. "No cane, Mama." The "Mama" had slipped out, and she shot him a haughty look.

"They gotta be apples then."

"No apples. Not unless they're brought in special for Christmas. Believe me, last week I rode all over this county, and there aren't any apple trees. The only fruit I've seen growing wild is blackberries."

"Going have another look around."

She walked back into the store and looked at the sacks of grain leaning against the wall. Jed followed as though it was the most natural thing in the world to be following the old black woman around. No, he decided, not old. Not young, either. He had no idea what she was up to.

She turned to the clerk. "That sorghum. It raised here, mister? Some man local bring this in? Or a freighter come toting it in? Which?"

"A local man. Lee Morrow. He fools with all kinds of crops. Keeps hoping to stumble across something he can ship back East that won't take a ton of water to grow."

"Where he live?"

"About a mile north of Nicodemus. Just him. No wife or youngsters."

She nodded, then pointed to the sacks of sorghum. "One. Just need one."

Then she saw a bolt of cloth. "Taffeta," she whispered. "Real taffeta. Out here." She walked over to the material and rubbed her fingers over the purple taffeta. "I want one half yard," she said.

Jed stared, then jerked to attention, like he was her personal servant. He nodded curtly to the clerk. "One half yard," he repeated. Curious, he studied Queen Bess's inscrutable face. There had to be a reason.

Jed paid Seth Leister, then hoisted the sack of sorghum seed over his shoulder and carried it out to the wagon. He didn't know a thing about raising sorghum, and he doubted if Queen Bess did, either.

They drove on over to the livery stable. There were a few men clustered inside, watching a slight man with a wispy, blond beard poke an awl through an old piece of harness.

Queen Bess waited outside.

"Is there a Tobias Gentry around?" Jed asked.

The man laid the harness on a bale of hay and stepped forward. "I'm him."

Gentry was a small, bandy-legged man. He still wore his Union cap and never passed up a chance to re-fight the war. He agreed at once to survey the land for Queen Bess's homestead. "I'll be there the first of next week."

They started back to Nicodemus. Pleased with the way the day had gone, Jed whistled and admired the hardy grasses carpeting the prairie.

"We is going by that Morrow man's place," Queen Bess said.

"What for?" Jed's good mood soured. "Lord knows you are going to have all the work you can stand breaking ground to plant that one sack."

"We going. Or you can let me off on the way, and I'll walk."

"Oh, you bet. That would be fun to explain, when I drive in without you." Nevertheless, when he got to the place he judged was about right to turn off, he could see a faint trail through the grass. He followed it to a dugout.

Queen Bess jumped down while he stayed in the wagon. He could not hear what they said, but the man led her to a pile of sorghum stalks. They were still green. She came back to the wagon and grabbed the old quilt she had used to cover herself.

She spread the cloth on the ground and put all the stalks in the middle. She gathered up the four corners, dragged the bundle back to the wagon, and heaved it onto the bed.

She carefully picked out three eggs and carried them over to the farmer. "They fertile," she said. "Here."

"Much obliged, but t'ain't necessary. Didn't have any use for them old stalks. Just the heads are good for livestock."

"Take them," she insisted. "It only right." She climbed up onto the seat. "I'se ready."

CHAPTER EIGHTEEN

On the evening before work was to begin on Queen Bess's soddy, Jim Black drove her out to the newly surveyed homestead. They selected a good level place to build; close enough to the creek that the sod blocks would be moist, but over an incline where the house would not catch the eye of strangers passing through the county.

Jim staked out the lines where they would begin placing the sod blocks. "This enough?"

"This a God's plenty," she said, studying the twenty- by twenty-five-foot rectangle. "Just so I'm square with the world."

"I'll make sure it trues up with the North star."

They hacked away grass and weeds from inside the area, then smoothed it down with spades. Jim had fashioned a sod cutter in his shop after studying the one loaned to the colonists by a white homesteader Teddy had befriended. But building a sod house was tricky. Folks from Nicodemus would come tomorrow to help.

They camped next to the wagonload of tools. Queen Bess breathed quietly, looking up at the clear, cloudless sky. She would soon sleep out here by herself, night after night. A coyote howled in the distance, and she shivered, not understanding where such an animal could be hiding itself on the barren plains. She trusted Jim Black like a favorite son she never had and was comforted by his presence. But soon she would be completely alone.

When the men arrived the next day, they set to work at once. The settlers had learned the process the hard way. Sod blocks had to be just right when they were laid. Too dry, they fell apart, so they had to be cut fresh every day. Too soggy, they were like working with slippery mud. Too cold, frozen blocks crumbled and settled when they thawed.

But by now they knew exactly how to gauge where the sod would be strong and deep. They knew to keep all the sod strips even so the walls would be regular. They laid blocks side by side, two deep, around the foundation, everywhere except the door, smoothing the layers with spades as they worked.

Then they built up the sides with the joints broken, like they were laying bricks. Jim made them reinforce the corners with boards when it was about three feet high, for he wanted it to be perfect for Queen Bess. For a roof, they tortured the bent branches of a cottonwood into the Kansas Car.

The womenfolk started coming mid-afternoon of the third day. They had searched their homes for gifts. Queen Bess had come to Western Kansas with the clothes on her back and a sparse collection of medicines. She needed everything, although the community had very little to spare.

LuAnne Brown had made a beautiful quilt, using a Bear's Paw motif from the few decent sized scraps she could find. Libby Hays had given her two yards of red calico in addition to wages when she helped take care of the new baby, and LuAnne used it for the borders and binding.

Patricia Towaday was as close to a friend as Queen Bess had ever allowed herself to have. She'd taken to the small, feisty woman ever since Patricia had put Norvin Meissner in his place. She still remembered all too well the plantation tragedies when black folks thought they had a friend for life in their own people, and they turned out to be spies for white folks. Nevertheless, there was something comforting about Patricia, who saw plenty and didn't mind calling a spade a spade.

Patricia beamed when she shoved her offering into Queen Bess's hands. "It's for your curing things. I noticed you hangs a whole bunch of stuff separate."

She had made little bags with leather drawstrings from deerskin. "We could find different plants to make ink. Draw pictures of what's inside, unless you wants your daughter to do some writing. I heered you say sometimes you've got to doctor fast, and I figured if you could see what was in them right off without having to open or smell them, it would help."

"It sure 'nough will." Queen Bess gently rubbed one of the little bags against her cheek. It was soft as pussy willows. "Where you come by such fine leather? How you learn to finish it so soft and wonderful?"

"Indian woman who passed through here last winter give me one. Then I traded her one of my pans for a whole big piece of this leather, and she told me how to get it to looking like this. She offered to teach me how to bead it like their folks do, but I ain't got time for that kind of prettiness. I just needed to know how to keep the skins soft so we could wrap stuff up right."

"Remember me telling you about the old woman who stayed with me, Momma?" said Bethany. "She knew things about plants that we need to know."

Queen Bess stared into the deepening night. She remembered Bethany telling her about the woman. With a jolt, she recalled something else.

"Bartholomew." That was the word Bethany had used. The Indian woman had said "Bartholomew" when she left. Bess knew what that word meant now. There was a person on the prairie who could tell them right off what plants was what.

As soon as she decided for herself what kind of person he was, she would tell Bethany about him. He had seemed like a right nice old gentleman. Right nice old doctoring gentlemen didn't fit into the special place in hell she usually sent white people.

Bethany turned one of the bags over and over. "There's plants out here I've never seen before and plants missing I've always counted on. It's what's missing that's killing us. But that Indian woman knew."

"That may be," Queen Bess said, "but those Indians sure don't depend on none of the stuff we got used to back in Kentuck'.

Back there, white folks used to give us everything we needed."

"What they thought we needed," Patricia said. "Not enough. You know that. Not nearly enough."

"Maybe so, but when we was slaves we had enough food to stay alive, and we got used to it. We're going to have to learn different ways out here."

"Or start depending on white folks again," Patricia said.

"Yes." The two women's gazes locked in understanding.

Bewildered, Bethany looked from one woman to the other, knowing she didn't understand what was being exchanged in their glances, and knowing she didn't like it either. She shuddered, wanting to break up this mysterious intimacy. "There's other gifts for you, Momma. Waiting outside, where everyone can see."

She led her mother out to a shiny new washboard and a tub and a bucket. Delighted, Queen Bess stroked the sides like they were made of silver. She felt the hide on a new buffalo robe. She admired the barrels and planks that would serve as her first table. There was a precious hoe and some seeds.

Dolly Redgrave presented her with a

needle stuck in a piece of cloth.

"I'll just put it inside on where you won't lose it," Dolly said, as though Queen Bess needed help tracking her possessions.

Once inside, they heard Dolly cry out like she had stepped on a snake. She stuck her head out the doorway. "Y'all got taffeta, old woman? Purple taffeta? How you come to have real taffeta? Like you was some queen?"

"My mother has always been full of surprises," Bethany said evenly, although her face flushed with fury. "But I'm sure she wants to go right on receiving her gifts right now. Don't you, Momma? Come on back outside, Dolly. We don't want you to feel left out."

Dolly gave a knowing snort but rejoined the group.

"I've got something for you too, Momma," Bethany said, with false gaiety as she tried to regain her composure. "Close your eyes. Close your eyes, Momma."

But her mother wouldn't do it.

Bethany sighed. "Momma, I just didn't have anything to wrap these new cook pans in, that's all. There's three. I wanted you to see them all at once."

Everyone had found something, given something. The only person missing was Jed

Talbot. He had ridden off the day before without telling anyone where he was headed.

After they had all come forward with their offerings, Sidney Taylor brought forth his precious drum. A steady rhythm resounded across the prairie, and they told stories. Stories passed down to their people, some going back to Africa and some reaching no further back than Kentucky.

From the back of the circle, a woman rose. Gertie Avery was huge and homely, her neck nearly hidden in the great folds of flesh. She started to sing, and the group parted and beckoned her forward. Her stunning contralto began as a low vibration, then soared to such a dazzling clarity, it was as though she could stop the grass from swaying with the power of her voice.

"Ain't gonna study war no more," her voice echoed. When she launched into "Beulah Land," the others joined in. They sang of freedom and sorrow and tragedies and lost families and grief.

Bethany closed her eyes for an instant, heartbroken at the sheer pathos. She always raised her own voice in praise and was grateful for the comfort it gave her patients, but it was not her talent. She needed to stay clear-headed and objective. If she ever gave way to the emotion her people put into music, she might break with the pain she saw around her.

She knew if her people ever lost their music, they would lose their souls, but if she could sing like Gertie, her mind would float up to the clouds. She was made to think, like Gertie was made to sing. Born to roll words around her mind. That meant not clouding another person's emotions with her own.

The evening was mild; there was little wind. She looked across the prairie when she heard a horse neigh. Jed Talbot spurred Gloriana toward the group.

He reined up and leaped to the ground.

"Sorry I didn't make it back sooner," he said, rushing over to Queen Bess. There was a package strapped to his back. "Didn't figure Gloriana would appreciate this bouncing around." He shrugged out of the cord and handed her a bundle wrapped in hides. "A little something to cheer your new home, Mama."

She shot him a look at the "Mama," then turned it over and studied it like she was unwrapping snakes. Queen Bess removed the hides to reveal a sixteen- by eighteen-inch window pane of real glass. It would be the very first one in the whole community. She slowly lifted it and held it up to the light of the campfire.

For an instant, her face held fear again. The fear of a person who has never allowed herself to become attached to things that could be taken or smashed. Ruined out of spite or to teach her a lesson or to keep her from getting uppity or just because, that's why.

There was a telltale bob in her throat, and she winked back tears, and Bethany did, too, because she had never seen them in her mother's eyes before.

Queen Bess ran her hands over the shiny surface. She turned with wonder from one face to another.

"Glory be," LuAnne Brown said. "Ain't that fine, now."

Shyly Queen Bess looked at one face after another, and then she looked at Jed. Her lips trembled into a smile.

"Thank you," she said finally.

Bethany looked at her with wonder. Even rarer than her mother's tears was her mother's smile.

The morning after she moved in, Queen Bess set to work. It did not take long to put her meager possessions in order. Jim Black had broken up ground for a small garden and a patch for planting the sorghum. The men had donated a rain barrel and filled it from the creek.

She dragged two stumps intended for chairs over to the side of the doorway and placed two boards across them. The height was wrong for a work table, but she was used to backaches.

She separated the boards so there was a good crack in the middle, then placed one of her new cook pans on the ground underneath. She went to the bundle of sorghum stalks she had brought back when she filed for her homestead. She dragged it over to the table and placed some of the stalks on the boards. She began to mash them with a small, smooth log. It was not as handy as a rolling pin, but it would have to do. As she worked the stalks, juice dripped into the pan.

It took her two full days to collect enough.

As always, she had guarded her starter of yeast well, not letting it get too cold or too hot. It just took a bit of sugar to start it fermenting, but she threw in a good measure, because she would need a lot of yeast working before she was done.

When she had worked the last stalk of sorghum, she carried the juice to her cooking trench and set it to boiling. When the syrup was just right she skimmed little pieces of stalk off the top.

That night, although she could barely drag herself around, she made a large batch of biscuits. After they baked, she took them out of the cast iron pan atop the trench and finally stopped for the day. She sat in front of her soddy watching the sunset and ate them dripping with her newly made molasses.

The next day she dipped out a quart of her molasses, and a whopping pint of yeast and three gallons of rain water, into one of her two precious kegs. She stretched a piece of gauze over the top to keep out flies and let in air. She studied the sun and decided the weather was perfect to keep the mixture outside. If it was too hot, she would take the keg inside. In winter, she would keep it by the stove. Warmth and air were the crucial factors.

In three weeks, she had good strong vinegar. It took constant tending because medicinal vinegar either worked or died.

One morning she warmed a generous supply of rain water and washed her hair. She dipped a cloth into a basin and washed herself all over, even her calloused feet, which she shoved back into ugly, misshapen boots. She changed into a spotless gray-brown dress, which she had made after coming to Nicodemus. She wrapped a snow-white turban around her head.

She took a tin cup and dipped a generous amount of vinegar from one of her pans. As she did not have a jar, she would have to carry the liquid carefully.

She walked.

She reached Stockton early in the afternoon and meekly asked for the whereabouts of a Mister Elam Bartholomew. She was directed to a small house, half sod and half limestone, on the edge of town. Three rocking chairs were lined up neatly in front.

He saw her coming and went to the door.

"Mr. Bartholomew. I'm known as Queen Bess."

"Ma'am, we met in the mercantile store at Oberlin."

"Yes, sir, we did," she said, straightening with his use of *ma'am.* "I heard you say you set back because you ain't got alcohol for your medicines."

"Yes. I need alcohol to preserve my tinctures."

"There's other ways, Mr. Bartholomew. Other ways. I'se come bringing you another way. This here my own special vinegar. It'll pickle a corpse. Keep stuff a long, long time. Keep herbs of all kind. Release their powers, then keep them from spoiling."

"I say, this is very generous of you. Quite generous, indeed." Confused by her lofty bearing, he stammered, which he had not done since he was a small boy. "Do let me pay you. I mean, of course I must pay you." He wondered if the mixture worked, if this extraordinary black woman with the dark, smoldering eyes knew what she was doing.

"You don't owe me nothing," she said quickly. She nodded, then turned to leave. He called her back, as she knew he would.

"Ma'am. Please. Tell me how you did this. How you would know to do this. Please at least stop to visit a moment," he said helplessly, not having the faintest idea as to what might be the proper behavior for a gentleman in such a situation.

He removed his spectacles and rubbed the bridge of his nose. If she were a white woman, he would invite her to rest awhile. Outside the house, of course. Never inside. One would never compromise the reputation of a visiting white woman. It was, after all, a warm afternoon. Just right for sitting outside and chatting a bit.

"Please allow me to fix you a cup of tea before you start on your way."

"That would be most kindly."

She sat down in one of the rockers and arranged her hands on her skirts. He stared at her for an instant, went inside, and tried to regain his composure. By the time he finished making tea, he had decided to be amused at the bizarre situation. He merrily carried out one of his precious china cups and turned his rocker to face her.

"I am quite curious, of course, how you would come to know how to preserve medicines. How you would come to be here to begin with."

She told him about her work as a healer and a midwife in the South. She told him about the doctors she had assisted on plantations. She told him about her confusion over plants and their properties on the plains. She told him about her despair that so many medicines were not available. They talked until early evening. It would soon be time for her to leave.

"Please come inside." He hesitated. "Beg your pardon." Appearances again.

"Sir, ain't nobody going to pay no never mind to some old slave woman. Truth is, old black women already so sullied in folks' mind, it don't matter none. But I gots to be gone by dark, that's all. Just not seemly for me to be here after dark."

"Truth is," he blurted suddenly, "truth is, old botanists are already viewed as being so crazy in some folks' minds that I stopped caring what folks think a long time ago myself. So we make a pair, then, Queen Bess. You and I. A deranged white man who collects and labels plants for no good reason and a woman of color who fancies herself a doctor."

He led her to a room inside where he had tiny little bottles arranged on a shelf. On a larger table were little sprinklings of herbs placed on squares of paper. There were other groupings of grasses and plants with whole leaves and stems. Some he had already sketched and labeled.

"Oh my," Queen Bess said. "Lord have mercy."

They looked at each other and began laughing.

"Now please, sir, tell me what all these is for."

When she started back for her homestead, with the moon lighting her way, she reverently held her empty pan, which was stacked with small folded papers containing crushed herbs. On each was a sketch of what the whole plant would look like blooming, and her own marks reminding her of its healing properties.

Inside also were three precious glass bottles with glass stoppers. She now had sealable containers with which to extract alkaloids.

In turn, Elam Bartholomew now had an ample supply of her medicinal vinegar.

CHAPTER NINETEEN

Word got around about Queen Bess's housewarming. Josiah Sinclair strode into the hotel at Wade City. Aaron Potroff sat by the window reading the *Topeka Daily Capital* as though he didn't have a care in the world. Well, Sinclair had news for the dumb son-of-a-bitch.

"You hear about the little party that took place for that uppity old colored woman?"

Potroff shook his head and removed his cigar.

"I knew those people spelled trouble from the moment they first came here, Aaron. I tried to tell you. Well, they didn't stay put. I knew they wouldn't. That godawful old woman sent straight from hell took out homestead papers."

Potroff slammed his fist on the table. "That's impossible. The ungrateful coons are supposed to stay in the town, goddamn it. Not file for homesteads."

"See, I said you don't know nothing about them. I tried to tell you. You know what I heard last night? Drums. Heard them clear like they were right there in my store. My people never allowed darkies to have drums. They can talk with drums. Talk in ways white folks can't understand."

Potroff rose, shoved his hands in his pockets, and clamped down on his cigar as he paced back and forth. "Just calm yourself, Josiah. Give me a little time to think."

"You've got to stop those drums, and you've got to stop their organizing. No one in their right mind lets black folks organize. I hear there's another load of them coming in. Bold as you please. They're all over Topeka. We've got to stop them from coming out here. You hear? Before others get the same bright ideas and your precious little town is scattered to hell and gone, and we're surrounded by a bunch of niggers owning the best land."

"I no longer give a damn about their little town," Potroff growled. "Nicodemus was a good idea at one time, but they turned on me. Ungrateful black bastards. Would have skinned poor Wade alive if they had caught him. He outsmarted them."

"From what I hear, he out-ran them. Smarts didn't have nothing to do with it."

"The important thing is to keep them under control." Potroff tried to relight his cigar. "We've got to keep them on our side until Wade City is voted in as county seat. That's the main thing. Then we can run them all off, back to where they came from. The black vote can wreck us."

Four weeks later, Tobias Gentry was on his way back to Nicodemus to survey another homestead. He stopped for an instant to let his horse graze in the tall bluestem grass that was encroaching on the buffalo grass. It was a moonless night with no wind. Stars like diamonds flung across velvet sparkled in the jet-black sky.

His horse, Daybreak, a sleek little paint, was not as fast as he used to be. He was in no hurry anyway. Just wanted to get to Nicodemus by morning. Since the war, Gentry no longer cared about owning fast horses. It was past time to put this one out to pasture. Daybreak had earned his rest.

Gentry pulled Daybreak's head out of the lush grass and studied the stars. Despite his sure sense of direction, the lack of any landmarks on the prairie still unnerved him. No trees, no rocks, nothing to show if a man was on the right track. God knew it was impossible to get lost with this many stars.

His spirits had been high after surveying the land for the feisty old Negro woman. At first he had been glad to rub salt in the wounds of the ex-Southerners in the county. Glad to see the incredulous looks on their faces when the paper came out with the filing notice. When folks' surprise escalated to molten anger, he decided not to go around crowing about being the surveyor.

The Topeka Capital was keeping folks riled up over the Voorhees Committee investigation conducted by the United States Senate. They were considering the causes of the removal of the Negro from the South to the North.

Damn fools. Any Negro could tell them. He could tell them. If the truth be known, there wasn't a Southerner anywhere who didn't know in their hearts why their "Niggras" were leaving. They didn't want to be starved and beat no more. Shouldn't take too many brains to figure that out. But no, the government was going to waste the taxpayers' money on a whole investigation like it was a damn mystery.

One thing sure — and it tickled him plumb to death — the exodus was ruining the South. Not that the war hadn't already, but they were all scared to death there wouldn't be anyone left to do the work.

Tobias tugged at his hat and started off again. Folks in this county were madder than they had a right to be over that little handful of people in Nicodemus. He hadn't fought a whole war to be scared off a little surveying job on their behalf.

At first he attributed the prickling he felt on the back of his neck to the goddamned emptiness that always gave him the creeps. It was an unnatural expanse of land. Even in full sun, he found himself imagining shadows that weren't there. Hidden things when there was no place to hide.

Daybreak whinnied and started. Gentry looked around. He could not see any reason why the old paint should be skittish, unless the horse simply sensed his growing uneasiness.

Then he twisted in the saddle and saw a dark shadow, a rider, swiftly coming across the prairie. The horseman had simply materialized out of surrounding blackness. Gentry's blood surged. His heart pounded.

Normally, he would have assumed the man was friendly. Called out to him. Invited him to ride on together. Chat a bit. But his heart was gripped by terror at the suddenness, the strangeness, the silence of the swiftly approaching stranger.

He froze, undecided.

A fierce rebel yell split the night air.

He whirled around and kicked Daybreak into a lunge. The horse streaked across the prairie as fast as he could run. The old paint's breath weaved in labored gasps like leaky bellows. He slowed, lurched, then regained his footing.

Faint with dread, Gentry clung to the horse. He didn't dare look back. His blood pulsed loudly in rhythm with his horse's exhausted heart. His own heart and Daybreak's heart drummed as one with the hoofbeats of the rapidly approaching rider.

When the single deadly shot echoed across the prairie, Gentry slid to the ground. He saw the black kerchief around the face of the silent stranger who walked toward him, holding his rifle in front. He struggled to speak through the blood already gurgling up in his throat before the man coldly aimed for the second time.

"Don't shoot my horse," Gentry tried to say. *Don't shoot my horse.* But the bullet was for him, and the words were only thoughts.

The assassin kicked him once and watched until he saw the death stare in Gentry's glazed eyes. Then he reached into his pocket and pulled out a note he had brought with him. The words were printed with a common piece of charcoal: *Niggers, go home.*

He raised Gentry's body and laid the paper underneath him so it wouldn't blow away.

Then he pointed Daybreak in the direction of Nicodemus and slapped the horse's rump.

Jim Black was the first to see the riderless horse the next morning. Teddy was already at Jim's place, helping mount a wagon wheel, when they spotted him.

"That looks like Gentry's Daybreak. Something's wrong."

Teddy walked toward the horse, hand extended, careful not to startle him. He spoke softly, then reached for the bridle and led Daybreak to the blacksmith shop.

"We'd better start looking," Teddy said. "Something is terrible wrong here. We'd better look fast."

A group of men fanned out and began walking. Jim rode Daybreak so he could see across the tall grass. Even so, it was a man on foot who first saw the body. Teddy reached for the paper poking out from under Gentry. He read the words silently. A tear slipped down his wrinkled old cheeks.

All the men gathered to hear. A few women had joined the search, and they waited for Teddy to speak the words aloud, their worn skirts billowing like tattered sails, their dark faces drawn, aged with despair.

"It say 'Niggers go home,' " Teddy said finally, in a low, trembling voice.

No one spoke. Then a keening arose from Patricia Towaday. A chorus of wailing followed, a dirge that floated up to heaven.

"So it started," Jim Black said bitterly. "It done commence. It followed us out here. Where all we want is to be left alone."

"Did you think it wouldn't?" They turned to look at the stony face of Jed Talbot, who had been searching a mile away and rode over when he saw the cluster of people gathering. "Did you think the white man's evil wouldn't reach out to here?"

They all looked at Teddy as though he could supply some answers. He was the one who had told them it would be different here in Kansas. He was the one who had said this was the Promised Land.

"What in the hell we going to do?" Henry Partridge demanded. "Someone has got to take this soul back to Oberlin. We can't just leave him here or bury him like we has something to hide. This is none of our doing. We just wanted a little land surveyed."

"You're right, Henry. No hiding. Not for any reason," Jed said. "We'll need to borrow your wagon. I'll go, and I want Teddy to go with me. I need someone to bear witness."

Henry and Silas Brown stood by the body until Teddy returned. LuAnne Brown had sent a blanket back with Teddy. He spread it on the wagon bed. Then Henry and Silas hoisted Gentry's body, and Teddy pulled the blanket around him.

"Going to be a long miserable trip," Jed said grimly.

The veins throbbed in Jim Black's neck. "Yonder on that wagon lies a good man. He just trying to help us, that's all. Just trying to help us get by."

Sheriff Casper Bogswell got shoved into the job of sheriffing when he first came to Oberlin looking for a no-good cattle rustler who had taken off with his brother's prize bull. He and Lewis had planned to start a nice little herd. Their dreams had vanished with the death of their thirteen cows during the ungodly bad winter.

Lewis had thrown up his hands and quit, saying anyone who stayed in the godawful state was a damned fool, and that's not what his mamma had raised. Bogswell let him go with a shake of his fist and a few good-natured cuss words, as the claim had been in Lewis's name, and he was willing to sign it over. Bogswell decided to stay. He sort of liked the unreasonable odds on the prairie. Made him feel more of a man to say he could stand Kansas.

However, the bull stolen right from under his nose had been the last straw. The bull had been worth some money. Besides, hunting down the bull gave him something to do while he figured out just where he wanted to fit in. When the trail led to Oberlin, and the people needed a peacemaker, it seemed to fit. He suited the folks just fine.

Bogswell was six foot four inches tall, big-boned with a long reach. This scared folks enough that they usually didn't notice the mild, blue eyes of a basically pleasant man. Strangers who did notice his eyes immediately assumed he was a pushover. If they had looked at him longer, they might have noticed the quick shrewd glances of a man who didn't miss much.

He was clean-shaven and scrupulously clean. He had fine, sandy hair, close, even sideburns, and a wickedly attractive cleft chin. The people of Oberlin slept better with him on the job. He had an uncanny ability to sort out real trouble from good-natured high spirits and didn't keep folks riled up all the time like some sheriffs did. He checked out strangers the instant they rode in and was known to help them ride right on out if he thought they weren't the right kind of folks to be hanging around. He nearly always showed up for church and socials.

Jed and Teddy drove down the main street and stopped in front of the sheriff's office.

"What we going to say?" Teddy asked.

"We're just going to say what happened," Jed replied. "This man was most likely murdered for helping us. Even if they won't admit it, it's that simple, and most of the folks here will know why he was killed as well as we do."

"I 'spect most of them will blame it on the cowboys anyway." Teddy glanced over at the sheriff's office. " 'Stead of their own folks what think we shouldn't be taking any land atall."

Bogswell was already standing at the door and saw the ominous outline lying on the wagon bed. Before Teddy or Jed could speak, he stepped out and went to the back of the wagon. He flipped the blanket open and looked at the body. A muscle leaped in his jaw when he saw Tobias Gentry. Tobias had been his friend.

"How did this happen?"

"We don't know," Jed said carefully. "As to the how, he's obviously been shot. We just don't know who." He looked squarely into Bogswell's eyes. "We want you to know, the people of Nicodemus will do anything we can to help you track down that person."

"We just found him," Teddy said. "His horse came dragging in, and we knowed something was wrong." He drew a deep breath. "He did some surveying work for us. We found this, too." He reached inside his old jacket, pulled out the crude note, and shoved it at the sheriff.

Bogswell read it, and his eyes flashed with anger. "I won't have this, by God. Not out here."

Teddy's face softened with relief. "We's sorry," he said simply. "We's sorry we's the cause of all this, because he was a good man."

"You don't have to tell me what a good man he was. He was one of the best," Bogswell said. "We spent many a sociable evening arguing. About a lot of things. You are not the cause of this, so don't blame yourselves."

"I guess we should start back," Teddy said. He turned, awkward now, wondering if he should say more.

"There's something I want you to know," Bogswell shouted as their wagon rattled down the street. "If any of the rest of you want to prove up, I'll personally see to it that nothing stops you. I won't have this, by God, if I have to get everyone who ever fought on the right side in the war to patrol the prairie with me."

CHAPTER TWENTY

Bethany snapped at Zach Brown and then, ashamed, went to her little board to illustrate the answer to the math question he had just asked. But in a flash her mind turned back to the murder again. There was so much land. So much space. So much of God's blue sky. Why would anybody care if black people took up just a little part of it? Why should anyone mind?

This was the third day since the discovery of Gentry's body. She kept waking up at night, hearing sounds, her heart drumming with terror.

There was no use in trying to fight white folks head on. It couldn't be done. It would just get her people killed. There weren't enough blacks for anyone to give a damn about; that was what was so strange. If there were hordes out here, like she was reading about coming into Topeka, lining the streets and the riverbanks, that would be different, but there weren't.

Her little schoolroom suddenly fell unnaturally quiet. One minute there were the usual whispers and shuffling of feet, then dead silence. Nerves on edge, she turned around and saw her mother standing at the back of the room. Bethany had not heard her come in, but, as usual, the children had sensed Queen Bess's disapproval.

"Morning, Momma."

Queen Bess nodded stiffly. She stood there, arms folded. Bethany concluded the lesson, then sorrowfully faced her class. "Children, please tell your parents that school will not be in session for a while."

"But Miss Bethany, what about these here multiplication tables? I just got started."

"I know, Zach. Keep on with the work on your own, please. For a while." Her voice trembled. She could not look Silas and Lu-Anne's son in the eye.

The children silently filed out.

"You've heard?" Bethany asked after the last one left.

"Patricia came over yesterday."

"I'm just sick, Momma, just heartsick. I didn't think this could happen out here. I thought things would be different."

"Things ain't never gonna be different."

Bethany bit her lip, covered her face with

336

her hands, and swayed from side to side. "It's got to be different. It's just got to be."

"Well, it ain't. I tried to tell you. You wouldn't listen. You keep dabbling in things you don't understand. Trying to go where our kind ain't supposed to go. And look where it got you."

"Are you saying it's my fault?" Bethany asked, raising her head. "Are you saying this was in any way my fault? You're the one that filed for a homestead, Momma."

Queen Bess's eyes flashed. "I was just trying to move away from the foolishness I saw going on in this town. Black folks acting like white folks, like they could slip into another world. We is what we is. What God made us to be. Ain't my fault that man died."

"It's not my fault, either, Momma."

They both stood silently, grieving for the good man who had died on their behalf.

"Why did you come here, Momma, if you're not trying to lay this death at my doorstep? Why are you taking it on yourself to trouble me?"

"I came here because you is my daughter, and you has a lot of sway over these people here. You has book learning, and you is a granny to boot. They all listen to you. Tell these people to back down. Live apart."

"And stay frozen? What am I teaching these children for? What is the point?"

"You teaching them all for nothing, child. I am trying to tell you. You should be teaching them to stay alive. That's all. Just stay alive and stay out of white folks' way."

"Stop it, Momma. Just stop it. You're driving me crazy. And scaring me to death. This was surely the doing of one person. One evil, crazy man. I didn't come out here to be scared all the time. I came out here to be free."

"Oh, you foolish, foolish child. You think there wasn't a bunch of people behind this? Bulldozers? Night riders? People who ain't never going to forget the war. You fool enough to think white folks don't still hate us?"

"Momma. This town is what I'm all about. Don't you understand this? If we can't believe this, then there's nothing left. Not now, not ever. I've got to believe that there's good people out there. Good as well as bad. If we can't believe that, there's nothing left for any of us."

Queen Bess quivered with fury. "You ain't hearing me, daughter. You ain't listening. I is trying to tell you, which way people go in this here town is up to you. You and Teddy. Better not make no mistakes, or you going to get us all killed. It started already."

After her mother left, Bethany slowly wiped the writing off the blackboard. Difficult as her mother's words had been, they jolted her like a bolt of lightning. She knew she could turn Nicodemus in the direction it would go, and, once turned, they couldn't go back.

Would they live apart from white folks, or would they keep on trying to work out an arrangement with them? Could they play a role in deciding the affairs of the county, or should they be content with survival? Was it worth the risk, the constant fear? Was it worth dying for?

She walked over to the window and gazed out at the prairie. Before the murder the openness had seemed to offer endless opportunity. Now the expanse seemed threatening. Too much empty space.

Exhausted, she walked back to her dugout. Before the murder she usually roamed across the prairie in the evening. It soothed her frazzled nerves. Now she no longer felt safe wandering alone. She stepped inside and went to the bag holding some precious chamomile leaves and fixed a cup of tea, then sat terrified staring out the doorway as the evening darkened around her.

The whole community was abnormally quiet. Children no longer played outdoors until full nightfall. Finally, she rose and decided to squander a match and light a candle. She could not bear to go to bed and risk having nightmares. Suddenly her hands started to shake. Her face tightened with fury. She went to the corner where she kept snow-white bandages, wide strips torn and sun-bleached from flour sacks. Painstakingly accumulated for her patients.

She reached for a needle and a spool of thread and placed the bandages end by end. Tears streamed down her face. Convulsive sobs racked her body. She keened like a wild woman as she stabbed the ends together with brutal uneven stitches. When the length reached about six foot, she stood and grasped her hair, twisted it on top of her head, and fastened it with an old broken comb.

Then she began wrapping the snow-white cloth around her head into a slave's turban. When she finished, she picked up the candle and carried it to the broken mirror hanging beside her hanks of medicine. She looked at her ugly, tear-stained face.

"This is the way you looks. You is still a slave," she said slowly. "This is the way you talks. Not fancy. You is still a slave. This is who you are. You is still a slave."

She went back to the schoolhouse and sat stiffly at her makeshift desk in the empty classroom. From time to time, her hand strayed to adjust her turban. She had closed the school. It might be closed forever, so heavy was the cloud of fear shrouding the town.

"Niggers go home."

She stared straight ahead with unseeing eyes at the ugly sod walls she once thought were beautiful. The door thudded open, shut, open, shut, with the irregular gusts of wind. Her heart was dead to the wind today. Numb, she didn't notice when the noise ceased.

Jed Talbot walked through the door, then stopped dead still. "What in God's name? What in the hell do you have on your head?"

She looked at him with sullen, heavy eyes. "You a black man. You don't know what this is? You ain't never seed this kind of wrapping before?"

He walked over to her chair and furiously yanked her to her feet, shoved his hand under the turban, and pulled it off while she tried to slap his hands away. "Don't think like that, and don't talk like that."

Her shiny, black hair tumbled about her shoulders. She looked at him with tear-filled eyes. "But it is how we talk. And I'm going to start talking like our people talk and thinking like our people think. It's what I should have been doing all along."

"It's not how you think," Jed snapped. "Not how you talk, now is it?"

"Not yet, no, not yet. But it going to be," she said grimly. "Now let go of me."

He loosened his grip, then helplessly let his hands fall, turned abruptly, and walked over to the shelf in the corner. Striving to control his outrage, he examined the titles of the books there one by one, nodding with familiarity as he came across old friends.

Bethany Herbert was one of the most beautiful women he had ever seen, black or white. The image of her ricocheting into the Browns' dugout the first night he came was seared into his mind. The wild hair streaming behind the kerchief, her lively, lovely face, the shining brown eyes. For the last six weeks, he had become enthralled by her quick wit, her almost childlike inability to contain her enchantment with ideas. Her transformation from a woman crackling with compulsive energy to an ugly, sullen, gray-black toad infuriated him. A vein throbbed in his temple.

He shoved his hands into his back pockets and paced around the room while he marshaled his thoughts. Then he picked up a book and faced her.

"And what are you going to do about this?" he said. The air seemed to vibrate, matching his intensity. He walked over and stood directly in front of her as he waved the book. "The thoughts, these ideas, are already in your head, woman. It's too late. You can't go back. Don't you understand that? *We* can't go back. We can't leave this state. And you, my dear lady, can't go backwards in your mind. You can't wipe out book-learning."

Shocked by her sudden gush of tears, he reached for her, but she twisted away. "What are we going to do?" she whispered. "What in God's name are we all going to do?"

"We're going to fight," he said. "Right here, right now, we're going to fight. With every last breath. It's the only thing we can do."

"How? We've already gotten one good man killed. Why did you come here? Surely not just to berate me."

"Bethany, I came here because I want to organize this township. The township and then the county, and I want this school to be the first legal school. Your school."

"It can't be done."

"It can. And it will. Your students are getting top notch instruction. I want your work recognized. Validated. When your students complete their education, I want them to have a certificate of their progress. The kind white children get."

"It can't be done," she said. "They would never, ever let us start the first school district."

"It can be done," he said. "It can, and it will."

She was deathly silent for such a long time, he was afraid he had lost her. Then she spoke with exquisite slowness, as if pushing every word from her throat. A schoolmarm's words, proper and measured.

"This evening then, sir, I shall call a meeting and let our people know school will resume Monday morning."

She reached for the unbound turban, folded it neatly and laid it on her desk. Then she grasped her long, shiny hair and twisted it into a bun. She anchored it at her neck with one of the chicken feather quills she had carved out for use in the children's writing lessons.

Her eyes never left his face. Never strayed from his luminous, gray eyes. Never drifted from his strong, fine jaw and his sculptured cheekbones.

"Now you get the hell out of here. Just get the hell out of my school." Tears streamed down her cheeks.

Stunned, Jed Talbot started to speak, then touched his cap with a slight nod and edged out the door.

CHAPTER TWENTY-ONE

Teddy watched Jed Talbot walk toward the blacksmith shop. The lawyer wore a fawn-colored broadcloth suit with a gold brocade waistcoat. His shirt was sparkling white with a separate snowy collar, accented by a black bow tie. He carried a fawn-colored hat.

For an instant, Teddy was stunned by the fine figure of this man, his friend, looking like a Greek god. Looking like he had the authority of a king to order people to do this, or to do that.

Our lawyer, he thought gloomily. *Don't need a god-damned lawyer to lead us straight to hell. Won't set right with the Rooks County commissioners to go in looking like a riverboat gambler.*

Jim Black finished checking Gloriana's shoes. The mare's coat shone, and every inch of gear was polished to a cavalry shine.

Since the murder, there had been no stopping Jed. He had visited every single black family living in Nicodemus and gathered more than enough signatures to petition for a legal voting township.

Teddy had turned down the use of a fancier horse to make the twenty-mile ride to Stockton where they would present Jed's petition. "I rides old Sherman. Always have. Reckon I always will," he'd said stubbornly. "That old mule kind of got used to me."

Being bullied into this trip against his better judgment was bad enough. Damned if he was going to let Jed Talbot or anyone else tell him what horse he had to ride. He, too, was wearing his suit, but it was so old and worn, just like him, that he couldn't imagine anyone would accuse him of putting on airs.

"Ready?" Jed asked.

"I reckon."

When they came to the end of the street, Dolly Redgrave came flying after them. "I've fixed you a little something to eat," she said. "And I've sewed up a couple of dusters to put over you if it starts to rain."

She wore a yellow dress sprinkled with little white flowers and had tied her hair up with yellow bows of the same material. She looked pretty in the morning sun with her weak-tea skin and her pale, hazel eyes.

"I thank you kindly," Teddy said, knowing

this offering was all for Jed's benefit. The woman had been making eyes at the man since the moment he showed up, but you'd think Jed was some blind old mule and Dolly was ninety years old.

"Oh, you is welcome," she gushed. "Just so completely welcome. It's just some jerky and some chunks of cornbread."

Jed reached for the package of food, which she had tied into a square of cotton. He fastened it to the roll of dusters behind his saddle. Then he touched his hat politely. "Much obliged."

Teddy turned back to look at Dolly's face as they rode off. A mean woman. Bone mean. He wished she was gone. But if they started running people out of town because they had a crazy streak, wouldn't be hardly nobody left. Their lawyer included.

They rode three miles without talking at all. Teddy saw things now he wouldn't have noticed a year ago. He heard sounds that had formerly escaped his sharp ears. In spring and summer there were more shades of green than he thought possible — from the pale under-skin of wild onions, to the emerald cast of the tall bluestem that was making inroads on the patches of scrappy buffalo grass.

Prairie dogs stood like sentinels bravely

warning other families of approaching danger. He'd come to love their shrill panicked bark. Hawks dove like lightning toward tiny rabbits that strayed from their holes. Sometimes he was tempted to look up and see if one of the birds was big enough to carry off a tiny, old black man.

"Well, Teddy, we're crossing the Rubicon," Jed said.

"Don't know what that means."

"It means the die is cast."

"Don't know what that means, either. If you means we is making a big mistake, you got that right."

Jed laughed. "Means there's no turning back."

"Right. Doing things you can't take back or wiggle out of usually is a big mistake."

"Well, it's quite clear we can't go back after we take this step. After dice are thrown you can't undo the toss. Julius Caesar once crossed a river, the Rubicon, into enemy territory. Once crossed, he couldn't turn back."

"Them is fine words. Just right. That what we doing, all right. How'd it turn out for old Caesar?"

"It worked."

Just then old Sherman brayed, and both men laughed.

When they were about a mile from Stockton, Teddy stopped abruptly. "Jed, you sure you is doing the right thing?"

"As sure as I've ever been of anything in my life. Don't quit on me, Teddy. We have to fight."

Jed swung off his horse and reached for the package of food. He broke off a piece of cornbread and handed the bundle to Teddy. Then he held Gloriana's reins while she lowered her head to eat buffalo grass. "What we're doing today is just the first step. Next, I'm going to petition for the first school district and then organize the county."

When Teddy was tired, his stained face splotched and grayed to a mottled, dusty yellow, and today his skin looked like an old rattlesnake hide left to dry in the sun. "Right now, white folks around here is playing like killing that man was the cowboys' doing," he said slowly. "Things has settled down. They is acting like they don't care if we is here or not. They is acting proud of us like we is they own personal house niggers. They saying if those poor starving bastards packing those riverbanks in Wyandotte had a little get up and go like us Nicodemus folks, they could be eating high on the hog. Bethany reads me some of them papers, and they is all the time bragging about our grit

350

and stick-to-itiveness."

"Well, we've all managed to stay alive out here, haven't we?"

"Just barely. And then we had help."

"You mean the aid Harrington and Tripp rounded up?"

"That and Indians. They helped us, too. We can't say we did this all by ourselves."

"A man was murdered, Teddy. That's what I'm trying to say. There's no turning back now."

"In the first place," Teddy said, "we didn't stay here by choice. Hardly a one of us that wouldn't have left last winter. Takes money to come here, money to stay, and money to leave."

"But you are here. If I had my way, we'd have fought them in the South. Tooth and toenail."

"You crazy, Jed."

"Eventually, the North would see to it that our power in the South amounted to something. Not because they love us, but for their own safety. If we had stayed and fought it out."

Teddy's shoulders drooped. "Eventually won't get it. We talking about men that are poor, naked, hungry. Wife, half dozen kids that hungry right now. Can't wait for politicians to make things work eventually."

Jed swung back into the saddle as Teddy awkwardly mounted his old mule. "A good man has been murdered. If we let this kind of tyranny get a foothold here, like it did in the South, we're doomed."

Teddy glanced at the town ahead. He carefully brushed some cornbread crumbs off his old coat and looked squarely at the full noonday sun. A pleasant breeze cooled his head when he removed his hat. Little grasshoppers skittered across the plants, disturbing swarms of ants.

"Jed, you ain't been here long. I don't know you like I know all these people who came here from Kentucky. There's not much I can't tell you about them. I can tell you most of the time what they are all going to say, what they're going to do, and what each of them wants. That's the big thing. Understanding what each of them wants. But I knows you well enough to know you a lot different from the rest of us. There's things about white men you don't know, can't know, and wouldn't believe if I told you."

Jed did not speak. He flicked the reins against Gloriana's neck. Before long, they were in tall grass, up to their mounts' stomachs.

Teddy started mumbling while they rode,

and Jed stopped up short to hear. "Can't see that town of our'n any more, but it's back there somewhere." He waved toward the horizon. "Our houses," Teddy said, his eyes full of misery as he watched Jed's face. "Our buildings. The most our people have ever had in their whole natural born lives."

Jed rode on, ignoring Teddy's monologue.

"Hear our songs, mister lawyer man? All we can think about is the hereafter, because God knows, there's never been a thing we could own or count on down here. May not be much. By most people's thinking, all those little pitiful things are is a handful of dirt buildings, but to them it like the heavenly city paved with gold. Better think about that, mister lawyer. Better think real hard."

"I'm going to help you keep it, not lose it."

"Maybe. Maybe so. No one cares if we have this. Don't make a good goddamn to white folks if a handful of niggers want to set up a few buildings on land nobody wants anyway in a state most people don't like much after they get here. You're fixing to change all that. If we petition for a township, people going to notice us plenty."

"It must change!" Jed said. "Some of what you're saying is true. That white folks leave

353

us alone. That they don't care as long as we don't bother them. But that's not good enough. I'm going to keep working until they look at us and don't see color at all."

Teddy stiffened.

"You know what bothers me most?" Jed asked. His handsome face was solemn above his snow-white collar. "If I can't convince you, I'm afraid I can't convince anyone. But you can turn around and go back. I'm not willing to drag you into anything you really don't want to do."

Teddy looked down at the ground, then back in the direction of Nicodemus, then toward the town of Stockton. He looked squarely at Jed, and his old jaw quivered for an instant.

"You're the one who started this, Teddy. Why did you lure people out here in the first place?"

"I moved them away where things weren't going to work no time never, to a place where things might work sometime, if we mind our own business."

"Then why did you come with me today, if you don't believe in what I'm trying to do?"

Teddy sat rigidly upright on Sherman, his dried tobacco leaf–face still as death. "Because you is too ignorant to let loose roaming around by yourself. I is afraid you going to get hurt."

Jed's lips quirked into a faint smile, and his heart broke at the old man's bravery.

"Besides, you right about one thing. We can't let it start here. Not here."

Jed grinned.

"Now, mister lawyer feller. Let's go cross that there Rubicon."

They rode on into town.

"Well, it's clear where we need to head," Jed said. At the end of the street was a beautiful two-story, magnesium limestone courthouse.

"How much you reckon that set these folks back, Jed?"

"Five thousand dollars. Read that in their paper, when I was trying to figure out when their commissioners meet. That's their jail off to the side. They used to have to take prisoners to Ellis County."

"They gots real law, then."

"Real law and about the same number of people we have, but Stockton has about a ten-year head start. They've got a creamery, two grist mills, whole bunch of businesses, and enough churches to save all of hell."

Jed looked up and down the street and decided it was safe to leave Gloriana tied to the hitching rail out front.

Inside, they followed the sound of men arguing. Jed knocked lightly at the open door. The commissioners stared at the two men like they were apparitions.

"Gentlemen," Jed said in his well-modulated bass voice, "allow me to introduce myself. I am Jedidiah Talbot, and this is my colleague, Mr. Theodore Sommers. We are from Nicodemus, Kansas, and we are here with a petition to organize a township."

The details of the events of that day, told and retold by the three commissioners to whomever would listen, became legend.

"Swear to God, Mabel," Commissioner Atkins said to his wife that evening, "as God is my witness, the lawyer's paperwork was flawless. Perfect; letter perfect."

"And then," Commissioner Klein said to the intrepid editor of the *Stockton News,* "and then they invited us to dine with them at the Rooks County Hotel just like they had all the money on God's earth, and of course we couldn't refuse their kindly offer."

When the astonishing move by the Nicodemus lawyer was duly reported in the paper — particularly all the details of the three commissioners dining in public with the two men who weren't too terribly black — Jed and Teddy had established the right to enter any business, any store. By extension, it was understood that all the people of Nicodemus were to be treated with equal courtesy.

"The man was white enough to trust," Commissioner Kerry swore to the dumbfounded whittlers in the mercantile store. "Not white enough to pass, but plenty white enough, and he could talk as good as you or me. All dressed up, too."

"Jesus, Hiram, you've been hornswoggled plenty good. Everyone knows niggers can't read or write, let alone study for law. Where did they get that many signatures? You must have been drinking. Bet the same person wrote them all."

Hiram Kerry looked soberly at the oldest man in the store, knowing he wouldn't believe in Christ on a crutch if he'd seen it with his own eyes. "Swear to God, Ike, those signatures were genuine. That's the first thing we studied after they left."

"What you going to do, Hiram?"

"We're sending out a government surveyor tomorrow morning, and in two days' time, we're going to declare that Nicodemus is a genuine township."

"God almighty. Bet I know some folks that

are going to have a fit over there in Graham County."

"It's not officially Graham County yet, but you're right about folks having a fit."

CHAPTER TWENTY-TWO

Bethany heard a man shout. She stepped outside. A white man rode up hollering for her before he even dismounted. "Miss Herbert, you're needed fast over at the Beckers. Miz Becker is in a heap of trouble. Baby coming early."

Her stomach plummeted. She had never met this woman. When someone came riding in this fast, in a state of agitation, it was always bad news. Better to prevent trouble than try to fix things when it was too late. Besides, she would simply never get over her fear of delivering white folks' babies.

"I'm their neighbor, Mark Church." His horse was soaked with sweat. "Got a horse you can ride?"

She shook her head. "But I can borrow one from our blacksmith. Go get it while I check my medicine bag. I'll throw a little food into a tote." She rushed inside and gathered her things. For a birthing call, she also included a bag of rags and pads of old quilts to protect beds. They were already prepared. After each visit, she soaked them in cold water, then boiled them clean.

Church trotted back holding the reins of the second horse. Although she still didn't ride well, it was certainly faster than walking, and clearly Church's horse wasn't up to carrying double.

Inside the Beckers' homestead, she swallowed hard when she saw the disarray, the filth. The bed appeared to be heaped with rags, but in fact they covered an exhausted woman. Anita Becker was beyond screams, beyond pain, reduced to whimpering. The odor of sour food permeated the room, and Bethany's stomach recoiled.

There was no stove, just a cooking trench about ten feet outside the door. *Another family taking a homestead. Unaware and unprepared.* Anger welled up in her. She looked at the three tow-headed, undernourished children huddled in a corner, then whirled around and snapped at the woman's husband.

"Get them out of here, all of them, right now. They don't need to see their mother in such a state."

No one questioned Bethany Herbert when

she gave orders. Beyond color, beyond sex, was the authority of the physician, with unseen powers and shrouded in mystery. In the presence of the sick, white or black, she became simply the doctor, first and foremost.

As she shoved the family out the door, she spied an old washtub. She checked the rain barrel, then handed the tub to Amos Becker. "Go fetch some water. I need plenty. We'll send the children to the creek with the buckets. It will give them something to do. First, though, it looks like they need food."

She tried to keep her voice neutral. She didn't know what had happened to this family, but she knew hunger when she saw it. She doled out biscuits, dried apples, and jerky to the children. It wasn't nearly enough, but it would have to do. She solemnly handed Amos his share. "It's all I have," she said. "I would have brought more, but I just didn't know."

"Give it to my children, and I thank you kindly." Amos swallowed convulsively.

"No," she said, "you must eat, too, or you're not going to have the strength to do the things I need you to do."

Mark Church stood helplessly to one side, watching. When she walked over to thank him for coming after her, his eyes were troubled at the stark poverty all around him. An earnest man with thinning black hair, he spoke in a rush.

"Didn't know these folks was so bad off or maybe I could of helped. Not doing so good myself. Trouble is, I just ain't around much, so I didn't know, ma'am, swear to God I would have helped. I found work loading buffalo bones on the railroad over at Buffalo Park. Came back to the homestead to make sure I didn't need to run no squatters off my place. Gotta watch that, you know. Just chance the boy found me home when he came running over. These folks ain't got no horse. Lucky for them I'd heard about you. Want me to stick around? I was just heading back to work when the boy came."

Bethany shook her head. "No. Thank you. Don't scold yourself. This was none of your doing. I'll send the oldest boy back to Nicodemus on the horse I rode here. He can return it to Jim Black. I want him to fetch a woman who helps me from time to time. She can come in the wagon and bring food."

"Guess I'll be on my way, then."

"Just comfort yourself with the thought that if it hadn't been for you, I wouldn't be here at all."

He smiled with relief.

"Thank you, and have a safe trip to Buffalo Park."

Mark Church touched his hat and rode off.

Bethany walked back over to Amos Becker. "First off, I need to build a good fire out here. Then I need you to round up all the pots and tubs you have on the place. Then get going to the creek while I tend to your wife. Have your two youngest ones carry all they can."

She gestured to the oldest boy to come over to Jim Black's sturdy mustang. "What's your name?"

"Edmund."

"Do you know how to ride, son?"

"I have before," he mumbled hesitantly.

"Wouldn't matter if you didn't, I guess, you'd have to go anyway. I can't spare your father. Besides, old Blister here won't give you any trouble." She made him repeat back all the supplies she wanted LuAnne to bring. "Hurry now!" She helped him mount.

After seeing Edmund off, Bethany set water boiling. Then she went back inside. She shrank from the rancid odor coming from the feverish woman. She felt Mrs. Becker's stomach, and her heart sank. The baby had already died inside. She would certainly lose the mother as well. Having something go wrong with a white woman's birth and everyone blaming her for it was her worst fear.

She tried to think. Teddy and Jed were in Stockton. She had heard the town had a doctor, but even if she had a way of getting him, he wouldn't be able to do anything, either.

Except take the blame, she thought bitterly. It would be a fine thing if someone else could take the blame.

There was only one person who stood a ghost of a chance of saving this woman's life — Queen Bess. Only one person she knew of who could cut open a woman's stomach. She hesitated. Could she trust her mother to do her best with a white lady?

She slipped outside.

"Mr. Becker, extra water can wait. We'll get by on what your children bring back." She drew a deep breath and hesitated. But there was no other way. "I want you to fetch my mother. She lives on a homestead fairly close by." She gave him directions. "Tell her to come, right away, and bring everything she has in her medicine bag. Tell her to bring all her plants. Everything. Tell her to bring everything. She'll know what I mean."

"My Anita going to make it?"

She looked into his frightened blue eyes and decided to prepare him for the worst without mincing words. "The baby is dead, sir, and you will almost certainly lose your wife."

"Then why are you sending for your mother when I could hold my wife's hand and help her pass?"

"There's a chance. A small, small chance, but there is one."

Queen Bess looked at Anita Becker's pale face, her bluish lips. She pressed her fingertips against the woman's wrist and clucked at her feeble pulse.

"See what you brought on us all, daughter?" she said softly to Bethany. She turned and looked at Amos Becker, outside the open doorway. The children had just returned from the creek, and Amos was on his knees, one arm around each of them, as they sobbed onto his shoulder. "See what you done? We is going to be blamed for this. That man going to have our hides."

"No one could have done anything for her," said Bethany.

"White folks going to blame us anyway."

"Momma?" Her mother's face was as still as a death mask. "Momma? You know what you have to try. You know you're the only

365

one who can do this. I know you've seen this done. Once on the Twin Rivers plantation and once on the White Forks. And other places, too. You told me so. No one else around here has had a chance to watch European doctors do this."

"White doctors don't know nothing about this. They think they do, but they don't," Queen Bess said scornfully. "Don't know nothing at all. Our people been doing this forever. Your old grandmother Eugenie showed me this. She knew. But it most generally done to save the baby when the mother's a lost cause. Usually don't have to worry about the mother. This backwards. This hard." Queen Bess's face was grave. "Does this white gentleman know his baby is dead?"

"Yes, I told him that right away."

"Just so they don't think we killed it." Queen Bess hovered over the bed. Bethany could see her lips move. She watched her mother's hands flutter with strange movements. She had always known there were things her mother had not taught her. Her mother had promised to teach her, but the war had stopped her.

Then Queen Bess felt Mrs. Becker's hard stomach and laid the palm of her hand on her dry, scalding hot forehead. The woman would die soon. She was long past being able to deliver, although Queen Bess had brought drugs to start that process.

Bethany went out to the cooking trench and lifted off a cast iron pot of hot water. She carried it inside, and Queen Bess poured a little into a pan. She fished a bar of lye soap and a tin of beef tallow out of her drawstring bag. She washed her long slim hands with the soap. She immersed the little tin in the hot water to melt the tallow, then dropped a cloth into the still steaming pan.

She carried the tin over to the bedside and lifted Mrs. Becker's gown. She rubbed the tallow on the woman and on her own hand and gingerly eased it inside Anita's vagina until she felt the baby's buttocks.

The baby was breech. Breech and dead. It couldn't be worse. No wonder the woman had been in labor practically forever. If Bess tried to pull it out and pieces of putrefying flesh stayed inside, this woman was doomed. Worse, she was in a white man's house with a daughter too naïve to see where it would all lead.

She rose and went outside to talk to Mr. Becker. He sat on an old stump, head lowered, staring at the ground. Beyond was a scrawny old milk cow grazing on a straggly patch of buffalo grass. There were no horses, no geese, no ducks. A garden, mostly dead in the hot sun. She sighed heavily. Hope didn't live there no more. Just dead things.

Becker's daughter and his youngest son sat on the ground. They leaned against the stump, their pale faces tragedy-tight.

"Sir, you know the baby's dead, and the chances of saving your wife aren't good?"

Red-eyed, he could only nod at her.

"There's only one chance I know of," she said doggedly. "Only a slim chance, and it probably won't work. I need to know if you want me to go ahead."

"Will she die if you don't?"

"That's the only thing I know for sure. She will most surely die if I don't, and probably will if I do."

"What is it you want to do?"

"I need to cut her open and get that baby out of there. Right now. It ain't been dead long. But she fading fast. We ain't got much time."

"Don't want my woman to go to her grave sliced up."

Queen Bess nodded. "I understand. Can't say how it would go anyway."

She started back into the house, then turned at his sudden, bitter howl. "Go ahead, damn it, if that's the only chance we've got."

She looked at him carefully, worried at the abruptness with which he had changed his mind. If he came charging in during the operation, it would be disastrous. She wanted him gone and his children with him.

"Mr. Becker, I need you to go back to my place. They is chickens roaming. Bring me three. Three's plenty."

By the time he returned, it would all be over. Then she would send the family and Bethany on back to Nicodemus.

"Be a while before I start. You have plenty of time. Take the children to help you catch them chickens." Her gaze faltered for an instant at the bald lie, as she intended to operate immediately.

She watched them leave, went inside, and drew a sharp razor from her medical bag.

"Have you ever done this all by yourself before, Momma?" asked Bethany.

"Twice," said Queen Bess. "Twice."

"Did it work?"

"No. Mothers died both times. But those times when I helped old Doctor Herbert, I watched and remembered. That's how I learned all the white doctor's ways. I handed him his tools when he needed them. Got so he counted on me to do right. I watched how he carried on when he did other kinds of cutting."

Queen Bess pressed her fingertips against Anita Becker's neck, paused, nodded, and walked over to the counter where she had left her bag.

"What I remember the most was how he cleaned and cleaned everything. He said most doctors didn't believe in it, but he did. He was a right smart old gentleman. He said he'd read those letters those generals sent back to England when they fought that war that made the white folks free. Said Redcoats claimed we was dying like flies 'cause we so filthy. Said they didn't get so much disease 'cause they clean folks. They change sheets, change shirts. Wash they hands all the time."

She found a pan, put the razor in it, went outside to the cooking trench, removed a pot from the tripod straddling the low fire, and covered the razor with boiling water. "I knows the same thing 'cause I watch what happens. What happens is what is.

"Can't hurt nothing," she muttered as she carried the pot back inside. "Might do some good. Want you to scrub off that table yonder with hot water."

Anita Becker moaned.

"That woman a bleeder, ain't nothing I

can do," Queen Bess said. "But we going to try. Now help me get her on that table. We going to swaddle down her arms and legs to where she can't kick or go to thrashing. Just hope she pass out."

The two women lifted her out of the bed. Bethany wrapped a long bandage around her chest and arms, under the table and back around to secure her torso. Then she did the same thing to her legs.

Queen Bess looked at her daughter for an instant. Bethany looked like a frightened deer ready to bound away.

"I is going to start."

"I wish to a merciful God we had some laudanum."

"Well, we don't, child. She's been hurting so bad so long now, this ain't gonna make much difference to her. That's a blessing."

Queen Bess took a deep breath and softly pressed the side of the razor against the distended skin, tentatively, reluctant to take the irrevocable step. She lifted the instrument and studied it dispassionately, with cold, wary eyes, knowing if she failed they both were doomed.

"When I is finished, there's some parts of her won't be good no more. Going to rid her of them, too."

She turned back to Anita Becker and began.

Some time later, she laid the dead baby boy beside its mother, who was alive and breathing shallowly.

"Child, I want you to take that big old butcher knife laying on that shelf. Go stick it in that fire outside. Heat it up real good. Wrap your hand so you don't burn yourself."

She took the knife from Bethany when Bethany came back inside. She glanced at her daughter's terrified eyes as she carefully inserted the knife inside the woman's body and pressed the blade against the incisions she had made to extract the uterus.

Only afterwards, when she had made the last few delicate stitches to close the original cut on the stomach, did Queen Bess's hands begin to shake. Trembling, she lowered herself into the wobbly rocking chair.

"I don't want those poor children to see that baby," said Bethany. "Or any of the rest of this, either."

She wrapped the baby in a bundle of cloth and carried him to a bare spot beside the cabin. She found an old rusty shovel with a splintered handle propped up beside the rain barrel. She began digging.

If the family wanted a ceremony later, she would dig the tiny infant back out of the ground and help them with a funeral. In the meantime, the little boy child would soon start smelling. She dug a separate hole for the afterbirth and the remainder of Anita Becker's womanhood.

When she went back inside, Queen Bess was hovering over her patient. "She going to be hurting something fierce when she wakes up," she said. "We've got to keep her husband and those dirty little children out of this house and keep her clean. Don't want her agitated at all. Don't want no one around her but me."

"LuAnne will be back soon, bringing food and the boy."

"Going to set her to scrubbing as best she can without making no noise 'til the father gets back with the chickens, then I going to send them all away. LuAnne and you, too. I don't want anyone around," said Queen Bess. "I don't want anyone upsetting her even with their thoughts."

"Me neither, Momma."

"No point. I has tended many a sickbed. Y'all go on back to Nicodemus. We have a wait, a long one, 'til she gets her strength back. If she lives. Her little ones and that sickly man can get some sleep and some decent food."

"He won't want to leave her."

"I is going to make him go back to Nicodemus. I is going to tell him she needs the rest, and that's the truth. She weak. We just lucky she passed out."

"Here they come," said Bethany.

Amos Becker came walking across the prairie with his two children, each of them carrying a chicken.

Queen Bess stood in the doorway, smiling broadly. He looked at her face and stopped, frozen in place for a moment. Then, dropping the chicken, he gave a whoop of joy and ran toward the house.

"Hush," Queen Bess said sternly. "Hush up, now. She still sleeping. She mighty fearful sick, but she alive. You go see for yourself. Just a look. The children can look. It'll keep them from pestering. When LuAnne Brown gets here with the things I need, I want you to all go back to Nicodemus in the wagon. Want you to stay there for five days. Then you can come back home."

Amos Becker nodded and tiptoed inside. His Adam's apple bobbed as he bent and kissed his wife's forehead. Silently the children filed in. He put his fingers to his lips and whispered for them to be quiet and not wake their mother.

"She's alive," he said with wonder.

Queen Bess stood in the doorway watching. Her eyes shone triumphantly. Then she gestured for them all to come back outside. She looked at the horizon. "LuAnne's 'bout here."

The wagon pulled up, and the oldest son hopped off. Bethany stopped him from rushing inside.

"Good news, so far, Edmund," she said softly, "but your mother needs rest. Lots of rest. You can see her for just a minute, but we want her to sleep long as she can."

He swiped at his tears, then entered the soddy. He tiptoed up to his mother and solemnly watched the rise and fall of her chest. He stretched his hands toward her in wonder at the visible sign of life. He touched her frail face with the back of his hand and then turned to Queen Bess, as stunned as though she were a visiting black guardian angel, and he was struck dumb in her presence.

They unloaded the supplies. LuAnne Brown's nostrils flared when she looked inside the house. She headed for the broom, but Queen Bess pulled her aside.

"I want all you people gone. We needed the food, and I'll send for you directly, but Miz Becker can't be bothered with no cleaning commotion right now."

LuAnne nodded, slowly. "Mr. Becker," Bess called loudly. "Time you get going. I gots stuff to tend to. And you all needs hot meals. LuAnne, scatter some of that oats out here in front, so those chickens won't go nowhere."

After they left, Queen Bess grabbed the nearest chicken, grasped its head, and whirled it around until its neck parted from the body. She watched the bird flop until it lay lifeless on the ground. She pulled a pan of hot water off the cooking trench and used it to scald the feathers so she could pull them off easily. Then she gutted the chicken, deftly cut it into parts, and set it to simmering on the cooking trench.

The second chicken began pecking at the oats. She wrung the third chicken's neck but left it whole, and cut a slit in its belly leaving the entrails exposed. She walked a ways from the soddy so she wouldn't be bothered by the flies and threw it on the ground.

Then she went inside and pulled one of Elam Bartholomew's precious jars from her tote bag. It contained the dried latex she had extracted from the insides of prickly lettuce stems. It was as close as she could come to a natural narcotic on the prairie. She had spent hours and hours cutting open the tiny stems and scraping out the sticky compound. Mr. Bartholomew had warned her it took so much time and work she needed to save it for her worst cases.

She took out a small bowl and placed it beside her jug of medicinal vinegar. She sprinkled the dried latex into the cup, added a small quantity of vinegar, and let it steep. Anita Becker would need a painkiller when she woke up. During the operation, knowing she couldn't take anymore, her mind had carried her body away. It would soon come back.

Finally, Queen Bess pulled the only rickety rocking chair in the soddy closer to Anita Becker's side and, clutching a cup of the prickly lettuce mixture, began her long vigil. When the woman roused with a sharp cry, Queen Bess immediately held the cup to her lips.

"Sip," she ordered. "As much as you can stand."

When Anita roused the second time, the chicken broth was ready, and Queen Bess alternated the prickly lettuce compound with sips of soup.

The next morning Anita's eyes flickered, then stayed fully open. Her voice thickened with pain. "Who are you? Amos? Where's Amos?" Tears trickled down her cheeks.

She just know, Queen Bess thought. *They always know.* "I is known as Queen Bess, ma'am. I is a healing woman. Your man done took the children to our town where there is good food and where they is going to be warm and safe."

Anita Becker took in the words "warm and safe." Then she swallowed hard and grabbed Queen Bess's hand. "My baby? The baby's dead, isn't he? It was a boy, wasn't it? I just knew it was going to be a boy."

"Yes, ma'am. It sure enough was."

Anita began to sob.

"Poor little lamb," Queen Bess crooned. "Just rest yourself. You is mighty lucky to have come through this. You have three fine children that is mighty glad their mother didn't go to Heaven with the baby. You just rest yourself now."

Queen Bess rocked and brooded as Anita fell back into a deep sleep.

She going to have plenty of other troubles soon. Milk for a baby that's not there. Pain like it's sent from hell itself.

The infection started the next morning. Tell-tale redness streaked from the abdominal incision. Mild now, by evening it would spread.

Queen Bess went outside and walked over to the dead chicken she had waiting just in case. She was a just-in-case kind of a woman. She knelt and examined the long cut. Maggots had already come. Her blessed maggots.

She went back inside and pulled out the piece of purple taffeta she had insisted Jed Talbot buy for her. She eyed the infection and cut a piece that would cover the wound where the flesh was puffing up.

She removed a hunk of beeswax from her bag and carried it outside to the fire. She reached for the nearest cast iron skillet and held it over the flames. She put the beeswax in it and watched it carefully so it wouldn't scorch. When the wax had melted, she dipped the piece of taffeta into it. After it was thoroughly coated, she fished it out with a stick and laid it on an old board.

She reached for a spare pot lid to use as a smooth surface, picked up the butcher knife, and walked over to the chicken. She knelt and scraped an ample supply of the maggots onto the lid.

Carrying the lid and the board with the cooling taffeta inside the soddy, she went to Anita Becker's bedside. The woman was stupid with fever, barely awake. Queen Bess mixed more of her dried prickly lettuce into the vinegar and added a dose of willow bark.

She lifted Anita Becker's head and coaxed her into sipping the acidic mixture. When she dozed off again, Queen Bess lifted her gown and scraped the maggots onto the incision. She dipped her finger into the melted beeswax and encircled the reddening flesh with the mixture. Then she carefully pressed the wax-coated taffeta onto the circle of wax, sealing in the maggots.

That evening, Dolly Redgrave stared in horror through the Beckers' doorway. She was coming back from Wade City where she had fit a wedding dress for the barber's daughter. Normally she went out of her way to keep from passing by this homestead. She disliked the unruly, starved children, but the yard was quiet for once. That was sure enough peculiar. Perhaps this clan of ne'er-do-wells had decided to give it all up.

She just naturally felt like it was her duty to check on the family.

Queen Bess dozed in a rocker. On the bed lay Anita Becker, with her stomach bare, sporting a purple patch. Dolly pressed her hand over her throbbing heart. Taffeta. It was the purple taffeta. The priceless purple taffeta.

She tiptoed in just a foot or two, before

she fled. But it was long enough to see a maggot, yes, a maggot; she would swear to that later. A maggot crawled out from under the edge of the taffeta.

CHAPTER TWENTY-THREE

Aaron Potroff re-read the article in the *Millbrook Wildhorse.*

> *The residents of Nicodemus have petitioned the commissioners in Rooks County to organize a township. Nationwide, those who fought for emancipation in the late war rejoice over this bold and stunning move by the brave citizens of this very first totally self-sustaining colored community.*

Potroff slapped the newspaper against his knee. He went to the hotel window and stared across the street at the Sinclairs' mercantile store. Not far down was the so-called lumber yard. There were only a few scraps of wood for sale, and hardly ever enough nails. Wade City had an aging barber who pulled teeth on the side. There was no saloon because the handful of temperance ladies, led by Estelle Sinclair, carried on like a little sip would lead straight to hell. The sorry hotel where he stayed was the most prosperous business in town.

His hands shook when he tried to relight his dead cigar. Calmed, he inhaled deeply, then blew a smoke ring into the hazy morning light. He had to think of a way to stop the black bastards.

He never dreamed those people were capable of organizing a township. Worse, if they got it into their heads to organize the county — if they beat him to that, too — he would have a hard time convincing newcomers that Wade City was the town with the most potential in Western Kansas.

Normally, Nicodemus wouldn't have a chance in hell of being the county seat, but with feelings running as high as they did in the country, those traitors might attract a flock of holier than thou do-gooders to help them out. The next thing he knew, the damned darkies would be wanting their own railroad. If that happened, he would be broke. All his money might as well be on a slow boat to China.

Naturally, the Sinclairs would see the Millbrook rag, and the old lady would go into hysterics. Sometimes he thought it would be worth letting the whole town go under just for the sake of getting rid of Estelle. However, he could count on Josiah to stay halfway calm and think of a plan. He stubbed out his cigar and stroked his temples. He had to think. He couldn't just lie back and let it happen.

Two days later, Aaron Potroff went to Oberlin and telegraphed a friend in Omaha to ask for the kind of money he needed. It was a bitter pill. Until now, he hadn't looked for outside financing because he owned all the lots in Wade City, and he thought it would be the only town in the area. Instead, Norvin Meissner was praising Nicodemus like blacks were as good as white folks. He'd also heard there were a few no-count mavericks trickling into Millbrook from time to time.

His answer came late that afternoon. The telegraph was short and veiled, but he no longer had to worry about money. He went to a printing office and had some flyers made up.

The growing town of Wade City, Queen of the Prairie, is looking for ambitious young men who want to get ahead. Why limit your talents and your energy in places that are going nowhere when you can have a business and a building all your own that is a sure-fire pick for the next county seat? You already know the joys of living in Kansas: the opportunities, the clean water, the fresh air. Now come on a little farther west to a brand new county that likes high-steppers.

He studied Oberlin's main street. He intended for Wade City to have every single improvement this town had. He lingered in Oberlin until the flyers were ready, then headed north for the struggling little town of Baynard. It was just two years old. People grew disillusioned after they lived in a town that long. He was counting on that. The grass was always greener in another town.

He went into every one of the few sparsely stocked stores and bought something. Folks remembered big spenders. After he had eaten a sorry noon meal at the boarding house that doubled as a café and post office, Potroff strolled toward the end of town. On the outskirts, he saw an old man, stained with sweat and dirt, struggling to saw a pile of mixed wood into planks of even lengths.

"Kind of a waste of your time, isn't it," Potroff said as he watched, "using any cottonwood at all? Seeing as how you haven't got much when you finish. It warps when just a speck of dew lights on it."

The man, who hadn't heard him ap-

385

proach, whirled around and wiped his sleeve across his tobacco-stained mouth. "Case you haven't noticed, mister, not much mahogany growing around here."

Potroff grinned, holding up his hands. "That's so. Didn't come to needle you, just want to know if you can get your hands on decent wood?"

"Hell yes, if you can get your hands on some decent money."

"My money's good. I need three wagon loads of pine delivered to Wade City."

The old man swallowed hard. His toothless mouth formed a large circle. "Name's Bidwell. Three wagon loads, you say?"

"Three, and one load of walnut."

"Walnut?"

"Walnut."

"Gonna cost you."

"I figured it would," Potroff said. "All the buildings going up in Wade City are going to be first rate and built to last. And I've always been partial to walnut for furniture."

"You don't say."

"Would you happen to know if there's any men around here who might be looking for work? I'll pay extra if they're halfway decent carpenters."

"You don't say." Bidwell tongued his wad of tobacco against his cheek and nodded toward three men piling scraps of kindling onto a wagon. "Reckon them will help you out."

Most of the men in the town were looking for work. Any kind of work at all. Many had gone a hundred miles away to find work on the railroad, leaving a town full of women trying to eke out a living. There were even more outside the town barely staying alive on hardscrabble homesteads.

"Lewis Tidewater is the best carpenter there is," Bidwell said. "Trouble is, he's gone to Clements to find work. His wife is in the family way, and he wouldn't have gone off and left her if he could have made a living around here."

"Can you get ahold of him?"

"Don't know."

"Try. I'll pay if you can."

"I know other men who are plumb desperate to find something close by. Had to go off. You know how it goes."

"Yes, I do. That's why I'm so proud that Wade City is going to be named the county seat. Give folks steady jobs."

Bidwell spit out his plug of tobacco and cautiously looked at Potroff. "The county seat? You know that for a fact?"

"I do indeed," Potroff said. " 'Course, I haven't exactly got that in writing. It will have to be voted on. But I'm sure you know that railroads only go through county seats, and I have every reason to believe the Union Pacific Central will have a branch line coming through our town. That's not for publication just yet, you understand."

"Mum's the word, mister."

Potroff reached into his inside coat pocket and took out a small sack of gold coins. He handed Bidwell fifty dollars. "Reckon this will get you started. Hire whoever you need, and bring the lumber to Wade City."

Potroff went back to the mercantile store and asked the clerk if he could leave a few of his new flyers behind. "Plenty of work and available lots in Wade City," he said. "If you know of any good men that needs a job or wants to get ahead, send them my way."

The next week, Bidwell's scrawny team of mismatched Percherons pulled into Wade City. Bidwell, two other old men, and five young ones leaped down from the wagon bed. They set to work under Potroff's direction. Five days later, Wade City had two new buildings with elaborate false fronts.

Potroff shook Bidwell's hand, then paid the man generously. "Let folks know that if they've a mind to start a business, I'll loan them the money."

"You don't say."

"I have people coming in as fast as they can get here, but I'd rather give the folks in Baynard first choice of lots. I know what caliber of people they are. Never can tell with strangers."

Clearly dazzled, Bidwell hitched up his team and headed back across the prairie.

Potroff waited. It would just be a matter of time.

The next day, a solemn group of men came and looked the town over. When they had finished, one of them walked briskly toward the hotel.

"Have you got any lots left?" he asked Potroff.

"Sure do, mister. Some of them prime. 'Course, some of the best spots have already been spoken for, but folks have been known to back out. I'll check around. Don't want to get your hopes up, though. County seat towns fill up fast."

"When will you know?"

"Most likely next week."

"I'm going to tell folks back in Baynard there's lots available."

Potroff grinned from ear to ear. "You do that, mister. It's God's truth, and I'll be happy to help them."

It was a prairie phenomenon. Arranging and rearranging towns made and unmade fortunes in the twinkling of an eye. In two weeks' time, the whole town of Baynard switched to Wade City, buildings and all. Each structure was simply jacked up, put on sleds of rolling logs, and pulled across the plains to its new location. Wade City doubled in size.

Josiah Sinclair looked up from his column of figures when Potroff walked in the door. He stuck his pencil behind his ear. His store was doing better, much better, since the Baynard folks moved in.

"Morning, Aaron."

"It is at that." Potroff looked around at the shipments of new merchandise stacked on the shelves. "I'll get right to the point, Josiah. I've come with a business offer. Wade City needs a newspaper. An editor."

"Shouldn't be much trouble to find one, Aaron. They sort of breed like fruit flies here in this miserable excuse of a state. If there's one in a town, before you know it there's five buzzing around causing trouble."

"Don't want one of those fly-by-nights, Josiah. I want you."

"You can't be serious." He looked up at Potroff. "Hell, I don't know nothing about

390

writing a paper. Used to know a few things. I knew how to plant cotton. I knew how to hunt and fish and play a few cards. Used to know how to look just right when I stepped out of an evening. Don't know nothing about anything anymore."

He looked around at his growing stock of merchandise. He was starting to care about his store when he had thought he would never care about anything again. "Used to know how to manage a few slaves," he added lamely. "More than a few, actually."

"And that's the point exactly, Josiah. You used to know how to manage a few slaves. And that's what I want you to go back to doing."

"I'm not a man of letters," Josiah said. He turned as Estelle came from the back room, looking like the Witch of Endor summoned from the dead. He could tell by the eager look on her face she had heard everything.

"You don't have to be a man of letters," Potroff said. "I'll send you back to Topeka for a week. There's folks there that will sell us everything we need and teach you to set type. Then, as to your lack of writing ability, that's not an issue. I'll dictate every word that goes into that paper."

Estelle's bony little chest expanded. She cleared her throat. "We are thrilled to accept your kind offer, Mr. Potroff."

Both men stared at her. Potroff had not counted on Estelle wanting to be part of the operation. But she had possibilities. She could organize. The temperance ladies were like a vigilante society in this town. Best of all, she hated black people.

"As Mr. Potroff pointed out, Josiah, you know how to manage slaves. You used to be good at that." Estelle's voice quavered. "And I think I know a few uppity niggers around here that need to be taken down a notch or two."

Potroff nodded, cocked his head to one side, and touched the tips of his fingers together as he studied the couple. He had never seen skin the color of Estelle's before. It looked like the oiled buffalo skins folks used in the place of window glass.

"Well now, Miss Estelle, I do declare. I believe you're going to be a wonderful asset in this venture. A social column, perhaps? Tips for the ladies? Your opinions on a variety of issues?"

Her pale eyes gleamed with a crusading light.

Doomed, Josiah looked at Potroff. "When do we start?"

"I'll send you to Topeka next week. And Miss Estelle? Would you like to go also? I understand you have folks back there?"

"Yes, a cousin," she said. "Oh yes, sir, I would. I would like to go. I would indeed. And while I'm there, I could go to a temperance meeting. A real meeting."

"It will be arranged, then," Potroff said.

"Oh, I don't think you need to burden yourself with a long trip at this time, Mother." Josiah's Adam's apple bobbed like it had been dunked in a tub of water. "It would strain your health, and someone should keep the store open."

"Nonsense, Josiah. I'm sure one of the temperance ladies will be glad to fill in." Estelle quickly walked over to the bolts of fabric sitting on the far shelf. "I need a new dress," she murmured, dismissing the men.

"Aaron," Josiah said softly, flinching at the thought of a long trip with Estelle. "Have you ever thought of simply buying out the Millbrook and Nicodemus folks? If it worked, it would be mighty simple."

A week later, three men came to Nicodemus with plenty of money to spend. Potroff had already drawn up maps of the most strategic farms to buy out. It would be painless and simple. It wouldn't make any enemies, and it wouldn't rile folks up. There were other ways, but like Josiah had said, this would be the easiest.

At the end of the first day, Eric Keegan came back and announced that the first man had laughed at him. "Had a notion to shoot the bastard. Don't much cotton to being laughed at."

The second man, Ted Duvall, had better luck. At least the homesteader had told him he wanted to think it over. The third man didn't come back at all. Potroff gave them a couple more names. Too late, he learned that it aroused suspicion when men suddenly came around wanting to buy up basically worthless farms.

Two weeks later, Norvin Meissner wrote in the *Millbrook Wildhorse:*

Citizens, beware! There are scalawags loose in this area who would deprive you of your worldly goods for a mere pittance. There are men who are attempting to buy our precious land when we are on the verge of a bonanza. It is with trembling wonder that we inform the citizens of this soon to be county that a railroad will be coming through the town of Millbrook and, by extension, Nicodemus, Kansas.

Shocked, Potroff stared at the words. He cursed the stubborn stupidity of the ignorant homesteaders who didn't know when they were licked. Buying them out should have been simple. A blessing. Good American dollars for their no-count, miserable hovels on their sorry, rock-hard piles of useless dirt. Folks who wanted to leave could have been helped on their journey.

His next steps were ones he didn't want to take. Not because he worried about the harm they would cause, but because of the risk to his reputation as a benevolent person dedicated to doing good.

He took out his watch and studied the hands as though they had some relevance to his moves. He slowly turned it over and looked at the inscription on the back. The casing was a soft rose gold with a beautiful luster. The words engraved there were *To Hiram from your loving Emily.*

The watch had been given to his grandfather by his grandmother. At times he was comforted by this watch, this sense that he had come from people who had done right well. But lately, he was seized with melancholy when he looked at it. It was a reminder that there was no love, no Emily, in his life and no prospects that he could see. No one to care what kind of person he was.

He was forced to take this path. He had tried buying the niggers out. Violence would attract far too much attention. There was a gentler way. He'd try that first, then if he had to ratchet it up a bit, they'd brought it all on themselves. He tucked his watch back in his pocket and considered all the whites who were taking their business to Nicodemus. Ruin the blacks' cash intake and he would ruin the system that was driving their town. He decided to go after them, one by one.

He tossed a coin into the air and deftly caught it as an idea struck. Their biggest moneymaker of all was the doctoring. The little wench with prideful ways and her conjuring mother took in money that should have been in Wade City. He had to bring in a white doctor.

There were no medical standards, no state licensing agencies. Nebraska had proposed a law making new physicians register at the county clerk's office. That state would be the first to require that new registrants graduate from a two-year medical school. Those who were already doctors would not be burdened by such strenuous requirements.

Trained doctors were nearly impossible to come by because the prairie starved them out. It was only natural that a doctor would go where he could make a living. Some-

times, however, the prairie attracted vision-
ary practitioners with inquiring minds who
filed claims, loved their patients, and re-
joiced in the raw energy of the empty waiting land. But to the prairie also came the
charlatans, the drunks and opium addicts,
the down and outs, and the filthy-handed
rejects from society.

Hands with broken, filthy nails. Careless
hands. Bruising hands. Cruel hands.

Such was the kind of doctor Aaron Potroff
managed to locate.

CHAPTER TWENTY-FOUR

Norvin Meissner couldn't decide which was worse: mornings when the sun came up pulsating with a fiery blaze that paralyzed the mind, the air, the grass; or days beginning with an eerie wind, when searing gales blasted the earth and nothing alive could escape the reach of their heat. A peculiar uneasiness came over him when the wind blew. He could not complete the simplest task. He lost his train of thought. He misplaced things. Broke things. Hated himself. Hated his life.

He picked up his bucket, went outside, and braced himself for the trek to the lone well in the center of Millbrook. A sorry old well and still a bone of contention. It took a long time to find this water. The well digger had to go down one hundred feet.

He poured water down the pipe to prime the pump, then wearily began pumping, pumping, pumping, growing more anxious with each stroke. If this well failed, they were finished.

Millbrook was just a miserable little wide spot in the road. Wade City had doubled its population when Baynard moved in. Nicodemus was exploding. Meissner had no idea where Nicodemus was finding Negroes who had some means to see them through the first year. But it was a common sight now to see families coming across the plains, heading for that black town. When they arrived, there were people to greet them, expecting them, or so he had heard from the man who delivered lumber to Millbrook.

None of the white towns had developed such a set-up. The Nicodemus newcomers were fed, assigned to a house, allowed to rest and get on their feet. Then everyone pitched in to erect a building to suit their occupation.

Most of the white folks who came to the area were farmers or merchants and jacks-of-all-trades, independent cusses by nature. Wicked rivals who didn't mind helping a neighbor as long as the neighbor didn't get ahead of them. The people attracted to Nicodemus came from a slave background. They were used to being servants, putting their own egos aside, and pooling their resources. It had worked against them in the beginning, but it was their biggest asset now.

Also, many of the ex-slaves had been specialists on large plantations. No one could touch Jim Black as a blacksmith. But that was all the man had ever done. His giant arm pounded, pounded the living steel. Even those who hated blacks on general principle found themselves going to Nicodemus for blacksmithing.

No one could sew as fast or as well as Dolly Redgrave, so white women ended up going there to have dresses made. Nicodemus had a man who did nothing but make wagons and a man who made harnesses and had never done anything else.

They demanded cash in advance of work done, and a percentage of their money was pooled and used to help a new family get started. Meissner snorted as he tried to imagine forcing that rule on his white counterparts.

One of the most familiar figures on the prairie now was Teddy Sommers crossing the land on his ancient mule, carrying God only knew what to the land office at Oberlin, to the courthouse at Stockton, to this businessman, to that politician. You'd think Nicodemus was a miniature of Topeka with all its government doings and comings and goings.

Water trickled from the spout. Relieved, he turned his back to the wind and continued to pump.

Meissner turned when a horse whinnied. The Samson family was coming toward him in a broken-down wagon piled high with everything they owned. They had arrived in Kansas with a fine team. Now there was just one horse left, and its coat was dull, its gait listless.

Hiram Samson pulled up; his wife, Susan, and their little daughter huddled beside him on the seat.

Meissner removed his hat and held it close to his chest as though he were paying respects to the dead. "Wish you folks could stay," he said wistfully.

"Goodbye," said Hiram heavily. His lips worked, and he touched his hat. That was all.

Susan Samson stared straight ahead, her lips a thin red line in her white face, like Meissner personally had ordered up the wind, the heat, the lack of water, the dead garden, the swarms of insects, their constant gnawing hunger.

The wind whistled angrily, as if trying to stop their departure as they plodded on down the street. Meissner's throat tightened. He wanted to call them back. Make them stay.

When he turned back to the well, he had lost his momentum, and the pump wouldn't work anymore without being primed anew. He accidentally knocked his bucket off the spout, spilling the precious bit of water he had worked so hard to accumulate. Furiously, he kicked the bucket into the angry wind, set it sailing down Millbrook's only street, and headed back to his soddy.

"Lose something?"

Meissner turned. The wind was so loud he hadn't heard anyone ride up. He looked up into the gray eyes of a tall Negro man standing beside the most beautiful horse Meissner had ever seen. He handed Meissner the bucket. "Mr. Meissner, I'm Jed Talbot."

Meissner shook his hand. Although they hadn't met, he knew at once who Talbot was. Everyone was talking about the smart black lawyer who beat out the best minds in the county and managed to sneak a township right under their noses.

"I'm Norvin Meissner. It's a pleasure. A pleasure indeed. Do come inside my humble abode, sir, where we'll be out of the wind and you can tell me the nature of this unexpected visit."

Just a short time ago, Meissner wouldn't have had this wretchedly awkward feeling every time he saw someone from Nicodemus. But ever since the night he received the thorough trouncing, he had felt like a street urchin watching a happy family pass by his rat-infested alley.

Inside the soddy, he hustled around, moved some books off a chair, and gestured for Jed to sit down. "I'd offer you some coffee, but I couldn't stand the thought of starting up the stove this morning. Hot enough already."

"No need to trouble yourself," Jed said.

Meissner sneaked looks as he cleared papers off an upright stump and sat down. Talbot wore homespun pants and a blue shirt of coarse cotton, but Meissner had heard all about the fine suit the man had worn to Stockton — his elegant bearing, his melodious voice.

"I would like to come straight to point of my visit." Jed reached into a bag he had slung across his shoulder. "Have you seen this?" He handed Meissner a newspaper.

Meissner unfolded it and began reading. He stopped, looked up at Talbot, and read the masthead again. The color drained from his face. "I don't believe this. I simply don't believe it."

"It's true."

"Josiah Sinclair, editor. Who would have thought? It stands to reason Wade City would conjure up an editor sometime. But I thought it would take a while. Never dreamed they would recruit someone from their own ranks."

Meissner's shoulders slumped. Dazed, he looked around the cluttered soddy as though seeing it for the very first time. Every shelf was crammed with tools and type and paper. Strings of dried food hung from the ceiling. He could hardly locate his own bed at night. He had given up a wife and life in the East for this?

"Everyone knows Potroff owns that whole town. Lock, stock, and barrel, Mr. Talbot. Wade City's not like Millbrook, where we have a whole town company behind us. I've always been up front about that." He picked up the paper again and scanned the insides. "And a woman's column," he said wistfully. "With housekeeping hints. Written by that stringy mean-spirited wife of his. A real paper. God, women will love these little social items. This will put Wade City in prime shape to go after the county seat. Two towns now, Wade City and Millbrook."

"You're forgetting about the third town,"

Jed said. "Or maybe I should say the first town. We were here first. Nicodemus."

Meissner stopped before he blurted out that Nicodemus didn't actually count. He didn't want to alienate this man. His face sagged. "Of course. Forgive my oversight, Mr. Talbot. I was thinking out loud. It's just that I barely had the wherewithal to put up a decent fight against Wade City *before* they had a paper. I don't know how I'll do it now. The folks backing me want results. They want to see Millbrook grow." He rose and began to pace, his hands clasped behind his back. Sweat popped out on his tightened forehead. "I'm at my wits' end. I can't find people and can't keep them. Why are you here, Mr. Talbot? Surely not just to bring me a newspaper that I would have seen anyway." He glanced over at his volume of Tennyson. "I got off on the wrong foot with your people a while back. I reckon you've heard all about it."

"Yes, I did."

"I did not mean to offend anyone. I swear to God, I'm the best friend you people have got in this county."

"I know that, Mr. Meissner. I'm here to see if we can work together. There's nothing wrong with you wanting to protect your interests."

"I don't want to hurt anyone. Or exploit anyone. I just want to make a life out here. I would like to have a little peace. And a little life. A little rest at the day's end."

"That's exactly what we want, sir. A little life and a little peace. That's why I've come to you. You can help us. We can help you."

"Have you seen Wade City lately?"

"No, I can't say as I feel very welcome there. We all generally go to Stockton. It's where we do all our business anyway, and they've made us welcome."

"Well, Wade City's growing like Topsy." Meissner flushed. "I didn't mean . . ." Even his freckles reddened.

"Please! You don't have to weigh every word with me. Speak your mind!"

"What I meant was, Wade City is growing like a weed. Potroff is coming up with plenty of money for lumber, cloth, grain, anything the people want. My little burg doesn't change. It's shrinking, if anything. But I've heard Nicodemus even put in a second well. By any measurement, you have the most organized town in these parts."

"Which brings us to the purpose of my visit. I'm a practical man. Until last month, no one regarded Nicodemus as competition. That changed when we petitioned for a township. Now white folks are scared to death of us. But you and I both know there's no chance at all that a black town will be voted in as county seat."

"I repeat, why are you here, Mr. Talbot?"

"We intend to back Millbrook as county seat if you'll help us."

Meissner rose and crossed over to his precious lines of type sitting against the wall. He ran a finger over the metal. His face flushed with excitement. He couldn't believe his luck. Just last week, he had gotten word from his town company that when it came time to vote on the county seat it had better, by God, be Millbrook that won. Colored folks could swing the vote.

He turned to Talbot. "Sir, you honor me."

"How many people are there in Millbrook now? No booming. I'm way past being susceptible to propaganda."

"About twenty families and a few bachelors and widowers. Say about one hundred people. We lost two more families to Wade City this month, and most of the rest would leave in a heartbeat if they had enough money to go."

"And why would that be, do you think?"

Meissner forgot he was talking to a colored man. A man who could make or break him. His frustration had been building ever since Hiram Samson's wife had ignored him like he was a loathsome insect.

"Because," he said tersely, "because I lied to them. Nothing I thought was going to be true was true, or came true." He swallowed like his misery was a lump of bread stuck in his gullet. "There's hardly enough water to go around. The heat. The flies. Ground as hard as steel. No trees." He teared up. "And the wind. This goddamn wind." He picked up a piece of paper and crumpled it in his hands. "Of course they're leaving. Of course."

"Do you want to leave?" Jed asked.

"No, of course not. Your place, Nicodemus proves that it can be done. It can, if people will stay."

"Then you weren't lying," Jed said. "You were simply telling them future truths."

"Future truths," mumbled Meissner, his eyes alight with new understanding. "Future truths."

"Before we launch our new campaign, we have to improve Millbrook," said Jed. "My people will come over tomorrow morning and decide what needs to be done about your water, and the way the town is laid out and the businesses you must offer."

Meissner's smile died on his face. He slowly extended his hands and examined his fingers. "There's a few Southerners living here, sir; if they think there's a bunch of colored people moving in . . ."

"Tell them we're hired niggers if you have to," Jed snapped. "I really don't care. We've got to get Millbrook on a solid footing. This town has got to offer better services and more services than Wade City."

"But we don't have more or better services. That's the whole point."

Jed's scornful look was that of the doer, the planner; Meissner's, that of the dreamer, the bumbler, men who were broken against the rock of reality.

"That's right," Jed said. "You don't have more or better services right now, but you can have, and you will have. We're going to see to it. I'll send a team over Monday. We're going to start with your water situation."

"Why are you doing this, Mr. Talbot?" Meissner asked. He might not be a doer or a builder, but he could think. There had to be a reason behind all this. "Why me? Why Millbrook?"

"Why you?" Jed's gaze softened. "Because you're a good, decent man, that's why. The people of Nicodemus are not naïve. You have a printing press, the almighty power of the press. You may have rubbed some people the wrong way, but they told me you gave us supplies to start our school. You're the one who has our trust. That's why you. Wade City would like to wipe us off the map."

Meissner tucked his thumbs under his suspenders and gave them a snap. His eyelids fluttered as he blushed with appreciation. He turned and picked up the crumpled piece of paper and lightly tossed it into the air, then caught it before he turned back to Jed.

"I'm not a fool all the time, Mr. Talbot. I am more often than I care to admit, but not all the time. What do you people want from me in return for backing Millbrook as the county seat?"

"A lot," Jed said softly. "Not only do we want you to be the official, if informal, mouthpiece for Nicodemus, we want a black person on every single political committee. We want you to back this idea from the beginning. This county is going to have to factor in our ideas, and our interests, not just our votes."

"Of course, Mr. Talbot. Of course your ideas will be honored." Meissner's heart swelled with righteous fervor. His mind whirled. His paper would be a beacon, a wonder of literary excellence for this great state. Might he expect just a smidgeon of recognition for his stellar contributions to the noble black race?

Jed did not smile, nor did his eyes leave Meissner's face. "We're going to organize a school district. It's going to be the first in this county. We already have the first school, but we're going after state funding. The ultimate official stamp of approval. That's going to mean that your people — and by your people I mean all the white folks around — are going to have to attend a school run by black folks."

He waited. Meissner struggled to find words, and then they came at a gurgle, a whisper. "That's never been done. Never. It's impossible. People will leave this town and maybe even this county."

"No, they won't," Jed said. "Some, perhaps. But not all. Besides, most of them can't afford to leave. Nicodemus has the very best teacher," he added. "The very best."

"God, don't I know. Don't I know."

"Build up Bethany Herbert. You've heard of Phillis Wheatley, the black poetess? Did you know the first patriot shot during the Revolution, Crispus Atticks, was black?"

"Yes."

"Well, educate the people out here."

Meissner listened. He watched Talbot's

411

face as he bragged about black intellectuals.

"Mr. Talbot, I know. I'm not the one who needs convincing. And God knows we agree on Miss Bethany. She's got the finest mind I've come across in my lifetime. But she can't be everywhere. And you can't, either. How many adults in your town can read and write? Realistically, what you are proposing just isn't possible."

For the first time, he saw Talbot flinch. He'd hit a sore spot, that was clear. Also clear was the look on the man's face when he'd mentioned Bethany Herbert.

Jed's handsome face became a polite mask. "That is a problem. One I intend to work out. When the white folks are forced to attend our school, I want them to find one equal to the best in other counties around."

"I don't mean to throw cold water on you, but it will never happen, sir."

"It will. I can promise you it will." Jed rose abruptly and picked up his hat.

"All right, Mr. Talbot. It's not like I have a choice. We've got a deal. I'll promote your Nicodemus, and you, in turn, will back Millbrook."

"Agreed."

They went outside. Jed mounted Gloriana.

"And another thing. Millbrook needs a doctor."

"You don't think I know that, Mr. Talbot?" the editor said bitterly. "We've looked high and low."

"Soon as we get your sorghum mill started . . ."

"A sorghum mill! Who said anything about a sorghum mill?" Meissner blinked. "Never thought of that, but no one else has one out here."

Jed laughed. "After we launch your mill, I intend to talk to Miss Bethany and her mother."

"Queen Bess," Meissner said dryly, as he swatted at the swarm of gnats around his face.

"Yes, Queen Bess. I believe the Herbert women can be approached about serving the medical needs of your community on a more official basis."

"Miss Bethany, maybe. But her mother, never."

"You've met, I see."

"Have we ever."

Jed laughed. "Good day, sir. I'll see you Monday morning with the crew."

Meissner went inside. Jubilant, he sat down, grabbed a piece of paper, and began composing the coming edition. From time

413

to time he paused and warmed himself with Jed's words. This fine colored man had judged him and found him worthy. Called him a decent man.

"A decent man." He whispered the words to himself. They warmed his heart to the very depths of his soul and gave him courage later when his bones turned to water and his hands shook so badly he could hardly set type.

CHAPTER TWENTY-FIVE

Teddy Sommers heard the commotion even before his team struggled up the short rise leading to Wade City. At first he had balked when Jed asked him to take a load of coal to the town on the day folks would be celebrating the launch of the Sinclairs' new paper, the *Wade City Chronicle*. Then he relented. He had a credible excuse to do a little spying because he wanted to inspect the cache of genuine walnut Potroff had for sale.

There was nothing like walnut for fine coffins. He planned to trade a wagonload of coal the men of Nicodemus had chipped from the short vein they'd discovered. They hadn't found enough coal to make a killing, but it helped with their own fuel situation, and there was enough to sell off a wagonload or two to white folks once in a blue moon.

And blue moon about got it, Teddy thought

gloomily as he jolted along. *Be a blue moon, all right, before anyone from Nicodemus feels easy about going to Wade City.* He didn't mind going to Stockton or Oberlin or Norton.

"You're practically invisible," Meissner had insisted. "No one can slip in and out like you. Folks simply don't pay a lick of attention to you."

It was hardly a compliment, but Teddy knew it was the truth. There was just something about a tiny, shriveled-up black man in a tattered suit that folks didn't get too excited about. He blended with the prairie monotony like an old, worn-out gray cloud drifting across an uninspired sky that folks had given up scanning for rain.

"And you notice things," Jed had said. "No one else has your eye for details that wouldn't mean a thing to someone else." So he had given in and agreed to the trip.

Teddy stopped at the edge of town. He was close enough to hear the speakers on the platform. He stood by the wagon, knowing if he left it unattended, half the lumps of coal would disappear.

Josiah Sinclair was ending his speech. Behind him sat Potroff, Estelle Sinclair, and the new doctor, Winthrop Osborne, who had brushed his Prince Albert coat, sponged the spots, and looked quite respectable. Josiah introduced his wife amid an enthusiastic round of applause from the women.

A sudden breeze rippled Estelle's skirts and cooled her small, strained face as she climbed up on a little block of wood, one hand firmly clamping her hat to her head. "Today," she began, "marks the launch of the *Wade City Chronicle,* but I also wish to announce that the grand crusade to end all consumption of demon rum in this region will begin right here and now."

Teddy splayed his fingers across his face, closed his eyes for an instant, and cursed the day he lured his people to this crazy murderous state — free land or not. It seethed with passion over one no-count issue after another.

Liquor again.

Kansas wanted to amend the state constitution to keep folks from drinking or selling booze. If it passed, the state would be the first to take such a step. Jed had read an article to him just last week saying that the governor of Kansas, John Pierce St. John, had said, "The eyes of the whole people are turned toward Kansas."

Seemed like the whole country was always poking fun at the state, and women like Estelle weren't helping.

"Crazy damn bunch of wild-eyed women," Teddy muttered as he watched the females clap for their leader. "Too tough to die and too shriveled up to live. Smashing women. They just can't figure out what to do with themselves out here, same as the rest of us. So they goes out and smashes something."

"And we will unite with the fine, noble ladies of Stockton," crooned Estelle, "to make this region and our paper, the *Wade City Chronicle,* a guiding light for all the women in the United States."

Her voice trembled with importance as she called for people to sign the temperance pledge. Mostly women came forward. Teddy jolted into a new alertness. Dolly Redgrave was among those climbing onto the platform. Right off, he couldn't think of any meaner two women than Estelle Sinclair and Dolly Redgrave.

He wished he had a bottle of whisky. It was the only sure-fire way for getting through the day. A band started up, but it didn't cheer him.

Had to be a ton of money in back of this paper. Potroff had ordered in oysters, and they were giving away little sacks of flour inscribed with the motto *Wade City will rise like good yeast bread.* There was a slew of foot races lined up. A baseball game was

418

scheduled for later in the afternoon, and there would be a dance that evening.

Teddy looked around at all the hopeful faces. He could see them brighten right before his eyes. They were starting to believe the lies they heard. The rains would come. Wheat would spring up like a miracle. The Lord would actually notice them.

Teddy picked up one of the free issues of the paper someone had dropped on the street. He glanced back at the podium, where Estelle was introducing the "fine lady from Nicodemus."

He climbed back onto the wagon seat. He still had his load of coal. Hadn't looked at the walnut. He drove the team back over the rise toward Nicodemus, his business unfinished. He didn't have no more heart for it no how.

Didn't need a special kind of mind to see this town was turning meaner than a snake. Crusades did that to people, whether they wore hoods or carried temperance cards for folks to sign. Worked out the same, either way.

He was going to tell Jed to stay away from Wade City. Just don't go there. Not that Jed would pay a bit of attention to what he had to say. Sometimes Teddy thought he was as invisible to blacks as he was to white folks.

■ ■ ■ ■

Exhausted, Bethany sat by the window in her schoolhouse. Her practice was growing to the extent that she no longer could do right by the children. When she was called away, it was often so sudden that she had to leave in the middle of a lesson. Then, too, she was being summoned to greater distances and couldn't say for sure when she would be back.

She'd had another fight with her mother just last week. Queen Bess had scolded her for dragging herself out of bed to start the school day, saying she ought to have slept when she had a chance so she would be fresh to tend to her natural business, which was doctoring, instead of trying to make white children out of little black ones.

Bethany had bitten her lip hard to keep from blurting out what she shouldn't say to her own mother, then lost her temper five minutes later and said it all anyway — that the children wanted to learn. It was their right. Their fights were of no use; neither of them would give an inch, but Queen Bess was right about one thing. Bethany did not have the physical strength to keep up both. It was just about to kill her.

The wind was coming up. She knew she should get up from the chair, go home, and rescue her drying clothes before they blew off the elk horn in front of the dugout. But just thinking about her mother managed to drain the little bit of energy she had left.

Her thoughts strayed to Jed Talbot again. She tried to push him out of her mind. She had thought she was invulnerable and trusted the madness would pass. She trembled, and her cheeks burned. Whenever he walked into a room, she did not know where to put her slim, capable hands. One look from him and she felt the air move, the cloth against her breasts. And her hands, her hands. She had never given her hands a moment's thought before.

She stared dully at the dying embers of coal in the stove, grateful that the men delivered it to the school now, so at least she didn't have to waste precious time and energy gathering cow chips. But her classroom was dirtier because of the coal soot, and she missed the grassy smell of the dried dung. Her eyelids grew heavier; her head drooped. She dozed off, then jumped to her feet fully awake when she heard a sound.

"Miss Bethany!" LuAnne Brown stood in the doorway. "I come to tell you the little Turner boy is breathing just fine again."

Disoriented, she reached for the back of the chair to steady herself.

"Miss Bethany," LuAnne said softly, "you know Silas and I ain't seen you around the campfire lately, so you don't know what he preached about last Sunday."

"I'm sorry," Bethany said. She had been off doctoring for the last three Sundays and was too exhausted to go to church midweek.

"He preached from Exodus," LuAnne said, "the eighteen chapter, when Brother Jethro has a little talk with Moses, same as I'm trying to have with you right now."

"I'm not familiar with that scripture," Bethany said. "I'm sorry."

"You knows about everything else that won't do you a speck of good. 'Bout those Greeks. 'Bout lots of fancy things. But don't know nothing about what's helped keep our people's heads together, and that is the word of the Almighty God. In fact, sometimes I think you know the least about what you should know of anyone here."

Hot blood surged to Bethany's temples. Someone was always pecking at her. Her mother was bad enough, but to have LuAnne turn on her too was more than she could bear.

"You may be right," she said evenly. At

least she was still capable of controlling what she said. "What was that scripture?"

"Look it up," LuAnne said. "If you own a Bible, and I'm beginning to wonder if you do. Look it up. What else you might come across might surprise you. Exodus 18."

LuAnne left, and Bethany trembled with fatigue. Then she walked over to her stack of books, dug out her Bible, and located the eighteenth chapter of Exodus. She read about a tired man, a man pushed to the brink of exhaustion, as she was. A man who tried to do everything by himself. Then Moses's father-in-law, Jethro, nailed him, told Moses bluntly that what he was doing was not good, and he could not keep on alone, for he was trying to act as a judge of all the disputes between the people of Israel whom he had led into the wilderness.

Bethany closed her eyes, imagining the heat, the animals, the swarms of exhausted people trying to make their way across the Sinai desert. A burning land where there were no people. The Hebrew children had been scared, worn down, and, like most people under severe deprivation, not knowing what they were doing, they fought. Over big things, little things. She could just imagine it.

Bethany read on. Jethro had instructed

Moses to only represent the people before God and to seek out other able God-fearing men to take over his earthly responsibilities. It was the beginning of the judicial system, thought Bethany. Judges over judges over judges. She no longer tried to settle disputes, and no one could take over her doctoring. Then she laughed as she realized LuAnne was talking about the schooling. How like the woman to make her discover it on her own, instead of telling her straight out.

There was not a soul here who could match her book learning. Unless it was Jed Talbot, she thought. He might not know as much as she did about philosophy or the classics, but he knew more about government.

She had to find other people to help teach. She could see the disappointment on the students' faces every time she had to leave in the middle of a lesson. She had heard of other ways to run schools. She knew a little bit about how colleges were run. Different teachers for different subjects. Why not try that?

She straightened her schoolroom, then walked home to her dugout. At the edge of town, men were clustered around the second well. The sides had collapsed again, and they were trying to figure out what to do. She smiled. The men again; planning, organizing, starting to boss their womenfolk around like white men. Like ancient beasts waking up from a deep sleep.

"Evening, Miss Bethany."

She turned. The banjo man, Tom Jenkins, called to her from across the street. She smiled and waved back. Tom had been one of the first September colonists forced to hunker into little ravines like rabbits, wherever they could find rises to create burrows. They hadn't time to plan or think — they just wanted to survive. A majority of the families still cooked outside. The settlers had ended up scattered along the Solomon for about twelve miles by the time they found enough places for them all.

Tom had moved his family into town this spring and built a proper soddy. She didn't think she had ever seen the man when he wasn't smiling. Tom's two children never missed a day of school, and even before he moved to town he found a way to come in every time the drums called folks to a meeting. The evenings were filled with singing and Tom's lively banjo music.

Now, whenever a settler started a new business, seemed like another one followed. There were six hundred people in the settlement. About one-fourth were taking home-steads, but many of the newcomers were staying in the town of Nicodemus and making their living with the skills they had developed on plantations.

Six hundred people. Certainly not enough room in the school for more children. She knew there were parents who lived farther out trying to teach their children on their own. She got ready for bed with the sound of Tom's banjo ringing in her ears, but instead of lying awake trying to figure out how to do everything herself, for once she fell into a deep sleep.

Bethany watched the people gather around the circle where Silas Brown did his preaching. It was cooler, sweeter outside. The ground around the campfire was bare as glass. Worn down by these gatherings. There were no benches as there would have been back home where there were logs available. No stumps to set on. Folks just flopped down on the ground.

She smiled and nodded as she walked toward an empty spot and spread out an old quilt.

"Evening, Miss Bethany."

"How do, Miss Bethany."

Zach Brown, Silas and LuAnne's oldest

boy, looked quickly at the ground as she drew near.

"Evening, Zach," she said, forcing him to look up. Although she was embarrassed by his stark adoration, she remembered how awestruck she had been by Miss Nancy's tutor. She would have followed the man anywhere.

She had coaxed and encouraged Zach when he started to read. He had struggled dutifully and made adequate progress. Then when she started on numbers, his mind raced ahead. He would soon need advanced instruction.

Bethany saw Jedidiah Talbot and remembered his neat ledgers of figures with land calculations. Impulsively, she went over to where he was sitting, forgetting for an instant that her heart beat too rapidly and she couldn't control her thoughts when he was around. Jed jumped to his feet when she approached.

"Miss Bethany?"

"Do sit back down. Really."

"Only if you'll join me."

Miserably self-conscious, she sank to the cloth he spread out and arranged her skirt. His eyes were questioning. And something else. Was that amusement she saw there? Was he making fun of her? Did he know that when he came near the very colors in the air brightened?

"Thank you," she said. Surely it had looked to him and everyone else as though she had headed right toward him. And so she had, but it wasn't to get an invitation to sit on his dirty old blanket. She got right to the point. "Jed, I have a student who needs advanced math instruction."

He listened carefully, his head cocked to one side. That endearing precious way he had of focusing perfectly. A courtroom habit, she supposed, of carefully following arguments. Then she blinked back tears as she realized she was thinking of his mouth and those beautiful gray, intelligent eyes instead of keeping her mind on finding the right words for Zach Brown's sake. It just showed what a poor job she did of looking after her students.

"Yes? He needs more instruction?"

"Yes, or will. Soon, not now. I mean, I'm fine for now."

"And?"

"And I was wondering." She straightened and looked at him steadily, all business now. "I was wondering if you would be willing to provide it."

"To a child?"

"To a child, Mr. Talbot. But he's no

ordinary child."

"I don't doubt that, Miss Bethany. You know of course that I'm extremely busy right now and likely will be even busier when the election for the county seat comes closer. Wade City isn't going to give in without a fight."

"Actually, I'm not asking for just the one child. I'm asking that you teach arithmetic to all the children."

Jed didn't laugh but looked at her soberly.

"I have every reason to believe you've been trained in higher mathematics."

"I am," he said simply. "I was first in my class in calculus and physics."

"I am away a lot, too, doctoring outsiders. And we can just hope my work holds up. We need all the money we can get until more people are self-supporting."

"So what is it you want from me, exactly?"

"I for sure want you to teach Zach Brown. If you can't take on the rest, I want you to find out just who knows what in Nicodemus. Please ask them to take turns teaching the children. At least ask. People pay attention to you."

"I will ask. I can promise you that much. Are you going to do the same thing with the reading?"

"Yes, I am."

"Like a college, then?"

"Yes, as close to that method as I can make it."

"I've never seen it tried with little children before, but I don't see why it wouldn't work." He hugged his knees and shoved back his hat. He reached for his pipe, then patted his pocket. "Out of tobacco," he said. "I seem to keep forgetting I don't have any."

"I hope you don't have to think too hard about what I'm asking you to do."

"Don't have to think at all about my part. That's easy. I'm just trying to come up with the others. You can count on me to teach your young man. Earnest Jones used to be a miller. He would have to understand simple numbers to know what to charge his customers. In fact, there's a lot of men around here who can do simple math. That's not the hard part. The hard part is going to be convincing them they should be school teachers."

Then Gertie Avery stood and walked to the front. Her ample body was clad in a linsey-woolsey dress of dark brown that just matched her skin. Quavering with controlled strength, she led them through chorus after chorus of a spiritual. The cords of her neck vibrated.

Her voice was powerful as thunder, then

as soft as sleet, then the crackling of little fires, then the vibrancy of a cello. Bethany and Jed were drawn into the spell; her rhythm, her echoes. Swaying, they responded to the call, filled the empty prairie with their own sound — creating their own shade of black, souls leaping to the stars.

Oh God, thought Bethany. *Before you split the world, before there was land and sea, before you even divided light from dark and day from night, there had to have been music. You brought forth music first, and for me and my people it's never stopped.*

It will always be there, always be there. It's the only thing the white folks haven't figured out how to take away from us. I'm going to do everything I can to keep us right here in Nicodemus. This Promised Land where we can sing our songs and even use our drums. Our place.

She scarcely heard the sermon. Her mind was filled with plans for her school. Having decided to give up control of every detail, she found it was easy to imagine other ways.

When the service was over, she quickly jumped to her feet. She didn't want to give Jed Talbot a chance to walk her home. Not only did she not want him to get any ideas, she didn't want other people to, either. She flushed at that mocking look in his eyes

again, as though he could see right through
her.

CHAPTER TWENTY-SIX

Jed sat on a stump outside his soddy, reading through the narratives he had spent eight years collecting. Some of the stories were so heartbreaking he could hardly bear to set them on paper. It was years of work for nothing. No one would ever be interested in them now. Everyone — including blacks — wanted to put slavery and the war behind them. The North just wanted to rebuild its industry, and the South wanted to reconstitute its exhausted economy.

He watched a hill of ants scurrying back and forth. Even little insects had a natural sense of order, unlike the people here. Nicodemus was becoming a squalid mess. God knew there were plenty of men and women willing to work long, hard days, but the colony now had a larger population than most small Kansas towns.

Some of the newcomers were from Mississippi and Alabama, and some of the emigrants brought supplies. Although the colony was mostly Kentuckians, there was a mixture of blacks now. With opinions. Six men arrived last week with two teams and seed and made it clear they didn't come to starve. Thank God, Nicodemus had hit two good water wells right from the beginning. He never thought he would see the day when he longed for a good overseer, but that was what they needed.

The ants just worked. They didn't want to argue stuff out around a campfire every evening.

He was burdened by his promise to Bethany to help with the school. They were all overworked, but he simply didn't have the time. Meissner's question about the number in Nicodemus who actually had book learning had hit a sore spot.

Slaves hadn't been allowed to learn to read and write. Even one of the town's founders bore a brand on his cheek as punishment for daring to sneak some learning. Most of those who had acquired some education came to it late and were just marginally literate.

Jed wiped the sweat off his forehead and glanced at the horizon, then peered again at a speck growing larger and larger. He never thought he would see the day when he dreaded more people coming, but Nicodemus was stretched too thin to take in another group of destitute and starving strangers who had heard about the miracle town.

Coming home to Nicodemus, the Promised Land.

He could see the newcomers more clearly now. Two men were perched atop a gaudy, green spring wagon with gold scrollwork. Jed scoffed. It was a silly contraption. Relatively useless for the prairie. Seats in front and back and not much room in the rear to haul merchandise from town. They pulled up at the blacksmith shop. A tall black man, slender as a young sapling, gingerly climbed down and stood next to the team.

Jed walked over to meet them. "Well, I'll be damned," he mumbled. "What do we have here?"

The man still sitting on the wagon seat was dressed in a gray three-piece suit and wore a bowler hat. He was light complexioned — nearly as white as Dolly Redgrave — with an elegant, perfectly trimmed mustache. As Jed strode toward them, the first man stepped forward and held out his hand. It was encased in a fawn-colored glove.

"Mr. Talbot, I presume?"

Jed nodded. The man's diction was perfect, educated, and Northern. "Yes, sir, I'm Jed Talbot."

"Please allow me to introduce myself. I am A. T. Kulp, Jr., and this gentleman here is E. P. McBane." Kulp laughed good-naturedly as his travel companion groaned and tried to climb down. "Although my citified friend here is a little worse for wear, he will most certainly be joining us shortly. He has had the dubious distinction of clerking on Wall Street, and no doubt is waiting for a bell to clang before he makes his grand move out of this vehicle."

McBane snorted, gave Kulp a look, and stiffly climbed to the ground. He stood with both hands atop a walking stick. "We are both attorneys, sir, like yourself, and my wordy friend here is a right fair wielder of a pen. When he's not talking your leg off."

Kulp bowed deeply. "I have come here from the city desk of the *Chicago Conservator,* where I read little snippets about your town from time to time. And like my companion here, I have heeded the call of the West. We have come to seek our fortunes. We have come to assist you in the settlement of Nicodemus. We are quite concerned, sir, that you might regard us as competition, being a lawyer yourself."

"God, no," Jed said. "God, no." He laughed. Too pleased to find words to match Kulp's elegant introduction, he couldn't stop smiling. Educated men. At last God had sent him educated men. Men who could help handle the myriad of business details plaguing him. Land claims and surveys and convincing the state of Kansas they had a bona fide school right here in Nicodemus.

A. T. Kulp looked more like a displaced African chief than an editor. His skin was a soft gray without a trace of brown — like black ink washed with water.

McBane groaned as he steadied himself against the wagon, straightened, and rubbed his fists into the small of his back. "It's a pleasure to make your acquaintance, Mr. Talbot. A pleasure indeed, but I can't say the trip was a pleasure."

"Welcome," Jed said. "I can't begin to tell you both how welcome you are."

That evening Kulp and McBane helped Jed carry his belongings outside his soddy to make room for the straw pallets he had borrowed from the community storeroom. The settlers would build a house and a business office for the two men in short order, but, in the meantime, they would stay with Jed.

They ate at the Browns, then walked back to Jed's. After the two men settled in, Jed decided to bring up creating a school district. It would be a gift from heaven for Bethany because they would receive state funding.

Her exhaustion showed in her tired eyes and her thin, weary face. There were too many students clamoring for attention. Jed's heart skipped a beat every time he thought of her. She had been terrified when he asked if he could walk her home the night she sat beside him at the campfire.

But for the life of him, he couldn't think of a thing he had said or done. That evening, her face, lighted by the flickering flames, was hauntingly beautiful when she talked about plans for her school. Then it lost all its animation in a few seconds.

He knew the look. Slave dumb, no expression at all, like he was out to trick her.

He studied the two men — McBane with his refined features and Kulp, broad-nosed with tight, curly hair like a buffalo — then took the plunge.

"Gentlemen, I would like your help in securing the first school district. The state of Kansas needs to see other men than me appearing before them for every request in the world."

McBane looked interested. "A school, you say?"

Jed laughed. "Yes, we have a school here." He proceeded to tell them of the growing number of children who were yearning for book learning, and their dazzling progress. "We can't keep up," he said. "We're out of manpower. Not just the teaching; we need help with everything that requires people with an education."

"Looks like we showed up in the nick of time," said Kulp. "The Scriptures say a three-fold cord cannot be broken. Who can stand against us?"

"Exactly," said Jed. He expelled his breath in a rush. "Who indeed?"

"Do you know the steps for accomplishing all of this, brother?"

"I do. I've got it all drawn up. Subject to revision, of course." He smiled, sheepishly aware of his day-to-day high-handedness.

Bethany's back was turned toward the doorway, and Jed hesitated as he watched her clean the slate Jim Black had rigged up. He didn't want to startle her. She was humming a song he had never heard before. He loved to hear her sing. Watch her sway. See subtle movements of her hips.

He stood a few more minutes, holding his

hat in his hand. Bethany went to the window and looked out. The intense afternoon sun was softening. Groups of people would soon begin gathering around the campfire to trade stories, and to nosily agitate each other with good-natured teasing.

He watched quietly. She was as expressionless as a sphinx now whenever he came near, and he knew it wasn't her true nature. Her cheeks glowed like over-ripe peaches, and a dark flush rose on her copper skin when she taught the children. Her dark eyes glowed with intensity on the days she discussed ancient Greeks and the power of ideas.

When she was arguing with Meissner the two went at it like wild cats — cheerfully gleeful adversaries thrilled at a chance to match wits. A couple of times when Bethany had been sparring with the editor, she seemed to forget Jed was even in the room. But when he had cleared his throat and tried to pipe up with his two cents, Bethany stiffened, as though she were frightened. Her lips closed in a thin, tight line.

She looked lonely now. He yearned to touch her skin, to run his fingers through her black hair, which he had never seen loosened from a tight bun since the day they quarreled over the turban.

Embarrassed at having stood silently so long, he slipped back outside the door, then made a noisy entrance, giving Bethany time to compose herself at her makeshift desk.

"Jed, how nice to see you."

"Miss Bethany," he said, wishing she meant the words. "You know that Kulp and McBane and I have been to Topeka. I just got back this afternoon."

"So that's where you've been these past couple of weeks. I do wish I had known. Momma has a whole list of medical supplies she can't find around here."

"It was careless of me not to check," he said, "but we didn't want to disappoint you if things didn't work out."

"Disappoint me? How could your trip possibly disappoint me?"

"It was all about you." He twisted his hat around and around in his hands. "You are now the first official schoolmarm of the first official school in Graham County. You will have state funding."

"Money for books? And my children will have real diplomas?" Her hands flew to her cheeks, her face bright with joy. "I can't believe you did this. Oh, you wonderful, wonderful man. How did you do this? Money for books!"

Then, for the life of him, Jed couldn't account for the change in mood and the fearful look on her face. "I forgot myself. Please forgive my unseemly conduct," she stammered.

To his dismay, she burst into tears and ran out of the building.

Estelle Sinclair was composing her column for the *Wade City Chronicle* when Josiah finished sorting the mail and handed her the *Millbrook Wildhorse.* She skipped through the patent pages that were shipped from back East, as they would be the same as the ones appearing in her paper. She turned to the local items.

The color drained from her face, and her pulse throbbed in her stringy neck. She rushed to the back of the store where they had set up their printing press. "Josiah! You're not going to believe this. Those damn niggras have organized the first official school district, and it says here, right here in this paper, that little white children will be welcome."

"My God," said Josiah. "Let me see." He reached for the paper, quickly read the column, tucked the paper under his arm, and headed off to the hotel to see Potroff.

Aaron Potroff read the *Millbrook Wildhorse.*

His jaw tightened. It had gone far enough. What these people were proposing for little white children was beyond the pale. Not only did little black children think differently, their blood was different. It moved sluggishly like cold oil down a river choked with rotting roots. Hell, it even smelled different. Smelled like copper mixed with rotten eggs.

Once he had cut open a vein on a little nigger boy's arm, just to see for himself if the blood looked like his, or if it flowed black or some other color. Their brains had to be stoppered up, too. Clogged with spooks and clangety noise. He sickened at the thought of dragging down the minds of precious little white children.

He relit his dead cigar. "We cannot have white children going to that school, Josiah." His voice was calm, reasonable. He controlled his breathing, not wanting to reveal his surge of excitement at the memory of the smell of black blood. The intoxicating sense of power when that pickaninny stood trembling, his lip quivering, rightfully sensing that to survive he must not make any sound at all

"Hell, I know that," Sinclair said. "Everyone knows we can't let our children go to school with a bunch of ignorant niggers.

443

Don't know how they managed this, but we've got to stop it. They'll be sorry they tried this."

Potroff flicked a speck of tobacco off his shirtfront.

Sinclair raged on, infuriated by Potroff's apparent calm. "Do you understand what I'm saying, Aaron? What this means? If any little white child wants to get an official certificate verifying his education, he will have to attend school in Nicodemus."

"I heard you, Josiah. But I don't want the *Wade City Chronicle* to attack the school. It wouldn't set well with all the white do-gooders buzzing around. Here's what you need to do."

Two weeks later, a brief item appeared in the *Wade City Chronicle:*

A little baby died during a difficult delivery assisted by Miss Bethany Herbert of Nicodemus, Kansas. The family was passing through this area, and, according to my source, the unfortunate mother was taken in the throes of labor out in the prairie, and her husband rode to Nicodemus for help. He reported that Miss Herbert at first was strongly reluctant to come, then agreed to for a hefty sum of money. But once there, according to the husband,

444

she put an ax under the bed to cut the pain and then a pan of water beside it to cool the fever and said there was little else she could do about the situation. "It's my mammy what knows 'bout birthin'," she said. "Dat's her business. Mammy knows lots of things I don't."

This information is a direct quote from the grieving husband, and they kept on with their unhappy journey to Denver, with his miserable wife cradling their dead child, as she refused "to bury her precious darling on this godforsaken prairie."

In addition to her doctoring, Miss Bethany Herbert is the school teacher at the newly formed Nicodemus School District No. 1, sanctioned by the state of Kansas.

The damage was done. Once news spread on the prairie, there was little hope of calling it back. Women from the South immediately believed that Bethany was too ignorant to deliver a baby, let alone teach school. There may have been darker forces at work also, they whispered.

They repeated common knowledge on plantations. That the niggras spit in the food, put ground glass in scrambled eggs. That they were all looking for sly mean ways to do a body in. And some of the black women, especially the ones from the West Indies, could kill with a look or cause your cows' milk to curdle or your corn to shrivel up or your well to go dry. They kept little dolls and knew how to stick pins in them so people died in agony.

So people who were worried about their family's health and missed living back East where things were a little more up to date now found themselves calling on a white doctor instead of the Herbert woman and her conjuring mother. When Doc Osborne came, if he could pull them through the crisis at all, he ended his house call by urging them to sell their homestead and move to Wade City, where they would be given a free lot in town.

Don Hays gave Teddy a copy of the *Wade City Chronicle;* he was then obliged to take the sorrowful thing to Miss Bethany. He found her in the schoolhouse. It was late afternoon, and the children had left for the day. Solemnly he handed her the paper. She read it quickly and raised her eyes with growing disbelief.

"That's an out-and-out lie." She touched a finger to her trembling lips. "As outrageous a lie as I've ever seen. There were no deaths, no difficult deliveries. Even if it were

446

true, you know I have never, ever relied on primitive customs." Stunned, she read the passage again. " 'An ax under the bed to cut the pain,' " she said scornfully. " 'A pan of water beside the bed to cool the fever.' " She slapped the paper down on her desk. "I have never used that kind of grammar in my life."

"Everyone around here know that, daughter."

Her mother had slipped inside silently as a panther. Her black face gleamed under her white turban. Bethany could not hold back the tears. She rose, and Queen Bess stepped forward and held her close.

"Patricia come over this morning. Told me everything, child."

"It's such a lie, Momma."

"Cry it out, child. It the only thing that will help. I know all about white man's lies. Ain't nothing I haven't heard before."

"It just hurts so much, Momma. I didn't know anything could hurt so much."

"Child, child. I has been blamed for things what don't even make sense to pass off onto an ignorant black woman. The scalding go so deep it like a sore that can't heal. It hell because it really don't heal, neither. Other things do, but wrongful blame nearly never does. It like a black, smoking rock beneath your heart. If you is a black person, you can't speak up or point out what ain't true. All you can do is shuffle your feet and look dumb and try to keep from aggravating white folks even more."

"Why would anyone say such things?" Bethany looked at Teddy as though she expected him to have a ready explanation.

He lifted his hands to ward off her queries. "I don't know what's going on here; I swear I don't. I swear I don't know how spreading this kind of lie would be doing anyone any good.

"I do."

Jed Talbot hurtled through the door like a tornado and slammed his copy of the *Wade City Chronicle* down on the table. "I know who would benefit." His face was stern, his gray eyes cold with outrage. "Who would benefit by this is that no-count white doctor."

"But making me look bad will not make him look good," said Bethany. "Not in a hundred years. The man simply doesn't know anything, and I've heard he's drunk most of the time. Drunk and dirty."

"Doesn't matter," said Jed. "Doesn't matter what's true. It just matters what folks think is true. That's all that counts. And if they think you're an ignorant black woman who puts axes under the bed to cut the pain, they're sure as hell not going to come to you for medicine."

"It's more than that, Brother Jed." Kulp and McBane walked inside. "Much, much more." Kulp's voice was thick with fury.

"It's not the doctoring," said McBane. "It's the school. If the Wade City folks can convince people you can't put two sentences in the right order, they sure aren't going to send their children to school here."

"It both. Sure enough," Queen Bess said.

Kulp and McBane had never met her, but they knew who she was, and she knew who they were. "Madam, your reputation precedes you," Kulp said, his face grave, his voice deferential. "Your abilities are well known in this community."

Queen Bess raised her chin and nodded graciously. She studied these two fancy black men, spitting smart, shiny as a rooster's wings. Patricia said they mammy fed them pages out of a dictionary 'stead of mother's milk when they was babies, and they just naturally digested all those long, long words.

Her own Bethany. Jed. Teddy. All of them. Mixed blood. Too many mixed bloods coming into Nicodemus. Causing trouble. Riling folks. She and Patricia couldn't see

449

nothing to do about it. All these fancy folks was going to drag all the black folks into hell for nothing.

"They ain't nothing we can do about this, you know," she said. "Nothing at all."

"Beg your pardon, ma'am, but there is. Edward and I are volunteering to help teach school and to organize all the other systems needed to run a school."

Jed choked back a lump in his throat. "My God, my God, A.T. What an inspiration you will be."

The men were already phenomenally successful. They were building one of the most amazing land location businesses in Western Kansas. The first week they came, they began advertising in the *Stockton News,* the *Millbrook Wildhorse,* the Topeka-based *Colored Citizen,* and other papers back in Eastern Kansas. They boasted that they not only located and surveyed, they were qualified to practice in all the courts of the 15th Judicial District. They had printed formal business cards and advertised they would take care of all business before the local United States land offices and even that involving Washington, DC. Whites and blacks alike were seeking their services.

Most amazing, though, was their immediate involvement in state politics. They had already lobbied to be admitted to the Republican convention at Topeka and were furious when they were turned away. They immediately gyrated toward the activities of the state's colored men's organizations.

Kulp had peppered Kansas newspapers with letters from Nicodemus showing the community in the most positive light. He had even presented a paper to the St. John's Literary Society on one of his visits to Topeka.

"This is not to minimize your credentials, Miss Bethany," McBane said. "Please do not misunderstand our intention."

"I don't. But absolutely no one, I mean no one, can perceive you two as being ignorant and uneducated."

"This is very generous of you," Jed said. "While we're discussing this, there's some state standards for what we have to teach the youngsters."

"Say no more, Brother Jed. I know both Greek and Latin, and Brother McBane here knows everything that can be done with numbers. I've always wanted to teach school, haven't you, Edward?" Kulp tried to keep a straight face.

"Well, not exactly," McBane said, "but one thing is becoming clear. Everything I ever wanted to be, and most of what I've never wanted to be, is going to be used up in this town."

CHAPTER TWENTY-SEVEN

Queen Bess, Bethany, Teddy, and Jed were en route to Stockton. Once there, they would all go their separate ways and shop quickly so they could start home before dark. No one ever went out from Nicodemus in a wagon without planning to bring back as many supplies as they could manage. Bethany had a long list of requests from the women. Teddy wanted to scout for off-price lumber, and Jed had business at the courthouse.

Queen Bess had saved enough money for another washtub. She wanted a separate one to process rabbit pelts and start a shoe business. She was getting more washtubs than you could shake a stick at for all her little ventures. She tried not to be too prideful, but in the evening, when she sat out, there was something about that little line of tubs. It eased her heart.

She hadn't figured out all the details yet,

but she got the idea a couple of weeks ago when Jamal Gray sailed past, running like the wind, and brought down a jack rabbit with a slingshot sure as David brought down Goliath. Up until that time, she couldn't for the life of her figure out what poor black folks — and a passel of them at that — were supposed to do about shoes.

Back home, when they were slaves, providing shoes was the master's problem. Then after they were free, back in Kentucky there were always little animals, deer running afield, even softened tree bark if you were plumb desperate. Or they had old rags or vines to weave together. But out here rags were snatched up right away for quilts and clothes. After watching Jamal, she'd struck a deal with the boy.

She sat in the back with Bethany, listening to Jed and Teddy. Jed hadn't eased up a bit since Kulp and McBane came to town. He was still striving, plotting, stirring things up. All hell had broken loose after he organized Nicodemus Township. The folks around Wade City started writing the governor, saying he never should have let it happen, and Jed was firing his own letters right back to Topeka.

What Jed was telling Teddy right now wasn't nothing she didn't already know.

Until Graham County was organized, they were doing without any kind of law.

"Just to show you how bad it is, Teddy," Jed said, "last month, there was a scoundrel going to homesteads asking them to sign a temperance pledge, which the poor old sons-of-bitches were more than happy to do. Then he asked them to sign a second card for his records, and it was actually a sight note signing over all their land."

"They couldn't read what they was signing on them cards?"

"No," Jed said. He was no stranger to injustice, but this was one of the most galling prices blacks had paid for illiteracy. Losing their land with a stroke of the pen. Hell, whites didn't even have to use a gun out here. Rooks County was treating Graham County like an errant stepchild whose needs were met last. Sending the sheriff their way was one of them. Rooks County had its own problems to deal with.

"And the hell of it was, if they could read, the bastard stopped with the temperance card," Jed said. "If they couldn't, he tricked them into making their mark on the sight note. There was nothing anyone could do about it, since we're in a territory that's outside the law. In this case, crime was color-blind. In fact, about half the people who got taken were whites, because blacks are immediately suspicious when a white man asks them to sign anything."

"Cold-hearted bastards," blurted Teddy.

Queen Bess stopped paying attention when they started talking about the delay in electing township officers. Kulp and McBane were carrying on over it something terrible, because they spent most of their time traveling to Stockton and Topeka for all their fancy lawyering. Seemed like those two men were all Nicodemians could talk about, day and night. She was glad when they finally got to Stockton, and she didn't have to study on politics no more.

The town had changed more than she thought would be possible in six months' time. There was a millinery shop. Hats. Enough women here now to support a shop that made nothing but hats! A shop with real glass windows sparkling in the sunlight.

Queen Bess carried her bag over her shoulder, and as she passed the cobbler's shop she stared wistfully at the soft leather boots within. She could never afford them, but there was nothing to stop her from wanting them. Her old shoes were nearly done for. The soles were paper thin now, and they couldn't stand one more trip to town if she had to walk.

A cluster of smart-dressed white women came out of the mercantile store and were headed her way. They were all dolled up like they were coming home from some fancy doings. Another temperance meeting, she guessed, because Estelle Sinclair was in front of the group. Queen Bess kept her eyes down.

"Well, I do declare, Jessie, if it's not the mother of the woman who killed that baby," Estelle said. "Bold as you please." Her eyes glittered with malice.

Queen Bess's heart pounded. Her blood surged. She did not want trouble.

"Could have killed her faster if this one had of been there, from what I heard. She's a witching woman, sure enough," said a lady in blue calico.

"That's the woman who cast the spell and cut that baby right out of that woman's body."

"Her?"

"Yes, her. She was trying to kill her, don't you know. But God stayed her hand," said Estelle.

Queen Bess raised her head. "I saved her," she said quietly. "Warn't trying to kill her. Trying to save her."

"Don't sass me, nigger," Estelle said.

Queen Bess drew back. Other women had

joined them now, coming out of stores, gathering, gathering. She stepped backwards off the crude board walkway, stumbled, caught herself, and started backing toward the center of the street. It was littered with horse manure that eased over the top of her shabby, worn, mismatched shoes and leaked through her soles.

"Witching woman. Witching woman."

Their words began as a soft chant, then rose in intensity. Her eyes widened with fright. Dolly Redgrave came up from the back. Relieved, Queen Bess dared to breathe again. Her own kind. A woman from Nicodemus.

"Oh, this here woman is evil, pure evil," said Dolly. The freckles on her face deepened on her pale-tan skin. "Swear to God, ladies, I seed this myself, with my very own eyes."

All the women turned to Dolly, the lovely little mulatto woman who already was known as the person to do their sewing. And was she not always clean and neatly attired? Not exactly one of their own, but someone they could understand. Someone who had signed the pledge that liquor would never cross her lips. Fine lips, they had all agreed, nearly white-shaped. Not thick at all.

"What I seed was" — Dolly twirled her

little parasol and raised her chin — "I passed by that house the day after she cut that little dead baby out of that woman's belly. And when that lady didn't die right off, like this old granny wanted her to 'cause she was white, she sent the husband and children off to Nicodemus where they would be out of the way. And then, and then . . ."

Dolly paused for effect and cast her eyes toward the ground as though she were continuing with great reluctance. "And then she put maggots on that woman's stomach."

"Where she cut? Put bugs where she cut?"

"Yes. And then she covered them with a piece of purple taffeta so they wouldn't get away."

The women looked at Dolly incredulously, then looked back at Queen Bess. One of the women stooped and reached for a rock. Then another. The circle tightened.

"That's the most despicable thing I've ever heard."

"Purple taffeta," Dolly blurted again. "A beautiful, beautiful piece of purple taffeta. I knowed what it was the minute I seed that purple. I first seed that fine, fine cloth at her housewarming. Can't imagine anyone cutting up a piece of purple taffeta like it was just nothing at all." She dabbed at a tear.

"She must be touched in the head, or she must have magical powers," said a woman in back.

"Must be powers. Magic. Witching powers."

Queen Bess's throat tightened. "You don't understand. There's medicine doings my people know about that your people don't."

"Quite right, your people know things," Estelle said. "Do you keep little dolls, old woman? Do you stick pins in them?"

"No," said Queen Bess. "I just praise Jesus's name. I belongs to Jesus. Just Jesus. I telling you, I saved her."

But her words were drowned out as the chants of "witching woman" grew louder and louder.

"No, no, no!" someone called shrilly. "Stop!" Bethany wriggled through the group of women like a little terrier. "Stop." She threw her arms around her mother, who was kneeling in the manure. She pulled Queen Bess to her feet and wrapped her arms around her. Then, trembling, too shocked to speak, she turned to face the women.

"What in God's name is going on here?" A man's voice vibrated like a clap of thunder through the air. Elam Bartholomew pushed through the circle of women.

"I asked you, what is going on?" Elam's voice boomed through the silence.

One of the white women said, "We were just talking to this woman about Miz Becker, Mr. Bartholomew. Everyone knows she tried to kill her."

"That is an outrageous lie. Outrageous. Whoever is spreading such nonsense should be horsewhipped."

"It true," said Dolly. "God's truth. I seed it with my own eyes. Maggots. She sealed in maggots with a piece of purple taffeta." Her voice trembled. "Taffeta. She ruined a fine piece of taffeta."

Bartholomew's little spectacles glinted in the sun as he walked over to Bethany and Queen Bess. He stood quietly beside them. Only the whiteness of his knuckles atop his walking stick betrayed his fury. He was a scientist, a man used to reasoning with fools. He kept his voice calm, his words measured.

"To begin with, ladies, I'm sure all of you know I have a few credentials for what I'm about to tell you. In addition to my degree in science, I was a medic in the Late Rebellion. A major. I assisted surgeons. I have seen things so terrible I shall never speak of them again. But I can assure you that many a life was saved on the battlefield because the poor soul was lying next to a dead man, because then sometimes the maggots on the corpse . . ."

He paused and removed his glasses, pinched the bridge of his nose, and closed his eyes for a moment before he could continue. "Sometimes the maggots would crawl over to the wounded man and cleanse the infection."

Bethany's arms tightened around her mother's bony shoulders. She looked at the white stranger with wonder.

"And as to the taffeta . . . It's nearly non-porous. It's so tightly woven that when it's coated with wax nothing can contaminate a wound further. Dirt can get around the edges though." He looked at Queen Bess curiously. "Unless Missus Herbert found a way to take care of that, too."

Queen Bess nodded and peered up at the proud old white man as though they were having one of their private conversations.

"Candle wax," she mumbled. "You waxes the taffeta, and then you makes a trail with candle wax to seal it. Gotta be careful you don't burn no flesh, though."

Bartholomew looked tenderly at Queen Bess. "Moreover, this woman is my friend."

No one spoke.

"I have no idea how she acquired the skills to perform an emergency caesarean, but she did."

Queen Bess's eyes sparkled with pride.

"Furthermore, I have no idea where she could acquire maggots in such a short order." At this, he raised his eyebrows. "You can't just call them up out of thin air. It takes death, and in this case it wasn't Mrs. Becker's."

Queen Bess sensibly suppressed a wee smile. She would tell him later about keeping a killing chicken handy to bring on the maggots. A doctoring woman couldn't do nothing without a killing chicken.

"Madam, clearly you sealed in the maggots with the waxed taffeta."

Queen Bess nodded.

"We have often consulted," Bartholomew announced to the group, feigning amicability. "Discussed methods, and traded medicines. In fact, if I'm not mistaken, I believe you intended to pay me a visit on this trip."

He extended his elbow to Queen Bess. She tucked her arm under it, the women parted, and the elderly white botanist and the old black granny walked toward his house on the edge of town.

Queen Bess's hands trembled beneath the buffalo robe Jed had draped over her and Bethany for the long ride home. Bone weary, she slumped listlessly and stared straight ahead.

Bethany had just finished telling Teddy and Jed about their terrifying experience with Estelle and Dolly Redgrave.

"Dolly's dangerous," Jed said. He looked at Teddy. They were both horrified. "We won't let this pass."

"Tried to tell you that little high yeller girl was no good," Queen Bess mumbled. "And that Sinclair woman, she meaner'n a snake."

"Momma, where did you meet that Mr. Bartholomew? Why did he stick up for you? I told you when you first came about the Indian woman. The last thing she said to me was 'Bartholomew.' I told you that. I know you remembered. You remember everything."

Queen Bess said nothing.

"I didn't know what she meant. Could have been a person, or a place, or something else. I wasn't even sure I heard her right. So why didn't you tell me you had come across someone by that name?"

"Daughter, I wasn't going to tell you nothing until I looked this man over myself. How I know he safe for you to be around? And you knows, I has always had white gentlemen doctoring friends. Like he said. We done been consulting for the last couple of months. He tells me things. I tells him things."

"Momma, why didn't you tell me you were learning new things about medicine?"

Queen Bess looked across the prairie and chose her words carefully. The truth was — and it was a growing sorrow like fluid around her heart — truth was, she was beginning to doubt if her daughter, her very own daughter, the last of the great Herbert women, had a true calling. If Bethany did not, she could not bear the grief. Truth was, she couldn't stand to know. Not just yet.

"You was busy," Queen Bess said finally. "Busy at your school. Don't see you much since I got my place."

Bethany reached for her hand and gave it a squeeze. "Momma, my teaching work is going to lighten up. We'll have time to visit. Kulp, McBane, and Jed are rounding up different teachers for different subjects." Bethany's face glowed in the setting sun. "And books. Fine, fine books. Kulp and McBane brought a bunch with them, and they have connections." Her eyes sparkled.

Queen Bess stared at her for an instant. Motherwit was passed on through the milk. This child of hers must have sucked printers' ink from her tits instead of granny smarts.

She all fired up. Bess had known other owl women. But hardly ever a black one came along. She was losing her daughter to scribbles on a piece of paper. Worse, Bethany thought she loved children, but Queen Bess knew she did not. She was not a natural comforting woman like LuAnne that little ones just naturally sidled up to. It was ideas Bethany loved. Seeing the children understand.

Lofty thoughts got her daughter going. Caused her to wander off from a cooking pot. Caused her to forget herself and leave clothes outside with a rain coming on. No motherwit atall.

Queen Bess looked away.

"Momma!" Bethany reached for her. "I'm going on about the school again like I don't care about what happened to you." She put her arms around Queen Bess's shoulders. "I nearly died when I thought those vicious women were going to hurt you."

Queen Bess reached up and patted her daughter's dear face. This truthful, ripped-

466

up, half-white child of hers. Truth didn't set you free. It pierced. Jesus tried to tell them, but they wanted it all prettied up.

"It done," she said heavily. "No point in getting all riled up again."

"But I am. Dolly is one of our own."

"No, she not."

"Maybe not in spirit, but she's from Nicodemus. She's supposed to be one of us. And she was ready to sell you down the river." Suddenly, Bethany burst into tears of helpless rage. "She was going to sell you down the river over a piece of purple taffeta. Purple taffeta."

"Betrayal from within," Jed said as he angrily flicked the reins across the horses' backs. "Can't tell you how many times I've seen it myself and read about it even more. Have you heard of Gabriel, Bethany? And others. Every time some slaves tried to do something, one of their own would pass their plans on to the Man. Ruin everything."

"But Gabriel's Rebellion was for freedom," Bethany said through her tears. "Something important. Our natural rights. And the ones who betrayed him did so out of fear. That little slut was selling Momma South over a piece of purple taffeta."

The next day, Bethany stood in the doorway

of her schoolhouse and watched Earnest Jones lead the class. True to their word, Kulp, McBane, and Jed had rounded up volunteers. Earnest had warmed to teaching arithmetic like it was his natural calling. He'd told Jed, "Can't talk real good, but I can teach little children how to figure well enough to know when someone is cheating them. Not *if*," he added, "not a matter of *if*, if he the Man. It's a matter of how much. Then I'm going to teach them how to figure out what to do about it without getting themselves killed."

Bethany was bone weary from a sleepless, haunted night. Rage-wracked and grief-stricken from the memory of her mother kneeling in manure. She shuddered. What if Mr. Bartholomew hadn't been there? What if her mother had never met this important white man? They could not let this go, but what could they do?

Wearily, she smiled at Jones's zest, picked up the basket she used for gathering plants, and headed out across the prairie. Little grasshoppers flew up wherever she stepped. She once saw the prairie as empty, but it teemed with insects. Life. For the rest of her days she would feel a subtle vibration emanating from the ground. She would never forget the drums and feet of that first

468

large September colony. Surging over the rise like a colorful cloud. Old folks, young folks. People throbbing with eagerness to start a new life. Denied Africa, they were coming home to Nicodemus.

Lulled by the swaying grass, the peace she now found in the emptiness, she spread her shawl out on the ground, stretched out, and fell sound asleep. She awoke to a roll of thunder in the distance. Startled, she watched the wind-spanked clouds, tucking in their tails, moving fast and high.

She brushed a tendril of hair out of her eyes, then gasped. She knew what to do. Somewhere between sleeping and waking and the first streak of lightning, it had come to her. She knew what to do. For all of them. Dream sure, it had come to her whole.

She leaped to her feet and watched the clouds whipped around like stampeding cattle. Lightning crackled, and her blood leaped with each bolt. Mindlessly, she reached for the bundle of hair secured at the back of her neck and pulled out the pins. She reached for her shawl and, hair streaming, ran for the schoolhouse.

She would not spend the rest of her life being rescued by white men, if they managed to show up at all. LuAnne had scolded her for not paying more attention to the Scriptures. Well, she was going to do exactly what the Bible said: fight the lying Josiah Sinclair and Aaron Potroff with the truth. Jesus had said, "The truth will set you free." People in the state of Kansas were going to get a stiff dose of the truth.

When she reached the schoolhouse, the children were dashing for their own homes, and Earnest Jones stopped just long enough to tell her he would come back in two days.

Bethany immediately ran to her dugout and hurried inside. She went to the shelf where she kept the precious sheets of paper Libby Hays had given her. Remembering the Founding Fathers, whose skill with words had freed a nation, she carefully sharpened her quill pen.

She first wrote what she wanted to say in the margins of one of Meissner's patent sheets:

"A great war is being fought right here in Kansas. A war of the angels. It is the age-old struggle of good and evil fought on the high plains of Kansas over a valiant Negro community. All eyes are turned toward Nicodemus, as they must be at this great juncture in our state's history. Unfortunately, this community of industrious and talented settlers is being threatened, besieged by a neighboring town,

Wade City, whose newspaper editor is bent on destroying Nicodemus. The people of Nicodemus plan to vote for Millbrook as the county seat instead of Wade City. Why would persons want to destroy Nicodemus? The answer, of course, is as old as the world: money. Therefore, a campaign of lies and disinformation has begun. Lies calculated to ruin the reputations of two of the finest medical women in Northwest Kansas."

She outlined the stakes involved in creating school districts, then exposed the treacherous nature of the letters protesting township organization. When the wording was perfect she copied it onto the heavy vellum paper and addressed it to the *Topeka Daily Capital,* where it would get the widest possible circulation.

She signed it *Sunflower.*

A week later, when Teddy went to Oberlin, she asked him to bypass the post office and carry the letter directly to the mail sack when the train came through. He glanced at the elegant envelope. Bethany saw the quick question in his eyes.

"Teddy, I know I can count on you not to tell anyone where you got this. Not even Jed. It's best to mix it in with a bunch of other letters."

471

■ ■ ■ ■

When Joseph Hudson, editor of the *Topeka Daily Capital,* received the letter, he did not consider the signature of "Sunflower" unusual. Many of his correspondents used pen names lifted from Greek gods or Shakespeare. Noting the exquisite quality of the stationery, the fine accomplished hand, and the well-reasoned words, he decided it had to come from an educated gentleman of good standing.

He was only too happy to print the letter from the mysterious "Sunflower" if for no other reason than to curry favor with Governor St. John, who was on a crusade to welcome blacks into Kansas. Editor Hudson scoffed at the pretense of disguising gender with the rather feminine pseudonym of Sunflower. No woman could have communicated so intelligently.

When the letter was published, the black elite of Topeka were outraged over the incident of the imaginary dead baby, and the white intelligentsia was incensed by the treachery of the Wade City politicians. Hudson wrote editorials about the underhandedness of white folks in Graham County. His circulation increased by at least fifty that week alone. Everywhere people were debating the effect of the Negro vote on Kansas politics.

Governor John Pierce St. John immediately began doubting the motives of white settlers in Graham County who had protested the organization of Nicodemus Township.

When the copy of the *Topeka Capital* containing the letter from Sunflower arrived at the office of the *Wade City Chronicle,* Josiah Sinclair stormed out and headed toward the hotel. Potroff was playing poker with Clyde McCall and Stanley Bradley. Josiah shoved the paper at the townsman and pointed at the article.

Potroff's face whitened as he read.

"Do you have any idea why this 'Sunflower' would want to turn people against us? Who is he, and why would he give a damn what we do out here?"

"If I knew who the sumbitch was, Josiah, I never would have let this happen," Potroff said coldly. He folded his cards.

"Well, we'd better find out before all Kansas starts watching the town of Nicodemus and sticking up for those uppity niggers."

"They owe me," Potroff mumbled. "Ungrateful black bastards."

"They don't owe you a damn thing."

"They wouldn't have come here if it hadn't been for me."

"You brought them here to make you rich, and it didn't work out," Sinclair snapped. "I tried to tell you those people have their own minds."

"Are you telling me it's wrong to want to get rich?" Potroff slammed his fist down on the table, scattering chips. "Isn't that why most of us came here? To get hold of some land and better ourselves?"

"Yes, but it was the lies you told that got you in trouble. Not just us wanting land."

"It's no different from the lies we tell white people," Potroff said. Other men had gathered around the paper. They laughed at what he had just said.

"Kansas is built on lies," argued Sinclair. "Nothing wrong with a little lie. It's what keeps most people going. Give a man a choice between the truth and a lie, and he'll take the lie every time, and mostly be better off for liking it."

"Some people," snapped old Pete Olive. "Some of us can handle the truth just fine."

Sinclair shook his head. "For a while, maybe."

Grant Peabody, who had kept quiet, spoke

up from his chair next to the stove. "Depends. Moving on kinds of people like lies the best. Stayers get plumb riled up when folks don't tell them the truth. I think we want stayers here in this town. In this state. Liars mostly move on."

"Those Nicodemus folks are stayers," Josiah admitted. "I've been there, and they have that look of people who are going to fight to the death. I know exactly how that kind of person thinks. That kind of thinking cost me my father and two uncles and my brother. Even knowing that now, we'd do it all over again to keep our homes and our way of life."

"Those niggers ain't got no natural way of life."

"Mebbe so, but they want one. They've got it in their minds they're entitled to one. That's what that town of theirs is all about," Pete Olive said. But then, Olive was a Yankee. A natural born contrarian.

"Ain't gonna be no town by the time we get through," Josiah said coldly.

"Shut up," said Potroff. "There's got to be that town. That's what I'm trying to tell you. We have to have that town to make us the county seat."

"No," said Josiah, "we have to have their vote. There's a difference. Towns don't vote.

People do. There's nothing that says we have to fall all over that town. People are watching that town like it's the new Eden. If we do anything to make it look like we're trying to do the town in, every reporter in the country is going to be out here."

"Are you saying we're going to have to vote right alongside of a nigger?" Clyde McCall's jaw tightened. He spit a stream onto a pile of sawdust, deliberately missing the spittoon.

"Yes. If we expect them to back us," Olive said.

"That's a fact," Potroff said. "Just don't do anything stupid again, Sinclair, like the mess you stirred up about that black woman killing a baby. Don't know who that Sunflower is. Sure as hell don't know how he found out about that story in your newspaper. But he came close to pulling the wrath of God down around us, and we don't want that to happen again."

"This wrangling ain't getting us nowhere," Grant Peabody said. "What you said about the vote — about a town not voting, people being the ones that vote. What do you mean by that, Josiah?"

"Just that. Talbot and everyone that's in cahoots with him think they're just one big happy family, but I'm telling you they're not. It's not human nature. There's plenty of people right there who don't like each other much. It's that way in every town."

"That's a fact," said Potroff. His eyes brightened. "There's folks in every town that'll do someone in for a dime. Never takes much, either. A word here, a word there."

Even as the words left his mouth, he saw Estelle Sinclair step outside the mercantile store and attack a stray chicken with her broom. Damned if the good woman didn't look like she could use a new dress. In fact, she deserved a fine new dress to wear for all her temperance meetings. Moreover, it would be good advertising for all the fine cloth she was selling in her store.

He would see to it that she got one, especially crafted by Miss Dolly Redgrave, who came and went like the pleasant south breeze, blowing here and there. Dolly, who had access to every house in both towns. Pleasant little Miss Redgrave. Nearly white.

Like he said, there were folks like her in every town.

CHAPTER TWENTY-EIGHT

Bethany walked toward the school. Two boys knelt at the side of the livery stable playing marbles. Little girls jumped rope, cracking out an off-beat slapping rhythm, with a double-dare rhyme, and a double-dutch loop that was timed real fine. Taunting, jeering. Her feet twitched as the familiar jingle wafted on the evening air.

Down by the seashore, down by the sea
Johnny broke a bottle and blamed it on me

She stopped and watched. Joyful little black girls who would never know the bonds of slavery. Children changed, brightened up after they came to Nicodemus. They lost their cringiness. Plenty good enough caretaking in their town. Plenty good enough. As much as most white girls had.

Another girl joined the jumper, carefully eyeing the stinging loop before she rushed under the high arc.

I told ma, I told pa,

Johnny got a whipping, ha-ha-ha
How many whipping did he get?
One, two, three . . .

The voices faded as she passed the hotel.

Tom Jenkins stopped playing his banjo long enough to call out a cheery hello when she walked past. Back behind the Browns' soddy LuAnne was scraping bits of flesh off a pile of rabbit skins. Her youngest boy was getting to be a dead aim with his little killing slingshot. He was nearly as good as Jamal Gray. LuAnne would have the skins turned into jackets in no time.

The people, the ebb and flow of people. Struck with wonder, she looked around her as though the scene were surreal, as though she had died and gone to heaven and the streets of Nicodemus were gold-paved and the sod walls of their houses and dugouts were shining with pearls and rubies and she could not, not, not get all of their music out of her head.

I'll fly away, Lord
I'll fly away

Unbidden, her heart thrummed with the tremor she had felt when the first wave of September settlers danced over the rise by the bank of the Solomon.

Coming home to Nicodemus.

She had never felt this way in her life

before and could scarcely keep her feet on the path toward the school. Her head understood joy. Knew what it was. But her careful heart couldn't find the room before. Didn't, couldn't, dasn't. She had always known her place. Now she could not contain joy. It welled up like a spring.

Music was constant, ever-present in Nicodemus. Music had always healed her people's hearts, and now it was breaking down hers.

Tom Jenkins's banjo and plantation songs and drums let loose and all the chanting little black girls clapping out bounce steps. In the evening, after the work was done, old men facing off with clickety-clackety spoons. Bunch of silly young ones on a washboard high, a-whacking out patterns too fast for the eye.

A calling people. Throwing the preacher's words right back at him. Agreeing, smiling at the man. *Amen.* Urging him on. *Send the words right back, brother, with just a little more. Amen.*

A little more religion, if you please, and we'll sway it right back at you with a clap and a shout. Amen. A little, little more right back. Because we know Jesus and you'd better, Brother Silas. You'd better, Sister Mary, or you won't be able to hear our song.

She stopped, radiant in the setting sun, to see if her skin was a new color. She pulled out a tendril of her hair, but it was the same shiny black. Her fingers were still long and thin. She was the same on the outside.

But Jesus had come to her last night. Came in a dream. Just as he had to the three kings who went scurrying off to find him when he was a baby.

Jesus came to her carrying a shining gold pen with a silver feather furl.

The point on the quill was sharp as a dagger, and the ink sparkled with stardust, and he reached for her, and she was so tiny she seemed to rest right on his arm, and she knew, just knew she had looked like that sometime before when she was just a little girl. She knew now he had always meant for her to become Sunflower. To pick up that pen.

A poor little black girl. Seeing darkly. She knew it was just about that time joy became buried so deep in her that only God knew how to drag it back out. But she couldn't remember why. She owned that pen once before. Jesus had given her that pen when she was just a little girl.

"Unnatural. A writing nigger. Causing trouble."

There had been a voice, a strange terrifying voice. She had tagged along with Queen Bess when her mother was out doctoring, and she had heard a white man speak from a far room. After that, she stuffed back joy like it would kill her if she tasted it whole. She gave the pen back to Jesus.

All day she felt the change from the dream. She was no longer afraid to look; the terror she felt when she saw her mother dragged off and the fire, the terrible fire. Her fury when she saw Estelle Sinclair forcing her mother to kneel in manure.

I'm free. Free, she whispered. Joy and pain alike, it didn't matter. Neither one would kill her, and she had always thought they both would.

Jesus had given back her bright gold pen.

Her mother came to Nicodemus because she had read one of Bethany's circulars written by her bright gold pen. And now, the most important newspaper in the state was printing her letters, and blacks and whites alike were making over this Sunflower.

The power. The heady taste of power.

Her mother. She stood dead still. Her heart pounded. Jesus and her dream pen. This was the way her mother felt about her doctoring. Doctoring was what Jesus had handed to Queen Bess.

Bethany sighed. Nicodemus needed the money her own doctoring brought in, because Queen Bess didn't want anything to do with white people. She could dash off opinions with her little gold pen until the cows came home, and it wouldn't bring one cent to the people here in this town. Not one cent. It was still her doctoring money that did them the most good.

She carried a bucket of coal inside the school, then wiped her hands and read some comments McBane had left for her consideration. McBane's immaculate handwriting emulated calligraphy. With his usual precision, he pointed out that he was ill-suited to help the younger children and that, in fact, there were only two children in the whole town who would profit from his advanced instruction.

She tucked a strand of hair behind her ear. He was right, of course. He did a good job of keeping those two children engaged, considering the time he was out of town.

In fact, Nicodemus might as well be an outpost of Topeka since Kulp and McBane came. Seemed like the whole town was coming from or going to Eastern Kansas. Some who had relatives back there spent the winter in Topeka and came back to Nicodemus in spring.

She picked up a copy of the *Topeka Daily Capital* McBane had left for her. She smiled. Too fastidious to underline, he had drawn an arrow on a discarded piece of paper pointing to the article he wanted her to read.

Now that the stream of Exodusters from the South into Eastern Kansas had turned into a flood of threadbare, sickly immigrants overwhelming the state with cries for aid and mercy, their colony was held up as a shining example: "Imitate the plucky settlers of Nicodemus."

Plucky settlers, indeed. The writer made them sound like trick dogs the state had coaxed into performing, when the town actually had three whirling dervishes of black men who could match wits with any white man in Kansas. Maybe the whole nation.

A new letter from Sunflower was taking shape in her mind, when Sonny Rayborn dashed past the doorway. Zach Brown stuck his head inside.

"Mr. Jed's back, Miss Bethany. They's all three back from Topeka."

Buoyed by the statewide reception given Sunflower's letters, Jed and Kulp and McBane had devised an equal rights ticket for township officers with positions divided equally between whites and blacks. Then

Kulp stunned them all by announcing that he personally wanted to take the required census for organizing the county.

Nothing could dissuade him. Not even when Jed pointed out the risks of a Latin-spouting, Shakespeare-quoting black man asking a nest of Missouri bushwhackers if they could read and write.

She remembered Jed warning him. "Half the whites in this county will be out to string you up if you come prying in their personal business, A.T. No one likes census takers even if they're white."

"I'll be just fine," Kulp had said.

"Don't count on it. There was a murder out here. Before you two came. A man from Norton got killed just for helping us get land."

She tucked back the memory and walked outside. The men were bathed in the fading rays of the setting sun. Golden men. Conquering heroes. People flocked around. Gloriana pranced like she was on military review. Kulp and McBane had a new black buggy. They had added gold lettering on the sides advertising their services as attorneys and their land locating business.

Kulp stood up and pumped his fist in the air. "We did it," he shouted. "It's done. Governor St. John has appointed me as the official census taker for the organization of Graham County. And E.P. here will be the temporary county clerk. Stand up, Edward, and take a bow."

McBane rose, removed his derby hat, and smiled at the cheering throng.

After the commotion settled down, Jed and Bethany went inside the schoolhouse. They couldn't stop smiling.

"And your little school, my Miss Bethany, your little school is going to be the site of the election for township officers," Jed told her. "The very first election in Graham County. After A.T. finishes his census showing there's enough legal voters to legally organize Graham County, Governor St. John will designate the temporary county seat. It's going to light a fire under the white folks."

Stunned, she forgot all the layers and layers of protection she always used against this man, like she required voodoo magic to keep him from invading her soul. Clean forgot herself until the words just flew out of their own accord.

"Jed. Do you know what this means? For the first time in the United States — the very first time ever — enough black people have gathered in one place to control votes on issues important to whites. This is the

486

very first time."

She reached for his hands and squeezed them. But when he started to pull her toward him, she tugged away, turned, and walked to her desk. "This election is going to take place here at my schoolhouse?"

"Yes. It's the only place in Nicodemus large enough."

"Then I want everything to look just perfect. In fact, I want this whole town to look spotless. Beyond reproach."

"Well, you've got a whole month. Then as soon as the official announcement of Kulp's appointment as census taker is published in the paper, he's going to begin. And after he completes this census he's going to hand carry the count back to Governor St. John. And then, by God, Graham County will be officially organized, and we won't have to run over to Rooks County every time we turn around."

"And it will be over. All over."

"Not quite," he said dryly. "Actually, then the real fight will be on to select the permanent county seat." He could not have stopped the big smile that crept across his face. "And all the fine, upstanding white people of both Millbrook and Wade City are going to go out of their way to make sure all of us black people know how thrilled they are to have us amongst them. We dey favorites," he mocked. "Sure nuff."

"I don't think these white men are going to like it much, having to come to Nicodemus to elect township officers."

"They may not like it, but if they're smart, they'll show up anyway. And vote the equal rights ticket. If they don't, they can't expect us to vote for their town for county seat." Jed picked up his hat and headed out the door. "I guess I don't have to tell you, we've practically had to tie A.T. down to keep him from floating off into the sky."

As Jed predicted, when they elected officers for Nicodemus Township a month later, Millbrook men came to their town all smiles, offering jobs and complimenting Bethany on the fine school. In fact, those who had intended merely to flatter came away impressed with the neat lessons she had cleverly left on the blackboard. They eyed her hefty pile of books. The Nicodemus women had worked themselves half to death cleaning every building in the town.

Only men participated in local as well as national elections, of course. Women of any race were denied suffrage. It was well known that when females thought about politics, it detoured blood from their uteruses to their brains. Letting women vote would be bad

488

for the country. It would ruin their ability to produce healthy babies.

The equal rights ticket for township officers, sponsored by Meissner and the *Millbrook Wildhorse,* won the election.

Editors of newspapers in neighboring towns were intrigued by the bi-racial composition and the novelty of Kulp's appointment.

"Graham County has a Negro census taker," mocked the editor of a Ness County paper. "We hear it don't suit the white trash much."

While Kulp began taking the census, the county seat fight began in earnest. Meissner charged that a number of Wade City people swore they would die before they allowed a black nigger into their house asking personal questions. The Sinclairs shot right back that Meissner was a damn liar, and they had affidavits to prove it. Which they dutifully printed.

Josiah pointed out that he had come from the South and always treated his blacks with the utmost respect, and in fact it took a Southerner to know and appreciate their worth. Estelle charged that Meissner had never made the acquaintance of a Negro in his life until he came to Graham County, and she assured all her fine, upstanding colored friends that the treacherous citizens of Millbrook didn't plan to have a thing to do with blacks after the county seat election.

One of the upshots of the raging controversy was that men from both Wade City and Millbrook were driving over a couple times a week to hire Nicodemus men.

No accusation of racism was too bizarre to print in the papers.

Bethany sat propped against the trunk of a cottonwood on the south bank of the Solomon. The day before, she and Jed and Kulp and McBane and Teddy had spent a hilarious afternoon poring over a collection of newspapers. They took turns reading the fawning rhetoric, with editors throughout Kansas suddenly discovering all manner of virtue in black people.

On Sunday afternoons the banks of the creek teemed with ambitious little boys trying to catch fish or frogs. If she tried to relax in her own dugout now, she was dogged by people stopping by to ask her advice or chat a moment.

Lulled by the rippling of the silvery cottonwood leaves, her mind drifted, and she fell asleep. She awoke with a start when a horse neighed. She jumped to her feet. She shielded her eyes against the bright sun, recognized the rider, and called out immediately.

"Cedric. I'm over here." She hollered again, hoping he would hear her before he passed out of earshot. She frowned. It was too early for Amity Berlin to deliver, or she would have stayed closer to town.

His horse was sweaty and exhausted. He trotted up, and she flinched at his look of despair. Cedric was a small man with a pinched, thin face that never seemed to tan. It just stayed as white as a dingy sheet. He was a constant worrier, with an annoying mannerism of plucking at his upper lip.

His gentle little wife was one of her favorite patients. She had urged them to get her at once since this was Amity's first baby.

He jumped down from the horse. "The baby's here, but she's dying," he gasped. "Dying. I tried to tell her that son-of-a-bitch was going to kill her."

Bethany's faced tightened with shock. "Who?" But even as she asked the question, she knew, and her stomach plummeted.

"That no good quack, Doc Osborne."

"But she's been my patient. How did he come to see her?"

"She asked. One of the women around

Wade City spread a bunch of lies. Claimed you were using magic and hexes and would cause little babies to go blind if you took a notion. Said you made the mother's blood go bad and crippled the little ones if they didn't suit you. Claimed you left spells in the house and buried stuff to ruin our crops."

Bethany tried to appear calm, but her insides quaked. "We've got to get moving. I need to see what that man's done to her, but I don't know if your horse can stand up to carrying double, Cedric."

"He can. It's only a mile further to go back through Nicodemus. We'll leave this one and pick up two more horses."

"All right. I need to get my bag, and I'll send one of the children for my mother. She's the best person I know of to have around if there's birthing trouble."

The horse's breaths came in harsh bellows by the time they reached the town. Cedric took off at a run toward the livery stable, and Bethany went inside her dugout. She grabbed an old sack and stuffed all the clean towels and blankets she had on hand inside it.

Not knowing what she would find, she went to the hanks of herbs hanging from the walls. She separated some, spread several small cotton squares on the table, and rolled the plants inside. She put them in her main medicine bag and ran outside.

Cedric cantered toward her, holding the bridle reins of a second horse. She mounted without saying a word, and they dashed off toward his homestead.

Bethany caught her breath at the odor when she walked inside. She heard the pitiful mewling sounds of a dying baby and took in the deathly sick smell of the frazzled-out mother. She went to the bed and lifted the hand of the delirious woman, who was so crazed with fever, she wasn't aware Bethany had come into the room.

Cedric had pulled a blanket up to her chin and tucked it around her, but Amity was trembling like she had been thrown into a snowbank. Bethany felt for her pulse. It was weak and erratic.

She reached for the baby lying swaddled on top of the covers and opened the wee girl's eyes. She gazed at the milky pupils. Her heart sank. Both mother and child were dying.

She turned and led Cedric over to a chair next to the bed and forced him into the seat. She placed her hands on his shoulders and begged him to control his harsh sobs long enough to concentrate. "I want you to take this little girl-child to Nicodemus and tell LuAnne I said to find the Alstead woman. She's just had a baby. I want her to start nursing this little one. We must try to save your little girl. My mother will be along shortly."

"I should be here," he said between sobs. "In case something happens. I don't want her to die alone."

Bethany squeezed his shoulder, knowing his dilemma and fearing that, in fact, that was just what was going to happen no matter what she did to prevent it.

"I'm so sorry, so terribly sorry. I'm going to tell you straight off, it's up to God. I'll do my best, but she's very sick and so is the baby."

"She thought she was doing the right thing. Hell of it is, Amity laid awake nights worrying about the best thing for the baby. She was plumb happy with you until folks started putting ideas in her head. Then she got to fretting. Wondering if she shouldn't just stick to her own kind. Her own people, you know."

His tongue was thick with shame as though he couldn't stand to say the words. "I just want you to know, I didn't egg her on. I didn't. But I didn't stop her, neither."

His voice was so low, Bethany had to strain to hear him. "Didn't stop her. Figured the women folks knew more about birthing. But I heard stories when I'd go to town. Doc's whisky mean. And I don't know if anyone's ever seen him sober."

"So I've heard. You don't have to explain. I know the stories that have been going around. But the baby. We've got to get milk for this baby right away. I don't want her to get chilled, and I'm not sure she can stand the ride back to Nicodemus, but I can't help her here. I don't think we have a choice."

In her heart, she feared Amity would die while he was gone and Cedric would never get over it if she did. But she had to decide on the best course of action quickly, or there wouldn't be any hope of saving either the mother or the child.

"We'll wrap the baby up against your chest so she won't jar so much. This baby needs more care than I can give her while I'm tending to your wife. Now open your shirt."

Wordlessly, he complied while she reached into her bag, pulled out some white cotton cloth and began tearing it into strips. "You're going to have to ford the Solomon," she said, "and I don't want to take a chance on you dropping this little one if you need both hands. This will help steady the poor little mite and keep her warm."

She gently picked up the baby girl, then laid her against the man's chest and wrapped the strips around them both, taking care to turn the tiny head to one side. Then she secured the wee bundle with another wide strip. She buttoned his shirt back up, leaving a gap at the collar.

She watched as Cedric swung into the saddle, holding one arm protectively in front of his precious burden. "Tell LuAnne to bring a couple of chickens, so she can start some soup."

He turned awkwardly and gave a little wave to let her know he'd heard, then he kicked his horse into an easy lope and started off across the prairie.

She looked at Amity, closed her eyes in dismay, and steadied herself. She immediately set water boiling and laid aside fresh cloths. She walked over to the bed, then peeled back the blanket from the woman's pain-racked body.

When she saw the damage, her mind quit as if it had been encased in ice. There was blood everywhere. At first she thought the afterbirth had not been completely expelled. Stunned, her hand flew toward her throat as though she could still her pulse.

One glance between the woman's legs and

the open wound told the whole story. Doc Osborne knew nothing. Nothing at all. Amity was a small woman. He had tried to cut an opening big enough. He clearly had either merely heard about this procedure, or didn't know how to sew her back up, or had been too drunk to try.

Then Bethany stared at the gashes on Amity's arms, the bloody crescent of a cup lip. He'd bled her. The bloody butcher had tried to fix this adorable woman by bleeding her. And he didn't know how to do that, either.

Then he had run off.

She shook with rage. Another woman the victim of a dirty, ignorant doctor who'd had his hands God knew where before he stuck them inside poor Amity.

She could not for the life of her think of anything to do. It was as though everything she had ever learned from her mother had vanished. None of her herbs would do a whit of good.

Nevertheless, she picked up a bucket of water sitting beside the stove and poured some into a large kettle. She stoked the fire. She untied her little cloth bundles and spread them out on the wobbly cottonwood table in the center of the room and grabbed three tin cups off a shelf to steep some herbs.

She tossed some dandelion stems into one, and echinacea leaves in another, then hesitated. Nothing would help or even give Amity relief. After she cleansed her, she would apply a compress of usnea lichen, which was the most powerful medicine for wounds she had in her arsenal.

She choked back a hopeless sob, then set her mouth in a grim line. She didn't even have laudanum for Amity's pain.

She set aside a cup for valerian leaves, to help the poor woman get some rest. But knowing her baby had lived would do her the most good. And the fate of the baby was in God's hands, and the women of Nicodemus.

There was a smoke house out back. With any luck, there would be some meat to boil for a strengthening broth. Reluctant to leave Amity's side, she decided to wait until Lu-Anne or her mother arrived.

When the largest kettle was boiling, she threw in a good supply of Kinnikinnick leaves and waited until the water was dark. Then she pulled the pan off to cool, dipped a rag in the mixture, and began to bathe Amity. It would be better if she could manage a sitz bath to reduce the pain and swelling of the woman's swollen, pus-encrusted vulva, but it would be too difficult without help.

She crooned as she worked, and the wounded woman's eyes fluttered open for a moment.

"Good. Good. I need you awake for a few minutes. I have some things I want you to drink."

"I'm sick. So terribly sick. And my baby? My baby?"

"Hush, you're going to be just fine."

"My baby?"

"She's in good hands. The very best of hands. It's a little girl. You're too weak to care for her right now. We've got to take care of you first, so I've sent her back to Nicodemus. Can't think of any people that know more about taking care of little babies than they do."

Amity Berlin closed her eyes. Her lids were blue veined, and there were dark, feverish circles on her cheeks. "I'm sorry," she said weakly. "Sorry I let that filthy old man near me. Sorry I believed all the lies about you."

"Hush. Don't waste your strength. I need to you to swallow some things for me, some teas. Just stay with me. Stay awake long enough for me to get some teas down you.

Hear now? You've got to stay awake long enough for me to fetch them."

Quickly, Bethany rose and carried the wash-pan to the table. She grabbed the first steeped cup of willow bark and echinacea and whirled back to the bed. "Now don't you quit on me. You've got to fight, and I need you to drink this. Right now. Drink every bit of this."

Bethany watched the fluttery little contractions of Amity's throat as she swallowed the tea. She kept talking, talking. "A sweet baby girl," she crooned. "Sweet little baby. You've got a sweet little baby girl to think about."

She started at a noise outside, but kept her eyes on her patient and didn't look up when she heard the door opening. Didn't turn her head until Amity swallowed the last drop. Didn't need to turn around, because when her mother was present it was like the air was charged with an unseen force. Bethany could have been blind, unconscious, paralyzed, or in a coma and still know the minute her mother walked into a room.

Queen Bess did not speak. She was too professional to say anything that would frighten the patient. She slowly walked up to the bedside. She trembled, and her hands tucked beneath her apron started to shake.

Her nostrils were distended from the tension of trying to control her face.

She reached for Bethany's shoulder and gestured at the door. Bethany wrapped the blankets around the woman, sealing in the warmth from the tea. She glanced at her mother, and the two women went outside.

"She won't live," said Bess.

"She must."

"She won't, and we will be blamed."

"But it was that incompetent fool who did this to her. You know that. As many good births as we've had around here, everyone should know that. This is not my fault."

"Folks is going to be plumb tickled to believe the worse," Queen Bess said.

"But why? When did this start? People around here were wishing us the best just a short time ago. Everyone in the country has been watching Nicodemus."

"It worse now because everyone watching us," Queen Bess said. "I didn't come here to be watched. Didn't ask to be watched. Bunch of Northern free-born strutters set us all up to be watched. Running people for office. Stepping too high."

"We can't just let Amity die," Bethany said.

"There's nothing we can do to stop it," Queen Bess said. "Nothing at all."

They went inside. Bethany looked at Amity's colorless face and eased her head up on the pillow. Queen Bess propped her up, and they tried to get the woman to sip a little tea steeped with witch hazel.

"If we could just get her fever down a little, maybe we could get her to swallow."

But the liquid slowly trickled out of Amity's mouth, and they laid her back down; before the hour was up, she died.

Bethany looked at Queen Bess. The two women were paralyzed with fear. Bethany closed her eyes.

Her mother had come into the Berlins' house like a pillar of fire, and Bethany had drawn back from the heat of her black, raging heart. The blue-black coal-fire heat of a race wronged.

Now that heat was replaced with pure fear. Her mother's face was the ashen-gray ghost color of haunts in the night. Dull dry as a scurrying spider. The dead cinder color of a people terrified and hounded.

"Momma?" said Bethany. Her voice trembled, and she reached for the old woman's hand. "Momma?"

Queen Bess turned away.

"See what you done, child? I tried to tell you. See what you done?"

CHAPTER TWENTY-NINE

The women of Nicodemus waited as Cedric Berlin rode up to the schoolhouse. They had heard about Bethany's hasty trip to the man's homestead. Knew it meant trouble.

Cedric dismounted, and LuAnne saw the tiny lump of the swaddled head sticking out of his partially buttoned rough shirt. She ran to him and unwrapped the strips securing the infant.

She froze. The tiny, lifeless body was already turning cold. She gently removed the little baby girl from Cedric's warm chest and pressed the wee, rigid bundle against her bosom. She turned to the women with a small, helpless shake of her head. She prayed for courage. She swallowed and turned back to the stranger, this white man. Not one of their own.

"Mr. Berlin, sir, this little baby girl is dead."

One of the women began keening. The

ancient sound wafted across the prairie.

"Lord have mercy," Patricia Towaday whispered. "He rode all that way with a dead baby."

Cedric Berlin said nothing.

His arms dangled helplessly; his shoulders slumped as he stared at the ground. He glanced at the cold infant in LuAnne's arms, gave his hat a savage tug, climbed back on his exhausted horse, and pounded off toward his homestead.

Jim Black raced to the corral and jumped on his horse without bothering to saddle up. He rode after Berlin, clutching the reins of a spare mount. "Wait," he called. "Wait up."

Berlin slowed, then stopped as Jim rode up.

"Your horse is half dead." Jim's stomach tightened. He wished he hadn't said *dead*. Wished some other word had come to mind. "This one's fresh. Use it. I'll take yours back to the livery stable, and some of our folks will come over to your place to help you."

Berlin nodded, dismounted, climbed on the fresh horse, viciously raked his spurs against its side, and lunged across the prairie.

Bethany and Queen Bess heard him ride

up just as they were closing Amity Berlin's eyes for the last time. They looked at one another helplessly as Cedric stumbled over the threshold.

The news of Amity's death spread at once throughout the white community.

"The black women cursed her. Killed her." The news spread like wildfire. "All their kind has just been waiting for us. Hoping to kill little white children while they're sleeping in their beds."

"A great tragedy has befallen this community," crowed Estelle Sinclair in the *Wade City Chronicle.* It was a great pity, she thought, that they had cried wolf once before when they now had hard facts to back up something so similar to what she had made up. It diluted it somehow.

A young mother and her adorable baby girl were killed through the incompetence and carelessness of ignorant and unskilled women who were called to minister to Mrs. Cedric Berlin after childbirth. The Berlins foolishly chose not to rely wholly on the judgment of our own fine white physician, Dr. Winthrop Osborne. Dr. Osborne has assured us that he had delivered a fine healthy baby to Mrs. Berlin the day before and both were in excellent shape when he left her bedside.

We can only speculate at this point, what would cause Mr. and Mrs. Berlin to turn their backs on their own kind and trust the most personal and holy of all medical events to primitive women who practice the dark arts. This needless tragedy could have been avoided.

"Not true, not true," Bethany whispered as she read the paper. "God in heaven. We do not practice the dark arts. We are not primitive. We do not set out to kill people."

There wasn't a soul in Nicodemus who didn't hear about the editorial. A pall settled over the community. Even the children stayed inside until their mothers chased them out; they sullenly started games they never finished.

On a cloudy night, a week after the article was printed, Jed went in search of Bethany. She had turned her classes over to Earnest Jones and A. T. Kulp and whomever they could round up each day, saying she had to tend to things.

No one had seen her step outside her dugout in broad daylight since the Berlin tragedy. But after sunset, nearly every evening now, she wandered up to the school.

506

Jed was acutely aware of her movements, the clothes she wore, her smile, her quick wit. Before the deaths, for the past month, Bethany had started wearing her hair down. One night she had even dashed under the jump rope and sang out the chants, much to the giddy delight of the older girls.

She changed back after losing Amity and the baby. Changed back like a ghost had crept inside her. She pulled her hair into a tight bun again, and she no longer eagerly set off across the prairie alone with her herb basket.

Jed found Bethany sitting by the window in the pale, white light, gazing at the moon. She turned when he came in, but her face was too shadow-dappled for him to see any expression.

"I came to see if there's anything I can do," he said.

"Nothing you can do and nothing you can say." Her voice was flat, devoid of any emotion. "Momma tried to tell me. Now they're gonna starve us out, or burn us out, or just flat kill us outright. Serves me right for stepping out of my place. For thinking we could be something we're never gonna be. There's just no place on God's green earth where we can live."

He crossed the room and gripped her by

the shoulders. He forced her chin up and made her look at him. "Listen to me, Bethany; there's something you've got to understand. You've believed that if you do the right thing, say the right thing, white folks are going to notice how smart you are. Well, they're not. Most of them are always going to have it in back of their minds that you're a dumb nigger. You can't change that."

"So what's the point? What's the point then in even trying?" Her voice caught. Jed gently smoothed away a tear from her cheek with the tip of his finger.

"I said most of them, not all of them. A few people can see, and they're worth it. That's what keeps me going. The few who can see beyond my skin and look at my heart. Those few people are going to see to it that blacks can hold office and have a fair say in this county. Important people. I believe that. Governor St. John is one of the finest men I've ever met, black or white."

"I don't care."

"Ah, but you do care. You just don't want to face up to everything that's in your heart. That's your trouble. You're going to ruin yourself if you try to keep your heart from beating."

"My heart was just fine a little while back," she said. Her tears overflowed now, and she didn't try to stop them. "For the first time since I was a little girl, my heart was just fine."

"Oh, sweetheart." He pulled her to his chest. "My darling Bethany, surely you know how I feel about you. Don't you know you can trust me? I want to take care of you. Please let me."

To his dismay, she began to sob.

"Don't," she said and pushed him away.

"What's wrong, Bethany? Don't you care for me at all? I think you owe me a bit of honesty. Is there someone else?"

Truth was, he had worried ever since Kulp and McBane came that she would choose one of those fine, quick-witted men. God knew he was resigned to the mystery of soul-matching, the unpredictability of the attraction between men and women. He knew they both admired her, and they brought out her rare streak of humor, which was almost as buried as the rest of her. But he had convinced himself there was no romance there. Perhaps he was mistaken.

"You're right, Jed. I do owe you a little honesty. No, not a little." She stared bleakly at the cold, distant moon. "Complete honesty. And no, there's no one else."

Jed slowly let out his breath.

"All right," she said. "Here's the whole

truth. Unadorned. But I don't think you're going to like it much."

He said nothing and waited, fearful of breaking the spell.

"It's not you. It's men, period. Not just white men but black men, too. You're an educated man. You have to know what has happened to black women. In Africa, women's chastity was honored and understood."

"My God, Bethany, do you think I'm trying to treat you like some octoroon offered in a New Orleans whorehouse? You know I would never do that." He ran his fingers through his hair. She turned and faced the wall, refusing to look at his face.

"I know you wouldn't, Jed," she said tersely. "But I'm trying to make you understand why I don't want to have anything to do with you or any other man."

He started to turn her around, but she kept her back toward him, then swayed against him, reached for his hands. They stood there pressed together, fingers interlaced, his breath harsh against her hair, the back of her neck.

"Jed. It's not you." Her voice trembled as though she could hardly bear to speak the words aloud. "It's not you. But when a woman sees too much, knows too much, especially if she's the wrong age, it does something to her. And I was just a little girl when I started following Momma around. So very, very little."

She shuddered and then became very still. "I helped Momma doctor women who had been raped by white men, and black men, too. Black men who hated themselves and then set out to prove how bad they really were. I heard old white men who came calling on Sundays after church talk about breeding black people like we were a bunch of dogs."

Her fingers tightened against his. A cloud moved over the moon, dimming the outline of the proud little pile of books, the rickety collection of boards set on stumps that served as desks for the children.

"You were never on a plantation," she said flatly. "I heard those fine, white, Christian men talking to Master St. James. Making deals. Money passed between plantations when one had a man that was good stock and the other owned a vigorous woman. Didn't matter if a woman had jumped the broom and loved her own man with every breath in her body. If the master said 'breed,' they had to breed."

She started to shiver, and it took every bit of restraint he could muster to stay quiet.

"I've known women to kill themselves,

Jed, before they would let that happen. Once I even knew a woman who killed her own little girl. Her own baby. Just because she loved her so much and was afraid she would grow up pretty."

Jed set his jaw, vowing like a lover, not a lawyer, that he would make this town safe for all the women. Not just Bethany — all of them. Cold logic turned to hot fury.

Once the floodgates were open, the words jerked out of Bethany in tear-laced spasms. "You're wrong in thinking I just want to fit in with white people. . . . God knows, I don't . . . I don't." She drew a deep breath. "There was a special kind of meanness to those old white masters. They had to see our women as loose and whores to work their evil."

Her heart beat like a wounded bird's, and his broke with sorrow for all of them.

"And the white mistresses, they were half crazy with hate. Why wouldn't they be? Seeing their husbands and sons slip off to the slave quarters. Seeing their own house servants gloat and smile, knowing their husbands loved them better. Why wouldn't they be crazy? Why wouldn't they be mean?"

"That's white men, Bethany. White men."

She yanked her intertwined fingers out of his and turned around. She poked at a tendril that had strayed from her school-marm bun.

"Black men have been ruined," she said flatly. "Some of them would just slink away and let white men do whatever they wanted to the women. They had no way to intervene. How could they? They were powerless. They were beat to death if they tried."

"That's not true. We're not ruined. Not all of us," Jed said. "You know how many fine men have flocked to this town."

She looked into his stunned, gray eyes. "I apologize," she whispered. "Truly I do. It was uncalled for to lump all black men together. All of you here in Nicodemus are good men. All of you. I just can't bear to see anything go bad for any of you. Teddy, Kulp, McBane, you. All the others. I just don't want it all to go bad on account of me."

"Bethany, what happened to you about a month ago? You changed. There's no way you would have even talked to me like this before then. I may not like what I'm hearing, but at least you're trying to make me understand. I don't want you to change back now. Please don't change back and shut me out."

She looked down and bit her lip. "There's something I'm doing that just Teddy knows about. It was really, really good for me. I thought it was good for all of us. Good for Nicodemus. But the wrong people started noticing us. I can't talk about it right now," she stammered. "Maybe never."

"All right." He carefully, tenderly, reached out and delicately touched her on her lips, slowly tracing the line as she shook like a fragile willow twig. Was accepting love going to be so very hard for this very difficult woman?

"All right. But I would like to know if there's anything, anything at all, any steps I could possibly take to win your affection? To show you how much I care?"

"Yes."

He blinked in surprise.

"If I haven't scared you off. I would be willing to try," she said shyly, her eyes cast down toward the floor. "What I'm trying to say is . . . I would like it very much, if we started keeping company."

Jubilant, he squeezed her hand.

"But if you are so inclined, I would like a proper courtship."

Giddy with delight that he had even coaxed out a teensy flash of her quiet humor, he started to respond in kind, but then when she raised her eyes and he saw her tears, he knew there was not a trace of levity in her mind. He took a deep breath and cast about for the proper words to say in this absurdly peculiar situation.

"Miss Bethany, actually, one of the reasons I came over here tonight was to inform you of my intentions to call on your mother and beg her permission to begin courting you."

It was a bald-faced lie, of course. He would just as soon ask a black bear for permission to take away its cub.

Bethany nodded. Regally, like this was to be expected. Encouraged that he had stumbled onto the fitting response, he decided he had better nevertheless get the hell out of there before he made a mistake.

"I wish you good evening, and, of course, I would like the honor of escorting you home." *As though she didn't walk herself home every day of the world,* he thought wryly. *As though she didn't roam half the countryside all on her own.*

"Thank you, Mr. Talbot, but I prefer to wait until you've spoken to my mother."

What the hell, he wondered. Where had she gotten such ideas? Had to come from all the novels she read. Then he was pierced to the core of his being with a flash of insight. She yearned for a tradition. Something more than just jumping the broom. Some sort of code honoring black women.

Some sort of ritual.

This was the best she could do. She was raiding another culture, and an archaic one at that, because her own had been destroyed. There was a defiant tilt to Bethany's chin, and although her eyes were clear now, he knew he was looking at a woman who could not take one more blow. His little willow twig would snap in half.

He kissed her hand, tipped his hat, and left. Tomorrow he would ride out to see Queen Bess.

Won't that be a deal, now, he thought gloomily as he walked toward his soddy. *Won't that be a deal.*

Three days later, Bethany walked over to Cedric Berlin's homestead. She found Cedric sitting on a stump in the sunshine, rubbing a mixture of tallow and beeswax into a set of harnesses.

He nodded as she came up. He looked her over, carefully and impersonally, as she stood rigidly in the noonday light, but he did not speak.

"Mr. Berlin, I came over here to see if there is anything I can do for you."

"No ma'am, there's not."

"And there's something important I want to ask you. Do you blame me or my mother for your wife's death?"

He set the harness aside and rigidly stared across the prairie, like he was being forced to look at sights he didn't want to see. He placed his hands on his knees. "You've seen the editorial in the *Wade City Chronicle,* then?" he asked.

"Yes, I have. I want to know if you're behind it?"

"No ma'am, I'm not. I've been thinking of nothing else ever since it came out. All kinds of people are asking me if I believe you and your mother killed my wife and my little baby girl."

"Do you?" she persisted.

"No, I don't. And I'm going to tell that lying son-of-a-bitch Sinclair so. He and that no-count woman of his probably won't print it, so I'm going to tell Meissner, too. He'll print the truth. Then I'm going to write to the *Topeka Daily Capital.*"

Tears welled up in Bethany's eyes. "I'm so terribly sorry. Believe me."

"I don't blame you or your mother for what happened. The thing I had to get settled in my mind was, could someone else have done better? And I don't think they could. That's the point. Osborne had done too much damage already."

"Way too much damage. Way too much."

"I lost my father and my brother in the war." Cedric propped his elbows on his knees and stared at the ground. His head drooped; his elbows stuck out from his folded-over body. "Amity lost people, too. That's one of the reasons why we came here. We thought it would be easier where the country looked different. Maybe it would make people think different."

He rose to his feet and looked blindly at the sun.

"Didn't happen. None of it happened. Worse here than it was back home. Lost my wife. The baby we should have had. People are just the same. No matter where. But there's one thing that's different out here. Black folks are trying to make their own way."

Bethany hid her hands in the folds of her dress and worked the cloth back and forth between her fingers. She waited for Cedric to go on.

"For some reason or another, the whole state is watching Nicodemus. If your people can't make a living here, if you can't make a life here, if things don't work for you here . . ."

His voice broke then, and his shoulders shook as he started to cry. Bethany yearned to reach out and comfort him.

He wiped his arm across his face and got himself back under control. "If your town don't make it, it will mean that it was all for nothing. My people died; their people died. All for nothing. Over a half million, I hear. Over a half million."

The sun shone on her face, warming her, warming her, and she knew she was hearing the truth. People wanted Nicodemus to succeed, not because they just loved Negroes — in fact, most of them didn't — not because of the kindness of their hearts. They wanted this because it would mean that all those poor soldier boys, both Union and Confederate, had not died in vain.

They actually cared and believed in what Lincoln had said when he prayed over the battlefield. If the war wasn't sanctified, wasn't hallowed by something good coming out of it, then it would mean their uncles', their fathers', their brothers' blood had drained into the dirt for nothing.

Just nothing at all.

And the good that had to come out of it, had to come from their little town. Folks didn't want it to get squashed.

Nicodemus.

That evening she sat outside her dugout until the moon rose high and white and looked at the woman in the moon that she had first spotted when she was just a little girl. Long before she knew about the man in the moon. It was a cool, clear night, and stars sparkled in the sky.

Inspired by Cedric's courage, she knew she could live with her fears. She could take it. It wasn't going to kill her. She rose, lit her kerosene lamp, removed a fresh sheet of the vellum stationery that she kept pressed between two books, and began the next letter from Sunflower.

As usual, she worked out the first draft on a tattered piece of Meissner's discarded misprints and labored over the words for an hour. When she was finally satisfied with the tone, she carefully copied it onto her good paper. She wiped away a tear when she re-read the words of her last paragraph explaining how Nicodemus's success would give meaning to the war.

She gave the letter to Teddy the next day.

That night, there was a meeting, and they gathered around the central campfire to hear Reverend Brown speak. He began with dark, haunting psalms before he even mentioned the deaths that were hovering over their little community.

Setting the stage, thought Bethany, with a

bleak smile. *Wanting to remind us that others have suffered also. More than my people, or maybe just like my people. That we are not alone. We have never been alone.*

Dolly Redgrave sat toward the back of the gathering. She eased away from the circle while the group concentrated on Reverend Brown. In the daytime, there were always too many children around for her to get into Bethany's house. Then, too, there were the unexpected comings and goings of Queen Bess.

She sneaked into Bethany's dugout while everyone was clapping and carrying on and began riffling through books and materials.

She could not read, but the Sinclairs and Aaron Potroff eagerly pored over anything with writing she had taken from other houses. She took a long time poking around all the little bundles of herbs. She noticed the fine paper between the two books and turned all the sheets over. They were blank. Nevertheless, couldn't hurt to take a couple.

She had turned to leave when she saw a scrap of paper lying in the bin containing hay cats and coal. She picked it up and turned it over. The page was covered with writing on both sides. There wasn't another place to put a single word. She guessed that was the only reason it had been thrown away to begin with. She folded it and put it in her pocket.

Tomorrow when she went to Wade City she would give the wrinkled piece of newspaper and the two blank sheets of the fine stationery to Aaron Potroff.

Teddy didn't like being out at night. But the train carrying the mail only came once a week, and he wanted to post Bethany's letter. He was a poor rider at best. Despite the reputation mules had for being surefooted and sensitive to dangers, sometimes he swore Sherman was the dumbest beast God had ever created.

There was a half moon, layered by clouds, and the stars were cold and distant. There was a natural cave up by the creek where some of the folks from Nicodemus stopped to spend the night. He rested there. He let Sherman graze, then dozed off himself.

He had been asleep for a long time when a sound jarred him awake. A sound or a feeling or a breath or a night bird or maybe just a deep knowing in his bones. All he really knew was that he woke up colder than he had ever been in his whole life. Cold, with his skin prickling and hairs rising on his arms. Cold, with his gut cramping in sheer terror.

One by one, they slipped out from the trees lining the Solomon. When he was able to breathe again, he couldn't speak. Couldn't scream.

The hooded men surrounded him.

"Y'all wouldn't be up to no good, now would you?" one taunted. "Ferrying some fancy words from that little trouble-making nigger wench?"

Still he did not speak.

"I'm talking to you, nigger."

Please deliver me, he prayed silently. *Please, God. Deliver me. Please, please spare me.*

"Boy, I'm talking to you," the man yelled.

Teddy knew he had heard that voice before, but he also knew it didn't matter. Nothing he could say or do would help.

The man who had been doing the talking suddenly slammed his fist into Teddy's face, and he felt the bones in his old nose crunch. He started to lose consciousness from the excruciating pain.

"No, don't make him pass out. We want him to remember this."

They dragged him over to a cottonwood tree and looped a noose-ended rope over the branch. Two men hoisted him up and pulled the rope down right over his head. Another man walked up and yanked down his pants, then pulled his knife from his pocket. His laughter echoed through the still, cold night.

"Well now, boys, these here aren't hardly worth messing with. Always wanted to see those huge black balls folks keep talking about, but these here is no bigger than teensy little old shriveled up black walnuts."

"Don't do that," a man said abruptly. "Don't want no part of this."

"Turning nigger lover on us? Getting soft?"

"Not getting soft. The coon needs killing, all right. We've got to stop these letters. But I won't go along with the other. It's not right."

"But hanging is?"

"Hanging is understandable. This other isn't. Makes us look like perverts. Makes people too mad."

"He's got a point."

"No, he ain't." Another man stepped forward, pulled out his knife, and ran the blade across his thumb. It was plenty sharp enough to cut two swift slits in an old man's scrotum.

Plenty sharp enough for old, thin black skin. Plenty sharp enough.

Teddy cried to heaven, but there was no one around to hear on earth who really gave a damn about an ancient black man whose days were numbered anyway.

The man who had lobbied for a simple hanging and not the other wanted to leave him decent. The debate was short and swift, but he won, so they clumsily tried to pull the pants back up while holding Teddy in the air. They knotted the frayed rope back around his waist. Teddy's eyes dulled with pain. They kept holding him. Not a single person wanted to be the first to let him go.

Sensing this, the man who had done the cutting decided it was just his luck that he had to take charge of everything. He stepped forward. "Do you have any last words, nigger?"

"Yes." Pain closed over Teddy like a curtain. His life was ebbing so fast that in a few minutes a hanging wouldn't be necessary. But he managed to force out the words that would haunt them for the rest of their lives. "Yes. You can kill me, but you can't kill all of us."

Enraged, the man who had done the cutting knocked the others away. He watched with satisfaction as Teddy Sommers's neck snapped.

Then they started toward the saddlebag lying beside his bedroll.

"Might as well take all this with us. Let

Potroff decide what he needs. Hard telling what all is in here."

"Just leave the note on that fancy sheet of paper and the other one with all the scribbling like we were supposed to. Tuck them in his pocket, so the wind won't get them. Soon as we're finished here I'll take the other note on to that nigger-loving editor's place."

The man holding the saddlebag opened the flap. "There's a letter in here. Might be some cash in it."

"Leave the letter. Leave the saddlebag."

They turned and looked at the man who had tried to stop the castration.

"Folks don't take kindly to messing with the mail."

Norvin Meissner discovered Teddy's body. No one saw the person who tacked the note to his door sometime during the night.

He read: *Go to the south bend of the Solomon. There's a surprise waiting for you.* What a waste of quality stationary!

Curious, he rode out at once.

At first, he didn't recognize the old man swaying from the branch of the cottonwood tree. Silver leaves dipped and rippled in the breeze. His eyes played tricks. He thought Teddy Sommers's slight black body was a dead, withered branch that had been broken off and set to dangling by the vicious prairie wind.

He rode closer, and his horrified eyes were telling him true now. He stopped, paralyzed like he had been struck by a rattler. Then he moved forward because he had to. His hands trembled as he reached for papers protruding from his friend's shirt pocket. There were two sheets. One, of creamy vellum contained the following note:

Tell the nigger bitch this is what comes of troublemakers and friends of troublemakers. Sunflower will soon be as dead as he is.

Stunned, he unfolded the other piece of paper and recognized one of his misprinted pages. He was still sending ruined paper to the children of Nicodemus so they could practice math problems. He recognized Bethany Herbert's elegant hand. Slowly he read the draft of a letter addressed to the editor of the *Topeka Daily Capital.* There were cross-outs and corrections, but there was no doubt about the content.

Bethany was the mysterious Sunflower. They had all assumed it was a man, but it wasn't.

He cut down Teddy's body, easing the fall, and draped the old man across the back of his mule. He placed Teddy's bedroll and saddlebag on the back of his own horse and went back to Millbrook. Reverently, he laid Teddy on his bed, then set off to tell the people of Nicodemus.

On the way, he saw Jed heading across the prairie on Gloriana. Meissner called to him, then kicked his horse into a canter.

Jed's face became corpse-still when Meissner told him about the murder.

Meissner removed his hat and fanned his face, then told Jed that Teddy had been killed because of the letters he was carrying. "Bethany wrote them, Jed. She's Sunflower. There's a letter in Teddy's saddlebag addressed to the editor of the *Topeka Capital*."

Jed gripped the pommel on his saddle so tightly the veins on his knuckles seemed about to pop out. "She can't be."

"You had no idea? I didn't, either. It's true. It's Miss Bethany, all right. I know her handwriting very well and so do you." He reached down into his saddlebag. "Here's the note that was on Teddy, written on fancy paper. Here's a piece of my newsprint that she wrote on, too. You'll recognize the words, Jed. There's a letter from Bethany addressed to the *Topeka Daily Capital* in Teddy's mail bag. What you do with all this is up to you, but I thought someone from

528

Nicodemus should have it."

A vein throbbed in Jed's jaw as he read the vicious note. His shoulders slumped. He nodded at Meissner and tugged at his hat in wordless thanks, then abruptly kicked his horse into a wild gallop and rode off to fetch a wagon to bring home the body of one of the finest men he had ever known.

The day was cold and without color. Bethany wished for one tree, one bird singing, one flower, to honor Teddy's life. But the prairie was bare and without sound.

The women's grief smashed their chests. As they washed Teddy's body and prepared it for burial, tears flowed down their cheeks.

"I'm going home," Sister Liza Stover said when she heard of Teddy's death. "Going home to Kentucky where at least we knows everyone hates us. We knows how to act to keep them from killing us. Can't take this anymore of having folks pretend to be our friends, then laying in wait for us. What did this poor old man do to anyone?"

Bethany stared at her with empty eyes. She had loved this man. This tiny wee elf of an old, shrunken black man who believed that life would be better in Kansas. Had honest to God believed he was leading them all to a land of milk and honey. Was just trying to help them.

She tenderly reached for his eyelids again. There had been no one to close them after his death, and by the time they collected his body, his eyes just wanted to stay open. They had tried just about everything to keep them closed, but nothing worked.

"Won't be any better back there," said Lu-Anne. "Folks hated us there, too."

"No, she's right," said Gertie Avery. "Back there we weren't all the time trying to fool ourselves. We were smarter back there."

There was a stir at the back of the room. Queen Bess walked in. Her face a fierce, shiny ebony mask, her head covered by her snow-white turban, her dress protected by an impossibly white apron. Funeral clothes somehow, despite the connection to slavery. Honoring the dead with exquisite cleanliness.

She held her hands quietly in front of her. Seeming to glide, she moved forward, saw Teddy's terrified, open eyes, and swiftly reached into the bag hanging from her side.

She closed one eye and rubbed a compound into it, then did the same to the other eye. Without speaking to any of the women gathered, she walked over to a collection of rags and clothes hanging from a small twig pounded into the dirt wall and tore off a strip. She went back and lifted Teddy's head and wrapped the cloth around the eyes.

"They'll stay if we leave them that way for a while. Won't take long," Bethany whispered to Gertie.

Still Queen Bess did not speak. Then suddenly the air was rent with a wild keening as the old woman threw back her head, splitting the prairie with a new sound. Different even from the anguished cry of mothers forced to leave their dead children along a lonely trail. Different from the Indian women viewing their dying warriors killed in their last wild sallies to save their tribes from the incursion of white settlers.

Different because it embodied the loss of hope of people everywhere. It pierced the hearts of all who heard it because they knew now how much better off they had been before.

Before hope.

Queen Bess's wail canted off the walls. Even the sod was not enough to absorb the sound, which was close to madness. Their souls trembled with fear before the helpless rage of this strong, fine woman who had always known what to do before as surely as if she were God Almighty.

A woman who didn't know nothing now. Same as they didn't.

This anger was a new feeling and threatened to send them spiraling toward the sun or to grab knives and axes and charge across the prairie in search of the terrible men who had done this ghastly thing to this wee, gentle little man, who was as innocent as a cricket.

No one tried to quiet her. The menfolk rushed into the soddy. Seeing Teddy all laid out, Jed sobbed openly. All the men's despair went beyond their grief for a man. It was their dashed hopes for the Promised Land, the victory forever to be denied.

Reverend Brown's shoulders shook, and no one could tolerate the smell already coming from the body.

"It's time," Jim Black said abruptly.

"His eyes," Bethany protested. "We want to wait till his eyes stay closed. Like they're supposed to."

Reverend Brown nodded.

An hour later, they loaded Teddy onto a single board, an old elm plank that had been used to make one of the benches in the schoolhouse, for he was even to be denied the use of one of his own coffins. Every one he ever made had sold at once. To the white folks.

Teddy's suit had been sponged off, his shirt washed. Bethany used strips of bandages to tie him onto the plank. She neatly arranged his hands and combed his hair. When they removed the cloth from his eyes, the lids stayed shut.

They trudged out singing. Gertie Avery's voice rose in supplication. The wailing mourners called the death dirge from one person to another.

A sweet breeze blew, rippling the grass, sending little showers of insects fleeing before their feet.

Reverend Brown opened his worn Bible and proceeded to read the black, grief-filled words from Psalm 22, " 'My God, my God, why have you forsaken me?' "

He had just reached the part about packs of dogs closing in and being surrounded by gangs of evildoers, when he saw people in the distance.

Two wagons were coming across the prairie. Reverend Brown stopped his sermon as they pulled up. The occupants were all white people, and he watched solemnly as Meissner hopped down. Cedric Berlin followed, then Betty and Donald Hays. There were others following on foot. Bethany recognized most of them as people she had helped.

The people of Nicodemus stood silent and unyielding. Reverend Brown's face was still and harsh as he looked at them hard. "This is a private ceremony," he said.

CHAPTER THIRTY

Norvin Meissner paused in the midst of the editorial he was writing. The mid-day sun scalded the parched earth, and the hot air pushed ahead by the dry, restless wind knocked a tumbleweed down what passed for a street in Millbrook. It caught against the base of the town well and hung there a moment before ricocheting on toward nowhere.

He glanced outside, then closed his eyes to shut out the sight of the timbers supporting the pulley that lowered the bucket. For the past week now, his stomach churned whenever he noticed any limb, crosspiece, beam in a house — anything at all — that would support the weight of a hanged man.

Anger was not new to him. But rage was. Cold fury was. A hundred times a day he saw Teddy Sommers's face before him.

The prowling wind shut out sounds, so he didn't hear the three men approach. Jed,

Kulp, and McBane appeared in the doorway like apparitions from a bad dream. None of them wore their lawyering suits. They all had pistols strapped to their sides. Kulp and McBane now rode horses they had acquired in Eastern Kansas. Not the equal of Jed's Gloriana, of course, but right decent horse-flesh for these parts.

Jed nodded curtly as they walked inside. Meissner's freckles darkened against his bleached skin.

He didn't speak, didn't move. Wished he didn't have to breathe.

The black men did not even bother to greet him. They just stood there silently; a whole world and a whole race apart.

He waited.

"We've come to ask for your help, Norvin," Jed said.

"Of course, whatever I can do." He expelled his breath in a gush, then trembled with eagerness.

Jed walked over and picked up the editorial, read it, then looked at him soberly. "This was going to be the first step. I see you've already taken it."

He nodded, his eyes wet with sympathy. "I mean every word of it."

"Here's the second step. Brother Kulp here is going to finish this census. And we're going with him to every single house — black and white — until he gets his work done. I want you to round up three white men from Millbrook to go with us. There's going to be a little delegation accompanying A.T. every step of the way."

"Three?" Meissner smiled for the first time since the men had walked through the door. "Three? I can assure you that half the town would go if you'd just ask."

They stopped a couple of miles west of Nicodemus.

"You two go on," Jed said, with a sad glance in the direction of Queen Bess's soddy. "I'm going to see how Bethany's mother is doing."

"Hate to see you go off by yourself, Jed."

"I'll be fine."

Kulp and McBane looked at each other, uneasy over leaving Jed unprotected, then nodded and rode in silence toward Nicodemus. Even Kulp, who normally talked everyone's leg off, had been knocked voiceless by Teddy's death.

If the nightriders had killed anyone else, the colonists' response would have been pure undiluted anger. But by killing Teddy, the devils had tamped down their rage with a blanket of grief so heavy the whole community had nearly stopped breathing. Like a widower who has lost his beloved after a brief, wild marriage, it was as though the town had lost its will to live.

Queen Bess sat outside. Listlessly she watched Jed dismount from his fancy horse. She stared at the prairie. He waited. She finally favored him with a look.

"Miss Regina Marie. I've come to ask your permission to court your daughter."

"She no good to you now. She dead." Her voice was hollow. Hard.

Jed flinched. "No, she's not. I'm not going to let that happen."

"Huh. She don't move. Won't talk. It done."

He removed his hat and ran his hand over his hair. He looked away in despair but made no attempt to hide the moistness gathering in his eyes.

Queen Bess's voice was thick, fog heavy. "She was just barely here anyway, you know. Before, I mean. Just barely. Not no good for nobody now. Tried to fool me into thinking she was a doctoring woman. Tried to fool herself. But I knowed better. She ain't had the call. She just smart. Took her a long ways, though. A right far piece, her being so smart," she said wistfully.

"Do I have your permission?" Jed asked

again, sharper this time. His mouth tightened with reproach. He couldn't stand to hear another word against his beloved. And from Bethany's own mother, at that. "Your permission to court her is all I want from you right now."

"Why?"

"Because having your blessing is important to your daughter. Your daughter, Mama."

Queen Bess sorrowfully gazed at the horizon, trying to make sense of the emptiness all around her. "She dead, I tell you. Same as. Warn't like she was going to make you no decent wife, no how. Filled with fancy ideas that warn't never going to do nobody no good. What you want with her anyway?"

Jed knelt down and reached for Queen Bess's hands. He gripped them tightly and forced the old woman to look at him. "I'm begging you, Regina Marie. Begging you. I want your permission to marry your daughter, and I want you to help me get her back." His voice broke. "She's the only woman I'll ever love."

"Well now, ain't that sweet?" Queen Bess absently shooed a fly away from the cloth covering her latest batch of vinegar. Clearly put out at being subjected to such nonsense from this fancy-mouthed colored man.

But her lip quivered. "Court her! Like she some fine white lady with slaves gathered around fanning her to keep off the flies."

He stared up at her mutely. Then Queen Bess began to sob. She pulled her hands away from Jed's and pressed them against her face. Jed put his arms around her. She cried against his shoulder until she was overcome with dry heaves.

"Help me, Mama. Help me. We can't afford to lose her. Neither one of us."

"She quality folk, sure enough." Queen Bess sniffed. "Yes, Mr. Jed, you can go a-courting. If you going to act like she's quality. She real special, you know."

Jed stood. "I know, Mama. God, yes, I know that."

Queen Bess sat up straighter.

"Then I also want you to trust me one last time with something else."

"To do what?"

"To obtain justice, by God."

She shivered when she looked at his steely, gray eyes, the blood of his warrior ancestors coursing through his veins. Done with words. Spear-ready to do whatever it would take.

"You going to go off and hang someone?"

"Yes and no," Jed said. "Not personally,

I'm not. But we're going to see to it that Kulp completes his census so we can organize this county. Then we're going to track down every single man that was involved in Teddy's murder and hang them legally by Graham County's own laws. We're going to show people that the law will apply to everyone. Black and white."

"Never has."

"This is the town and the state and the time," Jed said. "Teddy's murder is all over the papers. People care."

"White folks?" she scoffed.

"Yes. Some of them. They may not know all the details, but Brother Kulp wrote an editorial for *The Colored Citizen* right away. How the white people came for Teddy Sommers."

"Do you know their names?"

"Not yet. Ultimately, we're going to find out Potroff was behind it, of course. But he always has someone else do his dirty work. That goes without saying."

"I heard about the fancy paper the note was writ on. Heard those letters all those white folks back in Topeka was making over was my daughter's doing."

"How did you hear?"

"Patricia come over yesterday. She the one what said. She knowed I'd be taking it hard.

Teddy killed is hard enough. Knowing Bethany might have caused it 'bout to do me in. Can't think of nothing else now. Knowing it was my own daughter's words what got him hung like some old hog."

"Don't blame Bethany," Jed said. "We know she was betrayed by one of our own."

"Who?" she said. "Someone from Nicodemus? Who would be so mean?"

"We're sure it was Dolly," Jed said evenly. "Because she's gone. Packed up her things and left the same night Teddy was killed. Wouldn't make sense for her to do that unless she was afraid to stay here."

"She take her children?"

"No. Just her sewing things. In fact, that's how we knew she had just left instead of something happening to her."

"Her."

"Yes, her. What kind of woman would run off from her own children?" he blurted. He slapped his hand against his thigh whip-crack sharp, and Queen Bess jumped.

"She mean as a snake."

"Yes, maybe so. But she's gone, and we'll never find her. We can't do a thing about it. We'll never be able to bring her to justice now," he said bitterly.

Queen Bess lifted her head, and her face smoothed into an inscrutable mask.

"Don't fret yourself none about that little high-yeller girl," she said.

After Jed left, Queen Bess stared at strands of gray-white clouds dripping from the sky like streaky foam from a mad dog's mouth. She shivered from the ever-present wind that kept pushing, pushing at the edges of her soul.

She looked for Jesus in the clouds. Any sign at all to pull her back from the next step.

Jesus wasn't in the clouds. He wasn't in the swaying grass.

His voice didn't sing through the trees like it did in Kentucky, because there weren't any trees. His face wasn't on the water, because there wasn't any water for him to stir.

Warn't no Jesus here in Kansas.

She gathered power to her. Her mother had taught the ways, and her mother before her. They knew it was against the law, but it didn't make them no never mind. Didn't her, neither.

She had never used them before. Hadn't needed to and hadn't wanted to. She had belonged to Jesus.

Before.

Jed had asked her to trust him to do

something about the white men, and she did. He had the look. But wasn't nothing that man could do about Dolly. He said so himself. It was up to her to bring that spiteful little bitch to justice.

She rose and went inside. She went to the shelf that held all the herbs and healing medicines she had brought with her. She had never taught Bethany all she knew. Never wanted her daughter to know the dark ways. She reached for the tattered, black, silk handkerchief.

She carried it to the table. She laid it there, then sat heavily in her chair staring at it. Slowly she untied the knot.

It was difficult. Her hands trembled. The knot was hard, resistant. It took her a long time. She opened the square and looked at the cherished elements within. She picked up a root and began.

On a street in New Orleans, Dolly Redgrave stopped pinning up the hem of a white woman's dress and stared at her arm. There were small, black splotches like large freckles on her skin. Her fine, fine skin. Nearly white. Everyone said so. A week later they had spread to the rest of her body until she looked like a soiled Holstein.

In a mere month's time, she was as black as Satan's fiddle.

■ ■ ■ ■

"If it's just the same to you, Brother Jed, I'd just as soon you and your merry band of men stay hidden," Kulp said as he, Jed, McBane, and the three white men from Millbrook rode up to a soddy.

They knew it was occupied by a half-starved white family who could neither read nor write. One of the sons was said to be touched in the head. He would be marked as "idiotic" on the new census form just rolled out that year. In the meantime, Kulp was just concerned with tallying the male voters in the county.

"Understood." Jed grinned. "No point in scaring these poor folks half to death."

He waved for the men from Millbrook to stay back. No doubt the family had already been brainwashed by the propaganda rolling out of Wade City and would take little comfort in seeing strangers of any race.

"They probably expect us to murder them in their beds," Jed muttered.

"It would be one less white family to contend with," McBane said.

Jed looked back at their neighbors, hoping they had not overheard. He studied the homestead. It looked safe. There were no outlying buildings.

"Everything looks clear for you to do your work, A.T. Fire one shot if anything goes wrong." He gestured to McBane to follow him back to where the Millbrook men were hidden.

Kulp trotted down the incline toward the soddy. A little boy saw him coming, dropped his bucket, and ran screaming toward the house. Seconds later his mother appeared in the doorway, took one look, then started to shove against the rickety, half-askew door.

"Ma'am," Kulp called sharply. "Please do not be afraid. I'm simply here to take the census so we can organize the county."

She stepped outside, shaking uncontrollably, and her terrified little boy clung to her thigh. An old, yellow mongrel dog growled, hair stiffening as it carefully eased along the ground on its belly toward Kulp.

"The dog, madam," he said quietly. "Please call off that dog."

"Rufus," the woman said sharply, never dropping her gaze from Kulp's face. "Quiet down, boy."

The dog laid its head on his paws and lay watching, watching and whimpering.

"I just need to ask you a couple of questions," Kulp said. "That's all. I'm the official census taker. We must do this to get this county organized. It's the law. It won't be necessary for me to come inside."

She was barefoot, clad in faded calico, and her skimpy hair looked like dried, moldy moss. Veins stuck out like dead earthworms on her brown, cracked feet.

"Don't know nothing 'bout no politics," she said, her eyes sparking with anger, her arms folded across her chest. "Don't much care if this godforsaken county ever has a county seat. Don't care what you pay me, neither. Just want you folks to leave us alone."

"Madam, I can assure you, my purpose here today is not to engage you in a political debate or to try to influence your vote on the location of the county seat. All I want to know is, do you have a husband? Is he over twenty-one? And do you have sons who can be counted as eligible voters? That's all."

She peered at him suspiciously. "That's all?"

"Yes. Later this year, if this county gets organized we will take a federal census. Then someone will be asking you a whole passel of questions."

"My husband's off working on the railroad."

Kulp made a note on his form. "And your sons?"

"Junior's just sixteen." She looked down, reluctant to tell this black man that her boy wasn't quite right. It warn't natural to have some nigger come poking around when her man was away no how. Let alone a smart one. "Willy here is seven. I ain't got no girls."

"Thank you, ma'am," Kulp said warmly. He smiled. "That's all the information I need."

He walked over to Gloriana, picked up the reins, and started to mount. Suddenly he stopped and walked back, his hat still in his hand.

"Mrs. Sungar? What did you mean when you said, 'No matter what you pay me'?"

"Why, to vote for your town for the county seat. Don't care if you pay us twice as much as the other one. Ain't going to take no money for a vote. Irwin done told that other fellow so, too."

"What other fellow?"

"That Potroff fellow."

CHAPTER THIRTY-ONE

Bethany looked around her vacant classroom. Soon they would have to resume lessons. Move on. The room looked old somehow. Abandoned. A mouse peeked out from the coal bin. Dust motes hung heavily in the evening air.

With one arm she hugged the remainder of her precious vellum paper and envelopes against her chest. In the other hand, she carried a little stick of cedar she had snatched from the campfire. A boy had stripped the branches from a tree growing on the bank of the Solomon. The colonists rationed the cedar, adding just a few twigs to the main blaze each evening because they treasured the odor.

She went inside and walked over to the stove. She opened the grate and reverently laid the precious cedar inside. A burnt offering. Her hand trembled.

A last purging. Her dreams, her soul. She

would feed in the paper one sheet at a time and pray for forgiveness with each one. Pray for God to remove all vanity, all will. Pray that he dampen her fiery core. Pray to become slave dumb.

It was fitting somehow that this ritual take place at the school where her hopes had risen every morning, borne upward on the black smoke arising from the stovepipe. A vision of little black children soaring, soaring to the clouds, the sky, up to the heavens.

She reached into the box beside the stove and picked up some hanks of twisted prairie grass. She tossed them into the stove, then reached into the box holding dried cow chips and watched the blaze take hold until it was hot enough to ignite pieces of coal.

Her head seemed to wobble on her body now, and some days, she feared it would go banging away across the prairie like a tumbleweed. She couldn't complete a thought. If she got up at all in the morning she couldn't remember why.

It was time.

She clasped her hands tightly together to stop their shaking and turned to fetch the paper.

She was so preoccupied with the fire that she didn't hear the three men enter the room. When she saw them, she jumped, and her hand flew against her chest as though she could keep her heart from flying out.

"We didn't mean to scare you, Miss Bethany," Kulp said.

McBane nodded, his eyes solemn, watchful. Jed looked at Bethany uneasily, not bothering to disguise his anger.

Kulp cleared his throat. "We've come here to ask your assistance, Miss Bethany."

"They have, not me," Jed said quickly. "This is their idea. Not mine. I don't want you to do anything that would put you in harm's way."

She slipped behind her desk like a ghost and clasped her hands. She examined her thin wrists as though to reassure herself there was a body there. Her face was as dry as an autumn leaf, finally devoid of tears. Surely, she had been drained of them forever.

Kulp always did the talking. The man had an instinct for striking just the right tone with people. Even the whites who resented having to deal with a black census taker had been charmed by the man's easy manners, his wit, and his endless supply of stories. McBane was usually the one who fired off inflammatory political salvoes, like a little bantam rooster spoiling for a fight.

"I can't offer you decent chairs," she said,

"but there's no need for all of you to stand. Please make yourselves as comfortable as you can on the benches."

"This is not my idea," Jed said again. "But they've persuaded me that it's up to you."

"Everyone around here knows you are the mysterious Sunflower," said McBane. "And we want you to write one more letter."

Her stomach plummeted. "Why, in God's name? After all the harm I've done?"

"Because no one in Topeka knows you're that person," Kulp said. "Now we want everyone to know. What we've done out here. What we could be if folks just gave us a chance."

Kulp leaned forward, his voice coaxing, persistent. On one of his trips back to Topeka, he had met a fine lady — a schoolteacher, the daughter of a preacher man. The family was entranced when he came to call. His Lavina played the organ, served tea in china cups painted with pink roses.

The *Colored Citizen* had published the paper he'd read before the St. John's Literary Society. How could he ask Lavina to come here to this place he had shamelessly described as the new Eden? A place where they had hung a wee black man who was as innocent as a cricket.

"We're not asking you to tell a lie,"

McBane said.

"You have no right to ask anything," Jed retorted. " 'Specially to ask her to do something that might get her killed."

"Killed?" Bethany raised her eyes. Her heart leaped inside her, and her pulse throbbed visibly in her throat.

"Yes, killed. And they are going to try to persuade you that some good could come out of Teddy's death. They want to convince you there's a chance to make Teddy's life count for something."

"That's enough, Jed," McBane snapped. "We agreed to let Miss Bethany make up her own mind."

"And how could writing another letter help?" she asked.

"Folks have pieced it all together," said McBane. "You, the letter. Despite the reservations of Brother Jed, you can do us a world of good if you'll go along with our plan."

She did not believe she could bear the rebirth of hope. Sickened, she tried to beat it back. But like a baby determined to be born, hope began pushing.

"You owe it to your people," Kulp said.

"You don't owe anyone a damned thing," Jed snapped, glaring at Kulp.

"The hopes of thousands are resting on

your willingness to do this," McBane said.

"This is the first step," Kulp warned. "There's more to follow."

"I'm telling you, it's a mistake," Jed said. "The only reason I'm here at all is to keep these two from twisting your arm."

"Gentlemen!" Her voice was sharp, commanding, and all three looked at her sheepishly. "Now, I would like someone to tell me precisely what you want done."

"We have the note that was left on Teddy. We have the last letter you wrote to the *Topeka Capital.* He was carrying it with him when he was killed. We found it in his saddlebag. Now we want you to write another letter saying exactly what happened to Teddy. Name names, give all the reasons, and explain what's at stake out here for the colored people."

"Or not," Jed said stubbornly. "Or not, if you so desire."

"And the next step?"

"The next step will be to go with us to Topeka," Kulp said. "We can arrange an audience with Governor St. John. He has been quite intrigued with the columns of an editor from Parsons who goes by the pseudonym of Kicking Bird. I've heard he would love to know about Sunflower. I have my sources, and they say he concurs with those views as much as he agrees with the opinions of anyone."

"St. John's an odd duck," piped up McBane. "His crusade for Prohibition is as well-known as his advocacy for blacks. He believes women should vote."

"Bethany," Jed pleaded. "What if exposing you causes whites to come after you like they did for Teddy?"

"And what if it does?" Her cheeks flamed. She would not hesitate to give her own now worthless life to atone for her part in Teddy's murder.

Jed's lips thinned. She responded with a tight, proud smile, and he looked away. He slapped his hand against his thigh repeatedly.

"Yes. I will do this. Yes. It will take me a while," she said softly. "And I'm going to do it right now, right here in this very room." She swallowed when she looked at the pieces of vellum. The precious pieces of stationery she had come so close to destroying. The paper that would prove she was Sunflower.

"We have some ideas we would like you to include," McBane said.

"I'm sure you do, but I'm not interested in hearing them."

McBane started to protest, but Kulp laid

a restraining hand on his shoulder. "I'm sure Miss Bethany has ideas of her own," he said. "After all, she is Sunflower."

"I'm going to stay here until you've finished," Jed said. "Then I'll walk you home."

"No, no. I don't need someone to escort me, and I can't even imagine writing something this important with someone else in the room. Please leave with your friends."

Reluctantly they all filed out. Bethany picked up a piece of the children's scrap paper and laid it next to the heavy vellum on her desk.

She sat down and bent to her work, carefully testing the words. The room became crowded with haunts vying with one another to have a voice. Women wronged, women ashamed; but they were outnumbered by women clad in red. Warrior women — Joan of Arc, Madame Roland, Harriet Tubman. They whispered, coached.

Like a phoenix, Bethany's ruined soul rose from Teddy's ashes.

When she had finished, she stood, placed the letter inside the envelope, sealed it, and picked up the precious remaining blank sheets. Curiously energized despite the lateness of the hour, she left the schoolhouse and walked toward her dugout.

She froze, sensing a presence, then relaxed

as she saw Jed watching from behind the hotel. He kept guard until she reached her own place.

Jarred by the noise and the press of people, when Bethany got off the train in Topeka, she reached for Jed's arm. He gave her hand a comforting pat. "Nervous?"

"A little, yes." She laughed. "More than a little." She clutched her traveling bag containing new clothes as they waited for Kulp and McBane to return with a carriage.

At first she had laughed when A.T. rode into Nicodemus with ten yards of taffeta. The blue-purple was so dark it was nearly black. He had also purchased black wool for a matching bonnet and a warm shawl.

"You won't understand until you get there," Kulp said. "We don't want St. John or anyone else to mistake you for one of the Exodusters."

"I'm surprised you would say such a thing."

"Sorry, Miss Bethany, but Topeka has always had a large free-black community, and they're a bit snooty. The town was an important station on the Underground Railroad before the war. The Negroes there have their own benevolent organizations, their own lodges, their own churches, and their own businesses, and, believe me, their own social clubs."

LuAnne Brown had gathered women to help sew the dress and made them finish in two days' time. Patricia Towaday had unearthed a hank of white cotton thread, and her shuttle just flew as she tatted a fine jabot to tuck around the neckline.

Now, as Bethany eyed two well-dressed black couples waiting to board, she appreciated Kulp's savvy.

"We're over here, A.T.," Jed called. He helped Bethany into the carriage, then squeezed in beside her. Kulp had wired ahead to Lavina's family, as they wanted a suitable place for Bethany to stay. He and the other two men would stay at a hotel.

Topeka was exploding with activity, buildings, people. Still jumpy from the train ride from Ellis, Bethany marveled at how well Kulp knew his way around. He seemed entirely comfortable hiring a carriage and giving directions to the driver. Clearly, he and McBane were making a great deal of money in their land location business, or they couldn't have paid for all their train tickets.

Everywhere Bethany looked she could see clusters of raggedy blacks loitering on the street, with white men picking their way around them.

"There's a lot of hard feelings between the Exodusters and the blacks who have been here since before the war," Kulp said. "At first, all the churches and charitable groups helped the newcomers. Then the emigration overwhelmed everyone. Now everything they've worked for is threatened by the ex-slaves pouring in from the South."

Jed's mouth tightened. He extended his hands, flexed them, and examined the backs of his fingers as though there was an answer written there. "On the other hand, imagine how these poor people from the South feel. They can't go back. Not now. Back to what? It isn't their fault that they're ignorant and poor and half-sick."

"Isn't there anything anyone can do?" Bethany asked.

"Maybe," Kulp said. "But when St. John sees you for the first time, he must associate you with the free blacks and not with the Exodusters who are causing him problems."

They reached Lavina Hardesty's, and Bethany gasped at the attractiveness of the pristine, white, two-story house. She had never been around communities of black people who had lived free before the war. In fact, Jed and Kulp and McBane were the first freeborn Negroes she'd met.

Born on the plantation, then subjected to the abject poverty of Freedom Town in Lexington, she hadn't realized it was possible for her people to live like this.

Suddenly she was aware of every article of clothing in her suitcase. Panicked, she looked at Jed. He smiled and squeezed her hand.

A tall, slender woman came out of the house and stood on the porch. She wore a long black skirt topped by a snow-white waist. Her black crinkly hair was rolled back into a circle around her head.

"That's A.T.'s Lavina," McBane said.

They waited in the carriage. Kulp walked down the brick pathway to greet his lady and Lavina, extended her hand. Then the door opened again, and a man and another woman stepped outside.

"And that's her parents," said McBane, "and believe me, they are doing a right smart job of looking A.T. over."

The reverend's face was as stern as Moses's, and Lavina's mother wore a severe, black dress. But they both smiled and then shook A.T.'s hand as he whipped off his hat. Kulp turned, then walked back to the carriage to get Bethany.

Inside the house, Bethany managed to stumble through the greetings, but she felt profoundly awkward. However, when she went upstairs and changed, she suddenly knew she was dressed just right. She could thank A.T. for that. There was even a pair of gloves to go with her dress tomorrow. Her natural poise returned.

The next morning, as they sat in the lovely dining room, light filtering through the lace curtains highlighted Reverend Hardesty's white hair, ringing his head like a halo. His black face was shadowed. Grace lasted forever and ever. Bethany was grateful. It delayed the moment when she would have to pick up a fork and eat in front of these elegant people.

Only a memory of how white people acted and looked got her through breakfast. She had never sat at an elegant table. Nor had she ever faced a bewildering array of silverware, had someone pour her coffee, pass her food, and ask if she would like seconds. The eggs stuck in her throat.

"Anybody ever lose a wheel on these streets?" Jed asked as their carriage hit a hole. "We'll be lucky if we get there on time. And I doubt if St. John thinks much of tardiness." The capital teemed with new businesses. Construction exploded. "Might as well be driving in Nicodemus."

"There's stone sidewalks along Kansas Avenue," Kulp said, "and they are getting serious about paving streets in some parts of town, but, as you can see, the town is growing too fast for the money to keep up with. Most of the smoke is coming from the Wrought Iron King Bridge Works. There's a distillery here now and a rolling mill."

A teamster pulling a wagonload of lumber cursed his pair of work horses. The horse pulling their own carriage tried to rear, and chaos threatened until all the animals were brought back under control.

Bethany pressed her hands over her ears to shut out the din of construction. They headed toward the state house. An enormous mound of stone was piled on the south side. Men were going back and forth between wagons and supplies like a stream of ants.

Bethany stared. She turned to Jed. "How can Governor St. John even think in such commotion?"

"He can't," Jed said. "He leaves details like thinking to our venerable legislators. St. John stays at the Copeland Hotel and mainly works out of his suite there. That's where he's agreed to receive us."

St. John's secretary did not bat an eye when the four blacks announced they had an appointment. He was used to the governor giving audiences to African Americans.

Governor John Pierce St. John was a crusading knight of a man who could stare down an eagle. A magnificent mustache embellished his stern, Roman-nosed face. He had mined, chopped wood, clerked, fought in the Indian Wars, spit in the face of danger, and fought for every penny it had taken him to pay for law school.

He could take the measure of a man before the fellow opened his mouth.

He was uniquely qualified to negotiate the treacherous undercurrents of Kansas politics. He understood the state's peculiar attraction toward adversity. Understood its ridiculously defiant motto, *Ad Astra Per Aspera,* "To the Stars Through Difficulties." As though anything acquired easily was not worthy of notice.

Kansas was proud of being a hard state. Hard to stand and hard to admire. Proud of its disdain for joy and its militant morality.

St. John was the epitome of the warrior ruler and typically Kansan in that not all his views were predictable. He was a century ahead on women's rights, fanatically idealist about black rights, and perversely determined to slay demon rum.

He was badgered constantly now over the Exodusters. Not only was the influx about to break Topeka financially, they could not begin to cope with the filth and disease. If he had doubts about the stance he had taken in welcoming the flood of immigrants, he did not let them show.

He had met with Kulp and McBane before, but not with Jed. He bowed toward Bethany, who had been coached by all three men.

"Come into my quarters, please," St. John said.

Bethany's mouth was dry as cotton. It was good that only men were expected to discuss politics and business, because she could not have initiated a conversation if her life depended on it.

Taking seats, the four blacks listened to St. John expound on the construction of the west wing of the state house, which he could see out his window.

"Now," he said, settling behind his walnut desk, "welcome to Copeland County, or so I've heard this place called. But I'm sure you've seen for yourself why most politicians prefer to meet here rather than at that unfinished monstrosity over there. When it's done, of course, it will be one of the finest capitol buildings in the United States. If it's ever done."

He folded his hands across his chest. "I've been told this visit is of some urgency, but not the reason for all the mystery." He looked expectantly at McBane, but it was Jed who spoke up.

"Sir, we bring two issues before you today. First, Mr. Kulp has completed his census. Graham County has the required number of voters. We would like you to designate Millbrook as the temporary county seat until we can hold our official election. It's crucial that we defeat Wade City. And we would like to introduce you to Sunflower."

"You've managed to unearth this mysterious person?" St. John said. "I'm amazed."

He didn't add that blacks living in a remote corner of northwest Kansas were unlikely to know the identity of the most effective and persuasive writer to ever hit the pages of the *Topeka Daily Capital.*

"Yes, we know this person," Jed said. "We have just now introduced you to Miss Bethany Herbert of Nicodemus, Kansas, and we would like you to know, sir, that it is she who is the mysterious Sunflower."

"A black woman?" St. John grasped the arms of his chair. He leaned forward, then stammered with embarrassment, "I beg your pardon, ma'am. Please. It's just

that . . ."

"It's quite all right, sir."

Later, Bethany would try to pinpoint why she felt so strangely comfortable with this white man. Comfortable enough to serenely withstand his intense quizzing without faltering and without hesitation. As though she were facing St. Peter at the Pearly Gates, justifying her existence. She had never known before and would never know again a white person she trusted so completely.

"Quite all right." She looked at him frankly. "I'm used to having my intelligence questioned."

"You understand of course, Miss Herbert, that I must be certain, because your friends here are asking me to make an extraordinary move in designating Millbrook as the county seat."

"I understand."

He rose, paced, then stood clutching the lapels of his coat. "In fact, I have a whole passel of letters from Graham County stating why I should select Wade City."

"Yes, I would imagine that is true."

"What can you possibly offer me as proof that you are Sunflower?"

"Jed?" Bethany turned, and Jed drew a leather document folder from his inside coat pocket. He stood and carried it over to St.

John's desk.

"Sir, I will leave this here with you so you can have this verified by the *Topeka Daily Capital*. These letters are on the same paper the editor there has received. As you can see, this is a blank sheet of paper. Note the quality."

St. John reached for the paper and studied it intently.

"This is a draft of the letter I'm about to show you." Jed handed the crumpled newsprint to St. John, who reached for it, then read as much as he could decipher before he gestured at Jed to continue.

"And this, sir, is the letter written by Sunflower, that Teddy Sommers was carrying when he was killed. It's the final copy of the letter you just read, written on the vellum paper, as I'm sure you can see by matching it to the blank sheet I gave you."

St. John read the first paragraph written on the lovely stationery and matched the words to the ones on the raggedy sheet. His eyes sharpened, and he drew a quick breath. He looked at Jed, his eyes alight with new understanding.

"That hanged man? Teddy Sommers was the carrier for these letters? They originated in Nicodemus?"

"Yes. This outrage was the work of Wade

City men. That's why you must designate Millbrook as the county seat. The editor there, Norvin Meissner, is a good man. He supports our equal rights ticket. Our people."

Slowly Jed extracted the final piece of paper. His eyes misted, but he kept rigid control. Kulp and McBane sat sphinx solemn. Tears trickled down Bethany's face, and she did not bother to wipe them away.

"One more," Jed said again, softly. Then his voice shook. "There's one more. One more I want you to see."

He unfolded the blood-stained sheet of the same vellum as the other papers lying on the desk. The note left on Teddy's body. His hand shook as he handed the paper to St. John.

The governor read the ugly words. His body jerked, and his face flushed with anger. The whole room grew deathly still. The world outside seemed suspended. St. John slowly expelled his breath. His eyes blazed with a deadly fire.

He looked at all four of the black people. Then he reached for his pen and extended it to Bethany. "As I said, madam, I shall require absolute proof."

Puzzled, she arose and approached his desk. He slid the original blank piece of paper toward her, then hesitated. "One moment, please, Miss Herbert." He went to the doorway and called for the secretary to come inside the room and to bring the official state seal.

"Now, Miss Herbert. Mr. Jones will administer an oath swearing that what you are signing is the truth, and he will officially witness your signature. I might add that it had better be the truth, and this signature had better match the signature on the letter Mr. Sommers was carrying when he was killed."

Bethany's right hand was steady when she raised it. Steady when she placed her left hand on the Bible, and steady as a rock when she wrote the following words:

"I, Bethany Herbert do solemnly swear that I am the author of the letters published by the *Topeka Daily Capital* under the pseudonym of Sunflower."

She signed both *Bethany Herbert* and *Sunflower* and steadily looked at St. John.

"I can assure you, Miss Herbert, that all this formality is for the benefit of other people. I have enemies."

St. John watched as his secretary carefully laid Bethany's statement on the desk and imprinted it with the great seal of Kansas.

"There is no doubt in my mind now as to

your identity. Editor Hudson at the *Capital* is a good friend of mine, and we have spent many an evening poring over these letters. I know both this particular paper and this signature quite well."

He smiled ruefully. "And I do confess, Miss Herbert, you have surprised me. You have indeed."

Bethany said nothing but didn't suppress the broad smile spreading across her face.

"Now, gentlemen," St. John said briskly, turning to the black men. "As to your request! Mr. Jones, if you would be so kind as to witness the following bit of business, I shall this day declare Millbrook as the county seat. Needless to say, I intend for McBane to continue as the county clerk until all the officers are officially elected."

The governor reached for a piece of official state stationery. Jubilant, the four blacks watched St. John write out the statement that would only take him a few minutes but would change their lives forever.

"Mr. Kulp, the federal census will occur this year also. It's considerably more involved than the one you just completed. I would like you to participate with this one, too, but would you agree to sharing the responsibility with two white men?"

Too stunned to assimilate all the developments, Kulp could just nod before he found his voice. "Sir, I'd be honored."

"The *Capital* will soon receive a new letter," Jed said. "Miss Bethany wrote it right before we came. All hell will break loose when it's printed. She named names. Spelled it all out."

St. John nodded, then rose and walked over to the window and stared out at the teeming streets of Topeka, hands clasped behind his back.

He turned. "There's one more thing you need to know, Mr. Talbot. About the death of your friend, Mr. Sommers." The governor's voice was dangerously even with suppressed fury. "All the resources of the state will be brought to bear to bring those murderers to justice."

CHAPTER THIRTY-TWO

Bethany covered her mouth to hide her smile. The spelling bee was down to the last two competitors. There were now four white children attending the Nicodemus school, and Zach Brown had met his match in a boy close to his own age.

"Zach, please spell 'infuriated,' as in, 'He was infuriated by her superior tone.' "

"E-n-f-u-r-i-a-t-e-d," he said solemnly. His forehead wrinkled from the strain.

"No, I'm sorry. You may take your place with the other children. Now, Tommy, please spell 'infuriated.' "

Tommy Stuart beamed. Having heard Zach go down, he knew that only the first letter was wrong. "I-n-f-u-r-i-a-t-e-d."

"Correct."

Hall and McBane walked into the room as she was writing the next week's spelling words on her slate. The two men were going to give a special presentation to the upper level math students. She looked forward to having the afternoon off, as she wanted to visit her mother. She was eager to catch Queen Bess up on all the events that had taken place in Topeka.

She wiped her hands. "Children, for the rest of the afternoon, your instruction will be in the hands of Mr. E. P. McBane, county clerk of Graham County, and his business partner, A. T. Kulp. I'm sure most of you know that Mr. Kulp was the official county census taker when we were organizing this county, and Governor St. John has just re-appointed him as one of the three men who will conduct the federal census."

The children gazed at the men with awe. Black like them, having important doings with the governor.

"And why do we have a federal census?"

A little girl's hand shot up. "Because the Constitution says we must," she said eagerly, not waiting to be called.

Bethany laughed. "Thank you, Lydia."

Their college format was working well. She was still amazed at the zeal with which the blacks in Nicodemus pushed their children toward education. All the parents wanted to help with the school, even if it was just to clean or to keep the coal scuttle filled.

And to have Jed and these other two wonderfully inspiring black men help plan lessons! It was unbelievable. Kulp and McBane were rapidly becoming wealthy, and they kept the school supplied with books.

"I'll leave these students in your capable hands," she said. She smiled as she waved goodbye to the children.

Since the trip to Topeka, energy just bubbled out of her. Although it was early afternoon and she had plenty of time to walk to Queen Bess's and get a good visit in before dark, she decided to borrow a horse and buggy from Jim Black and take a pile of rabbit pelts to her mother. Queen Bess had begun making moccasins for the children to wear during the winter.

When she pulled up, her mother was sitting outside. "Brought you some work, Momma," she called cheerily, "and some news."

"I done heard your news, daughter," Queen Bess said.

"How?"

Queen Bess ignored her question and helped Bethany unload the rabbit pelts.

Bethany laughed. "Well, I'll bet you haven't heard *all* the details about our governor. Bet you don't know *everything* there is to know about A. T. Kulp's lady friend. And I've brought you some tea. From Topeka."

Queen Bess chuckled. "I always got time for a cup of good tea, daughter." They walked inside her soddy and her black eyes shone with contentment as she studied Bethany's lovely face, alive with joy. Her daughter was back from the dead. All fired up again with whatever it was that Bess would never understand and sure as hell didn't want for herself, either.

They were on their second cup, and Bethany was in the middle of telling her about Lavina Hardesty and her parents — black folks who lived like whites — when they heard the men approach.

Queen Bess knew. She had always known. There was no place on God's green earth. Not in the South, not in Kansas, not even in Heaven, where a black woman would be safe from white men.

Aaron Potroff and Dr. Winthrop Osborne walked through the door. Silently, like a pair of jackals stalking two gazelles. Queen Bess's heart fluttered wildly in her chest. Potroff carried a whip. How many times in this life had she seen such a whip? Heard the sound, the screams?

They did not wear masks, which could only mean they did not intend to let her and Bethany live long enough to say their names.

Queen Bess closed her eyes and trembled. Bethany's back was smooth, unblemished. Her daughter had never felt the lash. Then she sorrowfully opened her eyes and looked at her virgin daughter, who had held on to her chastity like she was protecting the last vestige of her African heritage.

She had told this precious, delicate woman too much. About the gold chains that indicated virginity, removed only at marriage. About the pride the women of their tribe once took in instilling virtue in their children.

She gazed at the pasty, evil face of Aaron Potroff. Like soured buttermilk. Then her eyes were drawn to Winthrop Osborne's filthy hands.

The whip would only be the beginning.

"Mr. Jed, you have a telegram. The man says it's from that powerful governor what's going to do us so much good."

Jed laughed as Jamal Gray eagerly jumped from one foot to another. "Anyone ever told you curiosity killed the cat?"

Jamal flushed. Jed grinned and glanced

around. He enjoyed sitting outside his soddy on sunny afternoons, catching up on little chores, and watching the children play after school let out. But it was too early for most of them to start their evening rituals. They all had chores to do first. He set the dress boots he had been polishing down by the side of the stump and reached for the message.

"Now do you suppose there's going to be anything in this you actually need to know, Jamal? Why aren't you in school, anyway?"

"Miss Bethany done give us young ones the afternoon off 'cause Mr. Kulp and Mr. McBane gots to work with the older ones. She done gone off to her mother's with a load of pelts." Jamal's eyes shone with pride. "Reckon I brought down most of those rabbits."

Jed smiled and ruffled the boy's hair. "That's a pretty safe assumption."

"Anyway, I was off trying to sneak up on some more rabbits." His slingshot stuck out of his back pocket. "Along came the telegram man from Oberlin. Said to give this to you, if I knowed who you was. Said he didn't want to take no chances on your being gone, but it would save him a couple of miles. I told him he could count on me for pert' near anything."

"He can at that."

Jed opened the telegram and read, then reread the contents as though he could not take it in. Governor St. John was asking him to testify before the Voorhees committee. The state of Kansas would pay his way to Washington.

The years, all the years he had spent collecting information. All the affidavits, the documents, the letters, the grisly tales of outrages; his wronged people would be given a voice.

He let out a whoop. Startled, the boy's eyes widened.

"It's all good news, Jamal. The very best of news, in fact. I'm going to Washington."

He dashed inside his soddy, grabbed his riding boots, and pulled them on. He wanted to tell Bethany and Queen Bess his good news while they were together. Sitting right there in his future mother-in-law's house. He intended to go to Washington with Bethany at his side, as his wife, his lawful wife.

He grinned. He would not give the stubborn old woman time to think. To work out any arguments for holding her daughter back. She'd already scolded him over the trip to Topeka. Made it clear she didn't like Bethany "gallivanting around."

Ecstatic that men of influence would be hearing his testimony, he sprinted over to the livery stable and saddled up Gloriana. His notes would be entered into the Congressional record. Preserved for the duration of the United States of America. The mare sensed his exuberance, and when she took off like she was in a race, he did not check her speed.

The grass waved him on. He laughed when Gloriana slowed to a trot, then a walk. He could see the faint tracks of Bethany's buggy.

Then he saw fresh horse droppings a few feet to the side of the buggy's track. They could not have been left by Bethany's horse. Puzzled, he dismounted and studied the ground.

There were two riders, but he would have known immediately if Nicodemus men had ridden off mounted because he had been sitting outside. Besides, nearly all of the colonists still walked. And anyone fetching Bethany to doctor would have come directly to the settlement, and he would have noticed a stranger, too.

Jamal said Bethany had left only an hour before he did. Edgy now, with his soldier's sense of danger, he stared in the direction of Queen Bess's soddy. There was no way a stranger would just happen by that place. It was too far off any natural trail.

No local white person would go seeking out Queen Bess for any reason at all. It was well known none of them were welcome on her property.

The riders were up to no good.

He grabbed Gloriana, mounting as she whirled, ears laid back. Then he stopped and turned in his saddle. About a quarter of a mile behind, he could see Jamal, trailing him as usual. The boy could run like the wind. Deciding quickly, he hollered at the boy.

"Jamal, I need you to do something for me." He kicked Gloriana high on the flanks and galloped to meet the boy, who was running toward him as fast as he could. Jed would rather be safe than sorry. These horses had to belong to two white men.

If he was wrong, he would apologize later.

"Run back to the schoolhouse," he told the panting child. "Tell Kulp and McBane I need their help. Ask them to round up all the men they can find."

Jamal turned to go.

"Tell them to use the drums."

He pointed Gloriana toward Queen Bess's soddy again, grimly checked his supply of ammunition, leaned low over the mare's neck, and spurred her into a dead run.

Winthrop Osborne slammed his fist into Queen Bess's face, knocking her off her chair. She lay curled on the floor. He walked over to the table, picked up the awl she had been using to make moccasins, and pulled the chair under the ridgepole that dissected the length of the roof. He stood on it and reached up, then scraped enough dirt away from the bare sod ceiling to thread his rope through. He tied the loop with a surgeon's knot.

He dragged Queen Bess beneath the rope, yanked her up, bound her hands together, and pulled her higher and higher. Stretched her out like a skinned, dark doe ready for gutting.

Her feet barely touched the floor. She cried out with each jolt, and her head fell back. Her turban dropped behind her. Osborne ripped her dress down to her waist.

Terrified, Bethany screamed. Potroff laughed, knowing there was no one to hear.

"Don't you know I've never let a nigger get away from me?" Potroff stood behind Bethany, clutching her wildly thrashing body. "I've brought them all back." His voice was whispery, raspy. "Not a one of them ever got away. Not one."

Bethany gasped, and her head whirled. She felt all the blood leave her brain and pool, down, down. She started to faint. She remembered, remembered that voice, that terrible voice from when she was out doctoring with Queen Bess.

Slave catcher. A slave catcher. Before the war, this man had made his living bringing back fugitive slaves. She had heard the voice before.

Unnatural. A writing nigger.

The same dry voice. Subtle like a snake's hiss. The same words: "They never get away from me." The same voice that had made her so fearful she'd handed Jesus back his gold pen. Told him to keep it. Didn't want to be an unnatural, writing nigger.

She had decided when she was just nine years old, there was nothing in this world worth attracting the attention of a slave catcher.

Queen Bess's cries pulled her back. Frantically, Bethany tried to break Potroff's grip. "Momma! Please, no, leave my mother alone."

Queen Bess's eyes were wild with fright. Tears trickled down her black cheeks. The first crack of the whip knocked her off her toes, and she could not regain her footing to support her weight. The lash cut across the old scars on her back and laid them open and raw. Scars left by the Yankees, her liberators.

Queen Bess set her teeth. She could not save herself or her daughter. But she knew men. They were saving Bethany for dessert. And they had the kind of evil souls where they would want to torment her first by having to watch her own mother being whipped to death. A cry of unbearable pain and raw fury ripped from her throat. Bethany lunged toward her again, but Potroff laughed and pulled her back.

Jed heard the scream and pounded his heels against Gloriana's flanks, urging the mare faster and faster. He reined up abruptly at the top of a rise, thinking like a soldier, an officer, assessing danger. His mind floating above the screams long enough to think, suppressing the impulse to dash recklessly ahead.

Only two horses were tethered a short distance from Queen Bess's soddy. Just two white men. The buggy Bethany had borrowed was out in front.

He slid off the mare and ran swiftly and silently as a panther toward the windowless back of the soddy. As he rounded the corner he heard another anguished scream and knew he could have made any sound at all and the men wouldn't have heard. They were too distracted by the women.

He drew his pistol and peered through the single glass window long enough to see that their backs were toward him. Then he burst through the doorway.

He shot Osborne in the shoulder just as the man was drawing his arm back to wield the whip again. Queen Bess's body jerked like the bullet had hit her instead. Her muscles were still quivering with dread of the next cruel blow.

Potroff did not have time to get to his own pistol lying on the table. But Jed's aim was spoiled when the man whirled around and darted toward it, and the bullet went high up on Potroff's chest. Jed kept his gun trained on him while Bethany ran to Queen Bess's side.

Jed dug out his knife and handed it to her, never taking his eyes off Potroff, who lay moaning on the floor. He was going to see to it that both men died very, very slowly.

Bethany cut the rope but she could not support Queen Bess's weight, and the woman fell heavily into the pool of blood and urine beneath her. Bethany cradled her mother's head in her arms and felt the faint pulse in her throat.

"It's weak, but she's still alive." Her eyes widened with fright. "I can't doctor this. He hurt her too much."

"Go get the buggy, and move it right next to the door," said Jed. "We've got to get her to the doctor at Stockton."

Bethany ran outside. She saw riders in the distance and shook uncontrollably. More of Potroff's people? More coming to back him up?

They drew closer. Terror gave way to bewilderment. Black men. All of them black. Men from Nicodemus. Some were mounted.

She shielded her eyes. She could see another group on foot about a half-mile further out. She cupped her hands around her mouth. "Help!" she called. "Please help."

The men on horseback began galloping toward her. Bethany's voice carried to the men who were walking, and they began to run.

"Get the buggy!" she yelled at the first rider when he came over the rise. "Bring it over to the front door. My mother. We've got to get her to Stockton. There's a new doctor there."

Earl Gray headed for the buggy, and Henry Partridge and Jim Black followed

Bethany into the house. A vein throbbed in Jim's temple at the sight of Queen Bess lying there, and he began to swear in a soft monotone. He went to her side and knelt.

"Need some help," he said to Henry. "Two more to help carry her." He turned to Bethany. "Want you out of here. Right now. You shouldn't be seeing this. Henry, you take Miss Bethany outside."

"No," she said flatly.

"It's too much for you to take," Jim said. "Go on now till we get her outside. Just take us a minute."

"No."

Earl came in with two more men.

"Grab a plank off my mother's worktable on the porch." Bethany's voice shook, but her training took over. She pulled a blanket off Queen Bess's bed. "Won't be good for her to sit in my buggy. We need to keep her flat with her back covered."

"Wagon's coming right behind us," Jim said. "Earl, go tell them to get a move on."

Jim looked over at Jed. Talbot's handsome mahogany features were stone still. He had dragged Osborne closer to Potroff where he could cover them both at once.

Jim had seen that look before, but never in a black man's eyes. Black men always knew that no matter how intense their rage, vengeance was beyond their abilities, out of reach.

This time, it wasn't.

As sure as he knew his own name, Jim knew what Jed Talbot was going to do.

The wagon clattered up. Jim and Earl went to the door.

"Peter, Sidney, need you inside here," Jim yelled. Then he went back to Queen Bess. She was lying on her stomach, her naked back carved into protruding strips of oozing flesh. Jim gently lifted her torso while Bethany slid half of the blanket beneath her. Then she lifted her mother's legs and hips and eased down the remaining length.

Queen Bess screamed, then fainted. Fresh blood rose to the surface of her back, which was scored like meat sliced for marinating. The four men covered her back, picked up the slab, and carried her outside to the wagon bed. Bethany climbed up beside Queen Bess and grasped her hand.

"Hurry," she called tersely to Earl. She pressed her fist against her trembling mouth. If her mother went into shock, there was nothing she could do. Earl climbed onto the wagon beside Elijah Woodrow. He turned and looked helplessly back at Bethany, then at Queen Bess, feeling every jolt of the old wagon in his own body.

Inside, Jed silently handed his gun to Jim. He walked outside around to the back of the soddy and got the rope he carried coiled on his saddle.

He needed two ropes for what he was about to do.

He went back inside and looped his rope over the ridgepole. The one Osborne had already put up would work just fine.

Jim's eyes widened with awareness. His hands shook as he watched Jed, but he kept the gun trained on Potroff and Osborne.

Jed grabbed Osborne first and savagely strapped his hands together like he was tying up a calf.

"You black bastards. You'll never get away with this. Never." The words jerked from Potroff as Jed yanked his arms away from his bullet ripped torso and savagely hoisted him upright.

Jed braced his feet and pulled on the rope looped across the ridgepole. He stopped when Potroff's feet were barely touching the floor, and the man was wild with pain.

There was a post outside the door. Jed went there and wrapped the rope around it. Then he went to work on Osborne.

The two men hung side by side like fresh game. Jed ripped the shirts off their backs and picked up the whip Osborne had dropped.

Jim Black said nothing.

The men from Nicodemus who had to walk were there now, and some of them filed into the soddy. They stared.

"Once for me. For this hand," said Henry Partridge, stepping forward. He thrust out his mangled claw. "And once for my sister who died because she was split near in half by men like this. She was just ten."

"And once for me," said Peter Jenkins. "For the man who slit my wife's belly open just to see if she was carrying a boy or a girl."

"Once for me," said Sidney Taylor, "for killing my uncle and my brother when they tried to vote."

Jed closed his eyes. The voices went on and on. Ghostly. Detached. From a world left behind.

Voices crying with the grief of lost, dark ghosts.

Do it for me, for us, they whispered in Jed's ear. *For all of us.*

Jed turned as though he were waking from a daze, but he could not speak. His fine, full lips trembled, and his gray eyes blackened with despair.

Kulp and McBane stepped inside the door, arriving late because they had come in their spring wagon.

McBane started forward, but Kulp held him back. Made him check his words before they left his mouth, knowing Jed's soul would be scarred forever if he didn't lay down the whip on his own.

As surely as Joshua stopped the sun in the sky, every dust mote, even the air, stilled. Slowly Jed looked at the two men. His friends who were moving heaven and earth to start a new civilization.

He had been part of that effort. He looked around at the other great, good souls who had flocked to Nicodemus. His people, joyful at last. Coming into their own. People who wanted churches and schools. Men who wanted to reclaim their manhood and their lost honor.

Their chances of making that happen would be ruined forever if he raised that whip.

Nicodemus. Kansas. This insanely idealistic state was their only chance.

As though seraphim rushed forward to seal his lips, he was unable to speak. Paralyzed with indecision.

From the past, he saw lines of blacks shackled together, broken, bleeding. Captured, torn away from their families. Ripped from their mothers' bosoms. Lonely, terrified.

Before him, toward the future, he saw men like Kulp and McBane. Ambitious, intelligent men determined to bring forth a new world of their own choosing.

Women, too. He saw the face of his beautiful Bethany. A maiden. An African maiden. He trembled. Nicodemus was their chance. Their only chance to turn their back on the horrors of the past and begin anew.

"Cut these two men down," he said softly to Jim Black. "Cut these two men down."

CHAPTER THIRTY-THREE

Elam Bartholomew was inside the general store when he saw the men from Nicodemus drive the wagon up to the new doctor's building. Bethany jumped off and pounded on the locked door. He stepped outside and crossed the street. "He's gone. For good, I'm afraid."

"No, please. No. My mother," she sobbed.

He followed her gaze to the wagon bed. When he saw Queen Bess, he paled and buried his head in his hands.

His soldiers had died of lesser and far fewer wounds. Pain and shock had killed almost as many as bullets. The chances of her dying of infection were astronomical.

Then he stiffened. "My house. Bring her to my house."

He sprinted toward the edge of town, and the blacks followed him with the wagon. Inside, he went to the closet and dug out a stretcher he had used during the late war.

Its canvas surface was still stained by old blood. He carried it outside, retrieved the poles, and inserted them into the sleeves.

Reverently, stiffly supporting the taut blanket, the men transferred Queen Bess onto the stretcher and carried her to Bartholomew's house. Bethany grasped her mother's dangling hand and felt for a pulse as she walked beside her. It was weak and rapid.

Queen Bess lay on her stomach, her head turned to the side. Her skin was dull. Her hair was thin, her skull mottled with blue-purple spots. Bethany had never seen her mother without a turban before.

Alonzo and Earl carried her inside. Bartholomew ordered Elijah and Silas to move his bed away from the wall and lay the stretcher on top of it so he could reach his patient from all sides. "I wish I had something higher, like a proper operating table," he said gloomily, "but at least we won't have to move her again."

"Mr. Bartholomew, I know you're not a doctor, but you were a medic during the war." Bethany's voice shook with despair.

He straightened and peered at her. "Miss Herbert, do you think you are going to have to talk me into doing my best for your mother?"

"Oh no, sir," she said, "that's not what I mean at all." All her training deserted her as she glanced at the bloody, black seepage of Queen Bess's back. It was too raw to bear the slightest current of air.

Bethany drew a deep breath, reached for Elam Bartholomew's hand, and held it in both of hers while she gazed intently into his eyes. "What I'm trying to say, sir, is that I don't know what to do. Where to start. If I had been able to think, I'd have grabbed every little bag of herbs and potions she had hanging in her cabin. But I didn't," she said bitterly.

He looked at her somberly, his eyes compassionate.

"I didn't. I couldn't. I just wanted to get her away. Even if I had gotten all her medications, I wouldn't have known what to do with them."

Bartholomew pulled his hand from Bethany's, gave her shoulder a comforting squeeze, and bent over Queen Bess's back, examining her, tracing a number of the wounds without touching them, his finger hovering over each one.

"What I meant, Mr. Bartholomew, was if you don't know what to do either, none of us will hold that against you. We just want you to try. You're the best we have."

He straightened, turned, and looked at her with a sad, wry smile. He gestured at all the little bottles neatly arranged on his shelves and the little deerskin bags hanging from a rope. "Actually, I know a great deal, Miss Herbert. Your mother taught me, you see. She taught me everything." He eyed all the bags.

"Everything."

Bethany stood at the edge of Nicodemus, her herb basket over her arm, and looked out over the prairie. She raised her hand to her throat and pressed her fingers against her pounding pulse.

It was the third time now she had started to gather plants and could not overcome her sense of foreboding. She always found some excuse to turn back. Wistfully, she looked at the swaying grass. It was such a short time ago that this land had seemed like the Biblical green pastures to her. She had felt no evil. The Lord had been with her, shielding her.

Now the grass was whipped around by a chilling wind. All the people in the town were edgy. Unsure of themselves.

Something terrible had happened at Queen Bess's soddy. And as horrified as they were by her savage beating, they were more stunned over that which they had not known existed inside themselves. A dark beast had been unchained.

One of the emotions that had always sustained them as a people, both men and women, was the certain knowledge that they were morally superior to whites. They would look at each other across the centuries with tragic, whip-crazed eyes and whisper, "At least we're not like them. Not at all. At least we have our humanity," they said smugly. "White bastards can't whip that out of us."

But they had.

The prairie seemed desolate now. The wind mocked. They were no longer willing to lean into it. And the colonists remembered the dark omen when they first left Kentucky. The fog, the terrible fog.

"Warn't natural," they recalled now as they sat around the campfire in the evening. "Knowed it warn't at the time. Always knowed you should do a leaving when it's green."

They nodded sagely, like they had always known the Lord was trying to tell them something with the fog. The way wasn't clear.

Any fool could see now what the gray had meant. As sure as if He had sent a bolt of lightning.

Unable to bear the grief, her own and the town's, Bethany turned to go back. Then she saw Jed walking toward her. Slowly, like he was savoring the sight of her.

He nearly always wore dark, store-bought pants during the day now and a coarse, blue shirt topped by a scarred leather vest. He carried a gun. She could not remember now when she had last seen him without a gun.

"You've been watching me," she said softly.

"Yes. I was hoping you would take the first step." He gestured toward the prairie.

"I couldn't. I'm not like I was after Teddy was killed," she said slowly. "I don't think I'll ever get to that state again. But I'm not quite the same as before, either."

"How is your mother?"

"Doing well. Against all odds, she's doing well. You know, Mr. Bartholomew was probably superior to any white doctor in the state to begin with. And since all the treatments he used on my mother were ones she told him about in their little chats — and they worked, they obviously worked — he now treats Momma like she has a medical degree from Cambridge. He waits on her hand and foot."

"They are the strangest alliance I've ever seen," Jed said.

"Aren't they? At any rate, he says she can stay as long as she likes. She's weak, but she's healing well. I saw her just last week."

"And her mind? Her attitude toward this place wasn't exactly ideal to begin with. I suppose she'll be making a bee-line out of here." He slapped his hand against his thigh repeatedly and gazed into the distance. "I suppose there's going to be one more claim up for grabs. At least she can get some money for it with all the improvements she's made. Enough for her to get a new start in Topeka or wherever she wants to go."

The wind ruffled Bethany's skirt and whipped it against her legs. "She plans to stay here in Graham County. In fact, she seems eager to get back out to her homestead."

"She doesn't want to leave? After all that's happened to her?"

"No. It's as though she had been braced for the worst, the very worst, and she doesn't have to worry about it happening now. It's over with." Bethany laughed. "She doesn't have to worry about it ever happening again."

"Who'd have thought," Jed said softly. "Who would have thought?" He shook his head. "Isn't that a deal, now."

"I give up on predicting my mother's reasoning."

Jed grinned. "And besides wanting to know about Queen Bess's condition, there's another reason I came looking for you today. I've got some good news of my own. I've just returned from Norton. I've had a long meeting with Sheriff Bogswell."

"Are they going to do something to those monsters? Or will it work the way it used to in the South?" she asked bitterly. "One kind of justice for white men and another for blacks."

"That's where the good news comes in. Dr. Winthrop Osborne, that no-good son-of-a-bitch, was only too happy to tell Casper everything. In great detail. Potroff was behind killing Tobias Gentry, that surveyor from Norton, too. Both of them. Teddy and Gentry. Bogswell has been looking for Gentry's murderer for a long time. They were friends. And the sheriff found proof," he added. "Of everything."

He closed his eyes for an instant. The proof had been in a little leather bag in Potroff's pocket. Within was a pair of shriveled black testicles. Potroff had been carrying them around like they were a good luck charm. He glanced at Bethany and decided she didn't need to hear all the details. "I don't think there's any doubt those two will be sentenced to death according to the laws of Graham County. And Kansas. We hang people here in Kansas."

It'll be a legal killing, this time, he thought darkly. *Legal.* He shuddered, knowing if he hadn't stopped that day, hadn't laid down the whip, he would have lost Bethany forever.

"They deserve to die," she said softly. "If two men ever deserved it, those two men do."

He nodded.

"Jed, do you know what you've done? Not just you, but all of us. What we've done? You've proven that black people can use the law to protect their own out here."

A muscle in his cheek jumped from his effort to disguise his pride. Then he looked at Bethany intently. "And I've proven that black men can use the law to protect their women."

She burst into tears and covered her face with her hands. He went to her and gathered her into his arms. They stood embracing each other for a long time until she stopped trembling. Her warm breath finally steadied against his chest like she was a sleeping infant.

"And I'm especially going to take care of you," he whispered into her hair. "With your mother's permission, of course," he added wryly. "With your mother's permission."

"She'll give it," Bethany blurted. "She's definitely going to give it."

He pushed her away so he could see her face. Then he bent and kissed her until they both were breathless.

"Darling, I was coming out to your mother's that day to tell you another bit of good news."

Her eyes widened when he told her about St. John's telegram. It was the chance of a lifetime for their people.

"And after our wedding, when I go to Washington, to testify before the Voorhees committee, I want you there with me. Watching."

Her eyes shone with adoration. "Your work. All those years of writing things down. It's finally going to get the attention it deserves."

Jed looked toward Nicodemus and held his hat across his chest. Like he were looking at a battlefield.

Bethany clutched Jed's arm. "This town. Just think what your testimony will mean to the people of this town. You must call a meeting tonight and tell everyone you've been selected to go to Washington by Governor John Pierce St. John, himself."

"I love that man," Jed whooped, throwing his hat into the air. "I love that name. Now that's a name for a man just naturally destined to do great things. How can a man not live up to a name like that?"

"Oh, Jed, Momma's going to about have a fit if I go traipsing off to Washington."

He grinned.

"The law," she said, "the law will work for us, too."

"Yes, the law. We have the power, right here in this town, to make the law work for us. In this great, good country, this loony state, this quarrelling county, and this half-off-the-ground town. Us. You, me, all of them. We can make it work."

She laughed at his exuberance.

Hearing a voice borne by the wind, they looked across the waves of grass. Jamal Gray was running, running, running, his words a distant plaintive wail. In front of him was the magnificent herd of wild black horses, necks thrust out, running across the prairie, their impossibly long manes streaming after them.

"Do you suppose he'll ever catch them?" Bethany asked wistfully as they passed over the horizon.

"No. But we were promised those horses when they came here," said Jed. "They're ours for the chasing."

"Now about this wedding . . ." Bethany said.

"Sweetheart, we're going to have the biggest wedding this part of the state has ever seen."

"And all the right words, Jed. All the right words. And all of our friends. Mr. Bartholomew. I want him to be there, too. And Norvin Meissner. Not just black people but all our white friends, too."

"I've been thinking the same thing." They stopped, and he kissed her again.

"You see? A marriage made in Heaven."

They strolled toward Nicodemus, their arms around each other's waists.

She stopped suddenly and shyly looked up at him. She bit her lip. He smiled tenderly, knowing he had better get used to this woman's whims.

"Jed?" Her lip quivered. "The wedding. I want us to jump the broom, too."

Shocked, he looked at her warily.

"Not in place of all the other stuff. In addition to it."

He said nothing but quirked his eyebrow.

"For Momma, Jed. For Momma."

Jed did not have to fill the settlers in on the importance of the Voorhees committee.

Every county paper in the state of Kansas had something to say about the investigation. Even if local editors were not interested in national politics, they still relied on the patent sheets forming the core pages of their editions, whether dailies or weeklies. These pre-printed insides shipped from the East kept up a running criticism on the daily testimony.

The settlers were summoned with the drums. The fire burned brightly with the healing scent of cedar wafting across the gathering. It was a tradition by now. They were comforted by the odor.

The fiery beams from the setting sun pulsed over the green grass and tinted even the blackest of faces with a touch of red. The clouds floated like a filmy layer of red gauze. A damp breeze cooled their faces.

The children, sensing something important was afoot, abandoned their games and plopped down by their parents. Families sat in little clusters. It was the largest group ever assembled in the town.

An unnatural hush fell over the gathering while Jed told them Governor St. John had requested his testimony. "The formal title of this investigation is 'The Causes of the Removal of the Negro from the Southern States to the Northern States'," he said.

"Senate report number 693. I spent years gathering information. It is our chance to be heard. To bear witness."

Henry Partridge rose slowly to his feet and stuck out his mangled paw. His eyes sparked with righteousness, and his voice trembled. "I want them to know about my hand. Somebody gots to know about this here hand. What they did. What they said. You gonna tell them about people like us?"

"Yes," Jed said. "About people like you. All of you. For the first time, the first time ever, this country is going to see on a witness stand a whole wide range of black men. All of us. Witness after witness. Some with tongues of angels and some treacherous as snakes. Some with lightning fast minds and some who had their brains beat out of them years ago, but this country will hear us, by God." His deep voice shook. "By the great, good God, the men running that investigation *will* hear us. The living and the dead. The mighty and the meek."

They were lighted by the afterglow of the sunset as family after family rose and told their stories. Evening deepened.

By the time the last person had given witness, their souls had crept back into their bodies.

Bethany sat quietly, flushed with hope,

giddy with adoration as she watched Jed's face. The tall, elegant man who would soon be her husband. Her mother had dreamed that their first child would be a girl. A great healer, knowing more than her and Grandmother Eugenie combined. Queen Bess was alive with anticipation.

Bethany looked across the prairie toward the Solomon. She would go there tomorrow and rest under a silvery-leafed cottonwood tree and watch the wind ripple through the sparkly undersides of the leaves.

Her prairie beckoned. Her green pastures after all. They had not forsaken the memory of green when they left the South.

She looked around at the people, their burned-out hearts restored. They had taken back their town. Their birthright.

And they would tell new stories to their children now. How they thought the fog was a bad omen, and they had been fearful of leaving. And for a while, a very short while, they thought they had made a terrible mistake.

But they came to understand they were told to steal away from the gray to a new land.

That's what the Lord had meant. Steal away to a land where there was no fog. Steal away to a state where a man could see into infinity under a sky so blue it hurt their eyes. Steal away to Nicodemus.

ACKNOWLEDGEMENTS

There are so many persons I want to thank. Some contributed to this book directly and some indirectly. Long discussions and my friendship with Angela Bates deepened my understanding of the heart of Nicodemus. She once referred to me as "my white sister with a black soul." She doesn't hesitate to straighten me out on issues regarding African Americans.

I was first attracted to Nicodemus through its music. Ernestine VanDuvall, one of the amazing Williams sisters, sent out a flyer advertising a fund-raiser for the church. I went on impulse. The rhythms, the call and response, went straight to my soul. I fell in love with the town. It inspired me to write a number of articles and short stories and even a nonfiction book published by University of Oklahoma Press. I love the energy that galvanizes the community during their annual Homecoming weekend.

I owe a special thank-you to Tiffany Schofield and all the people at Five Star who launched the frontier fiction line. Tiffany regularly attends the Western Writers of America convention and has supported countless writers on the journey to publication. I appreciate the editing contribution of Diane Piron-Gelman and that of my primary proofreader, John Crocket. Graham County historian Lowell Beecher responded immediately to any requests for information.

I'm grateful to the staff at the Kansas State Historical Society, local historians, friends in Nicodemus, and countless persons who responded to my requests for information about African Americans in Kansas. Five Star's organizational system is outstanding. I appreciate the time and effort involved in bringing *A Healer's Daughter* to publication.

As with all my books, I thank my agent, Phyllis Westberg, for her support of my ricocheting from one genre to another.

AUTHOR'S NOTES

The Healer's Daughter is fiction. Nevertheless, most of the elements of this book are based on facts. The town of Nicodemus is real. It was the first all-black town established on the High Plains. It exists today, and the site is now a national park. There is an exhibition focusing on the town in the new African American museum in Washington.

It would be impossible to exaggerate the courage it took to establish this extraordinary community. Three talented men shaped Nicodemus at the very beginning: Abram Thompson Hall, Jr., Edward Preston McCabe, and John Wayne Niles. Their deeds inspired some of the characters in the book.

Jed Talbot is a fictional character, but his multi-year task of gathering information and testimonies from African Americans in the South parallels the horrendous undertaking of Henry Adams and others on a committee of freed slaves who spent several years searching for an area where they could live in peace. Many of the families wanted to stay in the South. But Adams regretfully decided they would have to go, for they were slipping into a new and worse kind of slavery. In Kansas they could obtain land.

Elam Bartholomew actually existed. After his death, his original herbarium of about 40,000 specimens was acquired by Harvard University.

Queen Bess and Bethany are fictional, but many African American women were adept physicians who could draw from the best of white practices and add techniques from ancient knowledge. The work involved with feeding, clothing, and keeping a plantation functioning was mind boggling. Occasionally, when the white mistress was not up to the task, an intelligent, well-organized black woman took over her job.

So many African Americans fled the South in 1879 that Congress formed a committee to explore the reasons for the exodus. After the investigation, Senate Committee 693 of the 46th Congress issued a 1,400-page report. Due to the breadth of occupations and viewpoints of those interviewed — black and white — it is one of the most remarkable documents in American history.

Words cannot express my admiration for Kansas Governor John Pierce St. John. He was a giant among men who was a century ahead of his time.

ABOUT THE AUTHOR

Charlotte Hinger is a multi–award win-
ning novelist and Kansas historian. Her
historical novel, *Come Spring,* published by
Simon and Schuster, won the Medicine
Pipe Bearers award from Western Writers of
America and was a Spur finalist.

Kirkus Reviews selected *Hidden Heritage,*
the third mystery in her Lottie Albright
series, as one of the best mysteries of 2013,
and one of the best fiction books. The first
book in the series, *Deadly Descent,* won the
AZ Publisher's Award for Best Mystery/
Suspense. She has published many articles
and short stories.

In 2016, University Press of Oklahoma
published her nonfiction book *Nicodemus:
Post-Reconstruction Politics and Racial Justice in Western Kansas.* She still calls herself
a Kansan although she now lives in Fort
Collins, Colorado.